Photo of Northampton City Hall from the collection of
Historic Northampton

Forever and Ever

*To Jeanine,
Enjoy!*

Louise S. Appell

Louise S. Appell

authorHOUSE®

AuthorHouse™
1663 Liberty Drive, Suite 200
Bloomington, IN 47403
www.authorhouse.com
Phone: 1-800-839-8640

First published by AuthorHouse 1/26/2009

ISBN: 978-1-4389-3821-9 (sc)

Printed in the United States of America
Bloomington, Indiana

This book is printed on acid-free paper.

Joseph Billieux (1850 - 1920)
m.1874
Rose Arquette (1857 - 1938)

Oscar (1876 - 1938)	Alphonse (1880 ----)	Maurice (1881 -)	Mathilda (1884 -)	Charles (1887 -)	Clara (1897 -)
m.(1896) Flora DuPont (1873 -)	-m.(1899) Grace Poulet (1873 -)	m.(1900) Simone Dion (1884 -)	m.(1904) Edward LaPointe (1881 -)		m. (1917) Auguste Pelletier (1898 –1918)
Helene Louis Jacque George Jean	Artur Celeste Phillipe (1913 -)	Anna Colette Henri Robert (1925 -)	Pierro (1908 -) m.(1928) Angela Ciccione (1911 -)		
			Marie (1930 -) Amy (1937 -) Peter (1945 -)		

For

Those who remember

and

Those who keep their promises

Acknowledgments

◇◇

This is the last of the trilogy I set out to write almost ten years ago. Along the way there have been wonderful friends and family who have encouraged me, provided suggestions and critiques and helped in the search for tiny bits of information that gave these books depth and character. My love and gratitude to them all, especially:

My mother, Phyllis Fortier, who always believed I should write and lived only long enough to see a finished manuscript for the first book.

Mike Errecart, best of friends and chief cheerleader of my efforts, left this mortal coil before the first book was published. His picture hangs over my computer to remind me to keep going.

Rachel Michaud has been my special friend throughout the writing of these three books, with just the right words when I needed them. She dispenses praise and prodding in equal measure. It's impossible to imagine a better BFF.

The women of the Greengate Women Writer's Conference and especially, the leader Eunice Scarfe, listened to my words and helped me gain confidence that I could write stories that would capture an audience.

SWG, the Sunday Writers' Group provided thoughtful critique and fellowship at monthly meetings. Naomi, Brenda, Constance, Lynne, Connie and Paula, I thank you.

Cochrane's Saloon, meeting every Monday, has been a forum for spirited discussions, contributing invaluable feedback on the third book. I wish I had joined this writers' group years ago.

My sister, Beatrice Erickson, is always willing to come to my aid when I need her. She keeps the fires of interest going with readers in Massachusetts. It's my good luck to have a sister who is such a loving friend.

Chapter 1

◇◇

Montreal, Quebec
1980

Marie sat on the hard wooden bench in the waiting room at the Sisters of The Sacred Heart Nursing Home in Montreal, every muscle tense, hoping that Uncle Charlie would let her visit. All the way from Massachusetts, through the bright sunshine on the snow in the mountains of Vermont, through the swirling flakes as she passed the border, she thought about these first few minutes of seeing Uncle Charlie and how he would appear to her, what she would say to him. Hard to believe that so many years had gone by.

It never occurred to her that the nun at the reception desk would question whether he wanted to see her.

1

Dressed in the black suit and white silk shirt she had worn to her Aunt Clara's funeral, she looked like the successful woman she was. Unfortunately, she had stepped into a puddle of melted snow getting out of her car this morning. Probably her expensive black alligator pumps were ruined. She wore her hair in a short easy-care bob, carefully colored to cover the gray hairs she had been noticing with increasing frequency. Her makeup was applied with a light, but skilled, hand. Marie was very aware of the importance of appearance and the impression it created.

The small room where she was told to wait had a strong odor of linseed oil, the old wooden furniture polished to a gleam. A large crucifix hung on the wall opposite the bench where she sat and a classic picture of Mary and the Baby Jesus was to its right. Marie wondered if Charlie Billieux had become more devout in his later years. He'd been known to be a two-fisted drinker, frequently too hung over to make it to Mass on Sunday.

The sound of footsteps in the hallway roused Marie from her reveries of the handsome, robust man Uncle Charlie had been. He always had time for her as a little girl, taking her with him into the forest to find a Christmas tree, teaching her to fish, sliding down Hospital Hill on the toboggan while he held her tight in his arms. And he played the role of Santa all the years of her belief, so perfectly it was hard when she learned it was a myth.

"*Madame* Graham, *Monsieur* Billieux has given his permission for you to visit. Do you know he cannot walk?" The nun looked at Marie sternly, as if she wanted to protect her uncle from unwanted intruders.

"Yes, I've been told that. Does he use a wheelchair?"

"Yes, he does. He's in the solarium now. I'll take you there. I warn you that *Mere Superieur* will not like it if you upset him. She does not like anybody to be upset, but especially *Monsieur* Billieux."

Marie raised her eyebrows, but the nun ignored the implied question and turned, moving quickly down the hall and calling out to her, "Follow me."

The sun was shining in the windows of the solarium creating a glare and for a few seconds Marie was blinded by the intense light as she looked around the room searching for her uncle.

"Ah, *chouchou*, you always had such lovely eyes as a child. I knew you would turn out to be a beautiful woman. Come and give me a little *bisou*."

Marie turned and saw him, smiling; his arms outstretched toward her and a little bubble of pure happiness propelled her forward. "Oh, Uncle Charlie, I was so afraid you might not let me visit, I could hardly stand it, waiting for Sister to come back." She bent forward to hug him, kissing his dear face, stroking his hair, now all white but still thick and glossy. She glanced around and saw a small needlepoint-covered hassock, dragged it closer to his chair and sat down, her hand still touching him.

He had been a large man, tall and well-muscled from his labors on the tenant houses and, although age and inactivity had taken their toll, he still retained an aura of strength, his eyes clear and bright, arms thick with ropy muscles. He was wearing a heavy gray wool shirt covered by an obviously hand-knit black sweater vest. Marie glanced down to his pants legs, one pinned up. The slipper on his remaining foot was fleece and she could see the hand-knit argyle sock he wore. Even though she had been told of Uncle Charlie's injuries, it was a jolt to actually see his disability and acknowledge what that meant to a man whose whole life had been one of strength and action.

"I was in Northampton last week because Aunt Clara had the director of the Lathrop Home call me. You remember the Lathrop Home?" Marie paused and Charlie nodded. "Aunt Clara had been living there for nearly a year and I didn't even know it." Tears filled her eyes. "I can't believe I was so busy with my own stuff that I didn't do a better job of staying in touch with her." Charlie took out a big white handkerchief from the pocket in his vest and wiped the tears sliding down Marie's cheeks. "Uncle Charlie, Aunt Clara just died. We buried her just yesterday."

"*Ma belle Clara, gentille soeur. Morte.*" Charlie's eyes filled with tears and he swallowed rapidly to stem their flow.

Marie dropped her head down and cried as if her heart was breaking. Charlie put his gnarled hands on her shaking shoulders and stroked her arms, murmuring soothing sounds, as much to console himself as to comfort her. It took a while until she could get herself under control. He had watched so many of the sweet sisters in this place die, and well he knew that every death of a loved one was hard to bear.

"It was at Aunt Clara's wake that I found out you were here," Marie said, still sniffling. "Hazel Boucher said she had seen you when she came to visit her brother-in-law. Do you remember seeing her?"

"Ah, *oui, oui.* Such a busybody, a chatterbox. Her brother-in-law was the priest here for a long time, but he died a few months ago. He got old and forgetful, a lot like my *Maman.* I tell you, *chouchou*, it's hard

5

to get very old. Do you know I'll be 93 years old next month?"

"I know. I was thinking about that when I was driving up here. And I just turned 50. Uncle Charlie, tell me what you did when you left Northampton and tell me why you felt you had to do that. I really need to know."

"First, *ma petite*, you tell me about all those years I missed, when your *Maman* and *Papa* had another child, a little boy, I think. And they bought a house and your *Papa* started a business. For a while there I was getting the Gazette. Did you go to Smith College? Do you have any children? How about Amy? And I did read the notice in the paper when your *Pepere* died and then your *Memere*, but not whether they were sick or had an accident or what. I've heard little bits about the family from a few of the people I knew back then, but never the whole story."

A sweet-faced young nun, her face scrubbed to a shine, glided into the room and stopped in front of them. In heavily accented English she said, "*Pardon, Madame*, but *Mere Superieur* says *Monsieur* Charlie has to go for his mid-day meal and after that, he will take a little nap."

Charlie sighed, smiling at the same time, "Well, *ma petite, Mere Superieur* is the boss here, so I must do as she says. Will you come back later?"

Marie stood up and bent to kiss her uncle. "Of course. I'll go and find a hotel near here. I plan to stay for a few days before I must go back. I'll ask when it's ok for me to return today. We'll have some time together and I will tell you all you want to know. Will you answer my questions also?"

"I'll try. Some questions are hard to answer, but I'll try."

* * * * *

As she was retrieving her coat in the front vestibule, mentally creating a list of tasks she needed to attend to, a tall nun, back as straight as a poker, came down the hall and stopped in front of her. Marie was caught at an awkward moment, struggling into her coat. Clearly, this was Mother Superior; the tone of command told her that.

"Mrs. Graham, would you step into my office, please? I would like a word with you."

Without a second of hesitation, Marie answered her, "Of course, Mother."

Louise S. Appell

When they were seated on two comfortable armchairs in front of a fireplace, the room scented with the smell of pine, a novice easily identified as such by her dress, came in carrying a tray with a teapot and two china cups, decorated with elegant roses. "Will you join me in a cup of tea, Mrs. Graham?"

Marie was not a tea drinker, but she answered, "Yes, thank you."

The silence while tea was poured, sugar and cream were offered and each had taken a sip of the brew was driving Marie crazy. What was this all about?

"Mrs. Graham, we are delighted to see a relative of *Monsieur* Charlie's come to visit him. We are wondering why it has taken so long for his family to show some interest in his well-being."

Marie opened her mouth to speak, the nun held up her hand in the classic symbol for stop. "Please do not misunderstand me You have no need to defend yourself here. I am aware that Charlie has chosen to isolate himself from his family for reasons he has never explained. But even so, as far as I know no one has ever written to inquire about his welfare and he has been here for over 25 years."

Marie was outraged at the accusation. She had to struggle to control herself, knowing that Uncle Charlie was right when he called this nun 'the Boss'. Trying her best to keep her tone neutral, she answered, "You may not know that it was my Uncle Charlie's very specific orders that kept us away. He had his reasons which he has not explained to me anymore than to you. But if I had known he was in a nursing home or that he needed the help of his family, I assure you I would have been here at once. As it is, I have only known for two days where to find him. What is important is that I am here now. I intend to take a hotel room somewhere in this vicinity and to visit him every day until I can determine whether he will permit me to move him closer to my home in New York."

The nun gave a dismissing wave of her hand. "You cannot do that. He is too old and too fragile to be moved. You see him in his chair. His mind is clear. You think he is more robust than he truly is. I will tell you he is dying. He has refused treatment for his very serious heart condition. It is only *le bon Dieu* that keeps him alive now. Maybe he was waiting for you to arrive. You may certainly visit him as much as you want, without altering his routine, but you may not take him away from us. We will care for him until the end. And we will be by his side when the angels come to take his soul to heaven. *Tu comprends?*"

9

Marie stifled the urge to make a snippy comeback, knowing that there was a lot she didn't know about how Charlie came to be in this place, about his physical condition and even about this woman, whose strength and determination were formidable. "I am going now to find a place to stay for a while. Can you recommend a hotel nearby?" Marie's voice was cool but polite. She stood and gathered her handbag and gloves, suddenly aware that she had never been invited to remove her coat. Clearly, Mother Superior did not expect her to stay and chat.

The nun stood and nodded. "Sister Boniface at the front desk will give you the names of some hotels in the area. I assume you plan to return later this afternoon. *Monsieur* Charlie will be able to see you from four o'clock until six. *Bonjour.*" Marie was dismissed.

*   *   *   *   *

It was easy enough to find a decent hotel nearby, but too early in the day for the room to be ready. The Hotel LaSalle had a European flavor, small lobby, a bar but no restaurant. Marie had stayed in a grim, ugly little room in a no-name motel just this side of the border last night, when the light had faded and she was too tired to continue on to Montreal. She was eager for a bath in pleasant surroundings but it would wait. The desk clerk directed her to a nearby café where she could have a quiet luncheon.

When she opened the glass door of *La Tomate*, the smell of delicious cooking made her realize she was very hungry. A glass of Pinot Noir, a bowl of thick pea soup and some warm crusty bread revived her nicely. She took out a small notebook and her pen, ordered coffee and began to make lists, calls she needed to make, information she wanted to get, personal items to be purchased if she was to stay a whole week. Clearly, Uncle Charlie was well cared for and didn't appear to be in need of anything. The hand-knit vest and sock told her someone cared very much. Ah, yes, there were mysteries to unravel here.

Marie wondered how much of Uncle Charlie's past the Sisters of the Sacred Heart knew. Had he told them of the tragedy? Did they know where he had been and what he had done in the years after he left Northampton?

She paid for her lunch and hurried out to find a place where she could buy pantyhose and a book to read before bed. Then, passing a store that sold candy, she remembered how Uncle Charlie had loved licorice. She bought a bag of licorice Scotty dogs, the same kind she remembered buying at two for a penny in her Uncle Alphonse's general store on Hospital Hill. In a bookstore across the street she picked out a book from the few choices in English.

* * * * *

The hotel room was large enough and comfortable and included a desk where Marie could organize some papers, make phone calls, and focus on the world outside of Montreal. She glanced at the clock and determined it was a good time to call her sister Amy in California.

"Hi, Amy, it's me. I'm in Montreal. Uncle Charlie is here and guess what? He's been here for 25 years. Do you believe it? That woman at Aunt Clara's wake was right about his injuries, though. He's in a wheelchair."

Amy's voice conveyed her anxiety. "I'm so glad to hear from you. I heard there was a big snowstorm and I was worrying about you driving up there in bad weather." She was a long time worry-wart and, living in Southern California, if she heard a newscast mention snow, she started envisioning the potential for tragedy. Of course, the fact that their father had perished in an automobile accident fueled that concern.

"Not to worry, darling. All the roads were clear and I got off the highway when it started to get dark. Anyway, I've visited Uncle Charlie and he looks wonderful, even though the Mother Superior who runs the place told me he has a serious heart condition and he's dying."

"Isn't he in his nineties now?"

"Yes. He'll be 93 next month."

"Does he need anything? Is there something he would like that I can send? How is he paying for this nursing home? Should we be helping with that?" Amy was married to a Hollywood producer and her financial resources allowed her to be generous whenever a family member needed help.

"I don't think he needs anything, Amy. He was wearing a hand-knit vest and an argyle sock on his one foot. And I don't know the answer to your question about paying for the nursing care. There's a lot I don't know that I hope to find out. I'm planning to stay for a week."

"I wish I was there with you. You know I would be if I could." Amy's voice was wistful.

"Of course I do. I'll call you every day to report on what I find out. Oh, by the way, the Mother Superior is like a character out of one of David's movies. Tell him I said that. Give my love to the boys when you talk to them. And my love to you."

"Love you, too."

As soon as she hung up, Marie remembered she had forgotten to ask Amy to get in touch with Petey. Oh, well, she'd do it later. What with the overseas operator and the time difference, it took a while to get him and she wanted to get back to Uncle Charlie.

* * * * *

Sister Boniface was at the reception desk when Marie entered. With a smile big enough to light the room, the nun greeted her warmly and invited her to hang her coat. "*Mon Dieu, Madame* Graham, did you not wear galoshes? You will get your feet very wet. *Monsieur* Billieux is in the solarium. Do you know your way there?"

"Yes, thank you. And you're right. I will have to buy a pair of galoshes." Marie smiled at the unfamiliar word and the big change in the nun's demeanor. Now that she was identified as a loving relative of Uncle Charlie's, she was not only accepted but welcomed.

Marie's uncle was not alone in the sunroom. Two elderly nuns played cards on a table in one corner and a woman lay on a couch, covered to her chin with a bright quilt. A television flickered with the volume low, but no one seemed to be paying any attention to it. Uncle Charlie's wheelchair was pushed to a window where the sun could stream in over his shoulder. She could see that he was whittling, his hands firmly around the piece of wood he was holding, a pair of glasses perched on his nose.

"*Bienvenue, ma petite.* Come and see what I am making." He held out his hand.

Marie kissed his cheek and took the object in her hand. It was just barely begun, but she could tell it was to be a sled, about four inches long. The curve of the runner on one side was clearly defined. "Oh, this is so perfect. Will you paint it when it is done?"

"Sister Sara will paint it for me. She likes to do it. I used to give them to *les enfants* with just a coat of shellac, but she started painting them about eight or nine years ago and they look much better. This one is for you, *cherie,* so you will remember when we were young and went sledding together."

Tears leaked from Marie's eyes and she brushed them away. "Oh, Uncle Charlie, what a wonderful gift." Rummaging in her pocketbook, she took out the bag of licorice. "Are you allowed to eat this? I remember how you always liked it."

Charlie Billieux's broad smile turned back time. His eyes lit up with mischievous sparkle; his whole face took on a look of childish delight. He reached out for the bag and quickly, almost furtively, tucked in into his vest pocket. "The Boss would probably let me have only one a day, but I'm going to fool her. You are a good girl to remember how much I love licorice." He chuckled. "Now you are going to tell me what happened to everyone. I knew before I left that Clara had gone to work at McCallum's store and that her friend Ray went into the Army. I heard that your mother went to work in the bomb factory and that your father came back from the war with a limp and started a business. "

"Oh, my, there's so much to tell. In the first place, everybody was shocked when you didn't come home the minute you were let out of prison. *Memere* and Aunt Clara cried. We all loved you, never mind what happened. You were, you are, very dear to all of us."

"I'll try to explain it to you, *chouchou*, but later, after you tell me what I missed."

Chapter 2

◇◇◇◇◇◇◇◇◇◇◇◇◇◇◇◇◇◇◇◇◇◇◇◇◇◇◇◇◇◇◇◇◇◇◇◇◇◇◇

Northampton, Mass.
1944-47

When Marie's father, Pete, came home from the war in the fall of '44, he had a pronounced limp from a wound that might easily have cost him his leg had it not been for the diligence of a skilled Army field surgeon. The experience of war had changed him in fundamental ways. While some men came back bitter, angry and unstable, Pete returned with a new confidence in his abilities. He was ambitious to succeed and deeply grateful to have survived. He realized how lucky he was to have a family who loved him and he was eager to show them that he was worthy of that love. In the hospital, recuperating from his wound, he formulated a plan to start his own business, using skills he had honed as a tank repairman in the Army. His wife, Angela, had saved all the money she made working in a bomb factory during the war and it was that nest egg that made the business venture possible.

Pete was determined to make his motor repair business a success. By the time the war ended, he was feeling that he had a good chance. He joined the Elks and Toastmasters and became an active voice at the VFW. If every guy in town knew him, he reasoned, they'd think of him when they needed their cars and trucks and tractors repaired. Two army buddies, Stan Borowski and George Corelli, came to work for him and they shared his enthusiasm for making Pete's Motor Repair Shop the best in town.

George was a quiet guy, small in stature with longish hair, pale blonde, almost white. His time in the service was spent typing up reports since he was one of the few enlistees who could type. He did a great job of keeping the books for Pete's Motor Repair Shop, doing the banking and all those administrative tasks that Pete hated. Stan worked side by side with Pete, mostly on their backs under one vehicle or another. When Stan came back home to Northampton after the end of the war, he looked for Pete, who had already opened his shop. Pete was so enthusiastic about the potential of the business, Stan decided to take advantage of the

GI Bill to get some technical training in motor repair so he could work for his old buddy. They all stayed alert for promising modern trends. Pete was quick to buy any piece of equipment or try fresh ways to bring in new business.

There was a pervasive sense of optimism in town and, according to the newspapers Pete read, throughout the country. Factories that had hummed with war production were converting to consumer goods. Pete was especially interested in the new cars that were coming out of Detroit to be quickly snapped up by vets as well as by those whose old cars had been limping along through the war years. Lots of vets took advantage of the G.I. Bill to go to college or get some technical training. They were buying homes with G.I loans, starting families, opening new businesses, bringing new ideas to old businesses. Sure, there were some guys who came back from the war depressed, battered and unable to get themselves going and some who stayed drunk all day. But mostly, vets wanted to put the war behind them and get on with life.

Pete came home one night lugging a big box, a huge grin on his face, calling out, "Angela, come get the door and see what I just bought."

It was the first television set in the neighborhood, a source of wonder to all their family and friends. After a great deal of discussion on where to put it, Pete decided he'd always wanted a pine-paneled recreation room in the basement. Angela fussed about it sitting in the living room she'd decorated with such care until the basement could be converted, so the work was hurried along.

*　*　*　*　*

Stan approached Pete one day with an invitation. "Pete, I joined a group of guys working to get Truman elected. You know how I thought it was a brave thing he did, sending that bomb to finish the Japs and now some dandy from New York is running against him. I want to help him win this and I was hoping you might want to join up, too."

"Jeez, Stan, I don't know where I'd get the time. Angela complains now about how many nights I go to one meeting or another."

"Yeah, I know. Ann's been complaining, too. But I think it's important. Cut back on something else, but do this with me." Stan had been an ardent supporter of FDR and he'd seen in his own family the good that local political parties did for their constituents. "Sure, we all know some of the political stuff is baloney, but mostly it's better to choose a side and fight for it than let some other guy win and gripe about it."

George decided not to join them. He was taking some classes in business management and he was courting a girl from Holyoke, which meant driving over there whenever he could find the time. "Sorry, guys, I need to get married and I think this is the one. Got to take care of that business first."

* * * * *

Angela joined a neighborhood garden club and set about making their small back yard a showplace. A rock garden on the little slope back of the garage was filled with unusual succulents. Climbing roses grew all over the back fence. When Angela saw a brick patio in a magazine, she was smitten, so Pete got his buddies over on a Saturday afternoon and they put a brick patio in for her as a surprise.

She was friendly to everyone, quick to organize charity events, holiday parties, class outings for Amy's school. Petey was an easy baby, going through the stages of babyhood with very few bumps in the road. Since he was a robust child, he handled the usual illnesses with a minimum of fussing.

Louise S. Appell

Occasionally Angela would reminisce with her coffee klatch friends about the experience of working in the bomb factory, explaining to them how she had enjoyed the feeling of reward she got from getting a paycheck, putting money in the bank, getting praised by her supervisor for a job well done. "I know it's important now to be home with Petey, but when he goes to school, maybe I'll look for a job."

"You must be kidding," her friend Kay said. "How about playing bridge or golf or going out to lunch?"

"I don't think that would be so great. What would I be doing that for?"

"Angela, only people whose husbands can't keep a job go to work." Kay was exasperated. "Your husband makes enough to support his family. People would talk."

"People are going to talk anyway, so what's the big deal? Some folks have nothing better to do than talk about their neighbors. I don't care about them."

* * * * *

One day, when Petey was still a tiny baby, not yet walking, Angela set him out on the porch in his playpen and went inside to begin making a batch of brownies. She was pouring the mixture into a pan when she heard a voice out on the porch. She hurried out to find out who it might be and was stunned to see her brother Sal sitting on the porch swing holding Petey in his big hands. He was crooning and bouncing her little boy, who was giggling with delight. "Sal, how wonderful to see you. How did you know where I lived? The baby's name is Petey. Isn't he wonderful?"

Sal looked up at her, his eyes wet with tears. "He's beautiful. See, I made him laugh. He likes me. I'm his uncle."

Angela opened the door wider and held out her hand, "Come in, Sal. I'll fix you a glass of iced tea. Bring the baby. You can hold him while you drink your tea."

"Papa told me not to come or he'd wring my neck, but I don't think he can do that. Do you, Angela?"

Since Sal was at least four inches taller and fifty pounds heavier than their father, the thought make Angela laugh. "No, Sal, I don't think so."

Sal put his face down to Petey's belly and made a bubbling sound, which caused Petey to squeal with exuberance. "I've got a new job now. I'm working with the janitor at the Bridge Street School. I sweep and take out the trash and stuff like that. I saw you go by one day and I watched to see which house you went into." He looked at Angela quizzically. "I wanted to see the baby. That's why I came. You're not mad at me, are you?"

"No, Sal, I'm not mad at you. I'm glad you wanted to see the baby. I'm glad you're here. You can come over anytime. I'll be happy to see you whenever you come by."

He may be retarded, Angela thought, but he's a good man with courage and conviction and the sense to tell right from wrong. She just wished her father and her other brothers would come around, too. Not likely, after all this time, but she still hoped for it.

* * * * *

Amy, a student at the Bridge Street School, joined a Girl Scout group where her *Memere* was the leader. It gave her a wonderful opportunity to see *Memere* and *Pepere* and Aunt Clara, too, when she went to West Street after the meeting in Peoples' Institute ended. *Pepere* always came to pick them up and drive them home. Besides, Scouts did all kinds of interesting things. She learned to sew on buttons and darn a sock; she cooked spaghetti, went on trips to visit the International Silver Company where they made cutlery, learned to paddle a canoe and had many, many other adventures.

Amy doted on her brother. She loved her role as big sister and, now that Marie was in high school and very much involved in activities that left Amy out, it was fun to have an adorable (and adoring) brother to play with. She was a pretty girl, with features more delicate than her sister, Marie. She'd had a hard time with childhood illnesses and a bout of rheumatic fever left her with a heart murmur. *Memere* always said she was too skinny, all arms and legs. She took tap dancing classes for a few years and loved performing, but the rheumatic fever put a stop to that activity despite Amy's pleas to continue.

* * * * *

Charlie's widowed sister, Clara, loved her work at McCallum's Department Store, enjoyed the challenge of helping young vets, some of whom had never owned a suit before, to pick out clothes that were well-made, stylish and appropriate. She made sure they availed themselves of the services of one of the store's two tailors so that their clothes fit them well. She was forever saying to her customers, "It's the fit that makes the difference."

Many of these guys had left home boys and returned as men, with muscles defined, chests expanded and new inches added to their height. Clara knew that she was helping them, knew that looking good was important to their view of themselves, and she took quiet pride in that.

Her commissions grew steadily with her sales. Customers told their friends about her. Men who had routinely gone to Harry Daniels Men's Clothiers came in to look around. Since Clara was now assistant buyer for the men's department, she urged the expansion of goods to include cashmere sweaters and fine leather gloves.

"Tillie, *ma soeur*, I am going to buy a car. I think I'll ask Pete to give me some advice. Do you think that's what I should do?"

Tillie was aware that it was a nuisance to take a bus every time Clara wanted to visit with Ray's sister Anna in Hartford. Tillie herself didn't drive and was a little afraid of cars, but she said, "Yes, *cherie*, I think that would be good. You could go visit Anna more often."

Pete was enthusiastic about finding a good used car for Clara to buy and in no time the deed was done. It was a maroon Ford, not flashy, but sturdy and in excellent condition. Clara exulted in the sense of freedom it gave her to own a car.

Clara's beloved Ray was still missing in action. No trace of him had been found. Through the efforts of Anna's husband Randy, who had connections to their Congressman, they got as much information as there was to get, which wasn't much. There was hope he might have been injured and was being cared for somewhere, maybe unable to speak; maybe the people caring for him didn't understand English. The last information they had was that he escaped from a prison camp in a heavily forested region of Austria. The Army believed he had been injured during his escape and efforts were made to search the area around the camp but to no avail. Clara and Anna met often to keep their hopes up.

One night in the winter of '46, the phone rang and it was Anna, "Clara, I thought you'd want to know. My mother died last night. She had another stroke." Anna's voice was clogged with tears. "I know she was crabby when she got older, but believe me, she was a wonderful mother to Ray and me. Even though she treated you badly, I still thought you'd want to know, but I'll understand if you don't want to come to the funeral."

"*Mon Dieu*, of course I will come to the funeral. Just tell me when and where and I'll be there. My dear Anna, you must be devastated."

"The wake will be held Wednesday and Thursday night at a funeral parlor across the street from our church, St. Steven's Episcopal on Lincoln Avenue. I know my mother wanted to be laid out at home, but Randy says that's ridiculous. Nobody does that anymore. Do you think that's alright? And we will have an open house after the interment for people to gather together. I'm going to do that at home. It's so much nicer than doing it in the church basement, don't you think?"

"How can I help you? Shall I come a day ahead of the funeral? I'd be glad to do that, Anna." Although Clara had a strained relationship with Ray's mother, who thought Clara was too old for her son and a Catholic as well, Clara would do this for Anna who was her good friend.

"That would be wonderful. I'd be so glad to have you here. You can stay in the spare bedroom." Anna said. Her mother went to live with Anna when Ray joined the Army, but had been moved to a nursing home in the winter of '44 after a stroke. "But how about your job? Will they give you the time off?"

"Don't even think about that. I'll have no trouble getting the time off. I'll get there on Thursday morning so I can start doing a little cooking for your open house." As soon as she hung up, Clara started making notes on what she would need to bring. What a good thing it was that she had a car now. She could never cart all that she needed on a bus. She went in search of Tillie to ask her to make some brownies and tarts tomorrow.

* * * * *

The class of 1947 at Northampton High School had its share of brilliant students with the promise of greatness in their future along with the slackers and the jokers and the plodders and the 'just let me pass this class' types. The majority, of course, were adolescents going through a rite of passage. Some would go on to higher education, a fair number to Ivy League schools since they were in Massachusetts, after all. And some would join a family business or go to work in an entry-level job doing whatever it took to earn a paycheck. A lot of the young women were headed to secretarial school or one of the hospital-based nursing schools in the area. Twelve of the girls took the SAT hoping to be accepted for Smith College.

Some of the boys who had entered high school with Marie left to go into the service, but mostly the graduating class of 154 were the kids she had known through three years of football games, final exams, drama club performances and scandalous whispering campaigns.

Marie had taken dancing classes at Mrs. Stewart's Dancing School every Friday night during her sophomore year. It was held at The People's Institute and either her mother or her father drove her there and then picked her up. It was an agonizing, embarrassing, painful period for her. Nobody wanted to be a wallflower, so the breathless waiting for a boy to come and ask her to dance was a dreaded event every week. Getting her hair to look just right, selecting clothes to wear and the right lipstick color was a cause of some measure of agony before she would set foot out of the house. But she had done it and when prom time came, it paid off. She could dance.

"Betsy, has anybody asked you to the prom?" Marie asked. The girls were walking down Elm Street toward Main in the bright spring sunshine, both of them carrying a load of books in their arms.

Betsy shifted the load in her arms and hesitated. "Well, not exactly."

"What do you mean, 'not exactly'? Either somebody has or nobody has. Which is it?" Marie, who had not been invited yet, was irritated and jealous.

"Ron Cutler said he would take me if I promised to..to.. you know." Betsy was blushing bright red.

"Damn him. What did you say?"

"I just told you. That's what he said. He'd take me to the prom if I promised to let him do it. What do you think he said, please, please? No, he was talking about a straight trade. Prom date for S-E-X. OK?" Betsy was near tears.

"You're not going to let him, are you?"

"Well, I didn't say yes and I didn't say no. I just sort of stuck my nose in the air and walked away."

"That miserable *cochon*. Who does he think he is? He's not even handsome or smart, either. We should warn the other girls we know about him."

Betsy was appalled. "Don't you dare tell anybody. I couldn't stand it for anybody to know. I shouldn't have told you. Cripes, I wasn't going to tell you because I knew you'd make a big deal about it."

"OK, OK, OK. Calm down. I won't tell anybody. But stay away from him. He's bad news. Better not to go to the prom than go with somebody like that." Even as she said the words, Marie wasn't so sure they were true. Wouldn't it be horrible if nobody invited either of them to their own senior prom?

Louise S. Appell

* * * * *

The night of the senior prom was balmy, the gym decorated with lots of balloons and crepe paper. The teachers who were acting as chaperones came dressed in formal wear, smiling a lot at everyone. The band was one Rick Clarey had put together a couple of years ago. Rick was tall, blond, always good-humored, and popular. Everyone, including Marie, and numerous other girls in high school, had a big crush on him.

Wearing a taffeta and tulle evening gown in brown and white with puffed sleeves and a sweetheart neckline, Marie felt very sophisticated. She had a string of pearls around her neck, white shoes on her feet and a corsage of pink and white roses pinned to her shoulder. Her date was Eric Schumer, a sweet guy who was dating a girl from the freshman class whose mother wouldn't let her attend the prom. Marie didn't care. She was there, laughing and dancing and having a good time.

Betsy was there, too. Her date was Mike O'Connell, a goofy guy who was the class clown. Everybody liked him because he never said a bad word about anyone. His comic routine was all self-deprecating humor. Betsy looked pretty in green organza, with a big white sash tied in a bow at the back.

Angela suggested to Marie that she invite six couples to come to their house after the prom. The pine-paneled recreation room was decorated with streamers; the record player was set up on the bar; ginger ale and fruit punch were served, along with pizza and strawberry shortcake. Pete and Angela came down the stairs with more peanuts and potato chips, just often enough to assure themselves that all was well. Some parents came by to chauffeur their offspring and were invited in by Pete to have a drink and a bite to eat. Everybody was smiling through their sadness, realizing that another milestone had passed.

Edward and Tillie had been sad to see Pete and Angela move out of the house on West Street, taking their beloved grandchildren away. Even though they knew that the young couple needed to get out on their own, both of them cherished their roles as *Pepere* and *Memere*. Angela was great about bringing Petey to visit and inviting them to come for dinner or sometimes on a Saturday night to play cards.

When Angela first mentioned that she might want to get a job, Edward was a little alarmed. He understood how women had to work during the war, but Pete had a good business and could provide well for his family. Why did Angela want to do this?

"*Mon Dieu*," Edward asked Tilly, "Why in the world would any woman want to go out to a job if her husband can take care of her? Does she think they need more money? I wonder how Pete feels about this."

Tilly was at the kitchen sink, elbow deep in suds, washing up the supper dishes. "Why don't you ask him? Maybe he likes the idea. Remember how proud Angela was when she showed him all the money she saved while he was gone to war? And he was glad to get it, too. Even though the work was hard sometimes, I think she enjoyed it, being out there with other people."

Edward looked at Tilly with alarm. "What do you mean by that? Aren't you happy you don't have to go out to work every day? Don't I earn enough for us?"

Tilly turned from the sink, put her soapy hands on her hips and frowned at Edward. "Don't be twisting around my words. If I were a younger woman, I'd love to go out to work, meet new people, get a paycheck, and not have to ask you for every dime I wanted to spend. That doesn't mean I'm not happy with you or worried you can't support us. It just means I'm sorry I didn't have any choices. I took care of *Maman* and everybody else and that was my job and I did it. Just don't go thinking it's so hunky-dory to be a housewife."

Edward picked up his newspaper and headed for the front parlor to read. Before he read a single word, he thought about what Tilly had said and what came to his mind was that Pandora's Box had been opened now. It was necessary for women to go to work in the factories when so many of the men were at war, but now they'd seen what they could do, some of them decided they really liked it. He remembered the song that was so popular after the Great War. "How're you gonna keep them down on the farm, now that they've seen Paree?" Was something like that happening with the women now? What next, he thought with alarm. *Mon Dieu,* what next?

Chapter 3

◇◇

Northampton, Mass.
1947-1948

Marie entered Smith College in the fall of 1947, fulfilling her parents' dream for her. She continued to live at home, riding her bike to the campus every day all through her first semester and then, when her grades were good, Pete surprised her by demonstrating his pride in her accomplishment. He gave her a car, an almost new one, a two-year-old bright blue Studebaker, its chrome gleaming and the cone-shaped front looking like a rocket ship. A guy had brought it in to the shop for the third time, after his wife had burned out a clutch and stripped the gears and when Pete asked if he wanted to sell it, the guy said, "Yeah, I'd better, before she has an accident and kills herself."

College was very different from high school. Of course, she knew the other girls from Northampton that entered Smith at the same time she did. There were twelve of them; all but one had been in high school with her. Loretta had taken a year after high school at Birnham School to bone up for the exams. There were others from town in the upper classes, too, but she hardly knew any of them. It all felt strange. There were the long walks from one building to another for classes; she had to carry around a heavy burden of huge books; the big lecture hall for her English lit class had over a hundred students in the room. The college was well-known for the superior quality of education for women, an old and venerable institution, established when few women even went to college, but also as a place that was very costly and drew its students mostly from wealthy families. Cashmere sweaters and pearls were everywhere. In the locker room at the gym, she glanced at the silk and lace under things of some girls and was mortified at her plain cotton Fruit-of-the-loom panties from Woolworth's.

Whenever she could, she caught up with Betsy and they went to a coffee shop on Green Street. "Are you going to the freshman mixer on Saturday night? I heard they're going to bring over guys from Amherst." Betsy sat curled up in corner of the booth, her hands tight around a cup of steaming black coffee.

"I don't know. I was thinking about it, but I'm scared. I don't know what to wear. I don't even know what to talk about to those rich boys who go there."   Marie's coffee sat there untouched; she only recently started to drink the stuff because drinking lots of coffee seemed to be one of the rituals of college life.

"Well, I don't see how we'll meet anybody to date if we don't go."

From a booth behind them there was a loud burst of laughter. "...and then he said, 'I promise you won't get pregnant. I'll even wear two rubbers just to be sure.' Let me tell you, I swatted his hand out of my panties and jumped out of his car right that minute. Who does he think he is, anyway? He's just a nobody that works at our tennis club. I only went to the roadhouse with him for kicks."

Somebody shushed the speaker and the voices from the booth dropped down low. Marie and Betsy were wide-eyed in shock. They slid out of the booth they were in and left the place to explode in laughter when they got out to the sidewalk.

"I've got a class in Seelye Hall in twenty minutes, so I better go." Marie said when she could catch her breath. "I'll go to the mixer if you go. At least we could talk to one another."

*   *   *   *   *

In the five years she had been working at McCallum's Department Store, Clara had come to know Mr. Barron, the head buyer in the men's department and her supervisor, quite well. Of course, she would not say they were friends, exactly. It was a cordial, respectful relationship and she continued to call him Mr. Barron, as he continued to call her Mrs. Pelletier. They had dinner at Rahar's or the Whately Inn now and then. And if they had reason to celebrate something such as particularly good sales for the quarter or a special sale that went well and brought many people into the store, resulting in commendation by the store manager, they might go to Wiggins Tavern.

They rarely talked about their private lives. However, Mr. Barron did know about Clara's nephew Pete's wounding and subsequent discharge. After all, this information was covered in the *Daily Hampshire Gazette*. He was aware of her affection for Pete's children and her friendship with Ruth Goldberg from the ladies lingerie department. He'd been told she lived with her sister and brother-in-law. And Clara had felt she needed to explain about Ray's missing status because she was sure she would want to respond immediately when any new information was forthcoming.

Mr. Barron lived alone in an apartment on Bedford Terrace, in one of those big houses with the bay windows and dark brown shingles. Clara had never been to his home, but she had heard from some people talking in the lunch room that the apartments there were very elegant, with high ceilings and marble fireplaces. Somebody told her he had come from Worchester, had graduated from Holy Cross College in 1914 and had come to Northampton as a very young man. As far as she knew, he had no family. At least he never spoke of any.

Sometimes she thought of inviting him to Thanksgiving or Christmas dinner, but she was never sure if it might be awkward. Once, when she went to St. Mary's Church for a Novena, she saw him there, but his head was bent low over his folded hands and it would have been unthinkable to disturb him. She was going to mention it to him the next day, but then decided it was too private. She certainly did not want to embarrass him in any way.

On a Friday morning in the middle of January, Mr. Barron was not in the store when Clara arrived. That had rarely happened in all the years she had known him. He was nearly always there to greet her when she came in, usually with a smile and a message of encouragement. When he had not arrived by the opening bell, Clara became alarmed. She straightened items on the counter that didn't need to be straightened. She checked the special displays already checked the night before. And she fretted. Someone from Personnel would have called her if he had phoned in sick, an occurrence that had happened only twice in the last five years.

Unable to calm her fears, Clara asked Mr. Dickey and Mr. Coles if they had taken a call about Mr. Barron or perhaps had a message for her. "No, Mrs. Pelletier, neither of us has heard anything. We were just talking now and wondering what was going on. Was there a management meeting or something?" Mr. Coles looked at her anxiously.

"I'm sure not or I would have known about it." Clara answered him and picked up the phone with some hesitation to call Mr. Barron's home. When there was no answer, she was struck by a terrible sense of apprehension. Her next call was to Mrs. Corrigan in Personnel, who then called Mr. Grimes, the General Manager. Jackson Grimes had been in his position of authority at McCallum's for only two years, but he had begun working there twenty-seven years ago. He knew Herbert Barron very well, even knew that he had considered the priesthood at one time because he, too, had gone to Holy Cross, though he graduated two years after Herb. While they had not been close friends, Jack had admired Herb's style and his beautiful singing in the choir, where he was often given the solo pieces. It had been shocking when he heard about the scandal at the end of Herb's senior year. Another member of the choir had discovered the Choir Director and Herb in an intimate embrace and when the story came out, it seems the two men had been having what was delicately called " a relationship" for over a year. Of course, the Choir Director was dismissed immediately, but Herb's father was an important lay member of the church and a close friend of the Archbishop. Herb had been allowed to graduate. The sad part was that Herb's family refused to accept him, tried to force him to marry and within the year after graduation, he had broken away from them and come to Northampton looking for a job.

Mr. Grimes appeared in the men's department, told Mr. Coles to fetch his coat and come with him to Mr. Barron's apartment. Clara's distress went up another notch. What was happening? She wanted to ask Mr. Grimes to call her immediately when he got to Mr. Barron's apartment and found out why he had not appeared, but she was not sure if that would be proper.

Not more than an hour later, an hour of extreme agitation for Clara, whose ability to smile and engage customers in conversation was an exercise in tight control, Mrs. Corrigan came down to the selling floor and called Clara aside.

"Mrs. Pelletier, I have a message for you from Mr. Grimes. He thought it would be better to hear it from me than by phone. Mr. Barron has suffered a stroke and been taken to Cooley Dickinson Hospital. It would be appreciated if you could carry on with his duties as well as your own for the time being. Is that possible?"

"Of course, I will do whatever is necessary. I know what reports are due and how to prepare them. I'll be glad to help out in any way I can. When can I go to visit Mr. Barron? Did Mr. Grimes say how bad a stroke it was? Will Mr. Barron recover?"

"He didn't give me any particulars about Mr. Barron's condition. Perhaps you can ask Mr. Coles when he comes back." Mrs. Corrigan put her hand on Clara's shoulder. "I know we can count on you, Mrs. Pelletier. McCallum's is lucky to have you."

Mr. Coles never did return to the store that day. Apparently he was so shaken by the events of the morning, Mr. Grimes gave him the rest of the day off. Clara, with only one clerk to work the whole department, had an exceedingly busy day, so much so she had little time to think about the consequences of Mr. Barron's stroke.

Three days later, Mr. Grimes called her at her (actually Mr. Barron's) tiny desk where she was preparing the monthly sales summaries to suggest it would now be appropriate to visit Mr. Barron. "Thank you, Sir, for letting me know. Is there anything I can bring him when I go? Is he able to read?"

Mr. Grimes hesitated. "I don't think he's reading yet, but you might want to bring something to read to him. I think he would like that. I know he likes the poetry of Robert Frost. Certainly, Forbes library will have copies."

"Thank you, Sir. I'll do that."

* * * * *

That evening, Clara drove up Elm Street to the hospital, a book of poetry on the seat beside her. Since she also knew that Mr. Barron loved beautiful things, she brought three hyacinth bulbs on a bed of stones in a shallow blue glass bowl. She had planted them for herself last week, but decided that watching them grow might give pleasure to her colleague as he recovered in the hospital.

When Clara stopped at the nurse's station to inquire whether Mr. Barron was receiving guests at this time, the nurse there reminded her that he tired easily, so she should plan to stay for a short time only. He was in a private room at the end of the floor, near the solarium. She entered shyly, unsure as to whether she would be welcome. She should not have worried. Even with the distortion in his facial muscles, it was easy to recognize his expression of delight at seeing her.

"Mr. Barron, I was so sorry to learn about your stroke. I will be praying every night for your swift recovery." Clara moved toward the bed, the book tucked under her arm and the bowl of bulbs held in front of her.

Herb Barron was a proud man, not happy to be seen diminished like this, but still, absolutely overjoyed to see his charming, attractive, endearing assistant. He opened his mouth to greet her, but what came out was not what he intended. It sounded more like "Wek" than "Welcome" and more like "Ca" than "Clara", but she seemed to understand anyway.

Clara put the bulbs on the windowsill, chattering away about their care, how enchanting it always seemed to her to watch them as they grew and how lovely they would be when they bloomed. She pulled up a chair, showed him the book and proceeded to read Frost's poetry to him with expression and dramatic flare for the next fifteen minutes. "I'll be back tomorrow to read more." And she kissed his cheek before she left.

When Clara got out to her car, she sat there with the motor idling and let the tears she had been holding back through a mighty application of willpower, fall freely. Whether Mr. Barron would be able to recover enough to return to work was certainly questionable and even if that happened, she was almost sure he would never be the same.

* * * * *

Three months later the senior staff met in Mr. Grimes' office to discuss the position of Head of the Men's Department. Even though Clara had been doing the job along with other duties as Assistant Buyer, there were those in the ranks of Senior Staff who thought it inappropriate to have a woman in that position. Mostly they were the same people who had opposed her promotion to Assistant.

"It's one thing to have women run the lingerie, ladies' dresses and babies' departments, but a woman managing the men's department is going too far." Spencer Soames had run the furniture department for seventeen years and had never been friendly with Herb Barron, privately thinking him somewhat of a dandy.

"She's only been with us for five years, you know." Helen Carpenter (used to be Carpentier, but she changed it) was the Head of ladies' dresses and proudly told everyone she had been there longer than Mr. Grimes. "Thirty-five years, if you please." She had been a stock clerk, leaving school at age 15 to go to work when her father died and her family needed the money.

"Does she even have a high school education? I think that's a requirement." Robert Poulet asked. He was in charge of the shoe department and had been at the store for thirteen years.

"Excuse me, Mr. Poulet, but you are wrong there. McCallum's has never had a requirement of a high school diploma. Maybe you are not old enough to remember when families sent their children out to work because they needed to eat, but I do." Helen's tone left no doubt that Mr. Poulet had just made an enemy.

Jack Grimes rapped his pencil on the desktop. "Do any of you have any reason to think she won't be able to do the job? That is the only question of importance right now." There were murmurs of "no" around the room. "Thank you, everyone. Remember that summer merchandise is arriving and invoices will need to be checked expeditiously. Mrs. Corrigan, will you please stay?"

When the room had cleared, Mrs. Corrigan moved to the seat next to the desk. "Here are the figures you asked for. You'll notice that Mr. Barron was promoted in 1938 when salaries were especially low and we didn't start offering commissions on sales until 1942, so there's that to consider. The average salary of department heads is there under the list of all the salaries, but you need to keep in mind that not all departments offer the opportunity to make commissions. And here's a list of the commissions Mrs. Pelletier has earned each month she's been with us, which you'll have to agree is quite impressive."

"Liz, you don't have to sell Clara Pelletier to me. I agree she's a terrific person and a great asset." Jack smiled and reached for the pages of typed figures. "What I have to do is offer her a decent salary without bringing the wrath of the entire senior staff down on my head."

"What do you care about them? You're the boss. When Ed Bullock was General Manager here he never asked anybody for their opinion. No senior staff meetings. Nobody entered his office except to deliver something he asked for or to get dressed down for poor performance."

"Well, I'm a different kind of guy. I have to do it my way. Give me a figure you think is fair. Let's start there."

"How about $50 a week? She's now making $38, so it's a nice jump for her. She usually makes somewhere close to $10 more in commissions. That would put her, depending on the commissions of course, over $3000 a year."

Jack frowned, tapped his pencil, and studied the figures on the list in front of him. "That's too much, especially for a woman, especially for someone new to the position." He looked up at his Head of Personnel, whose face registered her exasperation. "I know how you feel about this issue of equal pay, Liz, but face reality, my friend, this is the way it is and probably will be for a long time. Maybe it will change some day, but I doubt it will be in my lifetime. Besides, you know I have to get approval from the owners and they'll give me a hard time about it. I don't want to have a big fight with them right now, especially when I'm trying to get them to agree to stay open at least one more night a week."

"I'm glad I don't have your job," Liz Corrigan smiled. "How about $48 a week? That's $10 more than she's getting now and, of course, she's facing a lot more responsibility. But I think she'll welcome it as a challenge. Will you promote the Coles boy to Assistant?"

Louise S. Appell

"No, Rick Coles is too immature. Cripes, you should have seen him when we went over to Herb's apartment and found him on the floor in his bathroom. I'll admit it wasn't a pleasant sight, but Rick just fell apart. I had to yell at him to help me lift Herb away from the mess." Jack Grimes shook his head. "You don't want to hear about it. But, no, I won't be promoting Rick Coles anytime soon. I think Arthur Hickey has more potential, anyway."

"I agree with you about both of those men. So, what do you want to do about Mrs. Pelletier? And have you talked to Mr. Barron about what he plans to do? I heard somebody say he's going to be in that nursing home for a long time."

"What really burns me up is that his family has money. They should step in and take care of him. I called them, you know, and his father said to me, 'You must be mistaken. We do not have a son named Herbert.' and he hung up on me. Miserable old coot. He's such a sanctimonious, pompous ass. Sorry to get sidetracked. Yes, I will call Clara Pelletier in here and offer her the position. Do we have anything else we need to talk about today?"

"Well, we're going to have to talk about the Simmons girl in the stock room, since I'm almost certain she's pregnant, but it can wait a few more days. We don't

50

have to decide right now. I'm hoping she'll leave on her own without waiting to be let go. And the delivery truck driver asked for a raise. I told him it was too soon, but I don't think he liked that. I'd hate to see him quit. Customers like him. He's very polite and very good looking, which is probably why so many ladies call to tell us what good service he provides."

Jack Grimes sighed deeply. "Some things never change. I remember when I first came to work here. There was a delivery guy like that. All the ladies called about how great he was. Some of us were convinced he was providing very special services to lonely housewives and when he left suddenly with no explanations, we figured we were probably right. I hope to hell this is not what's happening now."

"Could be. Lots of war widows in town now." Liz Corrigan raised her eyebrows, grinned at her friend and boss and left his office.

* * * * *

"Hey, Stan, how about you and George join me for a beer and a pizza over at Joe's when we finish up that Buick?" Pete punched Stan's arm in a friendly gesture as he passed by the rack of fan belts where Stan was selecting one from a large array.

"Sounds like a great idea. It's been hot as hell today. A beer would go down real good."

Joe's Pizza was a little hole in the wall on Market Street that drew a crowd for its outstanding pizza as well as its welcoming bar. It was popular during the day and early evening with working men, most of them locals who had been going there for years. Later at night, especially on Wednesday date night and weekends, it drew a huge mixed group from all the colleges in the area. Of course, everyone knew that many of the students were really too young to be drinking; most of them carried fake ID cards. But the police rarely bothered Joe, since he served only beer and wine and he was quick to cut off anybody who he judged had had enough.

The three guys went in the bar entrance and inhaled the rich odor of olive oil, tomato, onion and herbs that always hung in the air at Joe's place. They sat down together at a chipped Formica-covered table. All the bar stools were filled already and it was just quarter past five. "Joe must be rolling in dough, packing them in like he does." George observed.

"It's a tough business, though. You have to spring for all the pizza ingredients every day, not knowing whether you'll get the customers coming in or not. He barely kept his head out of water during the thirties." Pete picked up a menu idly and scanned the list of toppings for the pizza. Out of the corner of his eye, he saw a guy get off a bar stool and come toward them.

"I know you. You're the frog that Angela Ciccione married, right? You're the big hero that came back from playing soldier as a gimp? Did you know I worked with her at the bomb plant in Florence while you were gone? We were great together. She always did have a fantastic pair of tits. Did she tell you she let me put my hand in her pants?"

Pete's brain told him this guy was drunk and lying, but still, the adrenaline started to pump. He was sitting alone on one side of the booth, facing George and Stan, who was on the outside. Pete rose and a scant second behind him, Stan rose also. "I don't believe we've met. What's your name, mister?" Pete's fists were clenched. He was aware this guy was at least an inch or two taller and about thirty pounds heavier.

"You mean Angela never told you about me? I'm Tony Scarlotti. I went with her in high school before she met you. She was the best lay I ever had." His eyes were red-rimmed, his sneer showed rotting teeth.

"You miserable sonofabitch, you're a fucking liar." Pete kept his voice low, but the room had grown quiet, everybody craning their necks to see, their ears sharp to hear the brewing fight. Stan's muscled arm shot out and grabbed Tony's wrist, quickly twisted it up behind his back and in a move so fast and so fluid the audience for this drama argued about it for weeks, hustled the drunken Tony right out the door. When Pete followed, Joe stepped around the end of the bar. He reached out and grabbed Pete by the arm. "Let Stan take care of it. Two on one is no good. And Tony's drunk anyway. He just got fired today. It won't take long."

There was some shouting, mostly curse words, heard from inside the bar and when Stan returned in a few minutes, there was scattered applause. "What did you do that for?" Pete asked. "I could have handled it."

Stan grinned and rubbed his reddened knuckles. "Yeah, sure, but you would have taken your time about it and I was in a hurry to get to my beer."

* * * * *

That night, Pete was taking off his shoes and socks when Angela came out of the bathroom. He looked up. "I met Tony Scarlotti today at Joe's Pizza joint on Market Street."

Angela stopped moving, her face entirely drained of color and she started to sway as Pete jumped to his feet and put his arms around her, sure she was going to faint. "What did he say?" she whispered.

"Angela, he was drunk. He didn't get to say much before Stan grabbed him and marched him out the door. It was over in a minute. C'mere." Pete sat back down on the little flounced bedroom chair and pulled Angela onto his lap. "Tell me about him. Did you go with him in high school?"

"Oh, *Dio mio*, no. He lived across the street from us and my mother was always warning me to stay away from him. But...but...he was working at the bomb plant and..." Angela stopped and dropped her chin to her chest, trembling. Pete stroked her cheek and tilted her up so their eyes were level. "What happened? Did he hurt you?"

With her face tucked into his shoulder, Angela told Pete the story of Tony's harassment and later, attempted rape. She whimpered as she recalled her fright and the awful feeling when he put his hands on her. She could not bring herself to say the words, "down my pants," but Pete could guess easily enough. When she described her brother Sal coming to the rescue, Pete's relief was visceral.

Pete rocked his wife in his arms and murmured words he thought might be comforting while she cried out her remembered terror, soaking his shirtfront with her tears. She was subdued and relieved to tell the story to someone at last. For his part, he vowed to avenge her in some way, but he couldn't think how at the moment. All he could do was thank God that she had survived. That big sonofabitch could have hurt her. And thank God for her brother Sal, too.

In some part of his head, Pete felt guilty that he had not been there to protect her. She worked hard while he was away in the service and socked away all that money that made it possible for him to have his business, to buy their pretty little house. Working with slimeballs like that Tony Scarlotti was the price she had paid. How could he ever make it up to her? He unbuttoned his wet shirt and dried her face with it, kissing her cheeks, her eyes, her nose, her ears, while he was doing it until she started to laugh and squirm in his lap. When she wrapped her arms around his neck and started kissing him back, he rose from the chair and carried her to the bed. *"Je t'aime, ma cherie. Toujours je t'aime."*

* * * * *

Marie heard from her friends that there was more money to be made in the fields where Hampshire County farmers grew the highly prized tobacco used for cigars than any other summer job in Northampton and she was eager to make as much money as possible. She desperately wanted to own at least one cashmere sweater, maybe two, and a tweed jacket, too.

She could have driven her car to work, but all her friends around the neighborhood were going to work in the tobacco fields and they went together on the rickety blue bus that picked them up at 7 in the morning and brought them home at 4:30. There was a lot of horsing around and flirting on the bus, so if you wanted a date for Saturday night, you pretty much had to be riding the bus.

She packed her lunch, usually a peanut butter and jelly sandwich, an apple and a cookie, in a brown lunch bag. Mom said almost anything else would spoil in the heat and she shouldn't be taking chances. A guy with a refrigerated truck came by at lunch time and sold sandwiches, milk and soda, but his sandwiches were too expensive. When you earned thirty-five cents an hour, it didn't make sense to spend almost half that for an egg sandwich, although some people did.

The tobacco was picked carefully leaf by leaf under shade tents made of white gauze, where the heat built up to nearly 100 degrees by noon. The leaves were brought into the big tobacco barns in large boxes, where they were strung on thick string about four inches apart. The string was attached at the ends to lathes, each a yard long, and then the lathes were hung inside the barn row after row, beginning at the top. The guys who hung the lathes were usually farm kids who had been doing it for years. They clambered up into the rafters when a barn began to be hung and worked their way down until they were almost on top of the girls and some grown women, too, working in rows on the floor of the barn stringing the leaves. It was necessary to wear thick gloves. Leather was best. Still, Marie's hands and hair and skin smelled of tobacco all summer. She scrubbed and scrubbed with Lava soap to get the stains out of her hands every night, always aggravated that she got stained even though she wore her gloves faithfully.

It was hot, smelly, hard work, but there was a camaraderie that made it acceptable. Often they sang while they worked. Groups ate their lunch together under the shade of big old trees bordering the tobacco field, talked about their plans for the future, bonded in their misery when a barn got close to being full and the air inside was suffocating.

The work crews were formed of boys who picked the leaves, boys who pulled the suckers, (extra buds that had to snapped off to preserve the plant's energy for bigger leaves), girls who strung the leaves and boys and young men who hung the lathes.

When a barn was completely full, everybody moved on to another field, another barn. At night the smoke pots were brought in so the tobacco could be "cured". Each barn had hinged panels alternating with rigid ones and these needed to be opened or closed depending on the weather and the status of the "curing", a delicate job that determined the worth of the crop.

* * * * *

Marie hated it and loved it at the same time. She hated the early morning start, the heat and the smell, the frequent needle sticks, the painful muscle cramps, the way her hands looked all the time. But then, she was making good money, the kids she worked with were lots of fun and she was seeing Rick Clarey, her high school crush, on the bus every morning and every night, sometimes talking and laughing with him at lunch. He was home for the summer from Boston University, still the same relaxed, friendly, good- humored guy. Now and then he'd stop by her house on the weekend, sit on the porch, drink lemonade and listen to records.

One night, sitting alone together on the porch in the dark, talking about the end of summer and going back to school, Rick put his hand inside her blue camp shirt, pushed aside her white cotton bra and closed his sweating palm around her breast. Marie was startled.

She sat very still, her thoughts racing. What should she do? What happens next?   Rick put his mouth close to her ear and whispered, "Jesus, Mary and Joseph, I've wanted to do this all summer. You are so soft."

They both heard the screen door spring. He pulled his hand away and licked her ear before settling back on the porch swing, laying his arm along the back. Amy came out with a plate in her hands. "Mom thought you might want some cookies. They're chocolate chip. She made them this afternoon."

*   *   *   *   *

Pete and Stan worked for the election of Harry Truman all summer, making phone calls, going to meetings of civic groups to talk about their man and to disparage his opponent, Thomas Dewey. They described Republicans as a bunch of lawyers and bankers, "Wall Street boys" and Dewey as "the little man on the wedding cake," a clear reference to his cold stiffness. Pete really enjoyed the public speaking and the opportunity to make fun of Dewey, feeling that the man represented the rich, elite, privileged people in the country. He often said, "It's the middle class guys like me who won the war, who are going to succeed with our little businesses, who are always going to need the power of the government to help us, because there's no Daddy Warbucks going to hand us anything."

Stan wasn't happy in the limelight, but he faithfully trudged neighborhoods, leaving pamphlets at doors, calling people he knew to ask for small donations to the campaign war chest and tagging along with Pete to meetings where he shook a lot of hands and thanked attendees for listening.

Both of them were enthusiastic about Truman's chances for winning the election. When some skeptics pointed out that Truman was no Roosevelt; he didn't have the ability to charm, he was a blunt, plain-spoken man and he had been a haberdasher of all things before he became a politician, Pete laughed and said, "Wait and see."

On election night, the Democratic Party faithful gathered at Rahar's on Old South Street, just off Main Street, to wait for the returns. It was to be a long night's vigil. Ears strained to hear the radios which were tuned in to any station that got good reception, a radio in each of the rooms of the rambling old inn. Once some static drowned out the figures coming in and people ran into the next room shouting, "What did they just say?"

Around midnight when the news looked bleak, Stan decided to go home. His wife was home with her sister to keep her company and she was expecting their second child. Even though he knew she understood his excitement about the election, he felt a little guilty about all the time he had spent on the campaign in the last six months. And since it looked like they were probably going to lose, he was less interested in being there until the end.

Pete, on the other hand, was determined to stay and remained optimistic even when many were not. He kept circulating through the rooms smiling, chatting, assuring everyone, "It's not over 'til it's over." He pasted on a fake mustache and did an imitation of Dewey that had people laughing. He started up the chant "Give 'em hell, Harry" that raised the crowd's spirits. He was drinking beer, as was nearly everybody else. But he was drinking cautiously, knowing that to get plastered here was to make an ass of yourself forever and maybe even hurt his business.

When it was all over and Truman defeated Dewey, some party leaders stopped Pete on his way out, slapping him on the back and thanking him for his role in leading the party workers with his upbeat refrain. A State Senator shook his hand and said, "If you decide you want to go into politics, Pete, give me a call." And the local party Chairman said, "Come see me sometime next week. I've got an interesting proposition for you." Pete thanked both of them, but was vague and noncommittal. Politics was exciting for a few months, but he loved his motor repair business and had no intention of doing anything else.

Chapter 4

Northampton, Mass.
1948-49

Clara was wrapping Christmas presents in her bedroom when she heard the phone ring. Then Tillie called up the stairs, "Clara, it's for you. It's Anna." She ran down the front staircase and picked up the phone, "Hi, Anna, how are you?"

"Clara, sit down. They found him and he's alive."

Clara sat down heavily in the little tapestry covered chair by the phone, her sharp outcry bringing Tillie rushing in from the kitchen.

"He's very, very sick, they said, but alive."

"Where is he? Can I go to him? Who told you? Where has he been?" Clara's mind was filled with questions. She ignored the pain in her stomach, the obstruction in her throat that made her words come out in a croak, the tears sliding down her cheeks.

"Somebody from our congressman's office called Randy a few minutes ago. Some kids found him in a forest. At first they thought he was dead. They saw the dog tags and recognized them as American so they bicycled into their little town and told the mayor who called a British Army base not too far away. All I know is that he's in a hospital and he hasn't talked to anyone. The guy who called didn't know for sure, but he said it sounded as if Ray's in a coma." Anna started to cry. "I'm sorry. I'm sorry. I thought I was all cried out. I waited to call you until I could get ahold of myself, but I'm just so...so...." Her voice tapered off and Clara, herself crying, heard big sobs and sniffles on the other end of the line.

"Anna, Anna, listen to me. I need you to give me the phone number of the man who called you. I have to talk to him myself." Clara exerted every ounce of self-control she could muster to calm down, stop crying and do what she needed to do.

Apparently, Anna had handed the phone to her husband, Randy. "The call came from the chief of staff in our congressman's office in Washington. He just lost re-election but I'm sure the staff is there and willing to help. The guy to talk to is Harry Brownell. His number is Locust 2-4000. You have to get the long distance operator first, of course."

"Thanks, Randy; tell Anna I'll call her back later."

It did not occur to Clara that it was 6:45 at night and the office might be closed. She placed the call and when it was answered, she took a deep breath and said, "I need to talk to Mr. Harry Brownell. He just called Mrs. Anna Parker in Hartford about her brother, Ray Carpenter. My name is Clara Pelletier and Ray is my fiancé."

"Ah, did you say Clara? The report says the man wearing Ray Carpenter's dog tags has a crude tattoo on his left arm, looks like it was made with a nail. Clara, that's the tattoo. I didn't want to say anything about it to his sister, because I didn't want to upset her anymore than she already is with a name she wouldn't recognize. What can I do for you? I already told Captain Carpenter's sister all I know right now."

"Well, no, you didn't if you didn't tell her about the tattoo. I want every scrap of information you have. I've got a pencil and paper here and I'm going to write it all down. I think she may not have heard everything you said clearly when she was so shaken by the news."

The voice at the other end of the line inhaled sharply, "You're right, of course. And you got me on the tattoo. I was only trying to protect her, though. What do you want to know?"

"Let's start by exactly where and when he was found and in what condition." Clara's tone was grim. She was holding onto her control with an enormous effort.

"He was found in a forest near the border between Austria and Italy, but actually in Yugoslavia. That part of the world is Communist now, in case you didn't know that. Some kids out hunting rabbits found him under a big fir tree. He was half covered in pine needles, which probably protected him from the worst of the cold. He was wearing clothes typical of the peasants who live in that area, although he also had on what looked like the remains of a U.S. Army Air Force fleece jacket, which also protected him. The kids saw the dog tags and recognized them for what they are. There probably isn't a kid in all Europe that doesn't know what they mean.

Even though the area is Communist, a lot of the people there aren't sympathizers and probably don't give a damn who's in charge of the government as long as they get left alone to do what they've always done. The kids went to the mayor in their town, who most likely represents the highest authority they know.

Fortunately for us, the mayor knew somebody at a British Army base not too far away in Klacenfurt and he called there. A small team took a hell of a risk of creating an international incident, went into the forest with the kids at dusk and carried Ray out of there. That was five days ago. Every congressman serving District 1 in Connecticut has had red flags on all Army records related to Ray for a long time...well, since late 1945 when the Army finally admitted they couldn't locate him.

Umm, what else did you ask me? Oh, yeah, he's now in a hospital outside London. They took him there yesterday. He doesn't seem to have anything broken, although he's got two bullet wounds, well healed, one in the buttocks and one in the shoulder. He was severely dehydrated and malnourished and it looks like he was beaten with a leather strap because he's got scars across his back that are consistent with repeated beatings. He's got a recent large bruise on his head, which means he may have hit his head from a fall or maybe somebody threw something at him. It sounds like he's in a coma, so he hasn't been able to tell the authorities anything."

Clara was writing as fast as she could. "Now tell me how I get to see him."

"Whoa, I sure don't know the answer to that question. Even if you were willing to fly to London, I don't know if you could see him. He's pretty banged up, you know. And a coma means he won't even know you're there."

"How do you know that? I read somewhere that lots of times people in a coma can hear and know what's going on around them. Anyway, if you don't know the answer to my question about seeing him, would you please find out and call me right away? As I told you before, my name is Clara Pelletier. P-E-L-L-E-T-I-E-R. I'm in Northampton, Massachusetts and my phone number is 2175."

"Sure, I'll get on that as soon as possible."

"How about tonight? I'd like to start making my plans right away."

The guy on the phone laughed, "You sure know how to push, don't you?"

"When it's this important, I do. Thanks for your help. I'll be waiting for your call."

When she hung up the phone, Clara was completely drained. She went into the kitchen where Tilly and Edward were sitting at the table, their anxious faces reminding Clara that they had only heard her end of the conversation. She sat down and, referring to her notes, recounted the story for them, thinking all the while what an astonishing story it was.

Edward reached over and put his hand over hers. "You must go, yes?" It was not really a question.

"I think the first thing I have to do is call Birdell's Travel Agency in the morning and find out how to do it. Maybe I can get an airplane in Boston. I read somewhere that they have planes that go to London almost every day now. Maybe Anna will want to go, too. I have to call her now and tell her about my call to Washington." Clara's thoughts were getting jumbled, thinking of Ray, bruised and battered. She was apprehensive about flying over the ocean, scared of the future, but determined to stay strong.

* * * * *

Pete wasn't in the house five minutes, barely had time to scrub his hands and face before Angela handed him a scotch and soda. That fact alone revealed something momentous had happened in her day. She sat him down in the big blue club chair and told him the amazing news about Ray.

"Pete, she can't fly over there alone. What if he dies while she's there and she has no family to help her? I can't imagine it."

"Why doesn't his sister Anna go, too?"

"Yeah, that's the first thing I asked, but it turns out Anna is terrified of flying. She won't even go on a Ferris wheel because she gets sick."

"So are you telling me you want to go with her?"

"No, no, I have to be here for Petey. I think you should go with her and maybe Marie, too. Clara's going to need all the family support she can get."

"Marie is just a kid and she can't be skipping classes at college. And I've got a business to run."

"Marie is 18, a young woman. She can share a room with Clara, be there when she needs somebody to talk to in the middle of the night. Christmas break starts next week, so maybe she misses a couple of days, so what? She'll tell her professors and they'll understand. And you are good at getting your way. Face it; sometimes it has to be a man to stand up to these military types. They'll just give her that old 'There, there, dearie, we know best' bullshit. Your business can get along without you for a few days, maybe a week. You have to help her persuade them to move Ray back here."

"This will put a big hole in our savings account, I think," Pete sighed.

"I know. But helping Clara is too important to worry about that right now. If it had been you, I would have...." Tears formed in Angela's eyes and she brushed them away.

"Yeah, I know." Pete took out his handkerchief and wiped her tears away.

There was the flurry of getting emergency passports, but Pete's political connections were a help in getting that done. Birdell's Travel Agency got the tickets on Pan Am and made reservations at a modest hotel near the Marble Arch in London. Congressman Miller's office arranged for a US embassy car to pick them up and take them to the hospital just outside London in Tunbridge Wells. Four days after learning that Ray was alive, Clara and her loyal family members flew across the Atlantic, all three of them praying Ray would survive. If any of them had qualms about the flight, it went unremarked in their anxiety and concern for Clara's beloved.

*   *   *   *   *

Dr. Klein shook his head when he got the call that Clara was coming accompanied by two family members. "Ridiculous. We don't need them hanging over our shoulders. Everything possible is being done for this young man. He's very, very weak. I don't see much chance for his survival. It's a waste of their time and money."

His colleague, Dr. Pitt, pulled on his lower lip, a gesture characteristic of him when he was thinking. "I don't know about that, Bob. Whatever has happened to him in the last three years, he had to be pretty tough to withstand it. God, I'd love to know where he's been and what he's been doing. And who in hell beat him like that? Maybe having his fiancé here will give him the extra strength to fight his way through."

"I doubt it. He's nothing but skin and bones. He looks as bad as those concentration camp survivors. And I don't like getting pushed around by politicos, either. Nobody asked about these visitors coming here. We were just told they were coming and that's that. No advice wanted. Just do as I say. I hate that."

"Let it go, Bob. We're both damned lucky we haven't had anybody in our families that went through anything like this poor soul did. If she gives him some solace, I'll welcome her every day."

Bob Klein sighed deeply. "His numbers are looking better today. I asked for a set of X-rays yesterday and they just came back. It looks as if his arm got broken a while ago and somebody did a pretty good job of setting it, so wherever he was, there had to be a person there who knew how to deal with a broken bone. Maybe the same person who applied a lash to his back. Did you notice the pattern of the scars? Somebody wanted to inflict pain without causing any real damage. Probably enforcing obedience or punishing disobedience, depending on how you look at it. I wonder why he carved his lady's name in his arm like that. Lucky he didn't get an infection."

"He probably marked himself with her name to give him the courage to keep going. Maybe to remember why he wanted to live. My guess is he met up with a band of people living deep in the forest when he ran away from the prison camp and they had a difference of opinion on whether he could keep going or stay with them. Some of the forests in Europe are so old and dense they have people living like cavemen, completely self-contained, needing nothing they can't provide for themselves."

"But what would be the reason they wouldn't let him just keep going?"

"Needing new blood, maybe? Afraid he'd reveal their presence and bring in authorities? I don't know. Oops, I've got to go. Meeting in ten minutes. See you later."

* * * * *

It was quiet in the embassy car taking them to the hospital, each of them lost in their own thoughts. Clara was caught up in a fantasy where she kissed Ray and, like Sleeping Beauty in the fairytale, he sat up and said "Clara, babe, I've been calling you and calling you. I'm so glad you're here." Pete was thinking about what kind of red tape they would face to get Ray transferred to a hospital in the States. Marie was dreading the possibility that Ray would die right there in front of them and Aunt Clara would collapse.

A short, slender, bald guy wearing tortoise shell glasses introduced himself as Dr. Pitt and sat down next to them in one of the waiting room chairs. The room was empty, pretty small as waiting rooms go, thought Pete. The doctor asked about their flight, their hotel, whether they had been in Britain before. Pete started to reply, but Clara cut him off, asking, "Can we see Captain Carpenter now?"

"Of course. I do want you to be prepared, though. He's still quite emaciated, although better than he was. We are feeding him nutrients intravenously; he's turned over on a regular schedule to avoid getting bedsores; he will look to you as if he's sleeping. Actually, he's in a coma; his body is trying to heal. We haven't been able to determine how serious a blow to the head he had. Some studies have suggested that some patients in a coma do hear and assimilate what's going on around them, so please don't say or do anything that will be upsetting."

Clara ran her hand over her short, thin hair. "What do you mean by upsetting?"

"We've had women come here and get hysterical with weeping and wailing. That sort of thing doesn't help at all."

"Don't worry. That's definitely not me."

"And not more than two of you at a time." The doctor glanced over at Marie, who responded quickly. "I understand. I'll wait right here."

The first thing that Clara noticed when she walked up to the bed where Ray lay was his chest moving up and down rhythmically. Only then did she truly believe he was alive. His cheeks were sunken, his hair was peppered with gray, his color was chalk white and he was very, very still. She covered his hands with hers and leaned over to kiss his brow, then his cheek, then softly, softly pressed her lips to his. She whispered, "Ray, my darling, it's Clara. I heard you calling me. I'm here."

* * * * *

Chapter 5

◇◇

Northampton, Mass.
1949

They stayed four days while Pete made the case for transferring Ray to a hospital in New England, either one in Massachusetts or Connecticut. He went from one office to another, patiently pressing for an early decision. When Clara called Anna, she suggested Randy get the newly elected Congressman Ribicoff to add his weight to the request. Marie listened to her Aunt Clara talk out her hopes and fears every night and woke her from her nightmares, too. One day they all three distracted themselves by going to visit the tower of London and another day they watched the changing of the guard at Buckingham Palace, both Clara and

Marie chanting together the verse from Winnie, the Pooh, laughing as they shivered in the cold. "They're changing the guard at Buckingham Palace..." Pete thought they were nuts, but he smiled to hear the rare laughter coming from Clara.

When they left Britain, they felt reasonably sure that Ray would be home soon, and though they were right that the wheels had been set in motion, it was almost a month before it happened. The shared experience brought Marie and her Aunt Clara closer than ever before. Also, Clara had recognized during the course of their time in Britain that Marie was no longer a little girl, but a woman, young still but maturing fast, thoughtful, introspective and compassionate.

* * * * *

Clara's friend Ruth Goldberg came back to town right after the New Year and Clara welcomed her return. She knew that Ruth would listen to her fears about Ray, provide her with sympathy and kindness, endure her moodiness. They could talk about anything as they always had and enjoy the solace of beautiful music together.

Ruth had been living in Cambridge for the last two years, with her husband, who used the GI Bill to get an advanced degree in architecture at Harvard. Already a trained engineer, a graduate of Columbia University with nearly five years in the Navy, he was thinking about starting his own firm. Bob Rhoades clearly adored his fiercely independent Jewish wife and he was willing to take on the whole world in her defense. When he told his father, a professor of Ancient History at Smith College and a widower, that they had decided to settle in Northampton, Professor Rhoades was delighted. However, he cautioned his son that Northampton was a small town and provincial in many ways. Their mixed marriage might raise quite a few eyebrows and could mean that they would be less than welcome in some places.

"Oh, I don't give a tinker's dam about that." Bob declared hotly. "I like small towns and so does Ruth. We've lived in New York and we really like it a lot better here. Besides, I like being near you."

"And I like having you near me. Do you think this town is big enough to support a firm like you propose to start?"

"What I think is that a lot of things are changing and a lot of growing is going on. I don't intend to work just in Northampton, but all around this region. More people going to college means more buildings will have to be added to accommodate them. You don't think this surge of interest in education is going to stop, do you? These guys who go to college under the GI Bill will want their kids to go to college, too. You wait and see if that doesn't happen."

"Yes, I'm sure you're right about that, son. A great middle class is being created right now. People who never expected to do other than skilled labor, at best, will become professional workers of all types, will start their own businesses, become homeowners, community leaders. A lot of the resources of this country have been lost by putting higher education out of reach for all but the children of the wealthy. Now we'll see how teaching more people to think deeply, question conventional wisdom, and solve problems with new ideas can impact on this country. It's an exciting prospect."

* * * * *

Tillie noticed that Edward hadn't been eating with his usual robust appetite, often leaving some of his favorite food behind on his plate. "Edward, *mon cheri*, how come you are leaving food on your plate? You've always enjoyed my pork roast with spiced apples. Are you not feeling well?"

"It's just a little stomach trouble. Nothing to worry about. It comes and goes. I do not mean to insult

your excellent cooking. Will you forgive me?" Edward
smiled.

Not more than a week or so later, Edward was getting
into his pajamas when Tillie noticed her husband bend
over, clutching his middle. His face was a grimace
of pain. She became really alarmed and insisted he
see Dr. Boucher. Edward dragged his feet and kept
putting off her questions about whether he had seen the
doctor yet. One night, when she awoke to his moaning
and writhing, she gave up her distaste for using the
telephone and made the appointment herself. "The
appointment is made for 3 o'clock on Monday, *mon
mari*, so you must go."

Dr. Boucher's office was right on Main Street above the
Woolworth's store. Edward found a parking space a
little ways down and, resigned to the inevitable, climbed
the stairs. He opened the door with the pebbled glass
panel that announced, in bold black letters, Herbert
Boucher, M.D., General Practice. Inside, on a cracked
brown leather sofa, a young child slept, her head in her
mother's lap, her thumb in her mouth. At the other
end of the sofa a woman, looking very tired and worn
and near the end of her pregnancy, turned the pages
of a torn National Geographic. On a straight backed
chair by the window, Edward spotted an acquaintance
he hadn't seen in quite a while. "Gaston, *comment ca
va*? I heard your boy got married last year. He is all

recovered, then?" and he sat down in the unoccupied chair next to his compatriot.

Gaston roused himself from his reverie. "Edward, *bien, bien, merci. Oui.* He got married and now he is getting a divorce. My wife is so upset. Ashamed, *tu comprends?* We've never had a divorce in our family before."

"Times have changed. These young men came back from the war and they're going to change a lot of things, I think. Are you here to see Dr. Boucher?"

"Non, no, it's my wife." Gaston lowered his voice and leaned closer to Edward. "It's the change. She's having a bad time of it."

Edward nodded and just then Gaston's wife came out of the door to the inner office, her face flushed. She gestured to her husband with her hand and moved toward the outer door. Gaston jumped up, shook hands with Edward and said, *"Bonjour."*

It had been many years since Edward had been seen by any medical professional and he was nervous and anxious. In his mind, unless you were a child or a pregnant woman, doctors meant death was on the way. He sat there waiting, unable to read the magazine he had picked up, thinking about the arc of his life, the things he had to be thankful for, the regrets for what he would never get to accomplish, his great love for his wife, his son and his family, especially *les enfants.*

After a wait of 30 minutes or so, watching people go in to the inner office and more people arriving to take their place, Edward's name was finally called. He had known Dr. Boucher for at least twenty years, but their relationship was as formal as it had ever been. Although the doctor called him Edward, he still greeted the doctor formally. He described his stomach problems, answered questions about his bodily functions and agreed that he probably should have come in sooner.

It was extremely embarrassing to him to remove his clothes and wrap himself in the cold sheet provided, but of course he did as he was told. The nurse took his blood pressure reading and left the room. When Dr. Boucher poked and prodded Edward's stomach, he groaned loudly. Edward's teeth were clenched in an effort to avoid groaning again, but the examination was truly painful. And when he was told that "opening up" his body was the only way to get an answer to what was causing the distress, the words made him tremble.

Tillie reacted with tears and prayers, but was mollified that the surgery must be done to find out the nature of the problem. When she told Clara later in the evening, Clara murmured soothing words to her sister, but privately thought it must be cancer, the most dreaded word in diagnosis, almost certainly a fatal condition.

Clara had no intention of voicing these thoughts, of course. Later, when Tillie asked her to drive to the French Church so they could light some candles for Edward's quick recovery, Clara was pleased to have an opportunity to do something. Anything was better than just waiting and hoping. If anyone knew that, she did.

On the day of Edward's surgery, both Clara and Pete joined Tillie in the waiting room. Pete chain-smoked and paced until his mother told him to sit down and stop making her crazy. Dr. Boucher came through the door in a surprisingly short time, his surgical mask dangling, his face grave. "There is nothing I can do. Cancer is spread all over, in his stomach, in his liver, in his pancreas, everywhere. I sewed him right back up. Take him home and make him comfortable. It will not be long. I am so sorry, *mes amis*. I know how hard this is for you. Some day maybe we will know what to do. I hope so."

* * * * *

Edward came home in an ambulance. The attendants carried him into the house on a stretcher. He was now much too fragile to walk any distance at all. Tillie, Clara, and Pete stood on the porch, watching his arrival, frozen with a horrible sense of doom. It had been Tillie's decision to avoid telling Edward the diagnosis. She said that, if he did ask her, she would answer honestly, but really, she thought he probably knew.

Pete had arranged for the rental of a hospital bed, and he had set it up in the dining room after he moved the beautiful old mahogany table and all but two of the chairs into the attic. Within a few days, the room was changed as the various items needed to care for Edward were brought in. A bedside table, big enough to hold the water pitcher, cup, and glass straw as well as the small basin and cloths Tillie used to clean Edward, was brought down from the front bedroom. Clara found a small stool in the housewares department at the store that they could put beside the high bed so the women, when they were alone in the middle of the night, could reach across and tuck in Edward's covers. Pete went back to the rental place to get a tray table on a stand that slid over the bed for easier feeding. Now unrecognizable as the family dining room, Clara wondered if it could ever look again as it had all the years of her life. Too bad they had rented out *Gran'mere's* old bedroom.

When Maurice's wife Simone heard the news she insisted on moving in so she could help Tillie take care of Edward. Maurice drove her up to Northampton from their home in Connecticut.

"Edward, *mon ami,* I think we are getting old, you and I. Remember when you first came to court my sister Tillie? How *mes freres* and I made a nuisance of ourselves, asking questions? Well, all of us except Charlie. He thought you were a splendid fellow."

Edward chuckled and reached out to grasp Maurice's hand. Later Maurice would remark about how lucky he felt to have had that time with his brother-in-law. In a few days Edward's skin began to turn yellow and he could eat almost nothing at all. Even his favorite foods did not tempt him to a single bite.

Father Dumont came to visit every day, staying only long enough to lead whoever was there in prayer at Edward's bedside. Pete stopped by every day, also, eager to do any tasks his mother assigned him. It took a lot of control on his part to stop himself from howling at God for letting this awful thing happen to his father. Each day he noticed his beloved Pa slipping away and, as the morphine given him for pain was increased, Edward was less and less able to communicate with any of them.

Marie came to visit, but could hardly stand next to the bed more than a few minutes, the tears falling freely and the sobs threatening to turn into loud wails of grief. She had to leave to avoid upsetting her *Memere.* Angela brought Amy and Petey, hoping that Edward would know somehow that they were there and that they loved him. Friends and relatives stopped by for a few minutes, mostly just to say their goodbyes and to console Tillie. When Alphonse arrived with his son Phillipe, Clara greeted her older brother sharply, "It took you long enough to show up, *mon frere.* Did you have to get permission from your wife?" Alphonse did not answer her.

Less than three weeks after the surgery, Edward died in his sleep, not, however, before he had touched Tillie's hand and whispered, *"Je t'aime, ma cherie, toujours, je t'aime."* Clara and Simone were in the room, tears rolling down their cheeks.

* * * * *

The wake was at Quinn's, still the funeral parlor closest to the Church of the Sacred Heart. Tillie had already picked out the clothes for Edward to be laid out in. She choose his favorite brown suit with the matching vest, a white shirt and a light blue tie with a small figure of a gold fleur-de-lis. After a lot of thought and asking everyone's opinion, she decided he would wear his gold watch chain across his vest, but not with the watch in the pocket and the watch chain was to be removed before the final closing of the casket. His plain gold wedding band was to be buried with him. Pete got the task of picking out a casket. He asked Clara and Angela to come with him, but Angela begged off, since Petey had a cold and Amy wasn't feeling well either. She really hated leaving sick children with someone else.

Pete and Clara looked at a dozen caskets in Quinn's showroom and decided on a rich mahogany with brass fittings lined with cream silk. Mr. Quinn showed him some examples of the obituary cards that would be given to the mourners who came to the wake and condolence books that would be put out to be signed by everyone as they arrived. Pete said "I don't care." and so Clara picked out a simple style. They stopped at the liquor store and Pete bought an assortment of booze for the back room where many of the men would go expecting to be offered a drink or two.

Tillie had had weeks to decide what she would wear and on Simone's advice chose a simple black silk crepe with a broad collar and elbow length sleeves, which was one of the three Clara brought home from McCallum's for her to try. She planned to wear a favorite black hat with a veil.

During both days of the wake a constant stream of people came to show their respect and offer condolences.

Pete and Clara took turns greeting mourners at the door. They were Edward's co-workers at the library, many men in the community who shared his love of maps and had met him at meetings, all the tenants from the alley, a far-flung collection of relatives, some driving down from *Trois Rivieres*, others from Maine and people he had met casually when he was an air raid warden during the war and they came because he was a gentle loving soul who always had a kind word and a smile. Pete's buddies from all the organizations he belonged to hardly knew Edward, but they came to offer condolences to their friend and he let them know how much he appreciated it. Clara's co-workers at McCallum's came for the same reason and were greeted with hugs that expressed her thanks.

The President of Smith College, who knew Edward from his interest in maps, appeared and, taking Tillie's hands in his own, told her, "Your husband, Madame, was a wonderful and generous man who will be missed by many." Tillie didn't know what to say to such an imposing personage, so she murmured, "Thank you for coming." The Mayor and the Police Chief paid their respects, also. The outpouring of sentiment was extraordinary.

Maurice took on the responsibility of pouring drinks for the men who said their prayers for Edward at the kneeler in front of the casket and headed straight to the back room, knowing liquor would be available there.

It rained the night before the funeral mass and interment, but when morning came the sun was shining. Father Dumont, who knew Edward well and respected him, gave a moving homily in a voice hoarse with emotion. The children's choir sang beautiful old French hymns, including the one with the refrain "*Au ciel, au ciel, au ciel,*" representing the soul's ascent into heaven, a special favorite that left few dry eyes in the congregation.

The burial plot was in St. Mary's cemetery, right next to Tillie's mother and father, a short drive from the church. The ceremony at the gravesite was blessedly brief. Sniffles and sobs were heard, but there was no intrusive wailing to distract from the service. When it was over, the mourners quietly dispersed, some stopping by to touch Tillie's hand, give her a brief hug or murmur a few words.

* * * * *

Back home on West Street Clara could see that Tillie was exhausted beyond her ability to cope with anything. She guided her sister up the stairs, helped her remove her dress and get into bed.

"Clara, *ma soeur*, how am I going to live without him?" Tillie asked plaintively.

Clara sighed and stroked her sister's hair. "You will because you must. Edward would not want you to despair. You know that. I'll just pull the shades down and you close your eyes for a little while. Rest now and we'll talk later."

Leaving Tillie, she shut the bedroom door quietly and stood there, in the upstairs hall, thinking of the pain of loss, wondering if she, too, would have to learn to live without her man. Would Ray come out of the coma? Would he be changed? If only we could know what lay ahead so we could prepare for it.

Downstairs, Pete poured drinks for his Uncle Maurice and Aunt Simone. Angela had decided to take Amy home, where a neighbor was watching Petey just long enough for them to go to the funeral. Marie went in to the kitchen and started making sandwiches of whatever was in the refrigerator and arranging them on a tray. When Clara came downstairs, she was surprised to see the initiative and she thanked Marie profusely. They all sat around the parlor, talking quietly of nothing important at all, numbed by their grief, but taking comfort in being together.

* * * * *

Four months later, with Christmas approaching, Pete thought about how to celebrate the season without Pa. He could not see the sense in letting it be gloomy for the children. He knew his father would never have wanted that to be. Maybe the children's delight at the old traditions would cheer up his mother.

Pete decided to take Marie and Amy with him to tramp the woods looking for a perfect Christmas tree, something they had not done since Uncle Charlie left. The day was cold, the wind a little brisk, but the sun was shining and they were all enjoying the exercise. Marie threw a snowball at her father and he quickly scooped up a ball of the wet stuff and pelted her back. In a second, they were all throwing snowballs at each other and laughing 'til the tears rolled down their cheeks. Amy flopped backwards to make an angel and when Marie came to pull her up out of the depression she made in the foot deep snow, they declared the tree next to her angel was the perfect one to bring home.

While Pete sawed off the lowest branches and positioned the tree in its holder (this done out on the porch), Clara and Angela went up to the attic and brought down the boxes of decorations and Tillie made penuche with a little help from Petey, who was especially good at licking the spoon. Clara brought her record player from her bedroom and put on a stack of Christmas music. Everybody helped trim the tree, even Petey, who wasn't old enough to handle the precious glass balls, but was very good at hanging tinsel.

* * * * *

On Christmas Eve, Angela brought a big pot of ravioli over to the house on West Street, Tillie went down to the cellar and brought up two Mason jars, one of green beans and one of zucchini. They ate around the kitchen table, chattering of local events, Pete's clubs, his business and Clara's experiences at McCallum's. All of them felt deeply the losses at the table, Charlie, Ray, Edward, but they refrained from mentioning it.

Angela put Petey to bed in Clara's room, promising to wake him up as soon as Santa arrived. Pete had cajoled George into donning Charlie's old Santa suit, though it was necessary to use a great deal of padding. When he arrived and Petey was retrieved from his bed to see him, there were tears in the eyes of the women, remembering all the Christmases past when this ritual had drawn them together. It was a powerful reminder that individuals come and go, but the family lives on.

Pete's gift to his mother was a television set, which she had resisted as much as she had the telephone. When it was plugged in and the rabbit ears adjusted, she sat staring at the screen, watching the flickering when suddenly the picture appeared of a group of children playing the bells in a Christmas concert. She clapped her hands and her eyes widened. *"Oh, Pierro, c'est merveilleux."* Pete refrained from mentioning how much he hated to be called Pierro, his legal name, but instead, kissed his mother's cheek and answered, "I hope you enjoy it, Ma."

Chapter 6

◇◇◇

Montreal, Quebec
1980

In the solarium of the Sisters of the Sacred Heart Nursing Home, Uncle Charlie and Marie were wrapped in embrace, both of them weeping quietly, each of them mourning Edward LaPointe, *Pepere* to Marie and much loved brother-in-law to Charlie. "He was always a good man, a very good man."

They were startled when the sweet-faced nun came to remind them it was lunch time. Marie rose from her seat and wiped her eyes, smiled at her uncle and said, "I'll be back at four. Have a good nap." He blew her a kiss.

As Marie sat on the bench, wrestling with her new galoshes, Mother Superior appeared. "Mrs. Graham, may I have few minutes of your time." Without waiting for an answer, she turned and walked quickly to her office, Marie following obediently, galoshes flapping.

"I've been told just now that you upset *Monsieur* Billieux this morning. I thought I made it quite clear that you were not to do that." Mother Superior's posture conveyed her anger as much as her words did, but Marie was ready this time.

"Mother, I am doing what my Uncle Charlie asked me to do. I am telling him what happened in our family during the years he had been disconnected from us. As I am sure you know, life is not all chocolates and roses. People get sick; they die; they lose their way. I am sorry you don't approve, but that will not stop me from telling him what he wants to know. I am mindful of his health problems and what I tell him is sometimes a bit edited from all I remember, but I will not avoid answering his questions, nor will I tell him any lies." Marie was shaking, her hands clasped tightly in her lap.

"You know, I could forbid you to come in here." The nun's face was stony.

"But you won't because that would upset him even more and I'm sure you know that."

"You really don't understand how much we love your uncle, do you? Tell me, have you noticed any other men in this nursing home?"

Marie flushed, "I have been in the waiting room, your office, and the solarium and I don't know whether you have any men in here."

"Ah, well, let me tell you then. There are no other men here, only your uncle. Do you know why?"

"I have no idea why."

"This order runs an orphanage in Maine, not far from where your uncle went to work in a logging camp in 1942. Every weekend, he came in his truck to work on whatever needed to be done in the church, the rectory and the orphanage. When the boiler burst in the orphanage and we didn't have the money necessary for a new one, he bought one with his own money and installed it as well. Every Christmas he dressed himself up in a Santa Claus costume and came to visit the children, bringing them the toys he had carved out of wood all year and candy he bought with his earnings. He never missed. Each child got a little package and a minute to sit on his knee, get a pat on the back or a little *bisou* on the cheek. Year after year, Mrs. Graham, offering his hands to labor for God, to bring a little cheer to sad little orphans. Mrs. Graham, I was one of

those sad little orphans. And when *Monsieur* Billieux
had the big accident in 1955, some of us who had joined
the order and dedicated ourselves to Christ, petitioned
for *Monsieur* Billieux to be brought here that we might
repay him in some small way for all those years of joy
he brought. I was not then Mother Superior, of course,
but I was one of the leaders of the group that convinced
the Bishop that this was the right thing to do. Now do
you understand?"

"*Mon Dieu*, I am overwhelmed. Of course, I am not
surprised at my Uncle Charlie's generosity. He was
always that way. And he played the role of Santa for me
as a child, too. But for your order to assume his care
all these years......it's extraordinary. I've never heard of
such a thing. And the Bishop let you bring a man into
an all-female institution............I am speechless."

Mother Superior smiled, "Well, don't think it was easy
to get that permission. We had to enlist a lot of help.
But people are kind and when they heard the story,
they responded."

"Mother, I understand your desire to protect my uncle,
but he is hungry for knowledge about the family he left
behind. It is not for me to tell you the tragedy in our
family that led to his decision to isolate himself from
us. I do suggest it might be appropriate for you to ask
him, especially since you are questioning the wisdom

of my imparting information that might upset him."
Marie had herself in control now and she was using the
skills she had honed in boardroom debates over the last
several years.

"I do not wish to invade his privacy." The look on
Mother Superior's face almost made Marie laugh. It
was so very prissy.

"But you don't mind controlling his right to know, do
you? How is it different?"

Mother Superior rose from her chair. "I will think
about it, Mrs. Graham. I presume you will be back this
afternoon?"

"Oh, yes, I'll be here."

* * * * *

Marie went back to the cozy café, Le Tomate, for
lunch, indulging in a glass of wine as well as a slice
of quiche. What a luxury over a quick salad at her
desk, she thought. I'll have to contact the office this
afternoon before I call Amy. Too many balls in the air.
But she was not in any way sorry that she had decided
to make this trip. Being with Uncle Charlie right now
was the most important thing in the world. It was hard
to believe that he was as fragile as Mother Superior

insisted. Marie made a mental note to ask to meet with the doctor who was treating Uncle Charlie.

Marie was president of a large commercial real estate firm, operating in the New York City suburbs. She was well known and frequently appeared on the Today television show. She led 240 agents working in the field daily and all the support personnel necessary to ensure their success. Working her way up from the bottom in real estate sales soon after graduation from Smith in '51, she focused all her energies on providing superior service.

When she called her office, her assistant reported every detail that Marie needed to know about day-to-day operations and she made as many decisions as possible immediately. Some required mulling over, so she took careful notes, reminding herself once again that she needed to investigate new technologies that would improve her communications with the office when she was not there. Federal Express was newly available and helpful for papers that needed to be signed and returned, but something more interactive and more immediate would be a great help.

The business was built on the contacts Marie had cultivated over nearly thirty years of schmoozing in the city and its close-in suburbs. She knew she could not be gone much longer than the week she had allowed herself.

She also knew that her staff was trustworthy, that she had trained them carefully. It would be alright.

When she got Amy on the phone and told her the extraordinary story of how Uncle Charlie came to live at the Sisters of The Sacred Heart Nursing Home, Amy wept. "I was too little to remember Uncle Charlie in the same way you do, but everything I have ever heard about him convinces me he is a special man. Now, how about I send a large check to thank the Sisters for their care of our uncle?"

"Not right now, sweetie. I think they are justifiably proud of what they have done for him and consider that they are returning his generosity to the Order, like it's their sacred duty or something. Maybe later. Now tell me how you are doing today."

"Pretty good, thank God. If I'm careful maybe I'll be able to go to David's premiere on Friday. Did I tell you his new movie is premiering this weekend? He's so excited. The boys are coming home so they can go, even if I can't. Have you told Uncle Charlie about what happened to me?"

"Not yet. I'm trying to tell him what happened to all of us more or less sequentially, from after the war ended and Daddy started the business. I have to struggle with some of the memories myself. It was really hard today to tell him about *Pepere*. All these feelings get dredged up in me. The memories are one thing and the story I tell him gets a little bit edited. Mother Superior doesn't need to remind me about upsetting him. I certainly didn't go into any of the gruesome details of *Pepere*'s last days, his turning yellow and all that."

"Yeah, I don't remember much about it myself, but I do remember that, and especially how much the moaning upset *Memere*."

"Take care of yourself, Amy, darling. I'll call tomorrow. Maybe you would like it if I went over to Notre Dame and lit a few candles for you? Can't hurt and it might help."

Amy's laughter cheered Marie, "You, lighting candles? The big doubter? I thought you said paying for candles was paying for the gold embroidery on the priest's vestments? Do go over to Notre Dame, though. Remember the first time we saw it? I was really little and you held my hand."

"Oh, yes, I remember. You forgot your handkerchief and I gave you mine. You were wearing braids then and the candlelight made your hair shine."

Amy sighed. "It seems so long ago, doesn't it?"

"Well, sweetheart, I hate to tell you this, but it was long ago." Marie laughed.

"Bye now, call me tomorrow. Love you."

"Love you, too."

* * * * *

Failing again to reach Petey, Marie went back to the Sisters of the Sacred Heart, walking the few blocks in her new galoshes, mindful of the patches of ice that appeared on the sidewalk here and there, easy to miss and result in a hard fall. When she entered the vestibule, there were three people standing at Sister Boniface's desk, two young men, neither of them old enough to vote, and an elderly woman. Marie slipped by the desk and went directly to the little anteroom where she had first waited to see Uncle Charlie, and where she sat now to remove her galoshes.

"I'm sure he'll want to see us if you just ask him." The elderly woman spoke in a quavering voice with a decided Maine accent.

"But he already has a guest coming to see him." Sister Boniface answered.

"Can't he see more than one person at a time?" One of the young men asked.

"I'll go and find out what Mother Superior says about that." Sister Boniface disappeared down the hall.

Marie didn't want to take it upon herself to go to the solarium without the acknowledgment of Sister Boniface. It seemed rude to do so and probably violated one of Mother Superior's rules about guests. Since she was an old hand at introducing herself to people, she walked over to the trio and extended her hand to the woman. "Hello. I'm Marie Graham and Charlie Billieux is my Uncle. I overheard you asking to see him. How do you know him; where did you meet?"

The woman gave a little gasp and answered. "My name is Olga Krakow. My husband worked with Charlie in the logging camp many years ago. After Charlie had his accident, he disappeared and we didn't know where he had gone until we just found out because my youngest son is dating a girl who knew about the Sisters' having a nursing home here. My husband, Steve, is dead now, but these are two of my grandsons. They've heard all their lives about Charlie Billieux who was the kindest man in the world. When we learned where he was, we decided we had to come visit him."

Marie put her hand on Olga's arm, stroking it briefly. "I am so sorry for your loss. Did you lose your husband in a logging tragedy?"

"No, he got the lung cancer. I suppose it didn't help that they all breathed that sawdust every day."

Marie turned to the boys. "I'm Marie. What are your names?"

"Introduce yourselves to Mrs. Graham, boys." Olga Krakow interjected.

"They looked down at their boots shyly. "I'm Jack." "I'm Paul." and then in unison, "How do you do, Mrs. Graham?"

Marie was impressed with the good manners but before she could say anything, Sister Boniface came back and announced that the Krakows could spend a half hour with Mr. Billieux, while his other visitor was in conference with Mother Superior.

Marie was a bit startled by this bit of news. A conference with Mother Superior? What did this mean? As soon as Sister Boniface left, leading the Krakow family members back to the solarium, Mother Superior appeared at the hall entrance and made a gesture, which Marie interpreted to mean she was to follow her.

Louise S. Appell

Once in her office, Mother Superior went through the tea ritual again and then drew a deep breath before saying, "I did as you suggested. I asked Mr. Billieux if he could tell me why he had isolated himself from his family for all these years. It was very hard for him to tell me the story and I'm sure he painted himself blacker than necessary to convince me he is undeserving of God's forgiveness. It is now my mission to assure him otherwise. You must fill me in with the details so I understand the circumstances completely, *oui*? *Bon*."

For the next half hour, Marie recounted the story as she knew it, emphasizing that she had been eight years old at the time of the tragic events, but could fill Mother Superior in on the family lore that surrounded it. She told about the animosity between the two brothers that was built on her *Gran'pere's* favoritism toward her Uncle Oscar and in turn Oscar's sense of entitlement developed at a young age. She remembered being told about occasions where the oldest brother teased and tormented the youngest. Then when *Gran'mere* was dying, Uncle Charlie was devastated by the impending loss of his beloved *Maman*. He had always been the one responsible for the maintenance of the tenant houses that provided the bulk of the income supporting the household where his sister Tillie cared for their *Maman* and where Charlie and his widowed sister Clara lived, as well as Tillie's husband, Marie and her parents. When he heard that Oscar was manipulating his mother to be sure she left her entire estate to him, Charlie became enraged at the unfairness of it. He was sure that Oscar would throw them out into the street. When he learned that Oscar had removed their mother's much-loved gold cross before her casket was closed, Charlie confronted his brother at the gravesite. There was no question in anyone's mind that Oscar made the first move, putting his hands on Charlie's shoulders and giving him a hard shove along with harsh words. When Charlie picked up a gravedigger's shovel and swung it at his brother, it was an instinctive response, not an intent to kill, but the blow to Oscar's chest stopped his heart. He was dead when he fell to the ground.

Mother Superior listened quietly, her head down, her hands fingering her rosary. "And he is still punishing himself." It was not a question, but an observation.

"Yes, I suppose so. He was sentenced to five years in the county jail, but he got time off for good behavior, so he was there for four years. He refused to let anyone visit him and he never came home again."

"*Mon Dieu*, what a tragic story."

Marie hesitated, but then decided she might as well know the rest. "Do you know about my Uncle Charlie's lost love?"

"What? I know he never was married, but I don't know about any woman in his life."

"He fell in love as a young man and was courting a lovely young woman, who chose to leave him for a life of piety. She became a nun."

Mother Superior's eyes blinked rapidly, as if she was controlling her tears. She dropped her gaze to the floor before standing up abruptly. "I'm sure he's waiting to see you now. Remember we will be serving dinner promptly at six." Marie was dismissed.

*   *   *   *   *

"Hullo, *chouchou*, I hear you met Olga Krakow and her grandsons. You know, that's only two of them. She has nine grandchildren now, only one a girl. Her husband Steve was a very good man. I was sorry to hear he has passed away."

Marie smiled and dropped onto the hassock by Uncle Charlie's side. "It's nice to know you had some friends there at the logging camp, but why didn't you let them know where you were? They could have been visiting you all these years. Maine is not so very far away."

Charlie Billieux looked embarrassed. He ran his hand over his face and sighed. "I suppose I didn't want anyone to see me like this, a cripple, and pity me. I never expected to live this long. Then the years go by and one day you come here and I'm so glad to see you I don't care that maybe you will pity me. What difference does it make, anyway? We all change, don't we?"

"What doesn't change is our love for each other, *n'est-ce pas?*"

"*Oui*, that has never changed." Charlie looked out the window and they were quiet for a few minutes. "You said that *Maman's* room off the kitchen was rented. Why did Tillie do that? I wouldn't think she'd want anyone traipsing through her kitchen."

"There were a lot of changes after my parents bought a house and we moved to the other side of town, on Day Avenue, off of Bridge Street, near the cemetery."

Chapter 7

◇◇

Northampton, Mass.
1949-50

When Pete and his family moved away, Tillie started thinking about how to replace the lost income from the $20 for room and board they had paid each week. She decided to plaster over the door to the room off the kitchen that had served as *Gran'mere*'s bedroom during her last years, cut in a new door to that room from the side porch and rent the space out. Of course it would have no access to the bathroom, but there was still a privy in the garden out back and she felt sure some laborer or newly arrived immigrant would pay for the use of the large room. It turned out she was sorry the room had rented so quickly. When

Edward came home from the hospital they had to set up a bed in the dining room; but there was no sense thinking about that. She was still glad to get the eight dollars a week for the room.

Then, after Edward died and they no longer had his income, she developed a plan to close off all the back bedrooms, moving Clara into the front bedroom that had been used by Pete and Angela. That still left the bedroom Marie and Amy had shared to be used as a guestroom. After some discussions with Pete, she hired carpenters to build a staircase to the second floor from the outside in back of the house for boarders to use and she converted one of the three back bedrooms into a bathroom. Now she felt sure she and Clara would have enough money coming in to pay the bills.

Sometimes Clara teased her about her frugality, but Tillie stoutly defended herself. Hadn't they made it through The Great Depression without any of them ever missing a meal? Clara kissed her cheek and solemnly declared, "You're right, *ma soeur*. You are a very good manager. You should have had a store to manage or a company to run." Tillie brushed her off, but still was pleased that her skills were recognized.

Even though Pete and Angela had their own house now, big holiday celebrations were still held at 144 West Street. Sometimes Angela bristled at that, but not often. Pete hugged her and reminded her that it was especially important to his Ma that she have the holidays to look forward to now that she was a widow.

* * * * *

Ray had been moved to the Veterans Hospital in Newington, Connecticut, still in a coma. Clara drove down there once a week, sometimes picking up Ray's sister Anna to go with her, but not always. Anna often got to visit Ray during the week and she understood that Clara liked to be with him alone, sitting by the side of his bed, holding his hand and reminiscing about places they had been together. Clara was obdurate in her belief that he could hear her. All the doctors said he was getting stronger. His battered and emaciated body was healing slowly, but they knew little about the working of the brain and could only speculate about the coma.

* * * * *

In late 1948, Jack Grimes' wife had died during surgery to remove her appendix. He was a widower in his early fifties who had a son in college, and a daughter training to be a nurse. His solution to loneliness and despair was to throw himself into his work as General Manager at McCallum's, staying at the store long hours, coming up with innovative ways to improve their bottom line and looking more haggard every time Clara saw him. One night, leaving late herself after preparing the monthly report, they came out of the door at the same time.

"Pretty cold tonight. Do you need a ride home?" He turned to her.

"No, thanks," she started, and then changed her mind, "Well, yes, it is cold and that would be great."

Clara was used to the walk home and really enjoyed it or she would have driven her own car to work, but the look on Jack Grimes' face told her immediately that he needed a friend. As he handed her into the car, he said, "I think I remember that you live out the other end of West Street, right?"

"Yes," she laughed, "I live with my older sister. Two widow ladies rattling around in a big house. We're renting out the extra rooms though."

"It's just me living in my house now. Both my son and my daughter are out of the house, launched into adulthood. It's not quite the way I imagined it would be."

"Why don't you rent out part of it to some junior faculty member at Smith or maybe Amherst? It could be great company for you." Clara suggested.

"I could, but I value my privacy. I don't know how much I'd want to give up. Still, it's a good suggestion." He hesitated. "I haven't been thinking very clearly for the last six months."

Clara turned toward him and smiled. "I'll bet the owners of McCallum's wouldn't agree. You've come up with some great new ideas for the store. I especially like the new arrangement for the men's department with a special section targeting young men. We're doing very well with that."

"My God, you're beautiful when you smile like that." He blurted out and then turned a deep shade of red. "Excuse me. That just popped out. I don't mean to embarrass you." And he groaned. "What a jerk I am."

"Oh, please, don't apologize. Every woman appreciates a compliment. Oh, here's my house, right up there on the left."

Jack stopped the car and came around to open the door for Clara, reaching out his hand to help her. "Thanks, Mr. Grimes. I appreciate the ride. See you in the morning."

"How about having dinner with me tomorrow night after work? We could go to Rahar's. I know you used to go there with Herb. Please say yes."

Clara hesitated a few seconds before saying, "Thank you. I'd enjoy that."

*   *   *   *   *

Talking with Tillie about the invitation later that evening, she speculated, "I think he's pretty lonely and I'm a safe choice for him because we've got lots to talk about. He knows I care about the store's future, just as he does."

Tillie sat in the kitchen rocking chair, her hair up in curling papers, knitting on a scarf destined for Petey. She waved in the direction of the coffee pot and Clara poured a cup for each of them. The table was set for two and the soup for their supper was bubbling on the stove.

"Clara, *cherie*, he's a man, isn't he? And not like Herb Barron, either. You are a lovely woman and alone." When Clara opened her mouth to protest, Tillie held up her hand and said, "I know you are still in love with Ray, but he is probably not ever going to be the Ray you knew before, so you should be seeing other men, going to dances, having fun. Jack Grimes might be the perfect man for you. You should think about that."

Clara got to her feet and faced her sister with a scowl. "There will never be another man for me. If Ray doesn't

Louise S. Appell

recover......." A catch in her throat stopped her words and the tears began to fall. "If he dies, I will be his widow as much as if we had married and I will mourn both my men for the rest of my life."

She started to go upstairs, but then came back to kiss Tillie's cheek. "Goodnight, *cherie*, I cannot talk about this anymore."

* * * * *

Rahar's was a very noisy place on Friday night. The exuberant shouts of greeting, the underlying buzz of chatter and the music from the juke box filtered out from the tap room to the dining room where Clara and Jack sat at a dark wood, heavily scarred table on sturdy captain's chairs. "Would you like to go somewhere quieter?" Jack asked. "I haven't been here in a long while and I forgot how it gets on Friday night."

"Oh, no, this is fine with me. I kind of like that background of young people enjoying their youth." Clara smiled over her upraised glass of Canadian Club and soda. "We had a very good day today. I predict the monthly figures will really surprise you. That special on tennis sweaters caught the eye of every high school student who aspires to be another Pancho Gonzales."

"Let's not talk about the store tonight. Tell me what you were like when you were a little girl." Jack leaned forward, resting his elbows on the table as he steepled his forefingers and smiled.

"Not much to tell. I grew up here in the house on West Street, got married very young and widowed at the end of the Great War. Did you hear that they're calling it World War One now? Remember when all the newspapers called it 'the war to end all wars'?" Clara took a sip of her drink and set the glass back down on the table. She had chosen her dress carefully this morning, knowing she would be having dinner with the store manager tonight. It was a brown georgette print with tiny sprigs of flowers in pink and yellow. The white collar and cuffs made the dressy fabric look more business-like.

"Yes, I remember very well. Did you know I was a soldier in that war? A half-assed one, but still....."

Clara was a bit flustered. "I thought you came to McCallum's right out of college. I never heard anything about you being in the service."

"I guess I never mention it because I was parked at a desk in Boston the whole eighteen months of my service, shuffling paper. Somehow I've always been ashamed of that. Of course, I wasn't given a choice, but still, when I think of all the guys who were gassed, maimed, killed while I was safe in Boston, I cringe." Jack grimaced and leaned back. "When did you go to work at McCallum's Silk Hosiery?"

"It took me a while to get on my feet after Gus died. I was a mess for about six months, and then I started thinking about what I was going to do for the rest of my life. The Hosiery was just a few minutes walk from my mother's house. I moved there right after......" Clara stopped, struggled to control her voice and coughed into her hand to cover up the sudden surge of emotion. "It was convenient. I liked having all those other women around me. I made friends. I stayed there over twenty-five years."

Clara sat back in her chair and looked around the room, all dark wood and old photographs of Northampton on the walls. The place was rapidly filling up with patrons; someone was having a party over in the corner. People greeted each other boisterously. The smell of bread baking wafted out from the kitchen.

"Did I tell you how glad I am that you decided to change jobs? You've been a big asset to the store and I don't mean just how good you are at selling. People like to see a pretty woman with a sunny smile when they come in. It sets a tone, you know."

"Thank you. That's a lovely compliment." Clara was embarrassed. Her face flushed just a little, enough to add another dimension to her prettiness, enough to make Jack think he was wrong about calling her pretty, when she was truly a beautiful woman.

Jack, in his fifties, was graying in an attractive way. He was almost six feet tall and very slender. He dressed conservatively every day in a well-tailored suit and silk tie, polished wingtips on his feet, the aroma of Old Spice aftershave noticeable only when a person got close, never too much. He wore rimless glasses with gold earpieces and a tie pin that signaled his membership in the Elks.

When the waiter arrived, they both ordered fish, reminding Clara that Jack was Catholic. She knew he had been at Holy Cross College in Worchester at the same time as Mr. Barron, but she hadn't thought about his religion. Of course, almost everyone who went to Holy Cross was Catholic. She felt a little strange sitting here with him, having dinner. Somehow it wasn't the same as having dinner with Mr. Barron. There was something about the way he looked at her. *Mon Dieu*, she thought, I hope I haven't been giving out signals myself without meaning to. It had been such a long time since she had felt the touch of a man, maybe it was an unconscious longing. She forced her thoughts to Ray, lying in the hospital, still in a coma. Would he ever be in her arms again?

"You do know that I'm engaged, Mr. Grimes, and that I would have gotten married in '43, except that all leaves were canceled and my fiancé, Ray Carpenter, was sent overseas the weekend of our planned wedding?" It was a question intended to inform, in case he didn't know.

"Yes, Liz Carpenter told me about him and also about his being missing for three years after the war. It must have been hell, the not knowing."

"I always knew I would have felt something if he had died, so I was less surprised than others when he was found. He's in a veteran's hospital in Connecticut. I go to visit every week, but he hasn't come out of the coma yet. I keep hoping." Clara looked out the window, her eyes unfocused, startled a bit when she realized she saw her face reflected there.

Jack Grimes reached across the table and touched her hand. "I hear what you are telling me. That doesn't mean we can't be friends, though, does it? I like your company. It's good to have a pleasant evening. Please don't tell me we can't have dinner now and then. Or maybe go to a show. Or a concert. I heard you like classical music. So do I. Do you play tennis? I could teach you."

Clara recognized the look on Jack Grimes' face, that need to connect she knew must appear on her own. We're social creatures after all, she thought. "I'd like that. I just wanted to be clear about ...about....anything more than friends."

"OK. And friends get to call each other by their first names, right? In the store it has to be Mrs. Pelletier and Mr. Grimes, but outside I'll be Jack and you'll be Clara. Agreed?"

Clara raised her glass in a toast and smiled, "Agreed."

* * * * *

In the tap room that same night, Marie sat in a booth with her friend Jean across from her. A guy she'd just met an hour ago sat next to her and across from Jean's steady boyfriend, Arty. Her date was Arty's older brother, Wally, back from service in the Army and enrolled at the University of Massachusetts. She figured he probably didn't want to talk about that so she asked, "What courses are you taking this semester?"

Wally was a handsome guy with a small scar on his forehead from a gash he got playing football in high school. His hair was nearly black and wildly curly, even more than Marie's, and his eyes were dark green. He was almost pathetically skinny. And he was a cynic.

Louise S. Appell

He answered her, "A lot of bullshit courses they tell me I have to take in order to get a degree. Not that I mind so much as long as someone else is paying for it. Mostly I don't see any sense to reading English literature or taking biological science when I only care about mineralogy. I want to be a geologist. What do you want to do with a college degree, marry some smartass Wall Street broker?"

Marie suppressed a flash of anger and answered sweetly, "First of all, I want to be an educated person who knows how to use the knowledge of the past to think and analyze and solve problems, but I don't know what career field I'll pursue. At least, not yet."

Wally laughed, reached out and stroked her jaw line. "Oh, you are quick. Great answer, but what about a husband and babies and a house to take care of?"

"Not everybody thinks that's the only thing women can do. Do you know my mom worked in a bomb factory all through the years of the war? And she made a lot of money so my dad could start a business when he got back. They're partners. That's what I want, a partnership."

"Sounds good, but not many guys want that. They want a wife in the kitchen when they come home, thinking about what they would like for dinner, not about some career stuff. They want to make lots of babies, which will keep a wife pretty busy."

"Are you talking about that old male fantasy of keeping the little woman barefoot and pregnant?" Marie was getting hot.

"Listen, sweetheart, this is a date, not a debate. Let's get out of here and go someplace where we can dance. I'd like to hold your soft little body and smell your hair and remember I made it home safe." Wally stood up and held out his hand to Marie. "Hey, Arty, how about going somewhere we can dance? It's too noisy in here."

* * * * *

Later, when Wally drove her home, Marie chattered about the band, trying to ignore the noises coming from Jean and Arty in the back seat. Wally grinned at her. "Are they making you uncomfortable? He's young and stupid. You just have to turn a deaf ear."

At her house, he surprised her by getting out and coming around to open the door. He took her hand and walked her to the front door, brushed her mouth with a friendly kiss and smiled down at her. "It was nice being with you. Next time, we'll ditch the lovers in the back seat, OK?"

"Thank you for an interesting evening. I enjoyed dancing with you." Marie reached out and touched his chin. "Goodnight."

Wally was amused. Young, yes, but not dumb like so many of the girls he'd been dating. And it felt good to hold her. He had to be careful, though. He was a long way from making a commitment to anyone. Too many guys were getting married right away, tying themselves down. He had places to go, things to see, wild oats to sow. He'd date Marie again, but keep it light and friendly. He didn't think she was the type to tumble in the backseat of a car. There were plenty of other girls for that.

Angela was awake when Marie came home, making a great show of pretending to be working on a sweater she was knitting for Amy. When Marie answered her questions about the guy she had dated, Angela's anxiety was apparent in her admonition. "These vets aren't like the boys you're used to, you know. They're men, often wanting more from you than you're willing to give. You have to be very careful, *cara*. I don't want you to get hurt."

"I know that, Mom." Marie was irritated. "You don't have to tell me. Sometimes you act as if you think I'm stupid. But this guy was so much more........." Her voice trailed off. "Interesting. No corny jokes or silly stuff trying to impress other guys. I hate that. When a date tries to behave like a comedian, it makes me want to get up and come home."

"Marie, you can always call and your dad or I will come and get you. Do you always have a dime for a phone call like I told you?" Angela paused, waiting for Marie's head to nod her response. "Don't ever forget that. It's important."

Chapter 8

◇◇

Northampton, Mass.
1950

Marie sat in the windowless carrel in the bowels of Neilson Library, fuming. Her mother was treating her like she was still a kid, always asking questions about the guys she dated, the places she went to and telling her it was because she didn't want her getting into trouble. Didn't she think Marie had any common sense? Dammit, she was nineteen years old. Pretty soon she'd be finished with college and she could get out of Northampton and out from under her mother's thumb.

Betsy came around the corner of the library stacks to where Marie was sitting, books and papers spread all over. "Wow, you look like you're mad at somebody. What's up?"

Marie scowled and tossed her long, silky curls over her shoulder with a gesture that clearly spelled out her frustration. "It's my mother again. She was waiting up for me when I got back from Amherst last night. She made a big deal about how late it was, how I need to get my sleep, how dangerous the roads are when it snows, blah, blah, blah. I hate it when she treats me like I'm twelve."

"What time was it when you got back?"

"I don't know. Maybe twelve-thirty or so. I wasn't paying attention to the time. It was a great party. My date was Ed Claremont. Remember we met him at the Deke house last week? Tall, red hair, big glasses, going to be an attorney like his father, he says."

"Oh, yeah, I remember him. I thought he was drinking too much. I remember you did, too. How come you went out with him?"

Marie shrugged. "He called and I didn't have anyone else to go out with this weekend so I said sure."

"I thought you had the hots for that vet at UMass. What happened to him?" Betsy set her armload of books down and sat at the carrel next to Marie's.

"Better watch out for that snob who sits there. She'll give you a piece of her mind if she sees you sitting in her space. And yes, you're right. I wish Wally Hinkle would call, but I haven't heard from him for a long time. I'd be dumb to stay home weekends waiting for somebody who hardly ever calls." Marie sighed and started gathering up her books and papers.

"Has he ever asked you to......you know......do it?" Betsy had lowered her voice to a whisper.

"No, but if he did, I probably would." Marie stuck her chin out defiantly.

Betsy's eyes got wide and her mouth dropped open. "You don't mean it."

"I am so sick of everybody talking about it and pretending I know what they're talking about. What's the big deal? If you believe all the girls who say they've already done it, we must be in a tiny minority, you and me. I'd do it just to find out what's so mysterious about it. Haven't you thought about it?"

"Yeah, but I'm afraid. What if I got pregnant? My mother would kill me."

"I heard two girls at the Green Street Coffee shop talking about an abortionist in Albany who's supposed to be very good. There's always that. And some people have gotten diaphragms from a clinic in Boston."

"If anybody found out, then you'd get called cheap or a bad girl. And my mother says guys all want to play with the bad girls, but they marry good girls. Do you believe that?"

Marie was exasperated. "Betsy, you know better than to believe all that crap mothers tell you to scare you. Remember Pat Schofer? Didn't everybody know she was doing it with Carl Bingham all through senior year in high school? Didn't he marry her last year? Mothers lie about that kind of stuff all the time. Same as don't go swimming right after you eat because you'll drown and don't eat snow because you'll get sick and a whole bunch of other don'ts."

"I guess you're right. Promise me you'll tell me all about it if you decide to do it? I'm probably too chicken, but I know you and you're never scared."

The two of them hoisted their book bags and set out for Green Street to get a snack. They were both dressed in dungarees bought at the Army-Navy store and heavy sweaters under their duffle coats. Campus was quiet as they exited the library. The earlier snow shower had stopped and the paths were cleared. Lots of people were away for the weekend. Sunday was a good day to come to the library for town girls like Marie and Betsy. There were always fewer people around and plenty of peaceful places to study.

"My car's parked on Green Street. I'll drive you home after we get something to eat." Marie assured Betsy. "Maybe I'll go back to the library, though. I don't feel like going home."

*   *   *   *   *

Angela brought Petey to 144 West Street often to visit with her mother-in-law. It was clear to her that Mother Tillie loved the little boy and enjoyed each visit. Sometimes they all went up to the attic and rummaged through the trunks and boxes to find a toy that had been Pete's. Sometimes it was a little truck that Charlie had carved years ago. Sometimes a book, lovingly cared for, wrapped in cloth, was found. The attic was a treasure house.

One afternoon, while Angela and Tillie were drinking coffee and Petey was playing on the floor nearby, Angela mentioned to her mother-in-law that she intended to take up selling real estate as soon as Petey went to school. As she described the potential she saw in selling real estate, she became more animated, her enthusiasm making her eyes bright. Tillie said to her, "Why don't you start now? I could take Petey and you could do what you have to do to get your license."

Angela was astounded. She would never have asked Tillie, although she had often thought about it. The offer was perfect, the answer to her longing to get out of the house, meet with all kinds of people, earn money, contribute to the family, be recognized for her abilities. Sure, she knew Pete appreciated the home she had created for them, but ever since she had worked at the bomb factory she had a yearning to go out into the world and make her mark there.

"Oh, Mother Tillie, would you do that for me? I would be so grateful." Angela jumped out of her seat and impulsively wrapped her arms around Tillie's neck.

"I would enjoy it very much. I love Petey. He's such a good boy. You can bring him here anytime and I will take care of him. You won't have to worry about him a bit."

First, Angela had to gather information about getting a real estate license in the Commonwealth of

Massachusetts. That turned out to be easy enough. A call to the agent who had sold them the house got her the information and also an invitation to visit with the guy who owned the agency he worked for.

Leo Borowski was a roly-poly guy with thinning hair, a ridiculously flashy tie and a lot of nervous energy. He'd never had a woman agent, but he thought it might be a good idea so he explained the steps needed to become an agent and was full of information about classes and tests and costs. He emphasized that agents were responsible for their own success. In other words, you made money in direct proportion to the work you did. "Some agents work hard to build their contacts through a social network and rely on referrals and money from listings. Others do more working with newcomers to town and polish their selling skills. And, of course, some real go-getters do it all," he smiled. "What kind will you be?"

* * * * *

When Pete came home at the end of the day, after Angela had met with Leo Borowski, she sat him down in the kitchen with a drink while she was finishing meal preparation. "Pete, I want to go to work as a real estate agent. Your Ma has offered to take care of Petey while I'm working, but some of the work can be done right here at the kitchen table. I have to make lists and a card file and phone calls, which I can do here. I don't have to go to any office." Angela took a deep breath. "What do you think?"

"I thought you were happy with this house and Petey to take care of?" He scowled. "Are you unhappy, Angela?"

"No, Pete. I love this house, but I've got it all fixed up now and I just wanted to get out and see what I could do. I'm restless, *cara*. I enjoy meeting people, making money, having somebody say what a good job I'm doing..."

"And I don't tell you what a good job you're doing?" He raised an eyebrow.

"No, you don't. You just take it for granted I'm going to do it. And that's OK. *Dio Mio*, can't you see it's not the same?"

"Maybe we should have another baby. What about that?"

"No, Pete, we've got our family. I don't want another baby. Oh, dammit, why can't you understand what I'm saying to you?"

Pete ran his hands over his hair. He fidgeted in his seat. "Angela, remember before the war when I couldn't get a steady job and we had to live with my parents to make ends meet? Well, that tore me up inside. I felt like such a total failure, not being able to provide for my family. Now, my motor repair business is doing great. We've got plenty of money to take good care of our family. It makes me feel like maybe you don't think it's enough."

Angela dropped the knife she was using and went to Pete, throwing her arms around his neck, kissing him all over his face. "Pete, Pete, please, please don't ever think I'm not thrilled that you came home to us and started a business and built it up and provided everything we need. You are the best man there ever was, a great husband and father, a big success and my very own darling. This doesn't have anything to do with making money to provide for our family. It's for me to spread my wings. I don't want to play golf or bridge. I'm not interested in gossip or the church sodality. I want to test myself. Is that so hard to understand?"

"I'd have to be nuts to tell you not to do it, Angela. If you've got the energy and you think you can do it and take care of all the house stuff and the kids are OK, you have to have your chance."

"Pete, *caro,* Marie is already grown up; Amy is already thirteen and your mother is going to love taking care of Petey. The rest is easy. Anyway, I'll only be working part-time."

"What if one of them gets sick, Angela? How will you deal with that?"

"Of course, the kids come first, Pete. You know that. But this is the kind of job that can be put aside if I have to. Please be happy for me. I think I've found something I could really get excited about."

Pete hoisted her onto his lap and put his arms around her. "Good luck with it then, *cherie.* I want you to be happy. If doing this makes you happy, it makes me happy."

＊　＊　＊　＊　＊

Clara came awake with her hands clenched so tight her nails were making half moons in her palm. She hurt all over. *Mon Dieu,* she thought, what's happening to me? She tried hard but could not remember the dream she'd been having, only knowing she'd been terrified. Time to get up anyway. The alarm was set to go off in a few minutes.

Downstairs in the kitchen Tillie was preparing oatmeal, with the radio turned on to a news station, but too low in volume to disturb Clara. The newscaster sounded excited, but Tillie didn't really hear what he was saying.

"*Bonjour, ma soeur.* I could smell the oatmeal when I came down the stairs. How come you're making oatmeal today?"

"Petey's coming soon and he loves oatmeal with maple syrup on it. Angela has to show a farm out in Haydenville early today, so she's bringing him over soon now." Tillie smiled broadly as she turned from her task at the stove and looked at Clara. "*Mon Dieu*, you are as white as a sheet. Are you sick today? Do you feel dizzy?"

"No. I just had a bad dream and it really shook me. I'll be fine as soon as I get some coffee and a piece of toast."

"What was the dream about? Do you remember it?"

"I only remember that I was very, very scared and when I woke up I was clenching my hands as tight as I could. It's nothing. I have bad dreams all the time. I wish I could remember, but I never do."

"I read in *Ladies Home Journal* that you should write down everything you do remember as soon as you wake up and if you do it all the time, pretty soon you'll remember all of it."

Clara looked at Tillie with one eyebrow raised. "Yeah, well I'm not so sure I want to remember. Maybe it's better to let it go."

Just then the back door opened and Petey came rushing in to fling his arms around Tillie's knees. "*Memere*, I can stay until this afternoon. Mommy says she'll come and get me about three o'clock. Oh, I smell oatmeal. Can I have some oatmeal, *Memere*?"

"Of course, *chouchou*, I made it just for you."

* * * * *

As soon as Clara arrived home for dinner, even before she could remove her jacket, Tillie said "Call Anna right away. It's not bad news, so don't get upset, but she does have some news to give you."

When Clara reached Anna, the news spilled out of Ray's sister breathlessly. "That nurse at the hospital who's been so friendly called me and told me that some government people came to see Ray. They're going to try to find out who kept Ray in the forest all that time and why. They didn't tell anyone for what reason they were going to do that now, but they met with Ray's doctors and had a conference with everybody who takes care of him wanting to know if there were ever any signs of his waking up. And when they left they took away a copy of his file, too. They came from that new agency. I forget its name but it's the one that used to be doing spy work during the war. Something about intelligence. Isn't that interesting?"

"Maybe if they learn something and tell Ray it will help him come back to us. I'm so sure he hears what's going on around him. If somebody could remind him where he was for all that long time, maybe it would jolt him awake." Clara said thoughtfully.

"Yes, I thought of that, too. At least it gets him some attention. Lately I've been feeling that he's been around so long they've taken it for granted he's never going to wake up."

"Thanks for calling to tell me what's happening, Anna. I'll be down to visit him on Sunday. Do you want to meet me at that little tea shop down on State Street? About three o'clock?"

"Yes. I'd like that. See you then."

Clara told Tillie about Anna's news over supper and Tillie asked Clara if she had heard that the country was at war again. "It's been on the radio all day. Some place called Korea. I don't even know where that is."

"*Mon Dieu*, does it ever stop? Can't these people figure out a way to get along? What happened to start it this time?"

Tillie huffed in exasperation. "I tried to get that TV to work so I could learn more, but no matter how I moved the rabbit ears, I got nothing but snow."

"I'll try after supper. Maybe it works better at night."

*   *   *   *   *

Friday was warm so Clara was wearing a peach colored cotton pique skirt with a jacket that had a peplum, fitting snugly on her slim figure. It was suitable for the day at work, and still an attractive outfit to wear for having dinner with Jack Grimes. As soon as they sat down and gotten their drinks, she told him about the visit from the government people inquiring into Ray's condition and taking a copy of the files with descriptions of his initial injuries as well as notes on his progress.

"I don't know much about medical stuff, but I'm pretty sure government guys don't travel to Connecticut asking questions about a single soldier who's in a coma unless it fits into something else that's very important. I can't imagine what it could be......" His voice trailed off. "Well, maybe I can imagine. Maybe there's something going on in that area where he was found. Maybe they need to know more about the people who were keeping him in that forest because they could be a threat. Or maybe even useful in some way to the government."

Clara sat up in her chair, her eyes widened. "Maybe it has something to do with the Cold War. Isn't that area one that's divided between our side and people friendly to the Communists?"

"Yes, I think so. And I think we never get much information from the press on all the back room stuff going on. There are a lot of secret activities we can't know because it would endanger people for it to be public knowledge. Well, I do hope they learn something more about where your fiancé was and why he was prevented from leaving. Even if it doesn't have any effect on his coma, it would answer questions you must have in your mind."

"Yes, you're right about that." Clara took a drink from her whiskey sour. "I can't believe we are really in a war again. How can this be? Whatever happened that couldn't be solved by sitting down and talking out differences between these Korean people?"

"I read a lot of history. It's always been a passion of mine. And it's shocking how the history of the world is dominated by one war after another. Most of them, of course, were conflicts between warring tribes and men fought in hand-to-hand combat. But now that we've unleashed the horror of the atom bomb, I thought that would scare everybody enough that they'd see the value of putting more effort into diplomacy." Jack sighed deeply. "I'm sure there's a lot I don't know, but what I do know is that ordinary people don't start wars, don't want wars and are horrified at the results of wars."

To hide the tears that came to her eyes, Clara looked down at the menu. They were in the Log Cabin Restaurant at the top of Mt. Tom, enjoying the view of the valley below where the lights were just now going on in streets and houses. "The view of the valley is always so lovely from up here."

Jack recognized her need to end this talk of war. "Clara, I heard about a chamber music concert in Greenfeld next Wednesday night. Would you go with me? It's at eight o'clock. We'd have time to get a quick supper in Greenfield if we left right after the store closes. Please say yes."

"Yes, I'd like that. Thank you for asking me." Clara smiled across the table.

*　*　*　*　*

The next morning at breakfast, Clara told Tillie about the invitation and her acceptance. "He's such a nice man and he's obviously lonely. I told him we could be friends but nothing more and he's been the perfect gentleman each of the four times I've gone to dinner with him."

"That's fine, I guess." Tillie frowned. "You don't need to keep pushing him away, *cherie*. He's a good looking man. You're a beautiful woman. You could make it more, you know."

Clara's anger was evident in her posture and her voice. "Why do you say that? Maybe some day soon I'll get a call from Anna telling me Ray has come out of the coma and I will have my darling back. Do you think I'm giving up on him now just because I'm having dinner with a man? What about you? I don't see you looking for somebody to replace Edward. Why is it any different for me? Stop trying to push me into something I don't want." She flung her napkin down and grabbed her jacket. "I'll see you later."

"I'm not pushing, Clara. Only suggesting you think about it." Tillie called out at Clara's retreating back.

Her answer was the door clicking shut.

* * * * *

In the fall, Marie returned to Smith for her senior year. It had been a busy summer. She had decided not to work in the tobacco fields and instead took a job with the recreation department, running the kiddie train at Look Park. And she had crossed a big threshold in an unexpected way. When she met Betsy at the Green Street Coffee Shop she had not yet decided whether to tell her about it. And she certainly was not going to tell her it was Rick Clarey.

"Wow, you got a fabulous tan. I'm jealous. Did you like taking care of Mrs. Cramer's bratty boys all summer?" Marie asked as Betsy slid into the booth.

"It wasn't bad. They had plenty to do at the beach and I love the Cramers' house in Dennis. They gave me enough time off to go to some of the summer theatre at the Cape Playhouse. No summer romance, though. How about you?" Betsy lit a cigarette and sat back.

"Uh, well, not exactly, but I did finally do it."

"Do what?"

"You know. It. The thing we talked about before the semester ended."

Betsy's expression was wide-eyed and shocked and made Marie giggle. Her voice was a little strangled when she asked, "You mean you had sex with that Wally guy?"

"Yeah, I had sex, but not with Wally. And I'm not going to tell you who. It was just the right moment and I thought OK, this is it."

"Did it hurt? Was it messy? Were you scared?"

"No, it didn't hurt and it wasn't messy and I was a little scared at first, but then I wasn't."

"You're not being fair. You promised to tell me about it. Are you just teasing me? Did you really do it?" Betsy's voice was rising in indignation.

"For God's sake, keep your voice down. Somebody will hear you. Ok, I'll tell you what I can." Now Marie was sorry she had mentioned it to Betsy.

"Start from the beginning. Where were you?" Betsy asked, expecting to hear that Marie had been in the back seat of a car somewhere.

"I was in a hotel in Boston."

"What!! How come you were in Boston? Did your parents know you went there?"

"A girl I met working at Look Park knew about a neat place in Boston that has jazz concerts every weekend. She said she had a friend who went to Mt. Holyoke with her and lived in Newton and we could stay at her house. Of course, she doesn't have a car, so the reason she asked me was because I could drive us there. My mom said OK, but be sure to get home on Sunday before dark."

"I thought you had to work on Sundays at the Park." Betsy interrupted.

"Yeah, except for one weekend a month. Anyway, when we got there it turned out this friend had a boyfriend who was bringing along a guy for Marianne, but nobody had given any thought about me. So I was supposed to be a fifth wheel, you know. And besides, I got the message that her friend, Babs, wasn't expecting me to stay overnight either. It was as if Marianne only thought about getting a ride and I was like a chauffeur. I was really p.o.ed"

"Ohmigawd, you were stranded."

"We got to the concert and it was a terrific jazz group. The music was fabulous. The four of them were paying no attention to me, but at least I loved the vibes in that place. I was sitting there, grooving to the sounds and somebody came up to the table and squatted down next to me. When I turned my head and looked at him, it was a guy I know, so I squealed and threw my arms around him. I was just so glad to see him. It was like fate or something." Marie sighed.

"So how did you wind up in a hotel with him?"

"We moved away from the table and stood over near the bandstand. He asked me if I was with anyone. Of course, he knew I wasn't because anybody could look at our table and see that I was a fifth wheel. When I told him the scene, he said, 'Don't worry about it. I'll get you a hotel room. You can go back to Newton and pick up your useless buddy Mariannne tomorrow for the drive home.' and I thought that would be great and it would show those snobby girls that I didn't need them to get a date for me."

"Weren't you worried your mother would be furious with you?"

"Well, I'm not going to tell her and neither are you." Marie scowled at Betsy.

"OK, OK. I'm not going to tell anybody."

"So we left the jazz concert a little before it was over and we stopped at a White Castle for hamburgers and then we went to a hotel. I thought he was going to leave, but then he came up to the room with me and as soon as he closed the door, he started kissing me." Marie shrugged and looked away from Betsy. "One thing led to another and he was so sweet and ...so tender, it seems like it just happened. He kept saying 'Don't be scared.' And I wasn't. And it didn't hurt at all."

"Are you sorry you did it? Will you see him again?"

"Oh, I don't know. He goes to school in Boston, so maybe when he comes home for Thanksgiving or Christmas... I just don't know. Anyway, I'm not sorry I did it."

"Weren't you worried you'd get pregnant?

"No, I wasn't. He had rubbers with him. Anyway, I've already had the curse since it happened, so I'm not pregnant. You can forget about that."

"Wow, I can hardly believe it. You really did it. I'll bet I can figure out who it is. Let's see. Who do we know who's going to school in Boston?"

"Stop it, Betsy. Just stop it. I'm sorry I told you if you're going to make it a game. It was a really, really wonderful experience and I don't want you to ruin it." Marie's voice dropped to a whisper. "I don't want to talk about it anymore."

* * * * *

Chapter 9

<><><><><><><><><><><><><><><><><><><><><><><><><>

Northampton, Fall, 1950

When Leo Borowski handed Angela her first commission check, she went directly over to Pete's Motor Repair on King Street. As soon as she got out of the car and Pete saw the big smile on her face, the glitter in her eyes and the piece of paper she was waving, he knew why she was there.

"Pete, look what I got. My very first commission. I'm so excited, I don't know what to do."

Pete, very pleased that the first thing she did was come to him, strode out of the shop and toward his wife in the parking area. He threw his arms around her, forgetting entirely the grease stains on his coveralls. "Maybe we should frame it, *cherie.*"

"Not this one, *caro.* It's for two thousand, one hundred and fifty-two dollars. It's going right into our bank account." She giggled when she saw the shock on Pete's face.

Mon Dieu, Angela. That's a lot of money. How did you earn so much?"

"I sold that big farm out in Haydenville and Leo says it's been on the market for a year and nobody could convince a buyer to take it because of the water problem, but I found a guy from Springfield who wanted to build three houses out there and then I got the zoning changed and the water problem only mattered to farmers and these houses he wants to build won't be for farmers." She took a deep breath. "So I got the sale. How about that?"

"Sweetheart, you got the sale because you worked hard to solve a problem when nobody else saw how it could be solved. Good for you." Pete kissed his wife right out there in the parking area in front of everybody going by on the street. Somebody honked their horn. "And you know, I think you need to open a special new account at the bank just for your earnings, because I know you're going to do very well."

"Do you really think so?" Angela's eyes were shining; tears were close and she struggled to keep them from spilling over, so moved by her husband's belief in her, his generosity and his love.

"Yeah, I do. Now look at what I did. I got grease on your skirt and on your cheek, too." He brushed his thumb over her cheek and made it worse. "You'd better go home and clean up. And get that new account set up today. I'll see you later." He turned her around and directed her toward her car, then reached out to pat her fanny, stopping just in time to avoid putting a grease spot there, too.

*   *   *   *   *

Just before Thanksgiving Marie got a letter from Boston, from Rick Clarey, telling her he wouldn't be coming home to Northampton for the holiday. He said he had a job (he called it a gig) with a small band that was booked into a Boston hotel over the weekend and he needed the money. He would miss seeing her, but maybe he'd be home at Christmas.

Marie was sorry he would not be home for the holiday, but she wasn't devastated. She never did think her one night with Rick was more than what it was, serendipity. Why make more of it than that? Besides, she was a little scared of Rick. He was so much more sophisticated than she was. She didn't want to have him think she was some booby. She tore the letter up and threw it away. No need to answer.

She drove up to the campus after supper at home, planning to spend a few hours reading in her carrel. The library was quiet. Most of the campus houses served dinner later than her family ate at home. The place would start getting crowded in about an hour. When she rounded the stacks to get to the bank of carrels, she noticed that her neighbor was already hunched over, coat on the floor, books stacked high. Carol was hardly ever there, but when she was, she acted as if she owned the place.

Marie slipped her coat over the back of her chair and flicked on the light. Just as she got settled down to study, Carol looked up. "There was some guy here looking for you a little while ago."

Marie was startled; Carol rarely spoke to her. "Did he leave his name? What did he look like?"

"Yeah, he told me his name but I forget what it is. He's a tall guy, with some kind of scar on his forehead." Carol raised an eyebrow, "Looks a little old for you."

"Did he leave a message?"

"Um, yes, he did. You're supposed to meet him someplace. He left you a note. Here." And she picked up the note from in front of her and handed it to Marie.

Marie was ticked. Clearly, Carol had read her note, but she let it go because all that was written there was 'Green Street Coffee Shop'.

"How long ago was it?"

"Not very long. I just got here about an hour ago."

Marie shrugged into her coat and picked up her bag. "Thanks. Don't take over my carrel. I'll be back. I think."

Wally Hinkle was lounging in a front booth, drinking coffee. He hailed Marie as she walked in. Only when she came toward him did she notice there was a girl sitting on the opposite side, obscured by the high back of the booth. A little startled, she stammered, "Oh excuse me. I thought...I don't know what I thought."

"No, no, excuse me. I'm leaving. I just saw this lovely man sitting here alone and I thought he might need some company. But, obviously, I was wrong." The girl got up and left. Marie slid into the spot she vacated.

"Well, of all the nerve....." Marie was sputtering.

Wally laughed. "Are there many Smith girls that are so pushy? I'd heard a few stories, but this was a surprise." Clearly he had enjoyed the attention. "I stopped by your carrel after I called your house and your sister told me you were studying in the library. The girl at the desk gave me your carrel number. I hope you don't mind."

"No, no. It's Ok. What are you doing here in Northampton on a Tuesday night?"

"Looking for you. I decided not to go home to Worchester for Thanksgiving. I've got too much work to do and I don't want to get tied up in my family's drama. But I thought you might like to go out with me Thursday night, you know, after you have dinner with your family. It seemed like too much short notice to just call you."

"Why don't you come to Thanksgiving dinner with me? We're going to my grandmother's and there'll be lots of people. One more will be fine with her. She likes to have a big crowd."

Wally chuckled, "Whoa. I wasn't angling for an invitation to a Thanksgiving dinner. I was just looking for a little company that night."

"We can go out after dinner. Say yes. You'll like her cooking. French-Canadian. Best turkey dressing you ever tasted." Marie smiled.

On Thanksgiving Day, Maurice and Simone arrived from Connecticut just in time to join the rest of the family going to church. They were all dressed for the occasion in their finery to honor the day, although as soon as they returned Pete and Maurice removed their suit jackets and loosened their ties.

Tillie took a Mother Hubbard apron off the hook in the pantry and wrapped herself in the voluminous cover-up to protect her best black crepe dress. (She was still in mourning for Edward.) She handed one to Simone. Angela covered her navy blue skirt and white blouse with a bib apron. She showed Tillie and Simone that her blouse might look like silk, but it was made of the new fabric, nylon. "Here, feel it," she said. "It's supposed to be easy to wash and quick to dry."

Clara wore a maroon dress in soft wool with a zipper down the back, fitted in the torso and flared in the skirt. With Marie helping, she was setting the table with an embroidered tablecloth and matching napkins and the best china. Both of them were also getting drinks for everybody.

Pete and Maurice were drinking highballs, Canadian and Ginger, in the living room, Petey playing with some cars on the floor in the alcove where Amy was reading when the doorbell rang. Marie took a moment to smooth down the skirts of her red wool shirtwaist dress and pat her hair before going to answer it.

"Hi, Wally. I'm glad you could make it. Come in and meet my family."

Wally was wearing a beautiful pin-striped suit that looked brand new. Marie had never seen him dressed so formally. It made him look a lot older and not much like a college student. He handed her a bouquet of dark red football mums. "These are for your grandmother." He leaned over and surprised Marie by kissing her on the cheek. Introductions were made and Marie left the room to get Wally a drink. "I'll be right back." She was a little nervous about leaving him with her father, but it couldn't be helped.

"Marie says you're a vet. Army?" Wally nodded and Pete continued, "Did you see any action?"

"Oh, sure, but Marie has told me that you were on the beach in Normandy for the D-day invasion. I congratulate you for your courage and your survival."

Pete waved his hand. "I was lucky. Got the million-dollar wound and came home early. But how about you? You must have gone in very young." Pete raised his brow, inviting information.

Marie came in and handed Wally a drink, Scotch and soda. He took a swallow before answering. "I enlisted right after I finished high school in '42. Just a grunt, you know. But I was lucky enough to get into a good unit. We fought our way up the boot in Italy."

Clara, listening to the conversation as she continued with the table setting, stepped around Petey's cars and into the living room. "My fiancé, Ray Carpenter, was in Italy, too. He got captured in the mountains and sent to a prison camp."

Wally looked startled. "Captain Raymond Carpenter? A tall guy with blond hair and really bright blue eyes? He came from Hartford, Connecticut He had a fiancée back home named Clara, who sent him lots of packages full of treats. Is that you? Is he coming here today?"

Clara was stunned. "*Mon Dieu.*" She cried out. "Yes, I'm Clara." Goose bumps covered her arms and she clasped them around her. "He tried to escape the prison camp. He wasn't found until '48. Nobody knows what happened to him because he's been in a coma ever since." Clara could feel the tears starting to run down her cheeks. Maurice got up and put his arms around his sister.

"Jesus. This is unbelievable. Captain Raymond Carpenter was my officer. We were ambushed. We were in the same prison camp." Wally put his head down and lifted one hand to cover his eyes. Marie reached over and took the glass from him. "Excuse me." He got up and walked out the door, standing on the porch until he could get control of himself.

Angela, Tillie and Simone came in from the kitchen just then and Pete explained briefly the incredible coincidence. Wally returned and sat down. Marie gave him his drink and put her hand in his. He continued, "We all knew the war was going to end soon. We could hear our planes overhead and anyway, you could tell how nervous the guards were, some of them disappearing overnight, probably deserted back to their farms, hoping to survive. The Captain had taken a beating that was so bad, he didn't think he could survive another. That's why he had to escape. They took after him with dogs, but he had already told one of the guys he expected that and he planned to run in streambeds to put the dogs off the scent. Anyway, when he didn't get hauled back, we all figured he got away. Where is he? Can I go visit him?"

Clara came over and sat down on the sofa next to Wally. "He's in a VA Hospital in Newington, Connecticut, just a little south of Hartford. I go visit him every week. You must go see him. Maybe it will help. I think you have to be put on a list of approved visitors, but that will be no problem."

Tillie was frowning, Simone's eyes expressed her shock and Angela went directly to where Clara was sitting and put her hand on Clara's back. Tillie pulled herself together and announced, "Dinner's ready. Do you want to come to the table now?"

Clara had herself in control now. "We have to talk some more about this. I need to know every little detail you can tell me, but let's wait until after we have our holiday dinner."

Pete said the blessing, invoking God's intervention to heal Ray, giving thanks for his own survival, his family and the bounty of the feast. He asked for blessings on "our guest" Wally Hinkle and thanked God for bringing him to the Thanksgiving celebration. He remembered those missing from the table, especially his father, Edward and his Uncle Charlie. He ended by thanking God for the good health and well-being of all those present at the table.

When Pete began to carve the turkey, Maurice started to tell stories about their newest grandchild. Bobby was married, working in Springfield as an athletic coach at a high school and very happy with his new son. They had gone to his wife's family for Thanksgiving. He chuckled loudly and gestured grandly. To Marie, it was obviously an attempt to inject some of the usual heartiness into the dinner conversation and others picked up on it immediately, all of them anxious to avoid casting a pall over the holiday.

Angela chimed in with talk about her experiences in real estate, sometimes telling amusing or comical stories that had them all laughing. Pete responded with how proud he was of his wife. Tillie's frequent admonitions of "*Mangez, mangez,*" reminded them of every other Thanksgiving they could remember.

Marie was quiet, thinking about the extraordinary coincidence of Wally and Ray together in a prison camp and when her mother gave her a poke she chimed in to the conversation with comments about her last year at Smith and her indecision about what to do with her education.

Wally politely asked questions about Angela's work and Maurice's family and offered his observations about being a college student at this point in his life. He ate with gusto, frequently commenting on the taste of a particular dish. "Marie told me you were an exceptional cook, Mrs. LaPointe, and she was right. She just didn't prepare me for the variety and abundance of your table."

Clara was mostly quiet, caught up in her own thoughts, although she did compliment Tillie lavishly for the splendid meal. She knew she had to get through with this meal and that her sister would be disappointed if she didn't eat with her usual appetite, but really, everything tasted like sawdust. Her stomach was tight, her throat constricted, tears lurking very close to the surface. She made herself answer questions that came her way, and smile when the rest of them laughed at something that was said, but it was a mechanical response. All the while she was thinking 'Please, God, let me get through this without upsetting anyone or disgracing myself.'

After they finished, everyone rose from the table, again murmuring their appreciation for the splendor of the feast. Tillie and Simone took over the clearing and urged the rest of them to return to the front parlor, but Angela went and got a pot of coffee and some cups and enlisted Amy to follow her with a tray holding cream and sugar. Marie took orders for liqueurs. Clara went to see what she could do to help.

In the kitchen, Tillie put her hand on Clara's arm and asked, "Are you all right, *ma soeur*?"

"*Oui*. But I need to know everything he can tell me. Do you think everyone will forgive me if I badger him with questions?"

Tillie waved her hand toward the front parlor. "Go, ask. I think that young man will answer anything you ask him. He seems very affected by this coincidence." She turned to Angela and Simone. "Let's leave the dishes for now and go hear this young man tell his tale."

When they all were seated around the parlor, Clara asked, "Wally, can you tell me more about how you and Ray came to be captured in Italy? I'd like to know as much as you can tell, although I'll understand if it is too painful. And you said he was beaten. Who did it? The doctors noticed the scars on his back and thought it might have been done by the people who prevented him from getting to the Allied lines." Clara had herself in control now, focused on getting information and listening carefully.

"No, I'm glad to tell you everything because I can imagine how you must feel." He took a swallow of his coffee and looked around the room.

"We left Rome in June '44, right after we heard about the big invasion of Normandy, and we headed north. We all knew the Nazis were entrenched in the Apennine Mountains and that it was going to be tough going. I had been such a greenhorn, scared all the time when I first came to the unit. But I looked up to Captain Carpenter and trusted him to tell us what to do and I got better, toughened up and learned to do what had to be done."

Pete nodded, recalling the young men he had seen turn into warriors in a few days of desperate fighting.

Wally continued, "We were a very tight unit, everybody looking out for everybody else. The fighting was brutal. Those Nazis in the mountains were very well equipped. It was up the boot around Bologna that we were ambushed. Four of our guys were shot dead right away. The Captain was tending to another guy with a terrible wound when he was shot in the right cheek of his ass. He kept going, though, until we were overrun.

They put us in trucks and took us to a prison camp in Austria called Stalag Eighteen at Wolfsberg. Captain Ray got dropped off at a hospital in Volkermarkt. We'd heard that wounded officers were treated to good medical care, but some of us were pretty skeptical. Anyway, later on, the Captain arrived at Wolfsberg and he said his wound was healed.

The commandant in that camp took a real dislike of Captain Carpenter, maybe because the Captain was everything a military officer ought to be and all his men looked up to him. That fat SOB was probably a reject from some unit that thought putting him in charge of a POW camp was a way to get rid of him. Anyway, he took to beating the Captain for every supposed infraction of his rules. And he did it with a whip, which is probably against the Geneva Convention. It made you sick to see what he did to the Captain's back. As I said before, after the last beating, Captain Carpenter said he had to try to escape because he didn't think he could survive another.

Before he left, though, he told all of us-there were only about 60 or 70 Americans in the camp-to stay put, that the war was coming to an end and we'd be liberated soon."

Pete said, "And that turned out to be the best advice, right?"

"Oh, yeah. It wasn't much more than a week later that they told us we were going to march to Markt Pongau, another POW camp near Salzburg in the central part of Austria. Some guys had gotten sick and the march was really tough for them, but I was lucky. We had been working on a road that was a forty-minute march from the Wolfsberg camp, not exactly fun, but good exercise unless you were sick with dysentery or something. So I was in pretty good shape for the march.

Some guys ran off along the way, but I figured that the war was almost over and it probably made more sense to keep going and wait for a rescue. The country around there was a mixed bag as to who would give any help to escaped prisoners. It took us thirteen days to go about 200 kilometers, some of it pretty rough terrain. When we got there, the camp was ridiculously overcrowded, but after a couple of weeks, we were liberated and I was on my way home."

"What a horrible experience." Marie was surprised someone could actually survive in a prison camp.

"Well, you know, the way I look at it, I'm alive and I got no serious injuries. I learned passable German while I was there and got really interested in geology. They had a pretty good library at that camp. Not that it was a picnic, you know, but if you kept your mouth shut and your head down, you got through it in one piece."

Angela, sitting on the arm of Pete's chair, held his hand so tightly, her fingernails were making little moons on his skin. She thought about how this could have happened to Pete. What if she had lost him?

Simone looked over to where Maurice was sitting and her eyes met his. They both had the same thought, gratitude filling them, that their youngest child and only one of draft age during the war had such bad eyesight he was rejected.

Tillie, seeing her sister Clara's relief from the pain of not-knowing was grateful that this nice young man had come into their lives.

Clara shook her head, "I wish I could understand why he felt he had to escape."

"I think he was really worried that another beating would kill him. And, another thing I forgot to mention, some guys in the camp knew that there were Yugoslav partisans in the forests and mountains around Wolfsberg, so maybe he hoped to run into them and get some help in finding his way to our own lines."

Clara put her hand over Wally's. "Thank you for telling me all this. I know it must be hard for you to talk about it. The doctors noticed the scars on Ray's back and guessed they were from beatings, but they thought the beatings might have been done by whoever kept him from making his way home. There are some men from the government who came to the hospital asking questions about Ray just a couple of weeks ago. I'm sure they'll want to hear what you have to tell. I'm surprised they haven't contacted you yet."

"No surprise to me. I've been trying to bury my name as long as I remember. I had a little trouble with that in the army. It's not really Walter; legally it's Johannes Walberger Hinkle. My mother was married to a guy named Walberger Hinkle when she had me and my brother, but he deserted her and she got a divorce. We don't know what happened to him, but she then married a nice guy who has always been a great father to us. His name is Walter. Anyway, if mail came to J. Walberger Hinkle, my mother would probably have thrown it out."

"We sure are glad Marie brought you to Thanksgiving dinner, Wally. Not only for this new information about Clara's fiancé Ray, but you seem like a nice guy and any veteran is welcome in our house, any time." Pete spoke sincerely, "Now I understand you young folks wanted to go off on your own, so don't let us keep you here if you're ready to go."

Marie was visibly relieved. "Thanks, Dad. We're going to Springfield to listen to Gene Krupa's band at the Roger Smith Hotel."

"OK, *chouchou,* just don't stay out too late. Your mother can't get to sleep 'til she knows you're safely home."

Louise S. Appell

* * * * *

In the kitchen, Simone and Tillie chatted as they washed and dried dishes and pots and pans. Simone said, "That fella, Wally, seems like such a nice young man, but really too old for Marie."

"Oh, I don't think it's that he's too old," Tillie answered, "He's only six years older than she is, not such a big difference. But he's been to war and that changes a man. He's very mature and she's still got some growing up to do."

"The war sure made a difference in Pete, didn't it?"

"What do you mean by that?" Tillie's feathers were a little ruffled at any suggestion her son was less than perfect.

"Well, we all noticed he was drinking a lot before the war and he seemed angry all the time. And don't say you didn't notice that, because we talked about it and I remember both you and Edward were worried," Simone insisted.

Tillie sighed, "Sure, but some of that was because he couldn't get a steady job and he was so ashamed not to be able to support his family. He hated taking money from his father and he hated feeling like he was a failure.

And you're right that he came home behaving different. And thank *le bon Dieu* that he came home with just the one bad leg. And Angela gets credit for saving enough money so he could start his own business."

"I remember when you thought Angela was the worse thing that ever happened. I thought she was a lovely young woman but you weren't very nice to her," Simone added to rile Tillie a little.

"OK, I was wrong about that. She's been a good wife to him and she's a good mother, too. I'll give you that."

*　*　*　*　*

As Wally helped Marie into his car, he kissed her on the top of her head and said, "I'm really glad you invited me to join you for Thanksgiving dinner. You have a wonderful family and your grandmother's cooking is great."

Marie smiled up at him. "Yeah, she has her special recipes, you know? And I can't believe this strange coincidence, that you were in the war with my Aunt Clara's guy."

"I've having trouble dealing with that, too." Wally backed out of the driveway and headed for Springfield.

Louise S. Appell

They rode in silence, both lost in their own thoughts. Marie was sure that her parents would think Wally was too old for her and Wally was thinking there was no way he was going to get a hotel room today and talk Marie into bed after meeting her family. It would seem like a violation of trust. Too bad about that but wonderful to meet the famous Clara, about whom Ray talked all the time. She, the sender of boxes of cookies and brownies and all sorts of other stuff, which Ray always shared with the men. It was strange to see her in person and yep, she was as beautiful as Ray always said she was.

* * * * *

Sitting in the rocking chair in her room, Clara could hear the television downstairs. Tillie was watching with Pete and Angela and their young kids. Annoyingly loud laughter came from the sound track. Privately, Clara thought a lot of the programs on the TV were asinine, but Tillie liked them a lot, so she kept her mouth shut.

Searching through the records in the rack on her dresser, she picked out the Sibelius Symphony number two, with Koussevitzky conducting the Boston Symphony. As she listened, its turbulent passages matched her own inner thoughts. Why couldn't Ray have waited just a few more weeks? Was it really necessary for him to make that escape? Where was he all that time?

When the music softened to the lyrical segments, it evoked her melancholy. Was she never again to have that wonderful experience of joy that she had shared with Ray? If he died, could she go on without him?

"God, are you listening to my prayers? Please don't take him. I need him to make my life whole. You took my first love. Let me have this one."

She laid her head back and let the tears dampen her hair.

*   *   *   *   *

Wally called the VA hospital the next day to ask what he needed to do to get put on the list to visit Captain Ray Carpenter and was told he'd only need some identification. Although he'd seen a lot of death and terrible injuries, Wally still didn't know what to expect when his Captain was in a coma and had been so for who knew how long.

It was the stillness that hit him hard. The only sound in the room was a respirator. Captain Ray Carpenter had been the kind of leader who was always in motion, making sure everybody in the unit was OK, giving information and instructions, helping some guy with a problem, whatever it took to keep morale up. Seeing him lying there was really unsettling. His strong arms were much thinner, his cheeks looked gaunt. There was no color in the face that had always been darkened by the sun. And his hair, once so thick and blonde, was cut short and was all white.

Wally pulled up a chair next to the bed and touched his hand to Ray's arm. "Captain Carpenter, it's Wally Hinkle here. Remember me? I was the skinny guy who was always asking questions. And when I apologized for being a pest you told me that asking questions was a sign of a good brain working. I never forgot that. You'll be glad to hear I'm in college now. Just like you told to all the guys who joined up right after high school, I decided to get more education. Mostly I like it a lot, learning new stuff. Some of it is just a load of BS, though." Wally sighed and thought how strange it was to talk to someone when you can't tell whether he's even hearing you or knows what the words mean. But Clara made him promise to talk because she believed it helped, so he would talk.

A nurse entered the room and checked the dial on the respirator and the IV hooked up to someplace under the covers. She smiled and nodded to Wally, then left.

After he reminisced about some shared experiences, related everything he knew about what had happened to the guys in the unit, described the march from one POW camp to another, he got up to leave and as he stood by the side of Ray's bed, he came to attention and saluted . "Thanks for keeping us all going, Sir, and please get better. There are lots of us who came home in one piece because of you." Wally's voice broke and he left the room, swallowing rapidly to forestall his tears.

Chapter 10

◇◇◇◇◇◇◇◇◇◇◇◇◇◇◇◇◇◇◇◇◇◇◇◇◇◇◇◇◇◇◇◇◇◇◇◇◇◇

Northampton, 1951

January was a merciless month. The weather was brutal, lots of snow and temperatures near zero. Angela used the slow time in real estate to organize her files, send notes out to people she thought might be planning to list their houses, remembering those who had already bought property from her with birthday cards and notes of congratulation when she saw something interesting about them in the newspaper. It was good that she was home because Amy caught a bad cold that lingered for almost two weeks. Mother Tillie came to visit offering to help if she could. When Clara dropped her off at lunchtime, she said, "You needn't bother to come and get me. Pete will drive me home later."

Tillie brought her special chocolate cookies with the faces in colored sugar for Amy and Petey. Amy was sleeping, but Petey took his and wandered off to play.

Drinking coffee in the kitchen with Angela, Tillie asked, "Do you think Clara is looking like she's lost more weight? And is her hair falling out again?"

"Yes, I've noticed that her clothes look a little loose. And she doesn't need to lose an ounce. I don't know how she got through the holidays without gaining. I'm up about five pounds myself. But no, I don't think her hair is getting any thinner. Hard to tell with that short bob and her curly hair, though."

Tillie was thoughtful. She glanced around to see where Petey was playing with his little cars in the living room and lowered her voice. "I hate to say this, but I almost wish Ray would pass on. This coma business is especially hard on Clara. She keeps waiting and waiting and nothing changes. That nice Jack Grimes takes her to dinner all the time and concerts, too. But she keeps holding him off."

"You mean he's pressing her for more than friendship?"

"No, I don't think he's the type to push her. He's too much a gentleman. But still, when you think about it, he's not an old man, you know. He must be dancing to her tune because he hopes for more, don't you think?"

"Well, you're probably right about that."

*　*　*　*　*

McCallum's had sale signs in nearly every department and there was a spirit of competition among the department heads to see who could exceed last year's January profit figures. Clara had worked hard with the marketing staff to come up with displays that were attractive and appealing, especially to young vets just finishing up their education and going on interviews.

She made sure no buyer left the store without her card in his or her hand. Repeat customers were highly valued. Sometimes young men stopped in just to ask advice on a tie. Women shopping for their men were assured of the generous return policy in case a choice turned out to be a mistake. Jack Grimes continued to think she was a remarkable and exemplary employee as well as a wonderful companion and friend.

*　*　*　*　*

Exiting John M. Greene Hall after hearing Artur Rubenstein in a piano concert they both agreed was an incredible experience, they walked down the steep stairs huddled against the icy wind, their breath visible. Clara took Jack's offered arm to steady herself on the treacherous sidewalk. Jack looked down on her green cap clad head and asked, "How about stopping in at my house for a cup of coffee or a drink? I'm only a few streets away from here."

Clara was startled. Looking up into his face, she could see the eagerness there. In all the time they had spent together, and it had become a weekly ritual, their Friday night dinners after the store closed, he had never invited her to his home. "Not tonight, Jack, but thank you for the invitation. Another time, perhaps."

Jack was disappointed, but not surprised. He would try again. "OK, I understand. I'll ask again, though. I hope that will be all right." He didn't want to push her. She had her reasons for saying no.

When Clara was preparing for bed, she looked at herself in the mirror and noticed some loss of elasticity in her flesh. Well, why not? She was getting older. Almost 54 now. She hung up her dress, put away her hair brush, closed the curtains and slid into bed, pulling the down comforter up to her chin. The warmth enveloped her. She thought about how it might feel to have Jack Grimes' arms around her, to feel his mouth on hers. Could there be anybody after Ray?

Immediately, she was horrified when she realized that for a few seconds, she had been thinking of Ray as dead. *Mon Dieu*, how could I? He will come out of it. He will.

* * * * *

It had snowed all day, making the roads slippery and visibility poor as Clara drove home from work. She looked forward to a hot meal and a cup of really good coffee, having had time for nothing but a sandwich and a Coke all day.

She stamped her feet vigorously on the back porch to dislodge as much snow and muck as possible, not wanting to ruin Tillie's always pristine kitchen floor. As soon as she opened the door, Tillie rushed toward her and helped remove her coat. "Call Anna now. She didn't want me to call you at the store, but she said you should call her as soon as you got home."

Instantly, Clara knew that Ray had taken a turn for the worse, or maybe, God forbid, had died. She dialed the number with clumsy cold fingers. "Anna, it's Clara here. What's happening?"

"Oh, Clara, I wanted to call you at the store, but Randy thought that would be an awful thing to do. Ray is fading away from us. The hospital called and said his heart is slowing down and if we want to see him before he ...he....leaves us, we need to come right away. That was nearly an hour ago, but I knew you would get home by now and I ....I.....wanted to tell you myself. We're going to leave now. Will you be able to get down here with the snow and all?"

"Go now, Anna, and tell him I am on my way. He'll hear you. I know it. Be sure to tell him I'll be there as soon as I can."

Clara hung up the phone and turned to Tillie. "I have to leave right now. Ray is dying and I need to be there."

"You cannot drive down there alone in this snow. I'll call Pete and he will go with you. I don't think you should be driving at all."

But when Tillie called Pete she learned that he had already left the house to go rescue Marie whose car had skidded into a fence and crumpled the front fender into the tire so the car was not drivable. He would tow her in to the garage.

Immediately, Tillie said, "You must call your friend Jack Grimes. I'm sure he will be glad to drive you. You are not in any condition to drive yourself."

Clara had just come down the stairs from the bathroom, where she had retched up the meager contents of her stomach and so answered weakly, "OK."

Jack arrived in less than ten minutes, wearing heavy snow boots, his face in an uncharacteristic frown. "The snow will slow us down some, Clara, but I have chains on my tires and I noticed the plows are out everywhere. Let's go."

Tillie handed Clara a thermos of coffee and a bag of sandwiches. She hugged her dearly beloved sister and whispered in her ear, "It is time, *ma soeur*. Trust *le bon Dieu* to make it alright."

Clara gave her no answer.

* * * * *

They drove mostly in silence, Jack concentrating on the road and Clara lost in her memories. The radio played softly, mostly tunes from the new musical "The King and I" and other show tunes, now and then interrupted by a weather report. Jack was right; the plows had been out and they continued to see them working to keep the main highway open. As they got closer, Clara gave Jack directions to the hospital grounds.

When they arrived, Jack pulled up at the front and said, "I'll go park the car and then you'll find me in the waiting room whenever you need me. I'll be there."

Clara turned to him and in a voice quavering a little, answered. "I know. And thank you, Jack."

She checked in at the front desk and went immediately to Ray's room. Anna and her husband, Randy, were standing by the bed. A white-coated doctor, one she had met there often but whose name she could not remember, and a stiffly starched nurse were just leaving. As the doctor passed Clara, he touched her arm. "I think he's waiting for you to tell him it's OK to go."

Clara and Anna hugged; Clara grasped Randy's hand. Anna said, "We'll leave you here, but we'll be right outside. We've already said our goodbyes."

Alone with Ray, Clara leaned over him and kissed his brow, his eyes, his cheeks. She took a deep breath and in a voice clogged with tears, she told him, "Ray, my darling, we are so lucky to have had each other, if only for a little while. Now it's time for you to let go. I give you up to the loving hands of *le bon Dieu* and someday we will be together again. Go, my love. Go to your rest."

She moved the bed rail down and climbed onto the bed, put her arms around Ray and stayed there with her head on his chest, listening to the erratic beat of his heart. She let herself remember small, tender moments between them, recalled the time he gave her the champagne glass charm, the look in his eyes when he first caught sight of her in the bar at the Astor that time they met in New York. She thought she could feel his spirit leaving his body slowly, the leaving gradual and unalterable. When she knew he was gone, she stood up and dried her tears, glanced out the window into the dark night and stepped into the hall. Anna was sitting on a bench with her hands folded tightly in her lap. She rose, her eyes asking the question she could not voice and Clara nodded. The two women clung to each other, sharing their grief.

* * * * *

Later, after Clara remembered that Jack Grimes was waiting, after she introduced him to Anna and Randy, after she called Tillie to tell her that Ray had died, they all noticed that the snow had stopped. When Anna invited Clara and Jack to come to their home, not far from the hospital, she added, "I have something to give you. It may not be the right time, but I don't know when it would be, so come home with us and I'll get it out of the strongbox."

When they got there, Anna bustled around, making coffee, setting cups and saucers and napkins on the kitchen table, taking banana bread out of the cake keeper and setting it on the table. Clara looked up at the sound of a cuckoo clock and noticed that it was ten 'til eleven. All the faces at the table looked exhausted.

After everyone had coffee in front of them, Anna said, "We've been thinking about something for a long time because Ray didn't seem to be getting any better and anyway, our Congressman's office called and well, they had an idea we hadn't considered at all. We could bury Ray in the same cemetery as our mother, but the plot would be in a new section, since the old section where my mother and father had their burial plot is now filled up. They had a plot for just the two of them. That would be convenient for visiting.

Then, when Congressman Ribicoff's office suggested Arlington National Cemetery, it seemed like a good idea. I know it's in Washington, or near there at least, and we couldn't go visit easily, but what do you think?"

"Anna, my dear, I have no say in that decision. It's up to you."

"Of course you do. Even though you didn't actually get married, I know you were married in your hearts. I'm positive Ray would want the final choice to be yours."

"But how about you, Anna, what would be your wishes?"

"Randy thinks that Congressman Ribicoff wants to get some good local publicity out of it, but I said that was too cynical and besides, his office really was helpful, so why not? Anyway, it would be done with full military honors and would be a way to acknowledge Ray's efforts in winning the war."

Clara stared off into the dark beyond the kitchen window, thinking for a few minutes, then she turned and said, "Yes, I agree with that. My husband, Gus, is buried in a cemetery in France and I've never been there, but that doesn't mean I've forgotten him. No matter where Ray is buried, he will always be with me in my heart."

"So it's alright with you if I let the Congressman's office do the paperwork to have Ray laid to rest in Arlington?"

"Yes, yes, of course. When will it be?"

"I don't know because it's necessary to get a request in with his records. We need to make some decisions about some other stuff like deciding if we want a service here or there, use our own pastor or the chaplain at

Fort Myers, where the soldiers who do the burials are stationed. Do you want me to do that?"

"Anything will be fine. Just let me know the date as soon as possible so I can make arrangements. I think my sister will come with me."

Anna sighed, "I'm glad that's settled. Now I'll go get the letter for you Ray sent me when he first shipped out. He said to hold onto it and give it to you only after we got word that he was dead. I kept hoping he would come out of the coma and that I could give it back to him." She left the room and Randy asked, "Anyone want a little brandy in their coffee?"

Anna returned and handed a sealed envelope to Clara. "You might want to wait until you get home to read it. He sent me instructions that relate to something in there, so I've got an idea about part of it. Call me tomorrow and we'll talk about it."

Clara took the envelope and hugged her. "Thank you, Anna. You have been so good to me. I'm lucky to have you for a friend."

* * * * *

Jack drove back to Northampton without incident, the roads clear, the night sparkling with new snow. Clara slept most of the way. When they got to her house, Jack came around to help her out of the car and Clara turned to thank him. He opened his arms and she stepped into them. He embraced her tightly and murmured into her hair, "I'm so, so sorry, Clara. If there's anything I can do to lessen your pain, please ask me. I'll be here for you."

"Thank you, Jack. Thanks for everything."

It was after one o'clock in the morning, but Tillie was still up, waiting to comfort, to share in the pain, to offer her love. Clara gave her a brief telling of the end and of the decision about burial, but she was too tired to do more than that. When she got to her room, she looked at the sealed letter, but did not have the strength to read it right then. Tomorrow would be time enough.

* * * * *

In the morning, Clara took her coffee back to her room and sat in the rocker there with the letter in her lap, hesitating, staring into space, thinking, before she opened it with a nail file.

My darling Clara,

I'm writing this on the ship that is taking me away from you and from the wedding I wanted so much for us to have. But even without the formality of marriage vows, for a long time we have been as close as two people can be.

God knows I hope to make it home again. I want us to live out our lives together, cherish the changes that aging will bring, enjoying the journey. But just in case that doesn't happen, I am sending this letter to my sister to hold.

I want you to know that, if I don't make it back to you, I believe you should find a new love. Just as you loved Gus and he loved you, when he was gone, you were able to love me, I hope you will still hold me in your heart, as you still hold Gus in your heart and be able to love another.

You are a very loving woman, my darling, full of life and strong feelings and beautiful, too. There will come into your life another man who will want to give you his love. I'm sure of that. Please don't let your love for me keep you from loving back.

I am also instructing my sister, as executor of my estate, to carry out my wishes that all my worldly goods go to you. I've written a will to that effect, but I want to be sure that happens without any snafu. I've saved a good bit and my share of the sale of my mother's house added to it, and Randy has handled some investments for me, so there's a fair amount. It will give you a little bit of independence and security if I am not there to take care of you.

If I have to die in this war, I hope I do so honorably, so you can be proud of me. If you are mourning as you read this letter, imagine me there behind you with my hands on your shoulders, kissing the back of your neck, saying my goodbyes. I have loved you fiercely, and I am setting you free to love again.

With all my heart,
Ray

Clara sat there in the rocker, tearing rolling down her cheeks, remembering when she first met Ray and how quickly they had connected. She thought about the way the sun shown on his blonde hair, about the way his eyes crinkled when he laughed. He had such a great laugh. His body was beautiful, strong and lithe. She loved the feeling of his skin against hers, the stroke of his long fingers. How he did love Italian food. And strawberry ice cream. And a good jazz band. She thought about the last New Year's Eve at the Roger Smith Hotel in Springfield, just before he enlisted. He looked so scrumptious in a tux. From the very first minute she set eyes on him, he always seemed so vital. How could she still be living and he was dead?

She had been so sure she could never love another after Gus died. Her wonderful knight in shining armor. Her Galahad. It was hard to remember herself at seventeen, so totally absorbed in her love for Gus. And Gus at eighteen was an idealist who was sure he knew what it would take to make a better world. Darling Gus was so passionate in his belief in the goodness of people, he swept her along in his fervor. Really, they were just kids, playing at being grown-ups. Without a photo in front of her, she could recall only vaguely the details of his features, except his mouth, with lips as soft as any girl and his red hair with the cowlick in the front. Funny that she could remember his mouth but not his kisses. Not so strange when you think about it. They were both virgins, fumbling around, trying to figure out how best to please each other. Clara sighed. It was so long ago. Thirty-three years he'd been dead. What had she done that both of the men she loved were gone from her?

Clara got up, went into the bathroom and washed the tears from her face. She could hear Tillie downstairs puttering around in the kitchen, probably making something to comfort her. And she thought how lucky she was to have a sister whose love and caring were always there.

* * * * *

In late March, it was already spring in Washington, daffodils and crocuses everywhere. Coming from still cold New England, the group following the caisson carrying the flag-draped casket up the hill in the Arlington National Cemetery was enjoying the balmy weather, as much as anyone can enjoy anything in such a moment. The eight uniformed pallbearers moved in slow cadence to the solemn music of the marching band. Clara's eyes were drawn to the flapping of the flags carried by the color guard.

The morning had begun with a service in the chapel at Fort Myers, conducted by a short, bald chaplain who had one of the deepest voices Clara had ever heard. Although the words washed over her in a reverent hum, she didn't hear them at all, lost as she was in reverie. When it was time to follow the honor guard out of the chapel, Tillie had to touch her arm to alert her.

When they reached the open grave, Anna and Randy were seated on folding chairs, their sons, James and Edward on one side of them, Clara and Tillie on the other. Pete, Angela and Marie stood behind Clara. When the casket was in place, Marie turned in the direction of a sharp command to see seven uniformed men doing some maneuver with their rifles. She also noticed Wally Hinkle standing a little apart with three other men.

A slight breeze came up. Tillie quickly raised her hand to her black straw hat, fearful that it might go flying off. Clara noticed, glad she had anchored her small navy blue brimless hat with plenty of bobby pins. The Army Chaplain was saying something, but again she was so lost in her own thoughts, Clara heard not a word. As he stepped away from the casket, the man who had introduced himself earlier as the commanding officer of the funeral honors detail took his place. Two soldiers stepped up to each side of the casket and picked up the flag, holding it taut over the top.

Sharply barked commands called the escort to full attention and, with another command that Clara did not understand, the seven riflemen raised their guns in the air and fired three shots. When the single bugle began playing Taps, its haunting, melancholy sound reverberated in all those present. Both Clara and Anna were grateful to be wearing veils that concealed their reddened eyes.

Two soldiers folded the flag that draped the casket. They handed it to the commanding officer who bowed in front of Anna and handed her the perfect triangle. Anna took it and turned to Clara, "My dear, this is for you. I know Ray would have wanted you to have it." Wordlessly, Clara accepted the gift.

When the ceremony was over, several people came over to Anna to express their condolences. They were Army people or staff from Congressman Ribicoff's office and she introduced each one of them to her husband, her sons and to Clara. Harry Brownell said, "I've talked to you on the phone, Mrs. Pelletier. Do you remember?"

When Wally Hinkle came up, he introduced the three men who were with him, all of them former soldiers in Ray's unit. He told them he had called the hospital in Newington to inquire about visiting Ray and was told what had happened and also the plans for an Arlington funeral. Then, he called the men who lived close enough to be able to make the trip. It turned out that they were all staying in the same Howard Johnson's hotel.

Clara felt like she was surrounded by vapor that kept her isolated from the people around her. They talked to her and she nodded and smiled and shook hands when it was appropriate, but all these actions were automatic. Every sound was muffled; everything she looked at was blurred. When someone touched her, she didn't feel. She kept putting one foot in front of the other, moving forward toward nothing.

Then, Tillie came up on one side of her, Marie on the other and each took a hand. She could feel the warmth on her skin. She heard Marie say, "Come on, Aunt

Clara, we're going back to the hotel now. Let's order room service and have lunch together in your room." It would be all right. Clara had her family and that would be enough.

Chapter 11

◇◇

Montreal, Quebec, 1980

Uncle Charlie took the folded handkerchief out of his pocket and wiped his eyes. He reached over to Marie, sitting on the little hassock in front of him and wiped her eyes as well. *"Ma pauvre soeur*, to have this happen to her twice, it is *incroyable."*

"Memere was very worried about her, but Aunt Clara was amazing. I heard she completely fell apart when her first husband was killed, so it really surprised me that she was able to go back to work at McCallum's only a few days after Ray died. She said that staying busy kept her from surrendering to melancholy. And she had her good friend Ruth Goldberg , too"

"I should have been there for her. I know that now. All these years gone because I was too ashamed of what I did to Oscar. I couldn't face any of you. It's too late....too late." Charlie had his head down, shaking it slowly.

Marie got up from the hassock and put her arms around him, murmuring, "It's all right. It's all right."

Just then, Sister Boniface came in to the solarium to tell *"Monsieur Charlie"* that his lunch was ready. Marie knew that was her cue to leave so she kissed his dear face and promised to be back later.

As she stepped out into the corridor, Mother Superior beckoned to her. "Your uncle's doctor will be coming this afternoon and I remember that you said you wanted to speak with him. If you are here at three o'clock, you may use my office for your meeting."

"Thank you, Mother. I'll be sure to arrive by then."

Marie hastened back to her hotel, picked up mail and messages at the desk and called room service for a sandwich. She was determined to reach Petey today. A phone message from her assistant provided a number where he could be reached in Aviano, Italy. It was seven hours later there, so he might be out for the evening, but she had to try.

"Captain Peter LaPointe's office," an officious-sounding voice answered.

"This is Marie LaPointe Graham. I'd like to speak to my brother, please."

There was a pause and then she heard, "Marie, where the hell are you? You left that hotel in Northampton before I could get back to you." Petey's voice was hearty, friendly, welcoming.

"After I talked to you, when you were in California, I found out where Uncle Charlie has been all these years. He's still alive, although he's ninety-three and has a heart condition. I'm here in Montreal, spending a few days talking to him. He's in a nursing home run by an order of nuns and he wants to learn all about what happened in our lives after he left. I'm meeting with his doctor this afternoon."

"Why don't you move him to a place in New York? You'll have him close and he can get the best in medical care."

"Well, it's a long, complicated story about why he's in this particular nursing home for nuns, the only man here. They are not about to let me move him. Anyway, he's probably too fragile. I just wanted to be sure to let you know that we've still got family alive. With all the rest gone, it felt so wonderful to know he was here and he.....he ......he still cares about us. Of course, you didn't know him, but you've heard so much about him, and now that we've lost Aunt Clara, I ...I thought you'd want to know."

"Of course I want to know, Marie. What can I do to help? Does he need money? Is there anything I can send? I know you had trouble understanding why I couldn't come to Aunt Clara's funeral, but with this assignment in the works, I just couldn't get away. Did the flowers I ordered for her get delivered all right?"

"Yes, I put the rosebud nosegay in her hands myself. And no, there's nothing Uncle Charlie needs, but maybe later I'll ask you to pony up a donation to this nursing home."

"Sure, no problem. What else? I know you, Marie; you've got something else to say, so say it."

"Well, you know Amy can't make the trip, but when Uncle Charlie goes, I want you to be here with me for the funeral. We're the only family left and we should be here for him."

"What about Amy's boys? Do you think they could make it?"

"I forgot about them, and of course they are family, too. I'll ask Amy what she thinks. But you didn't answer me."

Petey laughed. "God, you are tenacious. No wonder you're such a hot-shot. Yes, unless we have a crisis here, I'll be at the funeral. OK? Satisfied?"

"Yes, and don't think I won't hold you to it."

"Goodbye, sweetheart. Love you."

"Love you, too."

Marie hung up the phone and sat, staring out the window, seeing her handsome, reckless brother as she had last seen him, straight, tall, striking in his uniform. It was such a surprise to all of them when Petey had decided to go to the Air Force Academy. Another part of the story to tell Uncle Charlie.

* * * * *

Promptly at three o'clock, Marie arrived for her meeting with Uncle Charlie's doctor. She had to stifle her laughter when she saw him. The Santa Claus image was unmistakable. White-haired, dapper, mustache and beard clipped just so, he bounced lightly on his feet as he came toward her, both hands extended. His eyes twinkled, his little belly shook as her grasped her hands and said, "*Eh bien,* so you are the famous Marie we have heard so much about for all these years. Your uncle was right when he said you probably grew up to be a beautiful woman."

"Thank you, doctor. I am grateful you could make the time to talk to me."

"Yes, yes. Now tell me what you want to know."

"Mother Superior has told me that my uncle has a serious heart condition and that he would be at risk if I tried to move him back to the States to be near me. Will you describe in more detail what his problems are?"

"Of course. As is often true in patients who are amputees, he has not gotten much exercise in the last several years. We believe that, when he first came here, there was someone who made an effort to get him to use his upper body muscles to retain the strength he had at the logging camp. But, you know how it is, as the years go by, some people leave and then new people come and they don't understand the value of working the body for a person's general health. So some systems deteriorate and that's what's happened to Charlie. We don't like to use much in the way of medication, but we did want him to try some of the more recently available drugs. Unfortunately, he was adamantly opposed and absolutely refused to take them."

"If I can talk him into taking them, will they do any good at this point?"

"We don't think it's worth making him upset or angry. After all, he is ninety-three and the body does slow down. In my practice I see a lot of cases like this where they've had a good life and we should let God make the choice. We really believe it is very unlikely that anything can reverse the damage to his heart. Did Mother tell you he has had six heart attacks?"

Marie was shocked. "No, she didn't mention that. I am amazed that he has been able to withstand that much assault on his body."

"We were, too, but he is a tough guy. He probably came from a line of men who worked hard and lived to a ripe old age. And maybe he was waiting for you to find him."

"Surely you, a man of science, don't believe that."

"Oh, yes, I do. We've seen it over and over again, people in terminal illnesses who hang on until the family has assembled. It's not all science, you know. Medicine is also a humanist calling. We believe there is something else to the living being that we'll never understand. Maybe it's the soul. Are you a Catholic, Marie?"

"No, doctor, I'm not. And I'm not a mystic, either. I just realized I don't know your name, although you know mine." Marie was getting very annoyed with this dapper little man and sick of the bouncing. Maybe it was a tic or nerves or something. Anyway, she found it distracting. And furthermore, she hated the condescension, the use of the royal "we." What made him think he could address her by her first name?

" Doctor Poulin, Robert Poulin."

"Well, Robert, thank you for your time. If there's any question of needed funds for procedures you think might help my uncle, please let me know. Now that I've found him, I want to do the best I can for him."

Dr. Poulin's face stiffened and he bowed slightly. "Of course, Madame, I understand."

* * * * *

Since the interview had lasted less than twenty minutes, Marie decided she needed to take a walk before seeing Uncle Charlie. She was angry and her anger was mixed with guilt and regret. Why hadn't she thought to search for her uncle years ago? How did she get so caught up in her personal drama that she let it go so long? She had already been feeling the pinch of remorse that she had been out of touch with Aunt Clara for almost a year before the Lathrop Home people called her. Could she have brought Uncle Charlie to New York years ago, gotten him better treatment, looked after him, and made him a part of her life?

It was easy to remember the hard words her ex-husband Chris had thrown at her when he left. "You don't give a damn about me or ever even give a thought to my feelings, my needs. All you care about is your prestige, your success, your effing business."   In the year since then, she had slowly learned the truth of that. Were the sacrifices worth it? Probably not.

When she first started in the real estate business, she had thought it was just a temporary job until she found a husband and started a family. Then, when she did marry, she was only going to work until she had a child. The disappointment when she didn't get pregnant was channeled into a strong desire for achievement at her job. But the more successful she was, the more she craved the accolades and so she stayed late hours in the office making phone calls to potential buyers, gave up going to the theatre and any other activity that didn't include making "contacts" and trolling for clients.

She was always careful to dress elegantly, to take buyers and sellers to lunch at restaurants where she was sure to be seen and to keep a permanent smile on her face, no matter how tired of worried or boiling angry she might be under the façade.

Her mother used to say, "The chickens come home to roost." And *Memere* always said, "No use crying over spilt milk." Marie squared her shoulders and lifted her chin. Thinking of those two women reminded her who she was and where she came from. She'd made her choices long ago and she'd live with the consequences. No sense moaning about it. What was done was done.

Noticing the time, she turned back toward the nursing home. She certainly didn't want Uncle Charlie to think for a moment that she wasn't coming.

* * * * *

The afternoon sunshine cast a light on Charlie Billieux's head that made him appear to have a halo. Marie told him so and he laughed. "I have to tell you, *chouchou*, I have never been an angel, not even when I was a little boy making my first communion. My *Maman* was very mad at me for dropping a marble on the floor of the church when all of us boys were going up the aisle to kneel at the rail. When we got home, she smacked my bare bottom 'til I couldn't sit down for the rest of the day." He grinned at Marie. "I have a surprise in my pocket. Close your eyes and hold out your hand."

Marie pulled over the hassock to sit in front of her uncle, closed her eyes tight, and held out her hand. He put something into it and when she opened her eyes there was the little sled he had made for her, polished and perfect, with the runners and the steering rod painted bright red, the boards varnished to a soft patina. "Oh, it's beautiful. It even has 'Flexible Flyer' written on it. Thank you, Uncle Charlie. Thank you so much. I love it."

"You should thank Sister Sara, too. She painted it and varnished it and wrote the name on it. I only carved it out of the wood."

Uncle Charlie leaned over and whispered in Marie's ear. "She likes licorice, too."

"Thanks for the tip. I'll take care of that before I come tomorrow morning. Red or black? Maybe a little of both?" and she smiled at his nod. Then she proceeded to make him laugh as she continued the story with tales of her misadventures during the final days before her graduation from Smith.

* * * * *

As Marie was leaving the building, Mother Superior was coming in. They both stopped. Mother asked, "Did you meet with Dr. Poulin? Did you find out what you wanted to know?"

"I learned that my uncle has had six heart attacks. If I was feeling guilty before, it is now twice as much. I regret I did not locate him sooner. And I have no faith that Dr. Poulin has done the best he could to help my uncle."

"I suppose it will surprise you to learn that I share your opinion, but he is brother-in-law to the Bishop here and that is all I am going to say about it. My hands are tied. I've been enough of a thorn in Bishop Frenier's side as it is. I can't ask for another doctor." Mother Superior sighed. "Would you like to come in for a cup of tea?"

"No, thank you, but I would like that another day. Today I have an errand and I must get there before the store closes."

"Let me guess. That rascal has made you promise to bring him more licorice. He thinks I don't know, but that's all right. He's entitled to his little pleasures. Go. I will ask you to join me for tea another time."

* * * * *

Chapter 12

<><><><><><><><><><><><><><><><><><><><><><><><><><><><><><><>

Northampton, 1951

The trees were all budding out, daffodils and tulips were blooming and the campus of Smith College was beautiful. Seniors had the privilege of wearing their academic gowns around campus; bicycles flew past with the black fabric billowing out behind them like sails.

The last week in April, Wally called to ask Marie to meet him at Joe's for pizza. She hadn't seen him since the funeral at Arlington and was eager to talk to him about it so, even though she was swamped with work, she agreed.

"Wasn't that a beautiful ceremony?" she asked. "I think it really made my Aunt Clara feel better to see him honored that way instead or a regular family funeral."

"That's what it's supposed to do, remind family members that our country appreciates the sacrifice made. I hope she'll be able to get on with her life. She sure is a beautiful woman."

Marie cringed a little at that, knowing that Wally probably thought of her as just a kid. Of course he was an older man than the guys she usually dated, but not that old. Aunt Clara was over 50, for crying out loud.

"Marie, I wanted to let you know that I'm transferring to Boston University next year. I didn't want to just disappear without saying goodbye. We'll both get bogged down with exams and you with graduation pretty soon, so I thought it would be a good idea to say thanks for everything. We had a few good times together and I want to wish you the best of luck in the future. You're real smart and you're going to be a big success in life." He hugged her tight against him and gave her a light kiss on the mouth. They were in a back booth with their beer, waiting for pizza.

"What are you thanking me for? I had a good time, too, so my thanks to you. And it was a great help to my Aunt Clara for you to tell her about Ray's capture and his escape. There's so much she doesn't know. Every little bit helps."

"It still amazes me when I think about the coincidence. You may think your invitation to Thanksgiving dinner was no special thing, but it was to me. Not just because you included me in your family, but finding out about the Captain......" Wally's voice trailed off and he turned his face away from Marie. She put her hand on his arm and he turned back, his eyes glittering. "There are things about war you don't want to know. I just pray you never have to find out."

Marie took a deep breath, pasted a big smile on her face and answered him, "One good thing, though, has been the chance to get a good education for a lot of guys who would never have gone to school. You're going to have a great career. I predict that one of these days, I'm going to see your picture in a magazine somewhere telling about great feats of yours and I'll say how we dated when I was in college."

The waiter arrived with the pizza and Wally said, "God, that smells good. I'm starving."

* * * * *

Marie hated her picture in the *Hamper*. She thought she had such a baby face and her hair was much too curly.

Ugh. On the day of her appointment to get her class picture taken, she would have forgotten it completely except for Betsy, who said, "Don't you remember you're supposed to wear a white blouse for the picture-taking?" And, of course, Marie had forgotten not only the blouse requirement, but the date of the appointment. She was just about to rush down to McCallum's and get Aunt Clara to find her a blouse when she remembered she had a white cotton shirt in her gym bag. So what, she thought, it will do. The wrinkles won't show because it would be just a head shot. But to her mortification the wrinkled collar did show and when her mother mentioned it, she said, "Nobody looks at those pictures anyway."

Between classes and studying for final exams, not to mention some silly meetings, Marie was more frazzled than she had ever been. The group of women who lived off campus usually met monthly, but during this last semester for graduating seniors, there seemed to be more than the usual number of meetings, some teary farewells, some passing the torch to the next group of seniors. Marie just wanted to graduate and move on.

"I don't need you to go shopping with me. Aunt Clara is going to help me," Marie informed her mother. Angela was more than a little chagrined at the announcement. She had looked forward to helping Marie pick out a white dress for her graduation, but she resigned herself to the snub. Marie had been so touchy lately, too quick to respond with anger or cold rejection when her mother offered her help. All of it had started when Marie proposed to leave home right after graduation to take up residence in New York City with her friend Betsy, and Pete had said, "Absolutely not."

Angela understood Pete's frustration. Marie seemed so young to them and they had always thought of New York as a fine place to visit but a truly frightening place to live. Crowds and noise and traffic and crime and temptations to a "fast" life were not what they wanted for their daughter. Still, Angela was sympathetic to Marie's desire to try her wings. "How about Boston, Marie," she suggested. And was met with a scoff.

Graduation day was June 11th and despite fears of rain, turned out to be sunny and pleasant. The silk shantung dress was perfect, the single American Beauty rose that Marie carried in the parade was glorious and her family was beaming with pride.

There was a small incident when the class lined up to receive their diplomas. One of the young women fainted. Angela and Pete craned their necks trying to see if it was Marie, but in fact it was the person ahead of her who hadn't eaten a thing for two days so she would fit into her graduation dress. Several people, including Marie, knew that was the cause of the faint, but some woman came rushing over and removed the girl, whose name was Sally.

For some reason no one got her own diploma. They just got handed a handsome leather-encased parchment printed in Latin and later there would be the big exchange on the grassy area of the quadrangle, everybody rushing around to find who had gotten theirs. It was a long day. It was a frantic day. It was wonderful. At last Marie was a graduate of Smith, a genuine B.A.

Clara had talked to Pete and Angela, urging them to accept Marie's decision to go to New York City with her friend. She pointed out that a major part of this desire to move to the big city was not rebellion, but a legitimate need to try her wings. If it didn't work out, she could come home. Privately, Clara believed Marie would make it work somehow rather than retreat in defeat. Marie was too strong-willed for that.

Pete wasn't very happy about losing his little girl, but finally, he conceded. "OK, you can go, but first you have to take the typing course at Northampton Commercial College. That's a simple enough request, isn't it? You'll be surprised how valuable that will be. It won't be all that hard to do and you can wait another six weeks to go to the big city, can't you?"

*   *   *   *   *

Betsy couldn't wait, though. She had a job offer from Bloomingdale's to become a management trainee and that required her to be in New York by the first of July and her parents were adamant that she not go to the city alone. After some harried searching, another roommate was found and the three of them agreed to find a place where they could live together. The new roommate had a brother who already lived in Manhattan and he had begun looking for cheap housing for his sister, so that was a head start. Her name was Natalie and she, too was to be a management trainee, but at Macy's.

Several New York Department stores sent recruiters to the college in the spring, but Marie wasn't interested at all. Ugh, she thought, it sounds like something you do until you find a husband, like working for the telephone company, as Alice was doing, saying "Number, please." all day. Some of her classmates got jobs with the big insurance companies in Hartford, calling delinquent clients to remind them to pay up and some who had education credentials, but not certification, went to teach in private schools. But most of the class of 1951 at Smith College got married shortly after graduation, mostly to the guys who had been coming from Harvard and Yale and Williams and Amherst on the weekends.

That's not for me, Marie thought as she drove to the commercial college on Pleasant Street for her first morning of classes. The place was a big building with a glass front where you could see the students at their typewriters concentrating on producing error-free copy. Of course, there were courses in shorthand, taking dictation, business ethics, and some other stuff Marie knew about only vaguely, but she was there just to take typing.

When she opened the door the sound of clacking keys seemed very loud. Oh, *merde,* she thought, I hope this doesn't turn out to be a disaster. Far from it; Marie came to enjoy her increasing competence over the six week period. There was something really satisfying about being able to turn out an error-free page. And she learned a lot besides typing skills, just talking and listening to the other students.

An unexpected and very welcome benefit from staying in Northampton after graduation was that Rick Clarey came home on leave after basic training at Fort Dix. He'd been drafted into the Army. He took her dancing at the Mt. Tom ballroom and to a great after-hours jazz club in Chicopee, where she tried smoking a reefer and got into a fit of coughing so painful and embarrassing, she never tried a recreational drug ever again. They made love on a blanket under the stars at secluded places off back roads in the country nearly every night and, after he left, Marie was in a panic until she got the curse a week later. It had been an exciting summer fling, lots of laughter and teasing, she learned a lot more about her own body and she became a better dance partner, but she was not in love with Rick and she was sure he was not in love with her. Friends, yes, even great friends, but that was it, nothing more.

When Marie finished the typing class, packed her things in her car and left Northampton, she was full of confidence and hope for her future. Her Dad gave her a hundred dollars and told her to find a bank and open a checking account as soon as she got to New York. Fortunately, one of the bits of knowledge that were a by-product of her time at Northampton Commercial College was a basic understanding of personal finance, something Smith College never offered.

* * * * *

The apartment Betsy and Natalie were in was located in Greenwich Village, a haven for artists and jazz clubs, where the streets were crooked, trees bloomed alongside the sidewalks and the pace was less frenetic than uptown Manhattan. Pete paid Marie's share of the July rent as part of the deal to get her to go to the typing class and Marie was glad of it, sure that there would be some resentment if the other two girls had been forced to come up with extra just because they were holding her place.

She arrived just after noon on August first to a day where the heat made the sidewalks shimmer. The drive from Northampton, picking up the Merritt Parkway all through Connecticut was pleasant; she found her way to the West Side Highway and down to Bleeker Street with no trouble. She even found a place to park that wasn't very far away from the building where she was going to live. Betsy had left a key in an envelope with a waiter at the little bistro down the street and Marie retrieved it without a problem. Her first reaction to the apartment that was going to be home was a muttered, "*Dio mio,* this is really small for three people." But she let go of her negative thoughts immediately, determined to stay optimistic.

As she began hauling her stuff from the car up the three flights of stairs, a really great-looking guy came out of the first floor apartment. He was medium height, maybe five foot ten and muscular, with dark hair curling over his ears and a wide smile. "Hi, I'm Sam. You must be Marie. Betsy mentioned that you would be arriving today. Let me give you a hand with that box."

Marie was grateful for the help and the obvious willingness to befriend her. Sam chattered about the neighborhood, pointed out the best dry cleaner, the restaurant to avoid, the quickest route to the tube station. Marie asked him how long he had lived in Greenwich Village. "Three years, going on four. I'm an actor, always looking for work in the theatre and keeping the rent paid by working as a waiter at Tony Pastor's. You've heard of Tony Pastor's haven't you?"

Marie was tempted to lie rather than appear to be a booby, but she decided against it and responded, "No. Is it a restaurant or a nightclub?"

"It's a jazz club. All the great ones show up there sooner or later. And besides, it's a place that stays open after hours where the guys that are playing in other places around town can come down here and jam."

"Gosh, I love jazz. I've been to an after-hours club near Westover Air Base in Massachusetts and I loved it."

"Good. You'll have to come some night. My roommate can take you. He's taken Betsy and Natalie already. It'll have to be some night when he's not working. Right now he's one of the gypsies in South Pacific."

"I thought that was a musical about an island in the Pacific. Do they have gypsies there?"

Sam laughed long and hard. When he got his breath, he said, "Gypsies are what we call people who form the chorus line in musicals. Cary is a dancer."

Marie was confused and mortified. "I never heard that before."

"Oh, don't worry. I never heard it before I met Cary. You'll catch on to some of this stuff after you've been here a while. Come on in and I'll get you a glass of wine. You do drink wine, don't you?"

"Sure, I'd like that."

*   *   *   *   *

It didn't take long for Marie to realize how right her father had been to insist that she learn to type. In almost every interview, at employment agencies and with potential employers, the first question was, "Can you type?" It struck her as funny. No one seemed impressed with her degree from Smith, but all were enthusiastic about her typing skills.

Sam took the time to show Marie how to make her way around the city using the subways and buses. He drew her maps for the first few trips, but Marie was a quick learner and she soon caught on. She dressed with care, always wearing a hat and gloves, stockings and low heeled pumps; it had been drilled into her that it was important to "look like a lady." The sidewalks were blistering hot, sometimes elevators didn't work, and Marie had to climb several stories to get to an interview. Even though she was bone-tired at the end of the day, she washed out her stockings and her white cotton gloves, put the Noxzema on her face like her mother taught her and lotion on her hands. When Betsy asked her how she was doing, she answered in her usual good cheer. Something would work out. She was optimistic. Within the first week of job-seeking, going from one interview to another all over the city, she got three offers.

On Saturday afternoon, the three roommates accepted an invitation from their neighbors, Sam and Cary, to drop in for wine and cheese. Natalie and Betsy bubbled over with their descriptions to Marie of the help and friendship the two handsome aspirants to the world of theatre had given them. The guys were very knowledgeable about getting along in the city and always willing to share what they had discovered.

The five of them sat around in the tiny living room, the girls in shorts and halters. The fan in the window was whirring blasts of cooled air into the room, but it didn't do much with the overall sticky heat. There were fat pillows covered in cotton prints for sitting on the floor and a low table was covered with cheese and olives, little pickles and a variety of crackers. Wine was served in pretty multi-colored glasses that Sam said he bought in Venice when he went to Europe after graduation from UCLA. "My dad's loaded. He hates my 'lifestyle' so he's glad to pay to get me out of his hair."

After they each talked a bit about themselves, their college experiences, their choice to come to New York City, they got around to discussing Marie's prospects and offering opinions on which of the jobs would suit her best. One was as a receptionist in a law office, where she would greet clients, collect and record time cards from secretaries, typists, filing clerks and temporary help and also fill in for anyone who was out sick or on vacation. Sam said, "My father is a lawyer and lawyers are real bastards to work for. They expect everybody to be as driven as they are. You'd hate it." This comment was followed by general whoops of laughter and then more soberly by general agreement that the job would drive Marie crazy.

Another job offer came from a modeling school. Again, the position was receptionist. The person who interviewed her was the office manager, same as in the law office, but in this place, it was an older woman, who made clear that Marie mustn't think of the job as a step toward modeling as a career. In fact, she told Marie, "You are much too fat and not tall enough to be a model, so you can forget it." Marie was surprised to hear herself described as fat, since nobody had ever suggested that and she didn't think she was. The duties were vague, but the pay was the best offer she got. Betsy and Natalie laughed and Betsy declared, "That woman sounds like a real bitch to work for. Do you want to be miserable every day?" Sam declared he thought she would be a fabulous model and Cary did an imitation of a model walking down the runway that had them all applauding.

The third offer was from a commercial real estate firm, where one of the owners of the company did the interview and told Marie, "I have a daughter who is going to be a freshman at Smith in September." He was a tall, graying man, dressed in suit and tie and a shirt with French cuffs. He impressed Marie with his relaxed, smiling elegance. He pointed out that the job was an entry level one and she would have to be flexible, doing work "as assigned." He said, "I realize you're a bright girl. You'll figure out where you are most needed, but basically, you'll work the telephone switchboard, take messages for the agents and greet people who walk in the door." Marie told him her mother was a real estate agent, but only part-time and selling houses and land.

"I can't offer you a lot of money, but I have a feeling you're going to take to this business like a duck to water, young lady. If you want the job, it's yours."

Marie had thanked each person who interviewed her and asked for the weekend to make a decision. The modeling school office manager was surprised that Marie didn't accept on the spot, but was willing to keep the job open for Marie until Monday.

There was general agreement among the wine drinkers that Marie would probably do best at the commercial real estate company, even though it paid the least. Marie figured she would have to put herself on a tight budget if she took that job. It would probably mean bringing her lunch in a bag, but after a lot of discussion among the others of how bad it would be to go to work every morning to a job and a boss she could barely tolerate, Marie decided she agreed with them.

Chapter 13

<><><><><><><><><><><><><><><><><><><><><><><><><><><>

Northampton, 1951-1952

In Northampton, it was a hot and sticky August. Look Park closed the pool because so many parents wouldn't let their children go there out of their fear of infantile paralysis, a virus some called polio. It was the disease that had crippled President Roosevelt and all knew to dread it. Angela had a woman friend whose son died from the dread virus in 1950, a year when it reached epidemic proportions in New England.

Petey had a summer cold and Amy was restless. She had gone to Girl Scout camp right after Marie left and when she came home she was unusually cranky. Angela was busy with real estate sales and didn't really know what to do about Amy.

"Come on, kids. Hop in the car and I'll take you over to *Memere's* house. She'll have some fun things for you to do. I've got to show two houses this afternoon, but I'll be back to pick you up before suppertime."

At 144 West Street Tillie waited for her precious grandchildren to arrive, getting out the big mixing bowl and measuring spoons, ready to make cookies. When they arrived, Petey was eager to be a helper in the cookie making project, but Amy asked if she could go looking to see if any of the kids in the alley wanted to play. "OK, *chouchou,* but don't stay out in the sun today. It's too hot."

A little later, Amy came back to ask if she could go swimming in the river where there were several people playing in the water. "Who's there watching the children? You can't go unless there are adults there."

"Mrs. Hughes and Mrs. Bolger are both there."

"OK. Don't go swinging on that branch, though." *Memere* warned her. "I don't think it's very sturdy."

When Angela came to pick up her darlings, Petey was carrying a bag of cookies and jabbering about his cooking skills. Angela noticed that Amy's hair was wet, but was interrupted in her questioning of her daughter by Petey's insistence that she try one of his cookies.

Two nights later, Petey appeared at Angela's side of the bed she shared with Pete and woke her up with urgency in his voice, "Momma, you have to come quick. I think Amy is sick. She's making funny noises."

When Angela got to Amy's room, she screamed for Pete, horrified at what she saw. Amy was in the throes of a seizure, arms and legs twitching and shaking. "Dio mio, my baby is dying."

Pete appeared at her side and recognized the spasms for what they probably were, signs of a high fever. He said, "Get a towel and soak it in cold water, then wipe her down with it. I'll get some pants on and we'll take her to the hospital."

They hustled Petey into the back seat and, with Amy in Angela's arms, drove the three miles to the hospital through the dark quiet streets in tight-lipped silence. The twitching had stopped, but Amy's breathing was shallow and labored. Petey, in the back seat, whimpered in fright and reverted to sucking his thumb.

When they arrived at the hospital emergency entrance, a nurse quickly took charge, taking Amy from Angela and instructing them to wait. Pete deposited Petey in Angela's lap and began to pace the small waiting room, then stopped abruptly, fishing in his pockets for dimes.

"I'll call Ma to come and get Petey and then I'll call Dr. Boucher to let him know we're here."

Clara, conditioned to fear a telephone call in the night, ran down the stairs to answer the ringing and when she heard Pete's voice, she came fully awake. "We'll be right there."

Tillie had heard the phone, but was still half-asleep and hazy when Clara came into her room to rouse her with the news that they were needed. "Let me wash my face and put on a dress first. It will take me no more than five minutes."

Deciding there was no time to fasten a corset and stockings, Tillie slipped on a dress over underpants and bra and a slip and declared she was ready, although in truth she was quite uncomfortable about appearing in the hospital so scantily clad. Her shoes felt strange on her feet. She thought to herself. "I'm being ridiculous. What does it matter how I look when Pete and his family need me?" But still, she could not get over her discomfort. She said nothing aloud.

Clara, who knew her sister well, sensed her discomfort, but decided to ignore it. When they got to the hospital, though, she said, "Why don't I go in and get Petey and we'll take him home? I don't think there's anything we can do for Amy and it seems like Pete wants to get Petey out of there and into bed."

Just as she came out of the hospital with a sleeping Petey in her arms, Clara saw Dr. Boucher walking toward her. "*Bonne nuit,* Dr. Boucher. Thank you for coming. We are taking Petey home." Her voice dropped to a whisper, "Please do not let Amy die." The doctor said nothing, just patted her arm as he passed.

Angela and Pete sat on a wooden bench in the waiting room, her head tucked into the curve of the arm he curled over her back. She was chilly and she was grateful for the warmth of his body. When they had gotten there about two in the morning, the place was empty. Later a man and woman came in arguing. His arm was wrapped in a bloody towel. He shouted at the woman, "If you didn't get me so riled up, I wouldn't have done it, you stupid ass." And she shouted back at him, "You're a goddam drunk. How many windows have you broken now?" And he flung back, "You're lucky I don't break your head, you idiot." A nurse came forward and shushed them. She led the man through the double doors. The woman was sleeping on the floor of the waiting room now.

Just as dawn came up, an ambulance arrived at the door. Two white-coated men wheeled a gurney in with somebody on it who was groaning loudly. "Automobile accident out on Route 9. Probably been drinking and missed the turn out there near the Crocker farm. We can smell the whiskey. He's pretty banged up, but not serious," one of the attendants told the nurse.

At six o'clock, three nurses in their starched caps and stiff white uniforms came in. Their rubber soles squeaked on the linoleum as they moved quickly through the double doors. A few minutes later, a different three emerged, their faces registering the long night's work, and they headed out to the world beyond the hospital.

Angela turned to Pete. "Maybe you should call Marie and tell her what's happened. She'll be really upset if we don't. Call now before she leaves for work."

"OK. Do you want a cup of coffee? There's a coffee pot out there near the phone."

"No, I don't want anything. Thanks." Angela was afraid she'd upchuck if she put anything into her stomach.

Pete returned in a few minutes. "She's going to call her office and tell them what's happened. She says she'll leave in an hour. I tried to tell her not to do that, but she wouldn't listen to me."

Not more than twenty minutes later, Dr. Boucher came out. Pete and Angela stood up, Pete's arm still holding onto Angela.

"We've got the fever under control now and Amy is sleeping. Her breathing and her heart are functioning well, so that is good. I believe she has polio."

Pete felt Angela's body tense beneath his arm. He asked, "But you don't know for certain?"

Dr. Boucher answered, "I have asked for a specialist to come see her because I want to be sure. I don't think she has the worst kind, but we may see some paralysis in a day or two and even that may diminish in six months." The doctor put his hand on Pete's back, "*Mon vieux*, it is not so bad. She is going to be fine. Best you thank *le bon Dieu* the virus did not get to her brainstem. Then it would be very serious."

"Can I go see her?" Angela interrupted.

"She's sleeping now. Why don't you go home and have a little nap yourself and come back this afternoon?"

"I just want to look at her. I won't wake her up."

Dr. Boucher frowned, "Angela, you look like you're going to collapse yourself. The nurses are taking good care of her, *cherie*."

"I won't stay long. Just let me see her."

With an audible sigh, the doctor led them through the double doors and turned them over to a nurse with instructions that they were to see Amy for "just a minute."

Amy's pallor was shocking to Angela. She was upset to see her almost fourteen-year-old, independent, smart, funny, adorable and much-loved daughter in the hospital bed with the sides pulled up, making it look like a crib. A nurse was exchanging towels wrapped around her right leg. The vapor coming off the new one gave evidence of its heat. Angela gasped and Pete squeezed her hand to remind her not to make a fuss. The woman who had led them to this room beckoned and they followed her out.

"Won't that towel burn her skin?" Angela asked Pete as soon as the door closed.

Their guide turned to answer her. "No, it's not as hot as you think. Dr. Boucher believes her lower leg may be affected and he ordered the compresses to see if we could stave off any damage."

Pete looked at the woman's nameplate pinned on her chest. "Thank you, Mrs. Cooper. We appreciate your care of our Amy. We'll be back this afternoon." And he steered his wife toward the hospital exit.

Outside, Pete said, "Angela, we have to stay positive for Amy's sake. Whatever needs to be done, we'll get it done. I know some guys who have connections to the Shriners' Hospital in Springfield. They've been dealing with this polio epidemic for a few years now and they've got specialists and new equipment. I'll make some calls when we get home. And Doc Boucher is right, you look exhausted."

"I want to go get Petey at your mother's."

"Not now, *cherie,* he's fine there, probably having a grand old time. You need to get some rest so you can handle whatever is going to happen."

"Well, you need some rest, too."

"I'm going to go over to the shop and tell the guys what's happened and see what business we've got today. I've got to do that first. But, if I can get away, I'll come home and catch a few winks later." Pete stroked Angela's cheek. "We'll take good care of her and she'll be fine. I want to hear what a specialist has to say, but whatever it is, we'll do what it takes. OK? Keep your chin up, *cherie.* We're fighters, you and I. And so are our kids."

* * * * *

Amy recovered with a weak lower leg, the muscles there flaccid and floppy. She was fitted with a special shoe attached to a brace that supported her leg from the ankle to the knee. The leather cuff that encircled her leg just below her kneecap was lined with sheepskin, but was annoying and hot. Angela drove her to the Shriners' Hospital in Springfield twice a week for treatments and after five months they realized with joy that the effort to avoid atrophy of her muscles seemed to be succeeding. By the spring of '52, Amy was walking around without the brace. She still had a slight limp, but, well aware that her father was totally unself-conscious about his limp, decided she would be, too. Marie called her at least once a week to praise her progress and encourage her. Their conversations always ended with Marie saying, "Keep your chin up, *chouchou*. Nothing can keep a LaPointe girl down."

"Mom, I joined the Drama Club today." Amy announced when she came in the door. "And guess what? We're going to put on 'Oklahoma' in June. And I'm going to try out for a part."

Angela was sitting at the kitchen table doing some calculations for a client. She looked up at her rosy-cheeked, excited daughter and thought for the millionth time how lucky they were. "Good for you. I hope you won't let that interfere with your class work, though. You have to keep your grades up if you want to go to college. What part will you try out for?"

"Well, not the leading parts, because those will probably go to seniors, but at least a part with a line or two. I know all the songs, anyway."

"How do you know all the songs?"

"Aunt Clara's got records from all the Broadway shows and she lets me play them even when she's not there."

Angela hugged her daughter, laughing, "You're pretty special, you know? I'll bet you get any part you want."

* * * * *

At the audition, Amy sat in the auditorium waiting her turn next to a girl who was biting her fingernails. Amy said to her, "I'm so nervous. How about you? Are you nervous, too?" And the girl turned to her and said, "Oh, shut up, gimp. What makes you think you can be on stage, anyhow?"

Amy laughed, "What does my limping have to do with it? Lots of people limp. My dad limps 'cause he was hurt in the war, but he doesn't let that stop him. Why should it stop me?" And when she got up to perform she belted out the show's tune 'Oh, What a Beautiful Morning' like a trooper. Mrs. Yates, the drama teacher, told her she had stage presence. Amy was none too sure what that meant, but she liked the sound of it anyway.

When the time came for the high school musical, Amy had her own cheering section. Clara invited her friend, Jack Grimes, and Tillie joined them. Clara's friend Ruth came with her husband and father-in-law. Marie drove up from New York and made the eight o'clock curtain just in time. Amy sang in the crowd scenes and had only one line of dialogue. Her whole family was proud of her.

After the show, they all went back to 144 West Street where Tillie had prepared lemonade and five different kinds of cookies. Mr. Grimes told Amy she was "enchanting." Marie hugged her tight and told her she had to take theatre classes when she got to Smith. Her father shook his head and said, "What are we going to do when you get to be a big star?"

* * * * *

Marie had been working at Metropolitan Commercial Properties for almost a year when Mr. Bates called her into his office and waved her into a chair. It was a very beautiful office on the corner of the building with big windows that looked out over Manhattan as far as the East River from the 30th floor. The furniture was polished and very grand. She was a little nervous being in there, but she certainly didn't think she was going to be fired. Everybody told her repeatedly how valuable she was, how organized, how efficient, how cheerful.

"Marie, I've been thinking about you. You've been with us for quite a while and you've done a very good job. How would you like to try something else?"

Marie's stomach gave a little lurch, but she smiled and said, "I'm always interested in a new challenge, Mr. Bates. What do you have in mind?"

"I think you should start taking classes so you can get your commercial real estate license. The firm will pay for them, but you'll have to take the classes at night and on Saturdays. We still need you to keep us all ship-shape here, but I'm pretty sure it won't take you more than three months to complete the preparation and take the test in September. We'll hire someone to replace you from the new crop of graduates who start looking for jobs in June and you can train the new person over the summer. How does that sound to you?"

It was an effort to sit still in the chair with her hands in her lap. She wanted to leap up and hug Mr. Bates, dance around the room, shout out her triumph. This was it, the chance she really wanted. She knew she would do well with the classes. She already had learned a lot. She was going to be a big success. She knew it in every firing synapse in her brain.

When she told Natalie and Betsy about her new status, Betsy said, "You're going to miss our high school reunion in June if you have to go to class every weekend."

"So what? You go and bring me back all the news. This is my big chance."

Natalie was shocked that anyone would want to go back to taking classes. She just wanted to meet somebody who would marry her so she could stop working. "I guess you won't be able to go to any parties or out on dates either."

"There'll be plenty of time to do that after I get my license. I'm not in any hurry to get married." Marie was too happy to let anything spoil her joy.

Chapter 14

◇◇

Northampton, 1953

On New Year's Day, 1953, the pale winter sun shone on the house at Number 20 Massasoit Street. The wide front porch was still decorated with fresh greens entwined along the banister and a wreath with a red bow hung on the front door. Inside, Clara sat in front of the fireplace in Jack Grimes' comfortable living room drinking Canadian Club and soda. The doorbell rang and Jack got up to answer. Ruth Goldberg, with her husband, Bob, new baby girl, and father-in-law, came in, calling out greetings. Clara rose to exchange hugs and kisses, taking the baby from Ruth and exclaiming over the tiny new person, not yet three weeks old.

"I think she'll sleep now. I just fed her. We brought her bassinet with us." Ruth was fizzing with her happiness.

After Jack got drinks for everyone, they settled down in the inviting atmosphere of overstuffed chairs and loveseats covered in velvet and chintz. Professor Rhodes announced that he had just finished Hemingway's book, 'The Old Man and the Sea' and found it to be a provocative piece of work. Bob asked, "Do you think it will win a Pulitzer?"

"Well, I don't know. Steinbeck's 'East of Eden' will be serious competition," his father answered. He sucked on his pipe for a minute and turned to Ruth, "What do you think, Ruth? I know you to be a big Hemingway fan."

Ruth frowned, "And I'm definitely not a Steinbeck fan. I know this will shock you, Papa Rhodes, but I haven't read the new Hemingway book yet. Of course, I've been a little busy." And she laughed, nodding her head in the direction of the bassinet in the corner. "Are either of them worth my precious time?"

Jack sat down next to Clara with his own drink and said, "You have to read them both, Ruth, even if you don't especially like Steinbeck. I'm betting they'll turn out to be important works in American literature. What do you think, Clara?"

Clara was always a little reticent to get into these discussions about books. Her lack of higher education still made her hesitant to voice her opinions. "I liked them. They're very, very different. 'East of Eden' made me cry, though, and I think somebody will make it into a movie one of these days."

"Oh, yes. You can be sure about that." Professor Rhodes nodded sagely.

Jack brought out snacks his part-time housekeeper had left in the fridge and, with Clara's help, set them out on the large coffee table. There were pretty little canapés, watermelon pickles, biscuits filled with ham and mustard, a tray of petit fours and some chocolate bonbons.

The conversation never flagged through the winter afternoon. The topics covered a wide range of their interests. Democrats all, they were wary of Dwight Eisenhower, who had just been elected president, questioning how his experience leading warriors would help him run the country. They dissected the pros and cons of the election campaign, finally agreeing that the public was mostly reacting to the emotional appeal of a war hero.

Professor Rhodes had been to New York City to see Samuel Beckett's play, "Waiting for Godot," and pronounced it a well worth seeing. Turning to Ruth, he said, "When you go down to the city to show the baby to your mother, you should take a little time for yourself and see this play."

They had all seen Jose Ferrer in the movie "Moulin Rouge" and been astounded at the actor's depiction of the stunted Toulouse-Lautrec, wondering how he must have endured extreme discomfort, doing all his scenes on his knees. Professor Rhodes rubbed his knees thoughtfully as they were talking, mindful of how aging was taking its toll. When the baby began to fuss, they were startled to realize how late it was. The light was already fading on this winter afternoon.

After the Rhodes family left, Clara said, "I'll help you with cleaning up and then I'd better be going, too."

Jack was carrying glasses and dishes on a tray, heading for the kitchen. He heard her, but said nothing. Clara followed him with her hands loaded with ashtrays and more dishes. She put it all in the sink and offered, "I'll wash and you can dry." Jack pulled a dish towel out of a drawer and picked up the first glass sitting on the counter.

They worked together silently for several minutes. This was a task they did often. "We didn't talk about our New Year's resolutions, did we? Have you made any?" Jack asked.

"No, not me. How about you?" Clara's hands were deep in the soapy water.

"Yes, I did." He took a deep breath. "I promised myself I would tell you how much I love you." Jack dropped the dish towel on the counter and stepped behind Clara, putting his hands on her shoulders and bending to kiss the back of her neck. "I need you so much, I can hardly stand to be civilized about it any longer." His tongue licked her ear and his hands came down to slip around her waist.

Clara hesitated, afraid to take this step, afraid not to. It had been more than two years since Ray died and nearly ten since he had gone to war. She and Jack had been friends for almost three years, going out to dinner or to the theatre or the concert hall. He had taught her to play passable tennis. And he had been her salvation when Ray died, always there for her, never expecting more than she was ready to give.

There had been goodnight kisses. Sometimes when they danced she could feel the evidence of his desire. Sometimes when she went home to her lonely bed after spending an evening with him, she thought about this possibility. He was a wonderful man and she realized he was very dear to her. But love? She was not so sure about that.

She lifted her hands out of the water and picked up the towel where Jack had dropped it on the counter. Deliberately wiping the suds off, she turned and lifted her arms around his neck. "I'm so scared of what might happen to you if I let myself love you." It was a husky whisper and, as she said the words, she lifted her head and opened her mouth for his kisses.

Clara was unable to stop the rush of desire. It had been so long, she had thought she might not be able to feel this way ever again. But Jack's lean body, pressed against hers, the stroke of his tongue on her flesh, the sensation of his hands caressing her body, brought it back to her in a lightning strike. She heard a little sound coming from her own throat. It was a yes, a plea, a signal.

Jack took her hand and led her up the stairs to his bedroom. The waning light of the late afternoon left the room in deep shadow. Clara reached out to unknot his tie; he pulled her sweater over her head. She reached up under her skirt and unhooked her garter belt. He pulled his shirt out of his trousers. In seconds, they were both naked. Clara shivered. Jack put his arms around her. He backed onto the bed and gently pulled her after him, caressing her body from shoulder to knee. "Yes?" he asked.

Clara couldn't wait. She needed him. "Yes," she said. "Right now." She needed to feel the incredible, soaring joy of physical connection. It was time. This felt right. She welcomed the sensation of spiraling higher and higher, of reaching out for something and then the spectacular moment when she felt the release thundering through her whole body.

Lying on her side, curled up against Jack, Clara could not stop the tears. Jack kissed them away from her cheeks. "Are you alright?" Clara reached out her hand to caress Jack's face. "Yes, I'm alright. A little surprised, maybe. I was afraid I might never feel desire again." She paused and smiled at him, "And now I know."

"I have grown to love you so much, Clara. This felt like a barrier that had to give way. Was I wrong to wait so long?"

"No, I needed time to heal the hurts. It's best that we've become such good friends. You've always been there for me and that's been so important." Clara kissed Jack lightly and brushed her hand over his brow. "I'm so scared, though. I've loved two men in my life and both of them have come to violent ends." Her voice dropped to a whisper. "Do you think I could be cursed?"

Jack sat up, shaking his head. "No, don't think that. The violence was the war. I'm too old to go to war, darling. I'm going to die of old age in my bed. Now, are you hungry? I make a great omelet. Gruyere cheese is the secret, along with chopped onions and ham, of course. Did I tell you my daughter got me the new Fanny Farmer Cook Book for Christmas? She must think I starve on the days Mrs. Tucker doesn't come in." Jack rose and dressed swiftly, leaving his tie on the chair. He reached into a drawer for a sweater and pulled it over his head.

He glanced over at Clara, still in bed, although she was sitting up now. He thought her very beautiful. It was hard to believe she was almost 56 years old. Her chin length hair was dark brown with no hint of gray. Her body was lean, but curved in all the right places. How could he be so lucky that he had her in his life? He was sure she felt something for him. Maybe not love, or at least not yet. But it would grow, he told himself. For now, they had come to a new place in their relationship and it was enough.

"You are very dear to me, you know." Clara said to him softly. "And yes, I'm a little hungry. I'll get dressed and help you with supper."

Over their delicious omelets, Jack and Clara talked a bit about Ruth and Bob and how they managed to live happily with Bob's father. It was a fortuitous arrangement for all of them. The house was quite large so there was no sense of tripping over each other, yet Bob was able to keep an eye on his aging father, whose eyesight had diminished so that he could no longer drive. Professor Rhodes was still teaching his classes at Smith, but he could easily walk to the campus. Ruth was serving as an assistant in the drama department as the result of an unexpected resignation there and she found it to be fun and exciting. Bob had taken on a second architect for his growing firm. The new baby was a wonderfully welcome addition to their family.

Changing the subject, Clara said, "I've been meaning to tell you something. Joe Daniels approached me about taking a job there." Harry Daniels and Sons was the premier men's clothing store in Northampton, located down near the railroad station at the end of Main Street.

Jack frowned, looked a little confused. "Why would you leave McCallum's, Clara? You must know how valuable you are to the store."

"Think about it, Jack. There has already been talk about our friendship. You know how people love to whisper about stuff. If we become..." she paused and looked Jack in the eye. "...lovers, the talk could get ugly. I don't think either of us wants that."

Jack's face turned bright pink. "No, I suppose not."

Clara reached across the kitchen table and touched Jack's hand. "Really, the offer came at just the right time, don't you think?"

Jack got up and came around the table. He reached for Clara's hand and gently pulled her to her feet, wrapped his arms around her and kissed her. "We are lovers now, darling, and yes, McCallum's will be sorry to lose you. But the store's loss means nothing to me as long as I have you."

* * * * *

Pete was stretched out on the sofa, his head in Angela's lap, counting up their blessings. "Our kids are doing great. Marie loves her job in New York, Amy's limp is hardly noticeable and she's getting really good grades. She won't have any problem getting into college. I'm none too happy about her plan to study theatre, but maybe that's just a passing thing. Petey's only problem is that he's too full of piss and vinegar, but as long as he's doing well in school, it's probably nothing to worry about. We're in great financial shape, mostly because you're such a hotshot." He reached up and pulled her hand to his mouth and kissed her palm. "So what do you have to say about all that?"

"I wonder why Marie hasn't brought any guys home to meet us. Do you think she is working too hard?" Angela frowned.

"Give her time. It's been less than two years. She doesn't need to get married right away."

"Well, I'd feel better if she started talking about something other than her work. After all, her roommate Natalie got married in less than a year after graduation and now I hear Betsy is dating somebody steady. With Marie, it's all about making contacts. She doesn't seem to stick with any guy for long."

"Angela, don't fret about it. I'm sure Marie can take care of herself." Pete was very proud of his daughters. "Where's Amy this afternoon?"

"She's gone to the movies with some girlfriends. She'll be back any minute now. I guess I should get up and start making supper. Are you OK with pancakes and ham?"

Pete sat up and put his arms around Angela. "Sure, anything is fine, but don't get up yet. I want to ask you something. How would you feel if I took some of our money and bought the lot next to the repair shop so I could start selling used cars?"

Angela looked at him, saw the glitter in his eyes and knew this was an important moment. "You already work too hard, Pete. Would you hire somebody to manage that?"

"Well, actually, I think George could do it very well. He's wasted doing nothing but the books for the repair shop. I'd give him the used car department to manage and he could train somebody to do the books for the whole shebang. He's been kind of chomping at the bit to do more and earn more now that he's got the twins. We'd work out some kind of arrangement for salary plus commissions. What do you think?"

"Pete LaPointe, you are a genius. What a great idea. I like it a lot. George will be perfect. Who owns that lot and how much will it cost?" Angela's real estate work was all in residential sales. She knew next to nothing about commercial property.

"I went over to City Hall and checked. It's some woman in Minnesota. Had it for a long time. She probably got it as part of an estate, maybe even forgot she had it. Don't you have somebody in your office that does the commercial stuff?"

"Yes. Barney Cooper. Do you want me to tell him of our interest?"

"If you agree we should do this, I'd like to get going on it. The lot would have to be graded and paved. I'd like to put up a cape cod house, only with big glass windows across the front, have a nice powder room for customers to use, a little kitchen for making coffee with a refrigerator for sodas and snacks, something classy, you know." Pete looked at Angela, grinning. "What are you laughing at? You know it's important that the customers feel comfortable."

"Pete, *caro,* you have already planned this whole thing in your head. What if I had said no?"

"Then I wouldn't do it, that's all. It's your money as much as mine. We're a team, *cherie,* and if you don't agree it's a good idea, we won't do it. But I thought you just said it was a great idea." Pete looked confused.

"I was just teasing. I do think it's a great idea and I love that you are so enthusiastic about it. I just know it will be a great success." Angela stood up. "Now I'd better fix some supper or nobody will be eating tonight."

"Wait a minute. Why don't I go down to the Chinese place and bring home some chop suey?" Pete stepped over to the basement door and hollered down the stairs,

"Hey, Petey, want to go with me to get some chop suey for dinner tonight?"

Petey came clattering up the stairs, a model airplane in his hands. "Look, Dad, I'm almost finished. It's a P-47 fighter-bomber, just like they flew on D-day. I have to finish the tail assembly and paint it, that's all."

"Good job, son. Now get your jacket and you can come downtown with me. We're getting chop suey for dinner."

Amy came in the back door in time to hear the plan. "Great. I love chop suey. Hi, Mom. The movie was great. You have to go see it."

Pete smiled at his daughter. "What did you see?"

Petey interrupted, "A lovey-dovey, kiss-kiss movie at the Calvin. I wanted to go see 'High Noon' at the Academy, but they said they were going to see 'Roman Holiday.'"

"Audrey Hepburn played the lead, Dad. She is so beautiful. I wish I looked like that. Maybe I should cut my hair."

Angela came over and hugged her daughter. "And maybe not. Next week you'll see Grace Kelley and want it long again. Come on. Hang up your coat and help me set the table while these guys go get chop suey."

Louise S. Appell

* * * * *

Fall was Marie's favorite time of the year. She always thought of it as the season of new beginnings. Betsy argued that spring was the time when all the buds came out and the earth seemed to re-new itself, but Marie, tuned in to the rhythm of a school calendar, continued to embrace fall as a time of renewal for herself.

Marie vowed she would make a special effort to be more sociable with the people who lived around them. She'd go to parties, hang around the jazz clubs, and maybe meet some guys who weren't either married or old enough to be her father.

When Betsy told her there was going to be a Labor Day party on their block with everybody bringing their favorite food, Marie said, "Great. I'll make a couple of meat pies. Do you think that would be OK?"

Betsy had been expecting her to say she had some country club party to go to with people from her office, so she was a little startled. "Sure, that would be great. You should tell Sam. He's the one doing the organizing. You know, just to be sure everybody doesn't bring the same thing. He's collecting three bucks to pay for the beer keg."

Marie knocked on Sam's door on her way out and, when he appeared, she handed him the three dollars and said, "Count me in for the Labor Day party. Will it be OK if I bring two meat pies?"

"Meat pies? Yeah, that would be wonderful. Nobody else is bringing any meat, except hotdogs, which Cary won't eat. Could you maybe bring three? We've got about twenty people coming."

"Sure, I'll be glad to." Marie felt good now. She was taking a positive step in her new plan. The past year had been a whole new learning experience, she thought. She'd had to learn about building codes and zoning laws and electricity costs and a whole lot more than she'd ever believed went into real estate sales. It took many evenings of serious study, many weekends of classes. But she was thrilled when she passed the test on her first try and got her commercial real estate license. And then she found out where the real work began, meeting people, making a favorable impression, knowing who was thinking about selling and who might be ready to buy. She smiled and smiled and made small talk and shook hands and stored a lot of information about people she met in her head. When the volume of information got too big to remember it all, she devised a system to keep track. Funny how she had ignored her mother working at the kitchen table with her stacks of

5 by 8 cards, never thinking how that activity was the crux of the selling game.

Early on Monday morning, Marie got out of bed and began making her *Memere's* French-Canadian meat pies, properly called *tortiere*. The kitchen in the apartment she shared with Betsy was tiny, so mixing and rolling out dough for the pie crusts meant clearing everything off the counter first.

She was humming a little tune, really enjoying the chopping and mixing, measuring out the spices carefully when the phone rang. "Can you get that, Betsy? My hands are wet."

Betsy came to the door of the kitchen and whispered, "It's for you. I think it's your boss. I can tell him I looked for you but you are gone out."

"No, I'll talk to him. Keep moving these onions around in the pan for a minute."

The call was an invitation to a lawn party later in the day. Mr. Gray apologized for forgetting to ask her on Friday, but said he got so caught up in the sale he was negotiating, it slipped his mind. "Oh, thanks so much, but I've already agreed to make some of the food for a neighborhood party and I don't feel that I can back out now. I appreciate the invitation, though. Have a great time and I'll see you tomorrow."

Betsy was amazed. In the two years they had been roommates, Marie had never chosen to party with the neighborhood group when there was an opportunity to make contacts in the real estate world. "Wow, you really turned him down. I can hardly believe it."

"Yup, this is my new plan. At least one weekend a month is going to belong to me. What do you think of that?" Marie smiled at Betsy's surprised look. "I'm making great meat pies today. Everybody will be talking about them for a long time."

Chapter 15

◇◇◇

Northampton, 1954

Nobody had ever given a birthday party for Tillie so she was surprised when Clara mentioned her intention to do that. At first, she resisted the whole idea. "I would be embarrassed to have people think I was getting above myself." But Clara persisted, pointing out that it was a shame families got together only for funerals, when everybody was sad but never for happy occasions. Tillie countered, "How about weddings? We always see family at weddings." And Clara scoffed, "How many weddings have we gone to lately? Maybe we'll all go to Marie's one of these days, but she might want to get married in New York."

After much persuasion, Tillie accepted the party idea. Clara would give a party for Tillie's 70th birthday, June 11. It would be in the social hall at the Church of the Sacred Heart. Clara found two women who had a small business cooking for parties. They would provide all the food and the servers. When Pete heard about it, he wanted to be included in the planning. He would provide the drinks and a bartender. Tillie thought they were going too far with this thing and doubted that the priest would allow them to serve liquor, but she was wrong. Pete went to see Father Dumont and made a generous donation to the church, then invited the priest to be a guest.

Angela took over decorating. With Amy's help, they made a huge sign to put on the wall. It read 'Happy Birthday, Tillie' and underneath '70 years young'. They located a balloon vendor in Holyoke who would come over the day of the party with his helium tank and blow up 250 balloons. The church owned all the tables and chairs they would need. Tablecloths and napkins, dishes and flatware, too. These were always available for church suppers; all that was necessary was for the dishes to be washed and the linens to be returned clean.

Clara called Simone and Maurice in Connecticut to invite them and Simone insisted she be able to contribute something. Clara had already ordered a big birthday cake from the Electric Bakery on Main Street, so when Simone offered to make the cake, she suggested making cookies frosted with the date on them for everybody to take home.

Amy and Petey were given the task of picking baskets full of daisies. Angela drove them out the Easthampton Road to a vacant field where the wild daisies were plentiful. Then she rounded up empty jelly jars from everybody she knew to use as vases on the tables.

Clara thought they ought to have some music, maybe even some entertainment. Jack knew a guy who played the piano and specialized in music from the past, so Clara called and arranged for him to perform at the party. The closer it got to the date, the more Clara got excited and Tillie got nervous. Forty-three people, including children, were invited; even Alphonse and his wife and son were invited. She drew the line at inviting Oscar's widow and his children, sure that they would not accept anyway and would probably make a nasty scene if they did come. Clara shuddered at the thought, remembering the encounter outside the church when Flora had screeched her venomous words at them.

On the day of the party, the sun shone bright, the forecast was for mild weather and Clara was frantic, trying to make sure that all the pieces were in place and the party would be the wonderful happening she had envisioned. Surprisingly, Tillie was cool and calm in her voile print and newly short hair. The rare trip to the beauty parlor buoyed her considerably. The florist delivered a corsage of pink roses that matched the roses in her dress and when Clara pinned it on her, Tillie whispered, "You are still my sweet little baby sister, no matter how old we may be."

Jack declared himself Tillie's chauffeur so he showed up just before the party was set to begin at 12 noon on Saturday. Clara had gone on ahead to attend to last minute details. Tillie blushed when she saw Jack, with a chauffeur's cap on, holding open the door to the back seat for her. *"Mon Dieu,* I am not a fancy rich lady to be sitting in the back seat."

"Today, my dear Tillie, you are a princess."

When the car pulled around to the front door of the building that housed the meeting rooms for the Church of the Sacred Heart, Tillie was astonished at the sight of an arch of balloons over the door, Clara standing there waiting for her. When they walked through the door, all the people inside were led by the piano man in singing the birthday song.

Tillie moved into the room, smiling broadly with tears in her eyes, hugging one after another of her much loved family and friends. Maurice and his wife Simone had brought along their son Bobby with his wife, Elaine, and their baby boy, Joey. Pete and Angela were standing behind a very grown-up looking Amy. Petey was all slicked up in his First Communion suit. And there was Marie, with her friend Betsy. They must have driven up from New York City last night. Four of Tillie's friends from the alley houses were there with their husbands, some with their children, and there were several of the ladies from the church sodality as well as friends from the Girl Scouts leadership. All of the sweet young girls in the Girl Scout troop Tillie led were there dressed in pretty party dresses. Father Dumont stood in the back, smiling broadly.

Tillie's thoughts turned inward, to her wonderful husband, Edward. If only he could be here... She stopped herself and remembered that he was now with God. Maybe he knew about this party and he was smiling down at her from Heaven.

Clara followed Tillie as she made her way through the room, taking her to the table set up for ten, decorated with flowers and balloons and a pile of gifts on a cart alongside. "Oh, my. I thought you told everybody not to bring gifts." Tillie said to Clara.

"I certainly did. But, you know, some people pay no attention to that. So just open them and enjoy."

There was an audible murmuring behind her, so Tillie turned around, surprised and pleased to see her brother Alphonse and his son, Phillipe, come through the door. He came toward her with his arms open and she moved forward to meet him, grateful for his presence and his gesture of affection.

Clara turned to Jack and smiled, her eyes misting, relieved that Alphonse had showed up after her none too gentle scolding last night when he told her he did not intend to appear. Clara's aversion to speaking to Alphonse's wife was the only thing that restrained her from telling that woman what she thought of her efforts to keep Alphonse from visiting his siblings.

The babble of conversation filled the room. Men went to the bar, brought back drinks for their womenfolk and drifted off again to join groups of men gathered here and there to discuss politics, sports, prices, common concerns. The piano played softly old tunes in the background. Pete handed his mother a glass of Canadian Club and ginger ale, bending to kiss her soft cheek as he did. "Happy birthday, Ma. I hope you enjoy your day."

Tillie was thinking she'd have to stop this tearing up every time something touched her. It just wouldn't do. Clara went to a lot of trouble to plan this big whoop-de-do for her birthday and she was behaving like a baby. No sense sitting there like a queen waiting for people to come to her. She got up and walked around, stopping to comment on a pretty dress, a new hairdo, or a handsome tie. She asked questions about events going on in her friends' lives. She told of how proud she was of her granddaughter Marie, working in New York City in a big real estate company and her other granddaughter Amy, going to Smith College in the fall.

"Do you know what Amy wants to do?" she asked. And without waiting for an answer she laughed and said, "She's going to be an actress, that's what. Can you believe it?"

Amy heard her *Memere* talking about her to a group of Sodality ladies and came over to where they stood in a little circle. "Now, *Memere,* you know I said I was going to study theater. Who knows if I'll be good enough to become an actress? Maybe I'll design costumes, or take up directing or some other job in the theatre. We'll wait and see."

When the serving ladies started to bring out the platters of shrimp salad and chicken salad and coleslaw, hot rolls and butter, the guests headed for their seats. Amy had made place cards with pictures of flowers on them for the head table, but others sat where they wanted. There were platters at every table and they were passed, family-style. Early tomatoes, grown in Mrs. Clary's own small greenhouse, were a special treat. And Tillie's favorite food.

After the dishes were cleared away, the Girl Scouts went over to the piano and, coached by the assistant leader, sang "O Canada" and "Let Me Call You Sweetheart" and "You Are My Sunshine." They urged all the guests to join them in singing "Daisy" and "Yankee Doodle Dandy."

While they were singing, Clara slipped into the kitchen and returned wheeling in a cart with a large three-layered cake covered in pink frosting roses. Written on the top was 'Happy Birthday, Tillie.' Seven candles flickered. There were murmurs all around as people stretched to see the cake.

"It's spice cake, Tillie, *ma soeur*." Clara whispered. "And one candle for each decade. Now you have to make a wish and blow them out." She held tight to her sister's hand as Tillie blew out the candles.

After the cake was served with coffee, Pete urged his mother to open her gifts. "Come on, Ma. Everybody wants you to open them now."

"Mon Dieu, a party and gifts, too. Really, people were not supposed to bring gifts."

Pete rolled the cart over to his mother, "Well, they did, so now you have to open them so everyone can see what you got."

The ladies crowded around Tillie's table while most of the men went over to the bar. Some of the children sat on the floor near Tillie's feet. There were books, some Dorothy Sayers mysteries, which all her friends knew Tillie loved, a pretty scarf, some embroidered handkerchiefs, a pair of gloves, some stockings, some Lily of the Valley cologne (Tillie's favorite) and a tiny box with a gold locket inside from Pete and Angela. The locket opened and three frames unfolded to reveal pictures of Tillie's three grandchildren. Tears ran down Tillie's cheeks and she looked up at Pete and Angela, smiling. "These three wonderful children are the most beautiful gifts you could ever give me. I am blessed."

The party ended with hugs and kisses as Tillie and Clara, Pete and Angela stood at the door to say goodbye to family and friends. Tillie hugged her brother Alphonse especially tightly and whispered in his ear, "Come to visit me at home, *mon frere*. I have missed you."

* * * * *

Two weeks later, Phillipe called, "Aunt Tillie, something really bad has happened. I thought I ought to call you.

Pa had a stroke last night. He's in the Cooley Dickinson Hospital. I hate to tell you, but the doctor says there is probably little chance that he will recover. I know you'll want to visit him. My mother will probably not go until she closes the store. I don't think she'll go this afternoon. She doesn't trust me to mind the store, you know."

"*Mon Dieu, mon Dieu,* this is terrible news." Tillie's chest tightened and her legs got weak. She sat down quickly. "*Merci,* Phillipe. You are so good to call and tell me. I will get your Aunt Clara and she will drive me over as soon as possible." She depressed the hook on the phone and called Clara at the Harry Daniel's Store only to find that her sister was in a meeting. Reluctant to take Clara away from business, she next called Angela, who was just preparing to go out, but agreed to come immediately and drive Tillie to the hospital.

"It's so lucky you were still home, Angela. Times like this I wish I had learned to drive a car. I wonder why we don't have a taxi in town."

"Oh, but we do. How do you think those Smith girls get from the train station when they go to New Haven or Boston for the weekend?"

Tillie was embarrassed. "I didn't even think about that. I never noticed any ads for taxis in the newspaper.

Well, maybe I just wasn't looking. I'm so spoiled. Clara drives me everywhere or I walk."

"Mother Tillie, I am pleased to be able to drive you whenever I can. You have been very good to me, especially in caring for Petey so I could work." As she drove into the hospital parking lot, Angela added, "Would you like me to come in with you or wait out here?"

"They may let visitors in just one at a time, especially if he is in bad shape."

"OK. I'll sit on one of the benches out here and enjoy the sunshine."

When Tillie asked for her brother's room number, the person at the desk asked, "Are you a family member?"

"Oui...I mean yes. Alphonse is my brother. I'm Mathilda LaPointe. Please, can you tell me, how is he?"

"He is very ill. You can stay for just a few minutes." The desk person motioned to a volunteer waiting to come forward and guide Tillie to the room.

Tillie was led down a corridor, past a door where she heard the person inside moaning, past carts with trays of uneaten food, where the scent of illness struck her forcefully. They reached a closed door at the end of the corridor. Tillie's guide tapped on the door. A voice inside called out, "Just a minute," and a nurse emerged carrying a covered basin. "You can go in now, but only for a few minutes."

Alphonse had never been a handsome man. He always seemed to be rumpled, in need of a shave and a haircut. But he was a kindly man with a smile for everyone. Lying now in the hospital bed, surrounded by white bedding and white walls, his color was gray, his face gaunt and distorted. His sparse white hair was sticking up in tufts. Tillie leaned over and smoothed his hair. She thought of him as he had looked at her party, just a few weeks ago, a little flushed from drink, smiling and happy. Now he looked smaller, older, and very, very sick.

Tillie kissed his cheek and took his hand. "Alphonse, *mon frere, c'est sa soeur.* I heard you were here so I came to visit you."

When there was no response, she said, "Can you hear me? Do you know I'm here? Squeeze my hand."

Tillie felt the slight tightening of Alphonse's hand in hers and she whispered, *"Je t'aime, mon frere, Je t'aime toujours,"* as the tears rolled down her cheeks.

A nurse stuck her head in the door to remind Tillie she must leave, but as she turned to go, she heard a sound from Alphonse. His mouth was moving, but the sounds were not words. His eyes were wet, the right side of his face pulled down. Tillie knew he was trying to say something. Then it came to her what it was and she said, "I know you love me, too, Alphonse. I never doubted that for a minute."

Outside, Angela was talking to Dr. Boucher, who had just come out of the hospital. When Tillie joined them, the doctor told her, as he had already told Angela, that Alphonse had had a massive stroke. It was unlikely he would recover. "He's had 74 good years, Tillie. I do not think Alphonse would want to live as crippled as he will surely be from this stroke."

Tillie wasn't sure Alphonse had had such good years. Marriage to Grace Poulet was no picnic, she thought. Of course, she said nothing about that to the doctor. She thanked him for telling her how it was and he left them, walking briskly to his car.

On the drive home, Tillie sat straight up, silent, clutching her handkerchief and dabbing at the quiet tears rolling down her cheeks. When they arrived at 144 West Street, Angela reached over and patted her arm. "Do you want me to stay with you, Mother Tillie? I could fix you a cup of tea."

"No, thank you, Angela. I need to be alone for a while. I want you to know how much I appreciate it that you took me to see my brother. You are a good girl." Tillie slid out of her seat quickly and hurried into the house.

As soon as she got in the door, Tillie called Clara again. When she was able to reach her, she explained what happened and urged Clara to go to the hospital. "I know you were never close. After all, he got married when you were only three years old. You probably hardly ever remember him at home. Still, he's your brother. You should go say your goodbyes."

Clara answered her, "Well, of course, did you think for a minute that I wouldn't want to do that?"

"Well, I wasn't sure. Lately you see more of your friends than you do your family." As soon as she said it, Tillie regretted the words. What had gotten into her that she would say such a thing to her sister? Especially after the wonderful birthday party Clara had arranged. "I'm sorry. I'm so sorry I said that. I don't know what's the matter with me."

"I've got to go right now, but I'll get up to the hospital sometime this afternoon."

* * * * *

On the drive up Elm Street to the hospital later that afternoon, Clara thought about Tillie's accusation. Was she ignoring her family? Certainly she spent a lot of time with Jack, mostly on Friday and Saturday nights and often all day on Sunday. But she went to early Mass with her sister every week and sometimes Jack took both of them out to breakfast afterwards. Even though Jack belonged to St Mary's parish, he now went to the same early morning Mass at the French church as they did.

Tillie spent a lot of time visiting Pete and Angela and her grandchildren. She had her Sacred Heart Ladies Sodality and the Girl Scouts. She loved bingo and canasta. Both of those pastimes bored Clara.

Jack joined Clara at every family celebration, so she was sure they all had figured out the relationship. She always came home at night, though, and Tillie never mentioned anything about how late it was or asked where she had been. Jack had stopped asking Clara to marry him. He seemed to understand and respect her need for independence and her fear that she was a jinx to any man she loved. And, of course he knew she would never leave her sister. He even suggested that Tillie could live with them, but Clara brushed him off, sure that her sister would not leave 144 West Street while she lived.

Mon Dieu, she thought, what a tangle. She just wanted to enjoy being with Jack and for other people to leave her be.

When she got to the hospital parking lot, she noticed Grace, Alphonse's wife, getting into her car and she sighed, grateful to avoid any contact with the difficult woman. The nurse told her someone was with Alphonse now and she would have to wait. Wondering who it could be, Clara went into the so-called lounge at the end of the corridor, a room devoid of any warmth whatsoever. Seeing torn cushions on the uncomfortable chairs, old magazines with pages ripped out, an ashtray overflowing with butts, her expression reflected her distaste. A young, blonde woman sitting there caught her look and laughed without mirth. "Pathetic, isn't it? At least it's better than standing in the hallway while I wait for my grandmother."

"Hi, I'm Clara Pelletier. I'm waiting to see my brother, but there's somebody in there now. He's in bad shape, so they're letting in only one person at a time."

"My gramma heard from her neighbor who works in this hospital that a man who was once very dear to her was here after a stroke. She said she hadn't seen him in a long time, but it was important to her to say her goodbyes. She doesn't drive so she asked me to bring her here. I think it's very romantic, don't you? Oh, by the way, I'm Stella Galusha. I think I met you once at a church fair. Don't you go to Sacred Heart?"

"Yes, I do. I think I remember you. Your grandmother used to have a butcher shop out of her barn during the war, right?"

"She did. When my grampa died, she took over slaughtering the animals herself. She stopped doing it a few years ago when her fingers got so bad with arthritis she couldn't use them for the cutting anymore. She lives with us now."

"Who did you say she came to visit today?"

"An old guy who had a store up on Hospital Hill. He bought all his meat from her. I'm guessing she had a crush on him...or maybe he was sweet on her. Anyway, she seems to remember him as a wonderful man. Maybe you know him. His name is Alphonse Billieux."

"Oh, yes, I do know him well. He's my brother." Clara smiled at the young woman and thought to herself, 'but maybe not so well at all.'

Stella's eyes widened; she put her hand to her mouth. "Gosh, I really put my foot in it, didn't I? Me and my big mouth. My mother is always telling me I talk too much."

Clara gestured with her hand to put aside Stella's concerns. "It's OK. Maybe I didn't know my brother as well as I should. If he's had joy in his life, I'm glad."

A nurse entered the dingy room, her hand on the elbow of a tiny woman with snow white hair. Her spine was bent and her movements slow. Stella came forward quickly and took her grandmother's hand. "Ready to go, Gramma?"

"Yes, I'm ready. Thank you, sweet child, for bringing me. It's so sad when we get old, isn't it? We have to depend on somebody's help too much of the time."

The nurse motioned to Clara with her hand and they both walked out of the room. "Remember, just a few minutes. He's had a lot of visitors today."

Clara began to shake as soon as she stepped through the door of her brother's hospital room. She saw him in the white bed, saw the white walls, heard the labored breathing and her stomach rebelled. Quickly, she entered the tiny bathroom and leaned over the commode. Oh, *merde,* how could this be happening again? She was back in Ray's room, facing the worst moment of her life. She washed her face with a paper towel, rinsed her mouth, and ran her hands through her hair. In the mirror above the sink she could see how stricken she was. I've got to get ahold of myself, she thought. With a huge effort and a deep sigh, she pulled herself together and walked out of the bathroom to go to the bedside of her brother.

She kissed his cheek and patted his hand, but Alphonse was totally non-responsive. "Goodbye, sweet brother. I hope you go to God peacefully. And I hope that dear little woman brought you some measure of happiness." Clara turned and left the room quickly.

* * * * *

Tillie dreaded going to the wake for Alphonse, fearful that Oscar's wife, Flora, would create an unpleasant, embarrassing scene. But Clara had an idea that taking Jack with them could deflect any potentially ugly encounter. She had long ago told him the story of the accident at her mother's gravesite and the bitterness that had torn the family apart in the aftermath. She felt sure he would intercede to stop Flora's anticipated harangue. And she was right.

When Flora approached the three of them as they turned from signing the guestbook, the expression on her face told anyone who looked that she was ready to spout venom. Jack stepped in front of Tillie and Clara and held out his hand. "Good evening, Mrs. Billieux, I don't believe we've met before. I'm Jack Grimes. I manage McCallum's Department Store and I know you to be one of our best customers and a woman of good taste and propriety. Please accept my sincere condolences on the loss of your brother-in-law."

Tillie and Clara slipped past Jack and went to kneel at the coffin of their brother. Alphonse's wife was weeping uncontrollably in a chair next to the coffin, surrounded by her friends and the new young priest, Father Gautier. Clara reached over the hovering group to touch Grace's hand and murmur, "I'm so sorry for your loss, *belle-soeur*." Tillie followed with the same message and they both hurried out the door. In a minute or so, Jack followed. "Let's go get some dinner, ladies. I think that worked very well."

The day of the funeral the wind and the rain forced all the mourners to huddle under their umbrellas and there was no chance for Flora to cause any mischief, although Jack was ready to play his role again if it became necessary.

Chapter 16

◇◇◇

Montreal, 1980

Uncle Charlie shook his head and stared out the window at the trees bending under the force of the wind. "Alphonse was always a sweet man. A little slow. Sometimes he had a bit of trouble following a story and he hardly ever got a joke, but he was a hard worker. And he wouldn't hurt a fly. Do you know why he married Grace? I'll tell you. Because she asked him, that's why. She was smart, that one. Some people said too smart. I guess she knew she could boss him around and he'd never argue. Hard to believe he's gone."

"I can say it now, I suppose. I knew about his little *affair de coeur* with Sophie Galusha, but I never said a word about it to anyone. I figured he deserved it and it was nobody's business, anyway. What do you think about that, *chouchou*?"

Marie hugged her uncle. "Everybody has secrets, Uncle Charlie. Some are more innocent than others. It wasn't until years later that Aunt Clara told me some of the family stories and by then, there was nobody left to judge."

Marie got up from the little hassock where she had been sitting when Sister Boniface came to get *Monsieur* Billieux for lunch. "I'll be back this afternoon after you take your nap."

Walking down the hall toward the foyer, she was startled as she passed the open door of Mother Superior's office. "Mrs. Graham, would you care to share lunch with me? I'm having a little soup and a sandwich here in my office. It's a nasty day out there. We can eat by the fire."

"Yes, Mother, I would like that. It's kind of you to ask." Marie lied smoothly. Actually, she'd been looking forward to an opportunity to collect her thoughts, return a few phone calls and put her feet up. But she must want something, Marie thought, or she wouldn't have had her door open, waiting for me to pass by.

A little table was set in front of the fireplace, set with lovely china and silver for two. Clearly, Mother Superior didn't anticipate a refusal. The fire was welcoming; a little hot soup would be good. Marie would make the best of it.

A novice came in with two covered soup bowls and a platter of sandwiches on a tray. When she set the bowls down and removed the covers, the aroma of rich pea soup filled the room. "Will you drink a little glass of wine with your lunch?" Mother Superior waved at a bottle set on the corner of her desk.

"Yes, thank you. I would like that." Marie was a little mystified at the elegance of this unexpected occasion. "Your table service is beautiful, Mother. I am admiring the visual delights as well as the scent of the soup. Especially since it is my favorite."

The novice poured the wine and Mother Superior settled herself into one of the brocaded chairs. She gestured to Marie to sit in the other. Lifting her wine glass in a little salute, she took a swallow of the wine and Marie followed suit. "I'm sure you are wondering why I invited you to lunch today and I'll explain later. First, enjoy the soup while it is hot. The sandwiches are made with our own ham. We raise pigs on one of our farms near Quebec City and we cure the hams there, too. I think you'll like it."

"The soup is delicious," Marie exclaimed, surprised to note that it was as good as any her *Memere* made. "You must have an excellent cook."

"Yes, when I first came here as a novice I was shocked at how well the nuns in this order were fed, as well as how luxurious some of the appointments are. I guess I expected to have to sacrifice all earthly pleasures in service to God."

Marie chuckled and said, "I learned long ago that Mother Church is very wealthy and most clerics and religious are afforded creature comforts if they want them. Of course, there are some monasteries and groups that are famous for their denial of such things."

"Have you ever been to Rome, Mrs. Graham?"

"Yes, I have been there four times, always awed by the beauty of the city itself and of course, nothing rivals the treasures of the Vatican or the splendor of the Sistine Chapel. Have you visited the Holy See?"

"No. I am sure it is glorious and that I, too, would be awed by it. But I'm not likely to be asked to go there. The Church still has a difficult time understanding and accepting the role of women in its work. I am saddened by that. Maybe it will change someday, but not in my lifetime."

The novice returned to clear their plates. Little lemon tarts appeared and tea was poured. Mother Superior leaned back in her chair and took a deep breath. "Would it surprise you to learn I enjoy a small brandy with your uncle every night after dinner? And that he recalls for me the stories you have been telling him during the day?"

"No, Mother, it does not surprise me, but I do wonder why you are so interested in our family's saga."

With eyes that looked by turns pained and adamant, Mother Superior recounted for Marie the story of how she came to the convent orphanage in Maine. When she was eleven years old, her father came to her bed and forced himself on her, threatening to throw her out of the house into the snow if she told anyone. She defied him and told her mother, who refused to believe her and took her to the convent, declaring her to be 'filthy-minded and uncontrollable.'

At first, the young girl was frightened, but then, when she told her story to the nuns, they believed her and assured her of a safe place in the orphanage. It was not the first time they had heard of such abuse. Most of the children were younger, but Michelle Ouimette, which was Mother Superior's family name, was glad to be a big sister to them. She had seven brothers and sisters back at the home she had been thrown out of.

The first weekend that Michelle was in the orphanage, Charlie Billieux came to do some replacement of a rotted door in the garden shed. She saw a handsome man who was kindly, patient with little children's questions, patting a little one on the head, offering gum drops or licorice sticks from his pocket. Immediately, she knew she loved him She concocted a fantasy that he was her real father, who had been forced to leave her with the Ouimette family when she was a baby. And now that she was here at the orphanage, he came every week so he could see her.

Even when Michelle got older and knew her fantasy for what it was, she still thought of Charlie as a surrogate father. So, then, when he was injured, she fought hard to get him accepted at the Nursing Home, so she could take care of him for the rest of his life. She called it "having the privilege of caring for him," because to her, it made her relationship to him more real.

"And now that you are here, telling him all he wants to know about the family he still loves, it is like he is giving me his family as well as himself when he recalls your tales for me every night. *Tu comprends?*"

Marie could not prevent the tears from rolling down her cheeks. "I do understand, Mother. And I now understand your resistance to my visit and your fear that I will take him away. He has spoken very little to me about himself or his relationship to you. Probably because he would never violate your privacy. Does he know about your real reason for being at the orphanage?"

"Yes, he knows. I wasn't going to tell him, but he refused to believe the story my mother told the nuns and when he asked me to tell him the truth, I could not lie to him."

"I appreciate your candor in telling me all of this, but why now? Am I a threat in any way?" Marie was genuinely puzzled.

Mother Superior stood up and Marie hastened to join her. "I want to be sure you understand that you cannot take him from me, now or when he dies. He will be buried here, in the small graveyard in the back garden, where I can visit him every day. No matter what you may be planning, it is of no consequence. I tell you of the strength of my relationship to him so you will not fight me on this." The nun's eyes were blazing as if ready to go to battle.

"I'm astonished that you would think I might do something so underhanded as to go behind your back to make arrangements for my uncle. All he has to do is tell me what he wants done with his remains. Does he know your plans?"

"Yes, but now that you have come here..."

"Do you think I would try to persuade him to let me take his body home?"

"Will you do that?"

"No, Mother, I will not. You have my word that I will do no such thing."

The smile that lit up Mother Superior's face was not the tight little polite smile she affected normally, but an expression of joy. "*Bon,* then we can be friends."

* * * * *

Marie thought about the story of Mother Superior's relationship to Uncle Charlie as she walked back to her hotel, buffeted by the wind and the sleet rattling her umbrella. How fortunate they both were, these two people hurt by events in their lives that shaped them ever after, that they had filled a need for each other. The strong desire for connection cannot be denied, or if it is, we are diminished.

Thursday already and she was planning to leave Sunday or maybe Monday, depending on the weather. She could really drive back in one day if there was no snow or rain, especially if she left early in the morning. She shook her head. That decision could wait.

Picking up the little pink slips at the front desk of the hotel reminded her to get moving and return at least a few of the most important calls before she hurried back to resume telling Uncle Charlie the family tales he seemed to want to know.

It was the housekeeper who answered when Marie called Amy. "I'm sorry, Mrs. Graham, she's not here. She went out to a luncheon with her friend Carol. I'll tell her you called."

Marie was cheered to hear that Amy had gone out. That meant her fatigue level was manageable. Maybe Amy would get to go to David's premiere tomorrow night after all.

Chapter 17

◇◇

New York City and Northampton, 1955-56

It had been four years since her graduation from Smith, and Marie could hardly believe how much she'd changed. At twenty-four, she had a job she loved and she did very well.   Not the really big money, but she was confident she would get there. She'd learned that hard work paid off. She spent a lot of time in the New York Public Library learning about the history of the city. Even hardened corporate types who went looking for a piece of property to match their goals and their wallets were impressed when she was able to tell them the histories of the neighborhoods and the buildings themselves, ticking off scandals and ceremonies and personalities of the past. They filed away her information in their heads so that they, in turn, could impress their bosses.

Marie learned quickly that appearance was important and she cloaked her youth in tailored suits she bought on sale at Klein's on the Square, the New York insider's place to go for high quality designer duds at rock bottom prices. It took true grit to shop there, but Marie learned how to meet the challenge, pushing and grabbing along with everyone else. The long curls that had been a source of many compliments when she was a college student were clipped short in a style that was easy to care for and went well with her hats. She carried a soft black leather briefcase that had been her Christmas present from her mom and dad, remembering her mother's admonition to polish it frequently so it would keep its luster.

She was still living on Bleeker Street, but Betsy had taken advantage of an opportunity for a job at Filene's in Boston in the fall of '54, so now Marie lived alone. Her income had gone up enough so that she could afford the hundred dollars a month for the tiny two bedroom walk-up. When her mother suggested that she might get lonely, she pointed out that having the extra bedroom meant family could come to visit more often because there would be a guest room.

Sam still lived downstairs, but Cary had gone off with a touring company of "South Pacific" and Sam had a new roommate, whose name was Paul. He was an assistant stage manager at Radio City Music Hall where the Rockettes performed every night. He seemed to always be angry, chain-smoking and ranting against this one and that one who didn't meet his high standards, and he wasn't as much fun as Cary. Usually Marie spent time with Sam alone.

They often went to Louis', off Sheridan Square, where the house special was a big plate of spaghetti and meatballs for sixty-five cents, including a lettuce and tomato salad. Marie loved the smell of hot candle wax dripping down the sides of empty Chianti bottles. It was dingy and noisy and none too clean, but the food was delicious as well as cheap, the sauce on the spaghetti heavily flavored with garlic and oregano.

Sam, a huge fan of Dylan Thomas, loved the White Horse Tavern, joining the group that sang loudly, if not well, the songs of the Irish rebellion. Marie thought that bar too raucous and filled with beatniks, who were famous for getting drunk, but she went to keep Sam company. Mostly, Sam was there in the hope of catching a glimpse of Dylan or any of the other famous writers who were known to be frequent patrons.

One night at Tony Pastor's, Marie was surprised to see a man she thought might be Tom Finkelstein, the sailor she and her friends had talked into coming to Esther's birthday party. He looked not much different than he had in the fall of '43. She waved at him, but he just looked puzzled. Marie was sitting at a tiny table with Sam and two of their neighbors drinking rum and Coke. "Who're you waving at, Marie?" someone asked. And Marie told the story of the scavenger hunt at a birthday party when she was thirteen. One of the items on the list to bring back to the party was a serviceman in uniform. Marie's team saw a sailor crossing the street and she, as forthright then as she was now, went right up to him and asked him to come back to Esther's house. Amazingly, he did. And then he dazzled the group of thirteen-year-old girls with his tales of being a submariner. He dazzled Esther's parents, too, with his good manners and sensitivity to the young teens.

Marie was shocked when Sam got up from the table and went over to Tom. She could see him talking and gesturing and then, there they were, walking over.

Tom leaned over and said, "I should have recognized you. Anybody would have known then that you would turn out to be a beautiful woman."

"Thanks, Tom. That's a sweet thing to say. Let me introduce you to my neighbors, Carl and Jane. Are you with someone? Would you care to join us?" Marie was blushing a bit.

"I'm here alone and I'd love to join you. Are you living in the city now? Did you go to Smith College? I remember you talking about that the night we met."

"Yeah, I graduated in '51 and came down here to work and I've been here ever since, selling real estate. How about you? Where were you stationed? When did you get to come home? Did you go to college? Are you married now?"

"Whoa. What a lot of questions. Let's go someplace a little quieter than this and I'll answer them all. How about it?" he asked, addressing the question to the others at the table. "Anybody interested in going over to the Peacock on Greenwich Avenue? They've got great cappuccino there."

Carl and Jane were both taking classes at NYU and begged off, needing to get up too early in the morning to make a late night. Sam asked if Tom would see that Marie got home safe. He decided to stay at Tony Pastor's.

Settled down with big, steaming cups of cappuccino, Tom told Marie about his adventures as a submariner, about the loss of hearing in one ear from an accident during a frantic dive, about coming home to matriculate as an engineering student at Stevens Institute of Technology across the river in Hoboken, then changing his mind and transferring to NYU to study architecture. He told her about landing a job with the Robert Moses firm, a really great place to be, even if he was stuck at the drafting tables. He said his parents still lived in New Rochelle. His sister, who had been in the WAVES, was married now, had two boys and lived near their parents. He said, "I got engaged a couple of years ago, but she broke it off after she got a better offer."

Marie was charmed. She thought this was the first time she had a date that talked about himself without bragging or trying to impress her with his superiority. Well, correct that, she mused, this isn't a date. When Tom asked her about what happened to the other girls at the party that night in '43, she gave him a straight answer as far as she knew and was chagrined to realize how many of them she had lost touch with.

"I got real lucky when I came here job-hunting. My dad had insisted that I take typing lessons the summer after I graduated, so I applied for receptionist positions. I got hired by Metropolitan Commercial, probably partly because one of the owners had a daughter going to Smith. But, anyway, after about a year as receptionist, I got to go to classes preparing me to take the commercial real estate exam. It's been nearly three years since I got my license and I'm still a greenie, but I'm getting better. I like it. And I like living in the Village, too. This is a fascinating city, isn't it?"

"I think you're a little too modest. I know how tough the commercial real estate exam is and how hard you must work. Not too many women are willing to do it."

"In case you haven't noticed, Tom, women's roles are changing. Haven't you heard about Betty Friedan's <u>Feminine Mystique?</u>"

Tom laughed and raised his hands in the air. "I give up. You're right. I'm a dinosaur, a chauvinist. Forgive me?" And Marie started laughing with him.

When they got to Bleeker Street, Marie warned Tom there was no elevator and he didn't need to climb up to her door, but he ignored her and followed her up the stairs. Marie said, "I'd invite you in, but I've got work to do tomorrow." He answered, "So do I," and gave her a hug and a brotherly kiss goodnight.

"Thanks, Tom, it was great to see you. I enjoyed hearing about what happened to you after that night. What a small world it is, though, to run into you at Tony's."

Tom started down the steps and then turned back, "Have you been to the Cloisters yet? I have to go there on an assignment for work Saturday. Want to come with me?"

Marie was a little startled by the invitation. She was thinking that there didn't seem to be any interest on his part in pursuing a friendship, but obviously she was wrong. "I may have to work in the morning, but I haven't been there and I'd love to go."

"Great. I'll call you at your office on Friday. I've got your card right here." He patted his breast pocket and waved.

* * * * *

Randy Parker left Pratt and Whitney in 1951, reminded by Ray's death of the importance of setting priorities. He was sixty and in good health and eligible for early retirement. For the first two years after retirement, he and Anna traveled around the country. They had a small camper that they hitched to their Buick and went wherever the spirit took them. They explored the Grand Canyon, the Mississippi delta, the Florida swamps. They didn't particularly like big cities; they loved the open road.

But in 1953, Anna slipped on a small rug in the foyer of a friend's home during a wedding reception and broke her pelvis. Even though she healed pretty well, she developed arthritis in her joints and found that traveling wasn't any fun anymore.

Looking around for something to do with himself, Randy decided to volunteer for the Democratic Party, at first stuffing envelopes and making phone calls, but during the year he did that, some people noticed that he could always be counted on and that he was a loyal, level-headed guy. As a result, he became more and more connected to the committees where discussions of strategy took place and decisions were made.

In 1955, the congressional delegation from Connecticut had only one Democrat, Tom Dodd, who replaced Randy's champion Abraham Ribicoff, when Ribicoff made a bid for the senate and lost. The Party regulars were determined to elect more Democrats. There were some who eyed Randy as a possible candidate. He was a quiet, thoughtful man, who listened and reflected and never raised his voice. That made him a very welcome contrast to the bombastic party elders.

One of the perks that came with his volunteering was being on the invitation list for several of the receptions the governor held for prominent citizens and potential donors. Randy was especially pleased to be included because Abraham Ribicoff was now the governor of Connecticut. These affairs were quite elegant. Anna loved getting dressed up in her best to attend. It was at one of these parties that Randy happened to see a man he recognized as having been on Ribicoff's staff when he was a congressman. He introduced himself. "Hello, I'm embarrassed to say I don't remember your name, but you were very helpful to my wife and me when her brother turned up after the war in a forest in Europe."

"Yes, I remember you. I'm Harry Brownell. Your brother-in-law's name was Carpenter, wasn't it? And he was buried at Arlington, as I recall."

Randy was pleased that his recollection was right. "We've always wondered what the CIA...I presume they were CIA...wanted with him. They hung around the VA hospital for a while, trying to get some information, but he never recovered from the coma. Do you have any idea of what that was about or any source of information to suggest?"

"It's interesting that you should ask. The Governor mentioned his interest in Captain Carpenter to me a while ago and some crisis or other intervened so I never pursued it. I'm on the Governor's staff now. He brought me along when he left Congress. I'll make some phone calls and see what I can find out." He took out a small pad and a pen. "Give me your phone number. I'll call you if I learn anything."

*   *   *   *   *

Three months later, when Randy was worried about Anna's persistent cough sapping her strength and he'd nearly forgotten his request, Harry Brownell called him. "I've gotten some interesting responses to my inquiries about Captain Carpenter. I'd rather not give you this information over the phone. Could we meet for lunch next week Thursday? My calendar is full this week, but next Thursday is clear."

"Of course. What time and where?" Randy felt excited, but a little shiver of apprehension ran down his spine. He wondered if he should tell Anna. No, it didn't make sense when she wasn't feeling well.

The luncheon meeting was to take place in an Italian restaurant across the street from the Greyhound Station, not in the heart of downtown Hartford. Randy had heard about it from some friends as a spot for excellent food, but he was not prepared for the beautiful pressed tin ceilings, the polished mahogany booths, the etched glass dividers. Pretty swanky, he thought. Harry was there already and hailed him with an upraised arm.

"What'll you have? You can see I already got my first martini of the day. I was early." Harry hoisted his glass in a little salute.

"Uh, well, I'll have the same." Randy addressed the hovering waiter. He was a little hesitant. It was not his practice to drink in the middle of the day.

"They have the best veal scallopini in town. You should try it."

"Sure. I love veal, especially if it's cooked well."

"I promise you can't get a bad meal here."

Randy's drink arrived and he sat back in the booth. He liked a nice lunch as much as the next guy, but he was here for a purpose. "So tell me. What did you find out about my brother-in-law?"

"I'm pretty sure you already know he was well thought of in the military, right?" Harry looked over the rim of his glass at Randy.

"Well regarded by brass and revered by the men under his command, too." Randy took a sip of his drink. "By pure accident, his fiancé met one of those men who told her about the ambush in the mountains near the Italian border and the later time in the camp for war prisoners."

Harry lit a cigarette and inhaled. "Yeah, that was in the file. The spooks interviewed that guy, Wally something, wasn't it?"

"Yes, Wally Hinkle. He's the one who explained the scars on my brother-in-law's back. They were inflicted by the camp commandant. Did you know that? When he was first brought to the hospital in England, the doctors thought they might have been done by whoever detained him all that time, but Wally was there. He saw it happen."

Harry struck the table with his fist, "Those SOBs ought to hang for that."

"Did you know that Wally Hinkle organized a few of the men in Ray's unit to come to the burial at Arlington? We met him there. Nice guy."

"No, I didn't get to meet him but the transcripts in the file make me believe he's a bright guy, taking advantage of the G.I. Bill. He'll go far." Harry drained his martini glass and signaled the waiter for another. "I'm going to tell you what I found out, but also some things need explanation before any speculation about Captain Carpenter will make any sense to you."

Randy leaned forward expectantly, his whole posture conveying tension. "OK, I understand."

Harry continued, "See, the OSS people were all over that area and they knew there were Yugoslav partisans operating in those mountains, sabotaging arms deliveries, blowing up roads, cutting communications lines, that sort of thing. When the war ended, it was chaos all over Europe and efforts to disarm those partisans were what you might call less than effective. So when the communists wanted to take over Austria, they had some of Tito's guys in position to put teeth into the diplomatic negotiations. We've still got a military presence in Austria. This damned cold war is draining our resources. Anyway, all that is by way of explaining to you why the intelligence community was hovering over Captain Carpenter's bed in the VA hospital. They hoped he could tell them something about these so-called freedom fighters. Every indication seems to point to his having been with one of these groups."

"Are you suggesting that he joined some gang fighting against U.S. interests? Because, if you are, I object very strongly." Randy put his glass down and scowled at Harry.

"No, no, quite the contrary. The conclusion of the CIA is that he was held against his will precisely because they were afraid he would tell about their activities. But wait a minute, there's more to the story. Some agents went into the little towns around the area of the stalag and talked to people. What they learned is that an old woman with a retarded son had heard about the Nazis putting people like him to death and she fled deep into the forest to save him. She was well-known by locals as a healer, which would explain the successful removal of the bullet Captain Carpenter must have taken during his escape. Somebody knew how to do it and how to prevent or at least treat infection."

Randy nodded and said, "We already know because Wally Hinkle told us that one bullet wound was a result of the ambush in the mountains and that one was treated in a German hospital before he was sent to the camp. The second one was probably a hit he took during his escape. From what Wally said they went after him with guns blazing."

The veal arrived, steam rising from the plates and the aroma of butter and lemon rich and inviting. Harry took a few bites. "Didn't I tell you this place had great food?"

"Yes, you did." Randy had lost his appetite, but he cut a small piece and swallowed it with some difficulty. "I have to admit, it's very good."

After a few minutes, Harry continued with his story, occasionally taking another piece of veal or forkful of the spinach that accompanied it. He seemed to avoid looking directly at Randy, who was gripping the edge of the table. "When the agents went looking for the old woman, they found the remains of her body in a crude structure in the woods. She had a Reising submachine gun lying next to her; also, a Garand rifle and a Colt pocket automatic were found in a hole in the dirt floor under a pile of baskets. There was no evidence of how she had died. Not much more than a skeleton left. They also found the bones of a very large man in front of the cabin, wearing the tattered remnants of overalls. There was no question how he died, though. Single shot to the temple. And...here's the shock. There were the remains of four other bodies on top of and around the big man's bones, all wearing what was left of their Nazi uniforms. They were riddled with bullet holes. We'll never know, but probably they shot her son and she retaliated by killing them with bursts from the submachine gun."

Randy shook his head. "Jesus, this is an incredible story."

Harry looked up at him and nodded, "Oh, yeah."

"But you think Ray was gone by the time the soldiers arrived, right?" Randy was trying to piece this all together, but it was so much to take in he was struggling with it.

"It would seem so. The report shows that he carved his serial number into one of the wooden supports of the shack. The old woman, her name was Olga, I think, was probably known to the partisans as a healer. They may have brought their injured to her for treatment. It could be that they showed up at her cabin and he left with them. Maybe they said they would lead him to an Allied base. And maybe they would have, but it was at the end of the war already, although Ray may have had no idea that it had come to such a quick end, and the communists ...these guys were almost certainly communists...were lining up their ducks to jockey for territory. We'll never know the whole story, of course, but most likely he tried to break away when he finally realized the war was over and they were deliberately holding him. The blow to the head could have been the result of a fall or he could have run head on into a tree limb. He was weak, maybe from hunger or dehydration, and he fell and hit his head in an especially vulnerable spot. "

"So there hasn't been any evidence that he was deliberately struck and left under that tree where they found him?" Randy was trying to think of questions Anna or Clara might want to ask.

"There's no way of knowing how he got the blow on the head that caused the coma, but there doesn't seem to be any evidence that anyone else was there where he was found."

Randy sighed. "What about the flight jacket he was wearing? You know he was wearing a fleece Air Force issue jacket when he was found?"

"Yeah, but that could have been something he found in the woods, discarded by some guy who parachuted into the area. Nobody has made much of that."

"Did anybody talk to the kids who found him?"

"Oh, sure. They were proud of themselves, but they couldn't add anything useful to what we already knew or had figured out."

Randy was gripping his fork like a weapon. "Godammit, this is so frustrating. There are so many unanswered questions here. But we owe you our thanks, Harry. We really appreciate your efforts to learn as much as possible. I guess some parts of this will forever be a mystery, but it helps to know every little bit. You can understand that my wife and Ray's fiancé were devastated at his passing. They had such hopes that he would come out of the coma."

The bill arrived and Harry plucked it out of the waiter's hand. "I was glad to be able to help. The Gov was interested, also. Some of these stories coming out of the war have shown us once again, if we needed showing, how valiant our men were. A bunch of ordinary American guys left their jobs and their families here and battled a formidable military machine and won. We need to keep remembering that."

Randy nodded solemnly and said, "Thanks for the lunch. I'll have to bring Anna here. I know she'll love it."

The two men parted outside the restaurant, Harry already thinking about his afternoon agenda and Randy deciding to walk a while and think of how to tell what he had heard to Anna and Clara.

* * * * *

In the days and weeks that followed, Randy found no opportunity he thought appropriate to tell Anna about his luncheon meeting with Harry Brownell. Finally able to convince her that she needed to see a doctor about her constant cough, neither of them was prepared for the diagnosis of lung cancer.

The prognosis was bleak. After her first experience with the side effects of chemotherapy, Anna declined to continue with that treatment. She decided to remain in her home and, as she said, "enjoy her last days with the people she loved." In three months, she was gone and Randy was devastated. He had no regrets for having withheld the information he got from Harry Brownell. There was nothing there that could ease the pain of the loss of her brother and she didn't need to hear the gruesome story about the old woman in the woods.

Clara came to visit with Anna several times during those last months, always bringing some little gift and her firmly positive personality. The two women chatted about inconsequential things, shared their distaste for shortened skirts, and enjoyed speculating on what to expect as a result of the emerging "women's movement".

At Anna's memorial service and subsequent reception for mourners, Clara was a huge help, organizing, comforting, and pitching in wherever she was needed.

Randy, although bereft, was, at the same time, relieved that Anna's last days of agony were over. His two sons, along with their families, hovered over him until he was seriously worried about losing his temper with them. He loved his daughters-in-law, but he didn't like to be treated like a needy emotional cripple and he definitely did not want to live with either of his sons.

He came into the kitchen where Clara was setting out little sandwiches on a tray. She looked up and was startled at his thunderous expression. "What's the matter, Randy? Is there anything I can do to help?"

"No, no. It's just that my son asked me for the fourth or fifth time if I was sure I don't want to come live with him and his family. Jesus, what makes anyone think I would want to live in a house with two kids under four? Visiting? Fine. But, live with them? Never."

Randy smacked his hand down on the counter.

Clara smiled. "I think they are probably feeling like they need to do something to help you endure your loss. We're all so helpless in the face of death. Even just making these sandwiches gives me the illusion I'm doing something when I know perfectly well that there is nothing I can do to change the awful fact of Anna's passing."

Randy sat down on a chair abruptly. "She was too young, you know. We were just beginning to enjoy my retirement. We spoke about going down to Washington in the spring...and now what do I do?"

Clara pulled another chair out from the table and sat. She reached over and put her hand on Randy's arm. "You go on, that's what you do. Even when you think you can't, you must and you will."

Randy raised his bent head and looked at Clara. "Of course. What an ass I am, to agonize about my loss, when you've been living with yours for how many years now?"

"Depends on when you start counting. But, yes, exactly right to remind yourself we all have losses to deal with. I know it's hard to believe it right now, but it does get more bearable with time."

"I have to tell you something, which I really should have told you before. It's just that I don't think it will help anyway. I never told Anna, but I met with a guy from the governor's office. You might remember him. Harry Brownell? He was with Ribicoff when Ribicoff was a congressman? He helped get you in to see Ray in that hospital in England."

Clara looked quizzically. "Yes, I remember him. What did you meet about?"

"Well, I had asked him about those intelligence guys that came to the VA hospital and whether he could find out what that was all about. I thought we might be able to get some more information about where Ray had been all that time after the war." Randy was a little apprehensive about how to tell this story to Clara.

"And did you learn anything other than speculation?" Clara fiddled with her watch and looked Randy in the eye.

"Actually, nothing that changes anything. He did tell me about our side knowing there were so-called "freedom fighters" in those mountains and that they were communists. He said they probably detained him to keep him from providing information about their activities after the war ended, since the commies were making a grab for territory. But, you're right. It's all speculation."

Clara got up and kissed Randy's cheek. "Thanks for trying, my dear friend. It's good to keep remembering Ray and mourning his loss. I do every day, as you will remember and mourn Anna. But we have to go on. And you will. Did I see the governor come in a while ago?"

"Yes, it was very gracious of him to show up. Several of the state senators did, too. I guess I'll keep up with my work for the party. Maybe even run for some local office. We'll see. And thanks, Clara, for being such a good friend to Anna and to me. You and Jack have to promise to stay in touch, OK?" Randy got up and walked back to the living room.

Chapter 18

<><><><><><><><><><><><><><><><><><><><><><><><><><><><><>

Northampton, 1957-58

Pete and Angela sat in Adirondack chairs on the new brick patio Pete had recently made in their back yard. It was the end of the day and they were enjoying a drink with a snack. Pete had cleaned up and changed his clothes since coming from the garage, but Angela was still dressed in her showing houses outfit, black skirt, blue blouse, plaid jacket and stockings with low-heeled pumps. She kicked off her shoes when she sat down.

"I got a note from the teacher. She wants us to come to a conference about Petey."

Pete sighed. "What's he done now?"

"The note doesn't say, but it was probably some prank. I think he's bored in that school, Pete. There's not enough to challenge him."

"I wonder how much it would cost to send him to Deerfield Academy? I know they have a great reputation. Or maybe Williston over in Easthampton?"

"*Dio mio*, are you serious? He's only twelve years old. That's too young to leave home." Angela was agitated, sitting up straight in her chair and glaring at Pete.

"Actually, he's not. There are boys younger than he is in those private schools. If he gets into Williston, he could be a day student or at least come home every weekend."

Angela responded hotly, "And who would drive him over there every morning and pick him up every afternoon? Would that be you? Or maybe you think I should give up my work to do that?"

"Stop getting riled up. I was just thinking about the options and now that you remind me of the difficulties, I don't think he could be a day student." Pete smiled and patted Angela's arm.

"You know he spends half his time on weekends hanging around LaFleur's airport, pestering those guys who keep their planes there." She took a sip of her drink. "He was always crazy about airplanes, but since you took him on that ride up over the Connecticut Valley, he's been more nuts about flying than ever."

"Yes, I know that. He told me some guy showed him how to change the oil in his Cessna and then he gave him a buck for helping. Petey was all excited about it."

"I wonder if they'd let him hang his model planes in his dorm room." Angela smiled.

Pete recognized an opportunity when he heard it. "Why don't I get some information about requirements and costs and whatever we need to know? We could look the stuff over and decide ourselves before we mention it to him. Is that OK with you?" Pete reached over and stroked Angela's cheek with the back of his hand. "I know you think of him as your baby, but he's growing up fast, *cherie,* and he's a smart kid. I want him to go to a good college and I don't think the public school is going to help him get there. He's not like the girls, who always knew they were going to go to Smith."

"OK. You get the information and I'll think about it. Fair enough?"

Petey came out of the house with two friends in tow. "Mom, there's nothing to eat in the fridge. We're starving."

Pete and Angela took Petey to visit the Williston campus in Easthampton. He declared it to be, "Neat-o." They got the application packet and filled out all the information, took Petey for a physical exam (Dr. Boucher pronounced him a healthy boy) and sent for his school records. His teacher was surprised to hear he was applying to Williston. "He was doing very well. His grades are excellent." Angela smiled and bit back her urge to remind the teacher how often she had complained about Petey's hijinks.

It was right before Amy's graduation from Smith that a letter arrived from Williston to welcome Petey for the fall semester of 1957. As soon as it was official, Angela started to have second thoughts. She was almost sure that Amy would want to go to New York and live with her sister. After all, that's where the theatres were and Amy was graduating as a theatre major. With Petey out of the house, too, she and Pete would suddenly be alone.

She was sitting at the kitchen table, papers spread out in front of her when Pete came in. "Pete, do you realize we are probably going to be here by ourselves all week starting in the fall?"

Pete, standing in front of the open refrigerator door, "Yeah, I guess so, except Petey will be home every weekend. What happened to the leftover apple pie?"

"Petey ate it about an hour ago. I know he'll be home on weekends, but during the week, we'll be alone."

"What are you saying?" Pete shut the fridge door and moved to a chair. "Do you want another baby? Because, if you do, we'd better go see Doc Boucher together and find out if that's such a good idea." He grinned. "If that's what you want, though, I'm all for it."

"No, that's not what I want and you know it. Quit teasing. I'm just saying it will be different. Oh, never mind. You just don't understand." Angela scowled.

Pete got up and stepped behind Angela, massaging her shoulders and then bending down to lift her hair and kiss her neck. "I think I do understand, *cherie,* but this is what's supposed to happen. Kids grow up and go off to have their own lives and you and I get to be there for each other. It's the big benefit of grower older."

"Except that maybe I'm not ready for that yet. Petey is still my baby." She sniffed.

"Hey, are you crying?" Pete lifted her out of her chair and put his arms around her. "It will be OK. You'll see.

He's really a pretty smart kid and almost as tall as you already. He needs to do this, Angela, and you need to be strong so he doesn't think he's doing anything that will hurt your feelings. He loves you very much and he needs to be sure you love him, too. Come on, *mon coeur,* don't cry. Sh, sh." He was stroking her back with one hand and holding her tight against his shoulder with the other.

"I'm sorry. I don't know what's gotten into me." Angela reached in her pocket for a hankie and wiped her eyes. She stepped back and glared up at Pete. "And you know damned well I'm too old to have another baby. What did you bring that up for?"

Pete laughed. "But it's so much fun to try." And Angela smacked him in the arm and grinned at him.

*　*　*　*　*

Graduating seniors at Smith got four tickets to the ceremonies and that was not enough for Amy. She needed a minimum of six. Her mom and dad, her brother Petey and sister Marie, her proud *Memere* and Aunt Clara would be really upset if they couldn't come to see her get her diploma. Well, actually, the diplomas still were handed out willy-nilly as they had been when Marie graduated. You had to go scrambling

311

around to find your own and give the one you got to the right person. Anyway, she had to find two more tickets somewhere.

She made a list of girls (women!) who came from foreign countries, Hawaii, Alaska and the west coast, figuring they were most likely to need only two. And then she hunted for those on the list who were in her classes and started asking. It took three days to get the additional two tickets. She was elated until her mom told her Marie was bringing a friend.

"Well, she certainly could have told me this before," she huffed.

"Amy, calm down, maybe she didn't know until now. And maybe he doesn't need to come to graduation, either. He can hang out here with Jack Grimes and Uncle Maurice getting the fire going in the barbeque pit."

"He? Did you say he? She's bringing a guy home? Is it her friend Tom? I like him. He won't care if he doesn't get to graduation."

"No, not Tom. His name is Chris Graham and he's an architect, like Tom, but that's all I know."

"Wow. What do you think it means? Has she finally gotten serious about someone? I like Tom, but that never seemed like a romance to me. He's always been a buddy or something. What do you think?" Amy pushed her long hair back behind her ears and glanced in the mirror. She picked up a silver barrette and set it in place.

"I'm not going to start guessing and neither should you. If she's got something to tell us, I'm sure she will. In the meanwhile, Miss Nosy Parker, keep your mouth shut. How would you like it if someone was sticking their nose in your business? Hmm?"

Amy laughed and slipped out of her cardigan. "Hah, I wouldn't like it at all and you know that's true."

Graduation was on Saturday, June 9 and the plans were for everybody, including the six ticket holders and the rest of the assembled family to come up to the campus to watch the alumnae parade in their colorful costumes, carrying banners with clever signs ("Class of '30 is still flirty") followed by next year's seniors in long gowns and then the graduating seniors in white dresses carrying long-stemmed American Beauty roses. It was a reunion year for Marie, but she was not joining the parade. She wasn't much of a parade person anyway and she wanted to watch Amy. Uncle Maurice and Aunt Simone, Clara's friend Jack Grimes and Marie's guest would go back to the house and start getting the feast ready while the family was listening to the graduation speaker, Ralph Bunche, Undersecretary of the United Nations, and watching Amy get her diploma.

When Marie walked in the door late on Friday night, Amy and her mother were sitting in the living room, both edgy with waiting. Amy jumped up and went to her sister. "Hi. Where's your friend?"

Marie set down her suitcase and walked over to the couch to give her mother a kiss. "He's staying at the Hotel Northampton tonight. He says he's always wanted to stay there and he figured there was enough going on here without having a stranger in the house."

Angela was annoyed. "I made Petey sleep downstairs in the rec room so we could give his room to your friend. You should have told me."

"Well, I didn't know he planned to do that until we were already on the way up here or I would have called you. Think about it, though. He's right. You've got your hands full this weekend." Marie was kicking off her shoes and peeling down her stockings. "We left right from work." She sighed. "Chris is a very sensitive guy. You'll like him."

Amy sat down on the couch next to Marie. "Tell us about him. Mom said he's an architect, but that's all we know."

"He went to Phillips Exeter and then Dartmouth. His father teaches history at Dartmouth. And then he went to Italy to study architecture before he started Columbia. I met him at a party I went to with Tom. He's working at the same firm. We like the same movies and music and especially avant-garde theatre."

"Well, when do we meet him, then?"

"I told him to come here at eight. He likes bacon and scrambled eggs for breakfast."

Angela raised her eyebrows. "Oh, yes? And you know just what he likes for breakfast?"

Marie's chin came up and she said, "Yes, I do."

Amy grabbed Marie by the hand and said, "Let's get to bed. It's late and we'll have to be up early in the morning. I need you to roll up my hair."

Angela watched her two daughters dash up the stairs and sighed. They were so grown up now, not her babies anymore. She was glad they had each other. Recalling her own childhood, the only girl with three brothers, she was a bit jealous of that closeness.

* * * * *

Chris Graham appeared at eight the next morning, Amy answered the doorbell. "Hi, you must be Chris." The guy at the door was wearing cream flannel trousers and a pale blue shirt with a white collar. His tie was striped, his cuff links gold and his blazer navy blue. He stood six feet tall, with an athletic body, short sandy hair and a wide smile.

He had a big grin and he was carrying a box of flowers, which he presented to Amy with a little bow. "For the graduation girl. That must be you, right?"

Amy was overwhelmed. She could hardly breathe. "Thanks. Wow. How did you get flowers so early in the morning?"

"When I made the reservation, I asked for the concierge and told him what I needed. Look at them. I think he got exactly the right thing."

Marie came into the living room and gave Chris a little hug. "I see you have met my sister, Amy, the graduating Smithie."

Amy opened the box. Wrapped in purple tissue was a bouquet of red and pink and white sweetheart roses. A card read: 'Congratulations. Now go break a leg.' Amy showed it to Marie and they both burst into laughter. Angela came into the room and looked at the card and frowned. "Is this some code I don't understand?"

Chris put out his hand and said, "Hi, Mrs. LaPointe. I'm Chris Graham. It's an expression among theatre people who are very superstitious, so instead of wishing one another success, they say just the opposite."

"Oh, well then...Welcome. Come in the dining room and get some breakfast. We've got scrambled eggs and bacon, toast, rolls, orange juice, grapefruit and coffee."

The door from the basement banged open and Petey appeared, his hair wet and his feet bare. "Hi, Marie. I didn't hear you come in last night. Guess what? I got into Williston."

"Petey, look at you. Is Mom putting fertilizer in the food? You're as tall as I am already."

Angela looked at him and said, "What's with the bare feet? You should be dressed and ready to go as soon as you have some breakfast."

"I guess I forgot to bring some socks downstairs last night. I'll go get some as soon as the guy..." His voice trailed off as he noticed Chris. "Are you Marie's friend who's sleeping in my room?"

"I'm Marie's friend Chris who is not sleeping in your room." And Chris put out his hand to Petey. "You must be the famous Petey, who's going to be an Air Force ace."

Petey grinned and shook Chris's hand. "Yup, that's me."

Angela tapped Petey on the shoulder. "Go get your socks and get back down here to have some breakfast. Your father went to get gas in the car and when he comes back, he's going to want to leave for the campus right away."

Maurice and Simone came in the front door, followed in the next minute by Tillie, Clara and Jack Grimes. Maurice asked, "Any chance of getting a cup of coffee before we have to go?"

Marie introduced Chris as her very good friend, an architect in a New York firm. Chris shook hands with Jack and Maurice. He made a bow of his head to Clara and Simone. "I'm happy to meet you. Marie has spoken of you often and it's nice to be able to put a face with a name." He put his arm around Tillie and said, "It's great to finally meet Marie's beloved *Memere*. I feel like I know you already."

It was decided they could all crowd into two cars and by 8:45 they were driving up Main Street toward the college. Pete had suggested they park on West Street and walk into the campus through the Green Street gate. Flowers were blooming everywhere and their perfume scented the air. They found a place to stand as Amy headed off to get her rose and get in line. President Benjamin Wright and his wife, as well as the Dean of the college and the Class Dean took their places on the steps of Neilson Library to review the parade.

All along the parade route, families gathered for the ritual that marked the end of one phase and the beginning of another. Many of the graduating seniors were getting married within the next few weeks. Proud fathers and proud fiancés clicked their cameras to record these moments. Pretty flowered summery dresses moved in the light breeze. White shoes and Panama hats were abundant. Here and there grandmothers raised lace-edged handkerchiefs to dry their eyes. For almost two hours they watched the pageant that embodied hallowed traditions, dear to the hearts of Smithies. When it was over, Chris joined the others to go back to the house and prepare for the party to come later and the six ticket holders went off to find Amy.

As they walked across the campus, Pete spoke quietly to Marie. "So, tell me about this guy, *chouchou*. Is he respectable? What does he do? Are you serious about him?"

"I think so, but he hasn't asked me to marry him....yet. He's an architect. A friend of Tom's. His father teaches at Dartmouth. He likes the same things I like. I'm going with him up to Hanover tomorrow to meet his parents."

"Sounds serious to me." Pete gave Marie a quick hug. "Does he make you happy?"

"Yeah. Yeah, he does. He's a really nice guy, Dad. He's the first guy I met in New York who seems to be more interested in what I like and what I think than the rest of them. That's important, right?"

"I don't hear you saying you're crazy in love with him, though." Pete's statement was half a question.

Marie looked at her father quizzically. "Well, sure, I love him. What's not to love? But you know me. Not likely I get crazy, right?" She grinned.

Pete sighed. "Maybe you need to get crazy now and then instead of working so hard."

Marie laughed. "Hah, look who's talking. I'm your daughter and didn't I learn from you about the rewards of working hard?"

* * * * *

Marie and Chris were married a year later in the Church of the Sacred Heart in Northampton. It was a small wedding with about forty guests, family and close friends. They planned to celebrate with their New York friends at a little party later, after they returned from their honeymoon in Paris.

Marie wore a tea-length white gown of silk peau de soie, embroidered with seed pearls on the bateau neckline and around the seam at the dropped waist. She had found it on sale at Bergdorf's. The veil was attached to a tiny crown, also embroidered with seed pearls and cost almost as much as the gown. The white silk high heels came from Klein's and Aunt Clara gave her a pair of long white kid gloves.

Amy served as her sister's maid-of-honor and Betsy as the only bridesmaid. They wore tea length cocktail dresses in a deep rose color, exactly the same as the color of the peonies in Marie's wedding bouquet. Tom was best man and Sam was groomsman. Marie was chagrined when Cary had called to say he couldn't make it to the wedding and then surprised and pleased when he showed up.

It was a lovely day in May and even though Marie was nervous, the only people to notice were her sister and her friend Betsy. She had always been good at controlling her emotions. Please, God, nothing should go wrong today. Angela had insisted that the reception be held at the Hotel Northampton, a suggestion she got from Clara, because they had a staff well trained in handling wedding events and family could all relax and let them do it. Pete had been all for holding a barbeque in the backyard, but Angela was appalled at that idea since she could just see herself in her wedding finery carrying out platters of food from the kitchen. Oh, no. She was having none of that.

When Pete held out his arm to his daughter as they stood in the back of the church waiting for the music to begin, he looked at her with tears in his eyes. "I don't care what they say, I'm not giving you away. I'm only lending you. And, if you ever need me, I'm always going to be here for you."

Marie turned and gave her father a quick hug. "Oh, Daddy, I know that."

Standing at the altar with Tom and Sam beside him, Chris looked up to watch Marie coming down the aisle on her father's arm. His athlete's body looked really good in a well-fitted tuxedo, his hair gleamed with the bit of some product he must have put on to tame it and when his eyes met Marie's, his smile conveyed his joy. Marie smiled back and thought him to be the most splendid man she'd ever met.

When Pete sat down next to Angela after he had done his part, she leaned over to whisper in his ear. "Where do the years go? I still think of her as a baby."

Pete took Angela's hand and gave it a gentle squeeze. "Yeah, I know."

Jack Grimes sat next to Clara in one of the front pews. When the organ began the recessional and the newly married couple turned to face the assembled family and friends, Jack whispered to Clara, "Any chance I could get you to change your mind?"

She looked at him ruefully and shook her head, then turned away to watch her radiant grand-niece walk up the aisle.

Tillie, sitting next to Maurice, whispered, "I wish Edward were here to see his *chouchou* all grown up, getting married to such a nice boy."

When the wedding guests arrived at Hotel Northampton, there was much milling about and chatting in the spacious lobby as they waited for the bridal party to make up a receiving line at the entrance to the ballroom. Everybody wanted to kiss the bride and shake the hand of the groom, meet the parents and head for the bar. A three piece orchestra, all members in white dinner jackets, was playing Broadway tunes softly.

Chris's older brother and sister came with their spouses and his two elderly aunts, both widowed, sat with his parents, these eight people his only family at the wedding. They were all congenial and seemed to be comfortable with the other guests. Tom, as best man, made it his business to circulate and be sure all the guests were enjoying the occasion. Cary got into excited conversation with Amy as he told her about his adventures in Hollywood and listened to her describe her experiences trying to break into the theatre world in New York.

She'd been living with Marie for the past year, but now that Marie and Chris were moving into a bigger apartment uptown, she didn't see how she could keep Marie's place on her meager earnings from waiting on tables at Jim Atkin's hash house in Sheridan Square unless she could find two roommates. Amy had met a lot of theatre people, mostly through her Smith contacts, but so far, had not made any close friends. She'd had a one line part in a small production of Tennessee Williams' play "Summer and Smoke" and got a mention by one critic as a 'luminous new presence.' She'd had a brief role in the soap opera, "All My Children" and she had done a toothpaste commercial. Cary assured her that was great for a first year, but he urged her to go west, where there were many more opportunities and a more relaxed atmosphere. "Better weather, too." He winked and smiled.

Clara, watching Marie with her new husband, noticed how often he touched her, his eyes conveying his love. Marie seemed to be less smitten, more concerned about guests enjoying themselves, watchful of the hotel staff, in control of herself and the event. Clara wondered how the goal-driven Marie would react to the changes in her life that marriage would require.

The bridal couple left Northampton right after the reception to drive to Idlewild airport on Long Island. They had reservations at a hotel close to the airport for that night and their plane to Paris didn't leave until the afternoon of the next day. Pete slipped an envelope into Marie's jacket pocket while he was hugging her and whispered, "Just a little mad money, sweetheart, so you can buy something special from your old dad."

Angela reminded them to take a lot of pictures. Petey told Chris how much he wished he could go up in a big plane that flew over the ocean. Amy kissed her sister and told her to have a great time. With all the hugging and kissing, Marie's little scrap of a hat was askew. Chris reached over and straightened it, touching the back of his hand on her cheek as he did so. Finally they were able to break away from happy family and get into Chris's Buick, start the engine and head out of Northampton.

Chris reached out to Marie and pulled her close to his side. "Well, now, Mrs. Graham, are you happy?"

Marie smiled up at him and answered, "Yup. How about you?"

"I feel like I just won the biggest victory in the world, getting you to marry me. When you came down the aisle in the church, I thought about how lucky I am." He lifted her hand to his mouth and started kissing each finger.

Marie frowned and pulled her hand away. "Chris, stop it. We'll have an accident if you don't pay attention to your driving." Then, aware of his startled reaction to her sharp words, she stroked his arm and said, "Plenty of time for that later."

* * * * *

Chapter 19

<><><><><><><><><><><><><><><><><><><><><><><><><><>

New York and Northampton, 1958-60

Chris and Marie moved into a one-bedroom apartment on West 96th Street and furnished it slowly in the contemporary style they both loved. A black leather hide-a-bed came with Chris from his old place and they bought two Eames chairs from a couple they knew who were moving to Chicago. They decided to buy a really good mattress and box springs and put them on a frame, but wait to get a headboard, and they found a beautiful triple dresser in walnut. Marie hauled the bookcases from her old apartment and a leather sling chair she put in their bedroom. It was fun to fill up the two rooms, making choices together, laughing at some of the stuff they saw in store windows, talking about the future.

"I like this place. It's cozy. A little tight for space, but that's OK for now." Chris sat on the sofa with a glass of wine. He was entirely relaxed at the end of the day. "It won't do for long, though. Where would we put a crib? There's hardly room for the dresser and your chair in the bedroom now."

Marie was sitting at the small round pedestal table that served for eating as well as a desk when the need arose. Right now it was covered with papers she was working on. She looked up. "Right. But when the time comes, we'll have nine months to look for a better place."

"Maybe in the country. What do you think? A pretty place in Westchester County, not too far?" Chris walked over to Marie and stood behind her with his hands on her shoulders. "Would you like that? I wouldn't mind commuting into the city every day and I think it's better for raising our kids."

Marie put her hand over his and twisted around to smile at him. "And how many do you have in mind, sir?"

Chris bent over and kissed her. "Three is a good number. But we'd better go right now and get the first one started." He pulled her up out of the chair and led her into the bedroom.

* * * * *

Amy was frustrated at how many call backs she went to only to be told she wasn't quite right for the part. Too young, too pretty, too fragile-looking, or some other nonsense. She knew a lot of people in the theatre through her Smith connections and Cary had been great about introducing her to more. But his focus was always on musicals and Amy wasn't a singer. Sam had more interest in drama and, although he helped her meet new people, their relationship wasn't as close. Cary had taken her on as a personal challenge.

In the fall of '59, Cary's agent called with great news. He had negotiated a part for him in a Hollywood production of the musical "The King and I." Cary would need to move west right away. It was an exciting opportunity.

"Come west with me, Amy. We can get an apartment together and you won't have to work because I'll be making good money. You can spend all your time finding just the right vehicle for your talent. I'll bet my agent will take you on. Say yes, darling girl. We'll have a great time."

"Cary, you are nuts. What would people say if we were living together? Anyway, maybe I just don't have what it takes. It's been an awful year. One walk-on in a play that lasted three weeks. One shampoo commercial and getting evaporated in the first two minutes on *The Twilight Zone*. What makes you think I'd do any better in Hollywood?"

"It's just a whole different scene. Acting is the only game in town. Not like here, where business is king. There the cin-e-ma (he pronounced the word in an exaggerated tone) is the business and that's it. Please, please come with me."

"I think I need to talk to my mom and dad and listen to what they have to say."

Amy was a little surprised when her mother and father supported the idea. Of course, they were apprehensive about having her so far away, but both of them had come to appreciate Cary's friendship with Amy. It had been long since they realized that Sam and Cary were homosexuals, but neither of them thought less of the pair. In fact, they were grateful for the help and support Sam had given Marie when she arrived in New York. And Cary had clearly become Amy's best friend. Maybe Hollywood was an inevitable move for Amy at some point in her career aspirations anyway. Better to do it with Cary's support.

Marie and Chris were less enthusiastic. They argued that she'd be too far away from family. Chris said, "Everybody says that Hollywood is full of degenerates, drunks, and shysters and that it's a cut-throat business. What's so great about that?" And Marie said, "You haven't given the New York theatre as much time as you should. It's only been two years, Amy. Give it at least another two before you make a move west."

Amy saw this as a big chance that might not come her way again. Having Cary there was like having a safety net. Anyway, if it didn't work out after a couple of years she could always come back. She'd been plagued with a succession of flighty roommates ever since she took over Marie's old apartment on Bleeker Street, so she felt no qualms about leaving there. Her dad drove down in a borrowed truck and took all the stuff she needed to store back to Northampton. It didn't make sense to pay for it to be moved out west yet. Maybe later when she got established.

Marie and Chris, her mom and dad and Sam came to the train station to see Cary and Amy off on the Twentieth Century Limited. Amy was as giddy as she had ever been in her life at the prospect of riding the train across the country. It was 1959, she was 22 years old, and she was having a great adventure.

* * * * *

As soon as the two of them moved into a charming two-bedroom furnished apartment in Pomona, Cary declared they needed to give a party. He had made friends and some good contacts when he'd been in the Hollywood area before. The party would be to announce he was back and to introduce Amy. He made up a list of forty people, which amazed Amy. "How did you get to know so many?" Amy asked.

"Some of them are gypsies like me, who decided to stay here, but also a lot are production folks. Most people don't realize that the movies have more technical support staff than actors, by far. They're the backbone of the industry. In some ways they're more important than the talent and they can make you or break you." Cary put his arm around Amy and hugged her. "You'll like most of them, darling girl, and they'll love you."

"Cary, I don't know what to serve or how to set up a party like this. I'm pretty sure a jug of wine and some cheese and crackers won't do it." Amy looked worried, her nose wrinkling.

"Don't even think about that. My agent gave me an advance to put on this show. I already called a caterer and a bartender. They'll take care of it." Cary seemed happy, positive, and full of energy.

On the night of the party, Amy was struggling to conceal her nervousness. She wasn't at all sure what to expect. Although in Hollywood for only a month, she already knew the atmosphere was far different from the theatre world of New York. She wanted to wear something spectacular to give her courage and confidence, so she'd taken Cary with her to shop for just the right outfit.

They found it at a little boutique in Pasadena. It was a flower printed silk jumpsuit, the pants and the sleeves flowing, tied with a sash. It would be a pain in the neck to get out of in the powder room, but she decided it was worth it. She wore spike-heeled pink mules and a pair of jade earrings that dropped nearly to her shoulder. The earrings had been a gift from her *Memere* on her graduation and it felt good to be wearing this reminder of family.

Astonishing that so many people arrived at once and in such good spirits, eager to welcome Cary back and to meet his friend. She got kisses galore and compliments on her appearance so lavish they made her laugh. Remembering all the names became impossible.

"You look like you're feet are getting tired. Can you leave the door now? Come sit with me on the balcony. Can I get you some champagne?" The guy who came up to her was slender, with sand colored hair and thick horn-rimmed glasses. He was wearing a white turtle neck under a dark gray blazer. "I'm David Epstein. Not an actor. Maybe some day I'll get to direct my own movie. Right now I'm assistant to a director."

"Thanks, I'd love some champagne and you're right. My feet are about to give up, so let's sit down, but not on the balcony. I don't want to get too far because Cary is determined to introduce me to everyone." Amy glanced over at Cary, who was in earnest conversation with a skinny guy whose head was bald and who was wearing jeans and a sweatshirt. When Cary looked up, she raised her eyebrows in question and tipped her head toward David. Cary nodded.

"That's Robbie Comack Cary is talking to. He's a choreographer and brilliant, but a little eccentric. Every dancer reveres him, though, so he gets away with it." David noticed someone vacate a chair and grabbed Amy's hand. "Sit here. I'll go get champagne."

In a very short time, David and Amy shared their experiences and their aspirations. David was born in California, in Santa Ana. His family owned a chain of furniture stores. He had two brothers and one sister. He went to film school at UCLA and dreamed of becoming a director of film spectacles, like the great Busby Berkley, who was his idol. He said he was 26 and Jewish. Amy told him about her family as well and then wondered how they had become so open with each other so fast. She gave a mental shrug and decided this was probably the way people did things in Hollywood, putting themselves right out there.

Later, Amy and Cary sat on the sofa surrounded by party debris and hashed over the events of the evening. Cary was especially excited that Robbie Comack had showed up. "Yikes, Amy, I never dreamed he'd actually come. He's really weird, you know. Brilliant, but weird. He invited me to visit him in his dance studio next week. Wait 'til I tell my agent. This could lead to something great for me."

Amy told him about meeting David Epstein. "He was so friendly. We got to talking and it felt like we'd known one another for ages. I don't know why, but I wasn't even a little bit nervous around him. He seems more... more normal than a lot of these folks."

Cary took her hand. "Be careful, though, darling girl. A lot of these guys are sharks. I haven't heard much of anything about David, except that he has some very good connections and a lot of potential. I just haven't any information about him personally, so go slow. OK?"

* * * * *

The next day David called and asked Amy out for dinner. She hesitated and he said, "Just dinner, Amy. I'm sure you've heard some wild stories about this town and probably Cary has already warned you to be careful. I promise you I'm harmless. Let's just have dinner and get to know one another."

That dinner led to another and then to a picnic and to a premiere and soon Amy was seeing David at least twice a week. She met with Cary's agent, a man so full of energy, he seemed to be in motion even when he was standing still. He agreed to take her on and she went to the auditions and general casting calls he arranged, always hoping for a break. When the break came, she was totally surprised to be cast as a down-at-the-heels streetwalker in a film noir, since all her previous work had cast her as a girl-next-door type. The director told her to project her delicacy and fragility. The make-up and tacky tight-skirted costume, white boots and plastic purse she saw in the mirror made her laugh at her image. The director told her she was great. He was smiling when he patted her butt. "Now go do it again, but this time, see if you can show me tears as you turn away."

Amy was learning that the film business was very different from live theatre. No worrying about missing a cue or flubbing lines, just do it over. And sometimes over and over and over. It was boring. It was exhausting.

It was exhilarating to see the end product. Even though her part was very small, Amy began to believe she could make it in Hollywood. It would just take time.

* * * * *

In September of 1960, Clara woke up and began getting ready to go to work. She realized something was missing. There were no sounds coming from the kitchen, no smell of brewing coffee. She called down the back stairs. No response. Still in her nightgown and wrapper, she descended into the kitchen. Empty. A shiver went all through her and a strange feeling of apprehension spread. She rushed back up the staircase to Tillie's room and without knocking, entered. Tillie Billieux LaPointe, 76 years old and the dearest person in the world to her family, was lying in her bed, hair in curling papers, hands folded, dead.

When Clara touched her sister's cold hands, she knew immediately that Tillie had died several hours ago and peacefully. Dropping to her knees at the side of the bed, Clara prayed for her wonderful, loving sister and wept for her own loss. She whispered, "God will surely reward you, *ma soeur*, for you have always been the best of us. And I hope Edward will be waiting for you with open arms."

First she called Father Dumont and Dr. Boucher. Then she dressed quickly and made coffee. She made a list of all those who needed to be called. Pete and Angela first. Angela could be counted on to help her with phone calls and arrangements. Jack could provide support and could be called on to run errands. *Mon Dieu,* she thought, I almost forgot I should call the funeral home right away. And Maurice. I'd better call him myself. She began dialing. When it got to be nine o'clock, she called Harry Daniels to let the store know of her family tragedy and that she would be out for a few days.

Clara sat down at the kitchen table, tears falling. Charlie, Charlie, where are you? You should be here. Why did you go away?

The doorbell rang. It was Dr. Boucher and right behind him came Pete. The doctor went up the stairs to examine Tillie and Pete gathered his aunt in his arms. While she wept onto his shoulder she could feel his tears dropping on her skin. "She was a beautiful person, *une ange,* and I think, *cherie,* she would not want you to grieve so. She would say it was time to go and be with Pa." Pete soothed Clara. "I had a feeling she was failing, you know? Remember how tired she's been looking? And falling asleep in the chair even when there were people talking to her."

Dr. Boucher came down the stairs. "It was her heart. It just gave out and that's what I'm writing on the death certificate. I don't think you want an autopsy, *non?* We'll put it down here and there'll be no question." He handed Clara the signed legal document and patted her on the shoulder. "She was a good woman. Everybody who knew her said that."

The priest arrived, apologizing for the delay and explaining that he had to attend two other deaths this morning. Clara and Pete accompanied him up to Tillie's room. Since Tillie was clearly already dead, it was too late for an anointing and the classic ritual of the Sacrament. Instead, the priest led Clara and Pete in prayer, asking for God's forgiveness of sin. When the doorbell rang, Clara hurried to answer it. Jack had arrived, ready to do whatever she asked of him.

Next the funeral director appeared to take charge of Tillie's body and to help Clara and Pete with making arrangements. So many decisions to be made. Which dress? Jewelry or not? Hours for viewing? Pick out a casket. Prayer cards? Guest book?

The church office called. What music should there be? Flowers for the altar? Did they want the choir or just the organ? Had they chosen pallbearers? Clara made a mental note to make all those decisions herself before her death so her loved ones would be free of this dreadful burden. Pete asked his aunt whether she knew if his mother had a will. No, she had never mentioned it. Pete said he'd call the attorney.

Jack went out and came back with a bag full of sandwiches. Angela showed up with a pot of soup. The four of them sat around the kitchen table to eat a very late lunch, each of them aware that it had always been Tillie who ruled this room, who made the food and served it, who urged everyone, "*Mangez, mangez*".

"Amy will be flying into Hartford tomorrow afternoon. Chris and Marie said they can pick her up. It's on their way. Maurice and Simone will get here by lunchtime. I told them to come directly to our house and I will feed them. Petey is very upset, so I'm going to pick him up this afternoon. I got Phillipe on the phone. He'll be at the wake. Maurice's kids will come for the funeral, but not the wake. I think that's all." Angela reported the results of her phone calls.

"Did you call that woman from the Girl Scouts? I forget her name." Clara asked.

"Oh, yeah, I forgot. I did that and also I called Mrs. Lemans, who's president of the Ladies Sodality this year."

Pete said, "I'll go tell all the folks who live in the alley right after we finish eating. It's easier to walk around than call all of them. I'm sure they'll want to know. Some of them played canasta with Ma."

When Pete and Angela left, Jack asked, "Clara, my dear, why don't you throw some clothes in a bag and come home with me. Surely you don't want to stay here alone tonight."

"No, I don't think that's a good idea. There'll be phone calls and I need to be here to answer them. But thanks for the offer. Anyway, I need to think." She smiled at Jack.

"Well, then, I'm going to the store and do a little work, but I'll pick up some Chinese for dinner and I'll be back later. OK?"

Clara stood up when Jack did and put her arms around him. She lifted her face for his kiss and said, "You're a dear man, Jack Grimes, and I don't know why you put up with me."

"Must be because I love you."

* * * * *

Marie and Chris stood together looking out the window of the airport, waiting for the plane to unload. They had driven up from New York and still had another hour or so to get to Northampton. They were both tired. Chris was lightly massaging Marie's shoulders. "Did she say if Cary was coming, too?"

"No, she told him not to even though he was willing. He's in rehearsal for some dance routine he's going to do in a movie and anyway, he hardly knew *Memere*. I told Sam she died, but I told him not to come. How about Tom?"

"Yeah, I told him and he offered to come up to support you, but I told him, too, not to come."

Amy emerged from the plane, her eyes looking tired. She looked around, saw her sister. And rushed to her. They hugged each other tightly. "I keep hoping it's not true. She can't be gone. She's always been there for us. How can she be gone?" Both women were weeping. Chris took each of them by an arm and led them to a bank of chairs.

"Wait right here. I'll go get some coffee for us." Chris set out looking for the coffee shop he had noticed as they came into the airport.

Marie rubbed her sister's back. "You must be tired, Amy. You can nap as soon as we get to the house. Mom says Petey is taking it hard. He's been so close to *Memere* since she minded him when Mom started her real estate business. I think now he's feeling bad because he hasn't seen as much of her since he went to Williston."

Amy sighed deeply and leaned her head on Marie's shoulder. "Yeah, well I feel bad, too. I was always going to stay in touch, you know, when I went west. I promised to write and I hardly ever did..." She started sobbing again.

Chris arrived with the coffee and sat down on the other side of Amy. "Come on. Have some coffee and then we'll get your bag. You probably ought to take a nap, Amy, before the wake. And Marie, your Aunt Clara will probably need you to do something."

They drank their coffee in silence, each of them dealing with individual thoughts, then Marie pulled herself together and stood up. "Amy, did you bring something warm to wear? I'll bet you've forgotten how chilly it can get here after the sun goes down. It'll probably be too cold for California clothes for the wake tonight."

"Oh, yeah, I remembered that. I brought a navy blue suit and a white silk blouse. Will that do?"

"Sure." Marie smiled. "Sometimes I forget you're a grown-up and not my baby sister anymore."

When they arrived at their parents' house, Angela was putting a tray full of little puffs in the oven. There were hugs and kisses all around. Petey came up from the basement rec room. Amy hadn't seen him since a year ago and she was shocked at how much he had changed. At fifteen, he towered over her. His gangly look was gone. His chest and arms were clearly expanding. "Petey," she exclaimed. "You're looking so grown-up."

He hugged her. "Yeah, and you're looking like a movie star."

Everybody laughed. Then they sobered, remembering what brought them together. Marie asked, "What can I do to help?" And Amy said, "I think I'd better lie down for an hour or so if I'm going to hold up for the wake tonight. I'm still on California time."

Pete and Angela arrived at Czelusniak's Funeral Parlor with Petey just before Chris and Marie came in with Amy. Clara and Maurice were there already to greet mourners at the door, although it was early and no one had arrived yet. The atmosphere was hushed. All of them signed the guest book and took a prayer card from the podium to the right of the door to the room where Tillie's casket was open for viewing. Banks of flowers surrounded it. Simone was in there, kneeling on the bench provided for that purpose.

Pete took Angela's hand and led her to the bench as soon as Simone rose. They both crossed themselves and kneeled. Pete put his hand over his eyes for a moment and Angela reached over to rub his neck. They rose and Pete leaned over the casket to kiss his mother. Angela touched Tillie's face and adjusted the small bouquet of roses, entwined with onyx rosary beads that had become askew in Tillie's hands. They rose and Pete headed to the back room where he was in charge of dispensing drinks to those who came there looking for one.

Chris and Marie were next to approach the casket, performing the ritual of prayer in tandem. Marie gazed at her much beloved *Memere* remembering all the years of love and attention that dear woman had lavished on her. The body in the casket looked so cold and still and unlike *Memere* that Marie felt a shiver of revulsion and vowed that no one would get to look at her body when she was dead.

Amy and Petey went to the casket together. After saying a prayer, Amy stood up and leaned over to kiss *Memere*. Petey followed, tears streaming down his cheeks. Dammit, he thought, I promised myself not to cry. Too bad, I can't help it. If somebody sees and thinks I'm a baby, they can go to hell.

Some of the cousins were arriving. Now there was a steady stream of people coming in the door. A florist arrived with more funeral tributes. The air started to smell too cloying. Petey and Amy went out to the porch.

Angela suggested Marie offer to take a turn at the door to relieve her Aunt Clara. Marie nodded and left to do that, annoyed with herself that she had not thought of it without prodding. Clara was grateful for the respite. She was going through the motions of ritual automatically, made again acutely conscious of the fragility of life.

Father Dumont came in to lead the mourners in prayer. Nearly everyone present dropped to their knees, some more carefully than others, some clearly finding it painful to do so. When he finished he went around the room, taking hands into his, murmuring soothing words. He spoke briefly to Clara and went to the back room where he expressed his condolences to Pete and accepted a glass of single malt scotch. (Pete knew Father's taste and made sure to have his brand available.)

Jack Grimes hovered near Clara all through the viewing hours, careful to be unobtrusive. He knew she did not want to cause talk about their relationship, but he felt that was probably inevitable in the long run and anyway, he wanted to be close in case she needed him. Some people greeted him, but most didn't have any idea who he was and in the atmosphere of the wake, accepted him without question.

When it was over, Marie and Chris went off to have dinner at Wiggins, a favorite of theirs. Pete took Angela, Amy and Petey out to the Whately Inn, far enough out of town that they were unlikely to meet anyone coming from the wake. Maurice and Simone were staying the night at 144 West Street and they joined Clara and Jack at Rahar's.

At dinner, Amy mentioned that she was surprised Marie wasn't pregnant yet. "She always said she wanted a family and they've been married two years already. What are they waiting for?"

Angela frowned at her. "It's really none of your business, Amy. You don't like it when anybody asks questions about you, do you?"

Pete said in a stern voice, "Now listen to me, young lady, do not ask her about that. You understand me?" Amy nodded, her eyes wide. Pete continued, his gaze fierce.

"Good. Don't let me find out you're poking your nose where it doesn't belong."

Amy was shocked at the reaction to her comment and guessed it was a very sensitive subject. Maybe Marie would say something about it to her while they were here, but she sure wouldn't bring it up herself after Dad got so huffy about it.

The next day was as splendid an example of perfect New England autumn as anyone could wish for. Tillie would be buried next to her husband Edward under a bright blue sky. The funeral service at the Sacred Heart Church was marked by the sweetness of the voices of the Children's Choir. Father Dumont's remarks reflected the thinking of all those who knew Tillie's good heart, her steadfastness in the care of her mother and her commitment to family and community.

At the grave site, all the members of the family clung to one another, comforted by each others' touch. Clara had asked that a minimum of floral arrangements be brought to the grave, the rest to go to the nursing home on Bridge Road. The priest sprinkled holy water and intoned the ritual prayers and too soon, it was over. The mourners returned to their cars, none wanting to wait for the casket to be lowered into the ground and covered over with dirt.

Clara invited the members of the family to return to 144 West Street for coffee and a snack. Most of the cousins declined, but there was a fair-sized crowd that filled the house. Chris assisted Pete in dispensing drinks; Amy and Marie served coffee; Angela and Simone set out a variety of snacks on the dining room table. Maurice, now 79 and having a little trouble walking, lowered himself into the big Morris chair in the front parlor and let others come to him. He announced to no one in particular, "We're all getting old, even Clara."

Clara came over and handed him a plate of little treats. She kissed the top of his head. "Not me, Maurice. Speak for yourself. I'm only 63."

"What are you going to do now, *ma belle soeur*? Will you live here by yourself with the three boarders upstairs?"

"I thought about that last night when I couldn't get to sleep and I've decided to leave here and take an apartment near downtown, maybe Bedford Terrace if one is available. I don't want to be here without Tillie. I'm not interested in cleaning up after boarders. Flora can do what she wants with this house. Burn it to the ground for all I care."

Hearing that, Marie and Amy looked at each other, startled at this declaration and dismayed by it.

Pete overheard her and stepped close. "Good. I'm glad to hear it. When you're ready to move, let me know. I'll get a truck and some guys to help and we'll move you."

Chapter 20

◇◇◇◇◇◇◇◇◇◇◇◇◇◇◇◇◇◇◇◇◇◇◇◇◇◇◇◇◇◇◇◇◇◇◇◇◇◇◇

Montreal, 1980

Uncle Charlie turned his head to look out the window, momentarily lost in thought. When he turned back to Marie, his eyes were bright with tears, but he was smiling faintly. "I remember when Tillie and I were very young. She was three years older than me, you know. She was always watching out for me. I remember when she was maybe nine or ten years old and I was so eager to go and do all the things the older boys were doing. She hovered over me, worried that I would get hurt. And she was there to kiss the hurts and wipe the tears.

"Then, when Clara was born....oh, *mon Dieu,* she was the little mother. *Maman* was so busy with the cooking and the cleaning and the caring for the rest of us, she was glad to have Tillie take over watching out for Clara."

Uncle Charlie grasped Marie's hands in his. She could see the emotions he tried to suppress play across his weathered face. He sighed deeply.

"We were all so worried about her when she was *enceinte* with your father. She had a very hard time. And when the doctor told her there could be no more babies, how she wept and how we wept for her. She named him Pierro, you know? He hated that name. She was never happy about calling him Pete. Ah, *Chouchou,* your *Memere* should have had a big family, she was such a wonderful mother.

"I was there when Papa was dying and he made her promise in front of all of us that she would take care of *Maman*, no matter what happened. I think she and Edward would have gone back to Canada if she hadn't made that promise. I often think they would have been happy to do that. But she promised. Do you remember how she took care of your *Gran'mere*? You were old enough to remember that, I think."

Marie nodded her head. "Oh, yes, I do remember that time." A little jolt of pain ran through her as she also recalled the horrible accident at her *Gran'mere's* gravesite, when Uncle Oscar and Uncle Charlie got in a fight and Uncle Oscar died. She hadn't actually seen the blow that did it, but she was acutely aware of how that event changed everything.

Sister Boniface came into the solarium and stopped in front of Uncle Charlie, her hands folded in front of her. "*Monsieur* Billieux, Madame Krakow and her grandson have come. They brought you something and she wants to give it to you. She says she'll only take a few minutes. She knows lunch will be soon."

"Of course, of course. Send her back here right away." Charlie leaned back in his wheelchair. A smile lit his face.

Nobody told Marie she had to leave so she stayed right where she was, on the little hassock at Uncle Charlie's feet. Olga Krakow and one of the two young men Marie had met earlier in the week came into the big, bright room. The grandson was carrying a large rectangular covered pan. It looked heavy.

"We were talking in the car on the way home after we visited you on Tuesday and I remembered how much you loved my *golubtsis*, Charlie. So I decided to make enough for everybody and bring it here today. It only needs to be heated up. I just told the Mother Superior they should serve it tonight because I made them fresh this morning and she said she would see to it. I hope you like them still." Olga blushed, her round cheeks a bright pink.

Uncle Charlie put out his hands and Olga placed hers in them. He squeezed lightly and pulled her toward him. She responded, bending her face for his kisses on both cheeks. "Olga, you are the prettiest and best cook in all of Maine. I will love the *golubtsis. Merci, merci beaucoup.*"

"We promised the Mother Superior that we wouldn't stay long. Now that we know where you are, though, we'll come to visit more." Olga glanced back where Sister Boniface stood by the door, as if waiting to escort them out.

Marie made a quick decision. "Uncle Charlie, I'm going to leave now. I want to talk a bit with Mrs. Krakow. I'll be back, though, tomorrow morning. Is that OK?"

"You be sure to come back. You have more to tell me, I know." Uncle Charlie lifted his head for her kiss goodbye.

* * * * *

As soon as they were out the door, Marie turned to Olga Krakow, "Mrs. Krakow, I would really like to see the place where my uncle spent all those years. I looked on the map and it seems to me it can't be much more than a couple of hours or so away. Will you ride in my car with me and I'll follow your grandson there?"

"Please, call me Olga. And I will call you Marie. OK? Yes, I'll show you where he lived and worked, but of course the camp has been abandoned for years so it's not the same now as it was then. More modern and the owners are more careful about safety. Steve, come back." She called to her grandson who was striding quickly toward his car. "I'm going to ride with Mrs. Graham and she's going to follow you to my house."

Marie helped Olga over the bank of snow and into the car, then got into the driver's seat and noticed that Olga's grandson was waiting for her to pull out into traffic and follow him.

"When did you meet my uncle, Olga? We know he left Northampton in March of 1942. Did he go directly to Maine?"

"I'm not sure, but I don't think so. My husband first mentioned that this new guy had come to the logging camp in the summer of '42, after the war started. Steve said the foreman was none too sure about hiring him, because he looked too old. Most of the men in the logging business get out before they get to their forties,

355

sometimes sooner than that. It's very hard work and dangerous, too."

"I didn't meet Charlie Billieux until quite a while after that. My Steve kept inviting him to come for dinner, but he always refused politely. Steve heard the story somebody told about Charlie spending every weekend doing work around the French church in the old town. They had a convent and a home for orphans, too." Olga removed her hat and settled it on her lap, patted her hair into place, tucking loose strands into her bun.

"My Steve liked him a lot. He kept saying how Charlie helped this one and that one and once he saved Steve from a log that was coming at him. So me and my kids really wanted to meet this guy. Finally after two years or so, he accepted the invitation to Thanksgiving dinner. We were so surprised. And when he came, he brought presents. We never expected that. For me, he brought a silk scarf. I've still got it. I'd never had a silk scarf before. And he brought chocolates and booze and toys for the kids. Did you know about his whittling? Our boys were crazy about him."

Marie turned her head to look at Olga. "I'm so glad he found some friends. I'll bet he really appreciated your cooking."

They were driving along a two-lane highway with very little traffic. Marie could easily follow Steve's car up ahead.

Olga chuckled. "He sure did and he was quick to say so, too. Well, after that he began to come more often. When Steve decided we needed to put an addition on our house, Charlie was the one who helped him. He knows a lot of stuff like plastering and plumbing and all kinds of things like that. Oh, here's my street. I'll fix us a sandwich and some coffee first and then I'll call my son, Charlie. He owns a hardware store in town and he's got a Jeep. You'd ruin your car on those rutted old roads to the camp."

It wasn't far. The roads were not only bumpy, but ice patches in the ruts caused skidding here and there. Marie was very glad she wasn't doing the driving. A clearing up ahead signaled that they had arrived. The place looked desolate and a little spooky to Marie, as if there were ghosts in the ramshackle buildings.

"Of course, it's been abandoned for quite a while, but you can see the log cabins where your Uncle Charlie lived while he was working here. They were sturdy enough, but still, a lot different than the prefab buildings they use now. No running water here, so no showers and no toilets. There was an outside pump. It may still be there. And a privy. We'll walk over there and you'll see." Olga's son Charlie led the way.

Marie carefully picked her way toward one of the log cabins, grateful for her galoshes. There was still quite a lot of snow on the ground. The three of them stopped before the first building, noticed the rotted wood of the stairs and stopped.

"If you want to see inside, I'll go check out the other cabins to see if there's one in better shape than this." Charlie set off at a lope to look at the other three cabins. He came back and took his mother's arm. "That one over there has steps strong enough for us to get in."

Marie was silently appalled at the primitive conditions, mentally comparing the place to the comforts of the house on West Street where her Uncle Charlie had grown up. The far end of the building was dominated by a huge stone fireplace, blackened from years of smoke. She could imagine him there at one of the wooden tables, bending over a cribbage board, feeling the warmth of the fire.

From the inside, light seeped through the holes between the rough-cut logs where the moss used to chink between them had fallen away. She thought about how cold it must have been in these living quarters in winter and she shivered. The beds lining the walls were made of wood; the heavy canvas webbing that had supported the mattresses at one time was disintegrating now, but no mattresses were left.

"Some of the men played cards or cribbage at those tables nearly every night." Olga said. She pointed to a rusty oil lamp that hung over one of the tables. "No electricity when your uncle lived here. Of course, the new camps all use generators now, but back then, the men rarely stayed up much after dark. And they got up at first light, too."

The three of them walked out of the building and looked out over the abandoned campsite. "Used to be they kept some horses for hauling the logs, even though they started to use tractors by the time Charlie arrived. When my Steve started here in '29, they used oxen, but for some reason, they changed to horses a few years later. I never knew why." Olga sighed. "It was a hard life. Worse for the men who lived here. My Steve came home at night, because our families lived close by."

"We were living with his parents when he first came here." Olga continued. "I was seventeen when we got married in June of '29. Steve was twenty and he had a good job in a hardware store. But, then, after the crash, he lost his job and they were still hiring in the logging camps, so he became a logger."

"What's that over there?" Marie asked, pointing to crude looking pyramid of logs with an opening in the front.

"Oh, that's the bean hole. It's where the cook prepared the beans in a huge kettle that fit into a hole in the ground. They raked hot coals over it and the beans baked in there. Those guys ate a lot of beans." Olga's son Charlie laughed. "Right over there is the cabin where they ate all their meals. Come on. We can walk over there."

Marie followed Olga and her son toward a bigger structure near the bean hole. She was learning what she came here to learn, but it was hard. She kept thinking of her Uncle Charlie, punishing himself for his brother's accidental death every day he lived and worked here, away from family who loved him, with no piano to play, no tantalizing smells coming from the kitchen when he came home at the end of the day. What a waste.

Passing a stone wheel set in a cradle, she called out to Olga and her son, "Somebody left a grinding wheel behind."

"That was for sharpening the axes. Must be they figured they don't need those anymore." Olga turned to Marie. "A lot has changed since this camp was abandoned. I guess a big part of it is how different it got after the war ended."

Olga's son made a dismissive gesture with his hand. "Some people think this was all glamorous. They talk about the old days with nostalgia. Well, they're wrong. It was hard, hard labor, dangerous, poorly paid and exhausting. There were no safeguards, no help for injured men. The owners treated them very badly. Now they have safety equipment, power tools, and laws to protect them. Back when this camp was active, it was a hellish place to work. I've heard the stories about the pride the men who worked here took in their strength and stamina, but, believe me, they paid a heavy price."

The three of them walked around the eerily quiet camp with either Olga or her son pointing out the different buildings and their uses. There was a repair shop, a stable for the horses, a blacksmith shop, a special house for dynamite (used mostly to break up log jams) and a storage shed. All of it was in a dilapidated condition. Marie was shivering obviously, partly from the cold, but also from her reaction to the starkness of the place. Olga noticed.

"Have you seen enough? Why don't we go back to my house, where it's nice and warm? I'll make some fresh coffee and maybe put a little whiskey in it to warm you up. OK?" Olga smiled and patted Marie's arm.

"Thanks for showing me where my Uncle Charlie lived. I'm ready to go. And I sure could use a cup of coffee."

Back at Olga's house, her son Charlie said goodbye, not even stopping for coffee. Marie was grateful for the heat coming from the wood burning stove in the kitchen and the steam curling up from the hot mug of coffee in her hands. The two women sat across from each other at the oilcloth-covered table.

"Olga, do you know how my uncle got injured? Did his leg get the attention it needed?"

"Oh, yes, my husband was there. It was in March of '56. Maybe you don't know, but it was easier to move the logs to the river when there was ice and snow. In March of that year we had a bit of a thaw and then it got chancy. They were using big dray horses to pull a sled with the logs piled on top, even though they had a tractor. I guess the tractor was somewhere else that day. Your uncle and my Steve had loaded the newly cut timber and put chains around the pile to steady it. The horses started off to the riverbank and one of the runners got stuck in a muddy rut. I guess the chains weren't tight enough or something, but the logs started to shift. Your uncle rushed forward to tighten the chains and the whole load came rolling off the bed of the sled and toward Charlie. It happened so fast nobody really could tell exactly what caused it. Steve was on the other side of the load, so he didn't know. Of course, he saw the pile of logs start to move and he heard several men shout and then he heard Charlie's scream. He had nightmares about that for the longest time."

Olga paused and looked out the window, blinking her eyes rapidly to forestall the tears that came with the memory. "I wasn't there and I didn't see it, but when Steve told me, I thought how it could just as easily have been him. People don't realize how dangerous logging can be." She wiped her eyes with her apron. "They could see that Charlie's leg was mangled and his other foot, too. And there was lots of blood, which always scares the guys even though they've seen plenty of injuries before. They knew to put a tourniquet on right away. They laid him on a board and put him in the back of the boss's truck. It was the boss that took him to the little hospital in Jackman. Steve went to visit him the next day, but he was gone, taken in the ambulance to someplace else. We heard a rumor that he went to St. Georges in Quebec, but when Steve called there, he wasn't there. Anyway, we didn't hear anything more until my grandson Paul started dating a girl who had been raised in the orphanage that's run by the Sisters of the Sacred Heart. She knew the story about Charlie because he's a legend to them. When

Paul was telling her about the summer when he was in High School and he worked in the logging camp doing repairs to the buildings, she asked him if he ever heard of Charlie Billieux. You can imagine how excited he got at learning where Charlie was. Well, you know the rest. I got my grandson to drive me to Montreal right away."

Marie had been weeping silently all the while Olga told the story of Uncle Charlie's injury. She put out her hand and covered Olga's. "Thank you for telling me. I don't think I would ever have known how it happened if you hadn't. Certainly my uncle has avoided telling me anything about his life since he left Northampton. All this week he's wanted to learn everything that I could tell him about our family, but he hasn't been the least bit willing to talk about himself."

"Isn't that the way men are, though. Except for the braggarts, most men don't like to talk about themselves."

Marie stood up. It was already dark outside. She looked at her watch and was startled to realize it was already 6:30. "I'd better get going. I want to get back to Montreal, have a little dinner and get to bed, so I can go see Uncle Charlie tomorrow morning."

"Why don't you stay and eat here? I can fix a little something." Olga offered.

"Oh, no, thanks. I'm not hungry right now. We had a late lunch. I've got to be going."

The two women hugged, both of them thinking how different their lives were, but not giving voice to those thoughts. It meant nothing. They were united in their care and concern for Charlie Billieux.

* * * * *

When Marie greeted Uncle Charlie in the morning, she was surprised at how gray his skin looked, but she said nothing about it. He smiled as she came in the door and the smile cheered Marie.

"*Bonjour, chouchou,* did you enjoy my friend Olga's company? Did she take you to see the old logging camp?"

Marie was surprised and amused that her uncle had guessed that she wanted to see where he had lived during those years in Maine. She had not told him when she left yesterday that she was going to do that, but he had somehow known.

"I did go to the camp with Olga and one of her sons called Charlie. Of course, the place is abandoned now and pretty much dilapidated. It looks to me as if that was a hard life, Uncle Charlie. How did you do it? You were not a young man when you went there."

"I remember Olga's son Charlie. He was a handsome young boy when I first met him, sticking his hand out and telling me his name. Did Olga tell you what a rascal he was when he was young? Always in some kind of mischief. She tells me he owns a hardware store now."

Marie sighed. "You don't want to tell me about it, do you?"

Charlie waved his hand as if shooing flies. "It was a long time ago. I have many regrets, but I don't regret the people I met there and the kindness of so many."

"Yes, you have a lot of people who love you, including family who never stopped loving you after you left and who missed you all the rest of their lives."

"And it is my biggest regret, that I was not there for them when they needed me. I guess I didn't think about that, only that I didn't deserve anybody's love. Now, *cherie*, tell me more about what happened to everybody."

*   *   *   *   *

Chapter 21

◇◇◇◇◇◇◇◇◇◇◇◇◇◇◇◇◇◇◇◇◇◇◇◇◇◇◇◇◇◇◇◇◇◇◇◇◇◇◇

Northampton, Paris, and Hollywood, 1961-62

Clara moved into 18A Bedford Terrace, a one bedroom and den apartment with high ceilings, beveled glass is the upper casements of the front windows and a fireplace in the living room. It was more luxurious than 144 West Street and it suited her perfectly. She could walk to work. She could accommodate Maurice and Simone on those few occasions when they stayed overnight and it was a short distance to Jack's home on Massasoit Street.

She missed her sister, Tillie, with a painful sense of loss, at the same time she reveled in her new surroundings and sometimes this made her feel guilty. Tillie would not have been comfortable on Bedford Terrace and Clara definitely was; it felt just right for her to be there. Decorating to her own taste was joy. She brought china and silver, lace tablecloths and pots and pans, a few treasured bibelots and the dining room set from the old house. But her bedroom was completely new, the living room was filled with a combination of new and antique pieces; and the kitchen, much smaller than the one she had known all her life, held a small round table and two chairs.

Clara and Jack were discreet in their relationship; anyone who knew them at all understood the nature of it. As long as it was not the cause for vicious gossip, Clara was comfortable. Jack had stopped entreating her to marry him, finally convinced that it was never going to happen. He loved her, she loved him. It would be enough.

Sitting in front of her fireplace with Jack, drinking coffee laced with Irish whiskey, Jack asked, "Have you ever thought about taking an ocean liner to France? We could go to Paris, go to Normandy, maybe look up some historic places?"

Clara, glowing from making love on this wintry Sunday afternoon, smiled at him and asked, "Where did that idea come from?"

"I've been thinking about it a long time. We could have a whole three weeks or so together without giving a thought to anyone else."

Clara smiled and snuggled closer to Jack on the soft velvet sofa. "You mean no busybodies to start gossip?"

"Well, yes, there's that. But I've been thinking about how much I want to hold you all night while you sleep and wake up in the morning to find you there, next to me."

"Maybe I'd get seasick and you'd have to hold my head while I retched into the basin. That's not very romantic." Clara sat up with a mischievous look in her eye.

"I'd do that, too, if it came to it. Clara, my love, I just want to be with you away from here. Even if it's just a few weeks, I want to do this. What do you think?"

"Oh, Jack, it's a great idea. I know I can take time off for a vacation. I'll need to renew my passport. Will you find out about ships going across?"

Jack hugged her; his eyes were bright with excitement. "Don't worry about a thing. I'll go to a travel agency in Springfield and get them to arrange everything. How about planning it for April? "

Clara told Ruth about the planned adventure and her friend was full of ideas and advice. Not that she'd ever taken such a trip, but her mother and father had done it before the war and had talked about it endlessly.

"Wait and see. It will be something you remember all your life. The ocean liners are even more glamorous now, with more modern conveniences. You do have to take evening dresses, though, because dress will be formal for dinner. What have you got? Maybe we should go shopping."

"Whoa, whoa, I'm not so sure I'm all that ready to spend a fortune on new clothes. I think a couple of long skirts and some interchangeable spiffy tops ought to do it."

Ruth looked chagrined, but then she brightened. "OK, so we shop for spiffy tops. I saw one in the window of Anne August that might work. And you have to get the right shoes, too."

"Not Anne August, Ruth. I'll go shopping in Springfield. I'm not eager to advertise to the Northampton biddies that I'm going on this trip, especially if they figure out I'm going with Jack."

Ruth looked disgusted. "I don't know why you care what people think. It's really none of their business. You get to live your life however you like. This is 1961.

Times have changed since the war ended. People aren't such prudes anymore."

"Sadly, my friend, I think you're wrong. In a small town like this, there's a lot of prudery. But, anyway, the only people I worried about are gone now, so what difference does it make? Still, I'd rather be discreet."

"Will you go to visit your first husband's grave in France?" Ruth asked.

"I don't know. I'd have to find out how to get to it. And, anyway, maybe that's expecting too much of Jack, to take me to visit Gus's grave."

As it turned out, Jack had already gone to the library to get information about visiting the Meuse-Argonne American Cemetery and Memorial where Gus was buried. It could be reached by train to Verdun and then by a 42 kilometer ride to the village of Romagne-Gesnes or by auto directly from Paris, a 245 kilometer trip. Jack decided they would hire a car to take them. He learned that the cemetery was staffed from 9 to 5 every day, so someone would be available to help them find Gus's grave.

When Clara got out of the taxi at the pier in New York, she looked up at the big ship in awe. She'd never imagined it would be so huge. Jack had booked them on an Italian owned feet, assured by the travel agent that it was renowned for excellent service and hospitality. The six-day trip was a time of unadulterated joy. Jack and Clara   danced every night, slept late every morning, savored beautifully prepared meals and enjoyed each other's company, whether playing cards, reading on deck bundled in warm blankets against an ocean still cold in the early spring, or sitting in the lounge people-watching. They were courteous to their fellow passengers, but declined to engage in anything more than polite dinner conversation.

They disembarked at Le Havre and took a train to Paris, where they stayed at the Hotel Prince de Gaulles, two blocks from the Champs Elysee and two more to the Arc de Triomphe. When they were brought to their room, Clara looked around at the marble bathroom, the silk-fringed draperies on the windows, the damask covered chairs beside a small round table and the box of assorted miniature bottles of cognac at the bedside.

"Jack, this must be costing a fortune. We could have stayed someplace simpler. This room is fit for royalty." Clara was already uncomfortable with Jack's refusal to share the expense of this trip.

Jack stepped behind Clara and put his arms around her. "Do you like it?"

"Well, of course, I like it. Who wouldn't? It's a really spectacular hotel, Jack."

"Then let's enjoy it." He turned her around and kissed her, tightening his embrace and inhaling sharply. "You are so beautiful. You should always be surrounded by beauty." His seduction was leisurely and Clara was receptive.

Afterwards, Jack suggested they change and go down to the lounge, which he told her featured an orchestra that played for the cocktail hour. The place was nearly full, but they were able to find a tiny table and Jack ordered martinis. Clara's eyes swept the room, looking at the dresses of the women, trying to guess nationalities. She listened to the cacophony of many different languages and wondered whether her Canadian French would be understood.

The days that followed were busy with sightseeing and delicious dinners in beautiful restaurants. They spent a hilarious evening at the *Folies Bergere,* took a trip to Versailles on a warm, breezy spring afternoon, strolled through the Louvre for a whole day, and admired the beauty of Notre Dame and the awesome view from the Eiffel Tower.

Clara reflected that lovemaking was somehow different, more relaxed in this place, removed from concerns for time, responsibilities and small town morals. She'd worried about the potential for discomfiture from too much togetherness, but that turned out to be unfounded. Jack planned well and with great sensitivity. He went off for a haircut one day, suggesting she might want to go shopping. He left her to her morning routines while he searched out a patisserie. Clara was not unaware of the efforts he made to insure her complete contentment.

The day the hired car and driver arrived to take them to the Meuse-Argonne Cemetery, Clara was puzzled. What did they need a hired car for? When Jack told her their destination, she was so overcome by her emotions, she cried. At first, Jack was startled and worried that he might have been wrong to plan this without discussing it with Clara. She assured him that was not the case. She had thought about visiting the cemetery when he first suggested the trip, but believed he wouldn't want to interrupt his vacation for this melancholy pilgrimage.

"Why would you think I would deny you this opportunity to visit your husband's gravesite?" Jack asked her.

"Because you were planning a trip full of pleasure and I didn't want to spoil it for you."

"This trip, my darling Clara, is for us to be together. Gus was a part of your life and I want to share that. How can I explain it to you?" Jack shook his head in frustration. "You are the most important person in the world to me. Don't you know that?"

The drive took about three and a half hours through small towns and farmlands with newly planted fields and meadows where cows were grazing. The countryside was bursting with fertility in the spring sunshine. When they arrived, the driver asked if they wanted to go to the Visitors' Center or to the memorial chapel first. Clara thought they should go to the Visitors' Center, where they could find out the location of Gus's grave and maybe get some information about the cemetery.

At the Visitors' Center, they learned about the battles fought near these fields and in particular, the final offensive that drove the enemy to seek an armistice. They leaned over a brass plaque set on a stanchion, written in French and English quoting General Pershing, writing of the last battle that it had been "prosecuted with an unselfish and heroic spirit of courage and fortitude that demanded eventual victory." They learned that out of more than are 14,000 war dead interred at Meuse-Argonne, 486 were unknown.

Louise S. Appell

A staff member helped them locate Gus's grave, with its headstone of white marble engraved with a cross, his name and the date of his death, Auguste Pelletier, 9-10-18. The headstones were laid out in rectangular plots bordered by square-trimmed linden trees, each grave surrounded by closely clipped green grass. It was very quiet, so much so that the sound of the American flag flapping in the breeze seemed loud.

Clara had bought a small bouquet of daffodils in Paris before they left and she laid it now at the headstone beside a bouquet of violets already there. At the Visitors' Center, they'd been told that families in the area often adopted gravesites to care for, so they were not surprised to see the floral tribute.

At the entrance to the chapel, the inscription carved into the stone lintel read, IN SACRED SLEEP THEY REST. Clara crossed herself and bowed her head as they entered. Jack put his hand on her shoulder. Candles were burning at the altar. Several people were sitting in the pews. They stood there in the back of the chapel for a few minutes before Clara turned to Jack and said, "I'm ready to go."

They got in the car and had driven a few miles when Clara broke the silence to smile at Jack. "Thank you for bringing me here. I am so grateful to see that Gus is honored. He went to war, you know, out of belief that it was his duty to help save the world. He was so young and idealistic. And war is so ugly. Will we ever have an end to war, Jack? Is it always going to be the fate of young men to battle other young men while some old politicians squabble over territory or ideas or power?"

Jack took her hand in his. "I wish I could tell you that there are always going to be sunny skies and conflicts among countries will end, but I'm afraid I would be deluding both of us to even think that."

They had three more days in Paris, spent mostly walking, dawdling over coffee in street cafes, people-watching, laughing at the antics of the small dogs so many Parisiennes brought with them everywhere. Clara noted the elegance of men's clothing, the tailoring precise, fitting closer to the body. She admired the way women used beautiful scarves to dress their outfits and the lovely scent of perfume in the cafes. Clara's Canadian French had been a help to them throughout their days in France, even though it was certainly different than the language spoken by the native French people.

They flew home on Continental Airlines in one of the new four engine jets, a Boeing 707, just beginning transcontinental flights.

* * * * *

Petey did well at Williston, making good grades, playing lacrosse, excelling as a member of the debate team, and every weekend when he came home, he rushed over to LaFleur's airport to hang around hoping someone would take him up in their plane.

As his sixteenth birthday approached on June 1, he dropped broad hints that his greatest wish was to get flying lessons. Of course, he had already been allowed by some of the pilots to take the controls, but that wasn't official stuff and wouldn't get him a license.

He sort of knew his dad was going to give him a car as soon as he got his driver's license because it was his dad who taught him to drive and had already mentioned that a car of his own was in his future. But flying was magical for him. He felt different when he was up in the air. Like he was on top of the world. Like he was a part of the sky.

Angela worried about him. He was so sure of himself, so tall, taller than his father, and so damned good looking. "I hope you've talked to him about sex and being responsible for his actions." Angela admonished Pete. "He's a good boy, but those hormones are pretty powerful. I don't want him getting some girl pregnant and then forced to marry too young. He's got a great future if he doesn't screw up."

Pete laughed at Angela's concerns. "Of course I talked to him. A couple of years ago, I started having those talks. At first he was embarrassed, but then when he figured I'd answer questions no matter what he asked, it got easier. Some of the stuff he'd heard from his buddies was the same stuff I heard at his age. The world doesn't change that much when it comes to sex. Don't worry, he'll be fine. Do you know he asked me to find out about getting an appointment to the Air Force Academy?"

"No." Angela cried out in agitation. "I don't want him to go fighting wars. Oh, Pete, you have to talk him out of that. We can afford to send him to college. The guys that come out of the military academies are the first to go."

"Angela, the wars from now on are going to be different. This Cold War we're in today is probably going to be the way countries handle their fights. Anyway, whatever happens, it's got to be a hell of a lot better flying in a plane than crawling on the ground. I think Petey could get into the Air Force Academy and do very well. I'm going to ask around to some of my political contacts to see what it takes to get him an appointment."

"What about getting him flying lessons for his birthday? How expensive is that going to be and is it a good idea?" Angela asked Pete.

"I'll go down to the airfield and talk to Bob LaFleur. Let's see what he says. I'm guessing it's just going to take paying for the hours he needs to get licensed. He probably already can fly. And I still plan to give him the used Ford coupe I fixed up for him. I got it painted red." Pete smiled at Angela. "You worry too much."

Petey came home the weekend after his birthday, tired from studying for final exams. His dad picked him at up at Williston and when they came around the corner of Day Avenue from Bridge Street, the red Ford coupe was parked in front of their house, with a big sign on it that read "Happy Birthday, Petey, from Mom and Dad." Petey jumped out of his father's car and opened the door of his birthday present. "Wow. Wow. It's a beauty." He ran his hands over the steering wheel and the plush gray seats, adjusted the mirrors, noticed the radio and the key dangling in the ignition.

Pete, standing on the sidewalk, was beaming. "Of course, you can only drive if one of us is with you until you get your license, but we'll figure out how to get that taken care of next week. I guess you like it, huh?"

Petey jumped out of the car and hugged his dad. He noticed his mom coming down the steps from the porch and loped over to lift her off her feet, hugging her tight and laughing. "Thanks, Mom. Thanks, Dad. It's a great birthday present. I really love it."

Aunt Clara and her friend, Jack Grimes, arrived soon after to join the birthday celebration dinner. They were carrying a big box wrapped in blue paper with a white bow, which they took into the house with them. Petey pretended not to notice as he went downstairs to leave his laundry bag and then took the stairs two at a time up to his bedroom to deposit his duffle.

In the kitchen, Angela was taking a pork roast out of the oven and chatting with Clara who was arranging asparagus spears on a plate. "I suppose he was excited about the car, even though he probably was expecting it." Clara looked at Angela with a lifted eyebrow.

"Oh, yes, he was very pleased with it. And not a single word about flying lessons, either."

"Of course not. You raised him right. He's a good boy. But I can't wait to see his reaction to the envelope under his plate."

Angela called them all to the table. Pete and Jack carried their martinis in from the living room. Petey came clattering down from upstairs and called out, "Oh, boy, I smell pork roast."

In the dining room, Petey's chair was stacked with gifts and peeking out from under his plate were four envelopes. "Hey, those sisters of mine remembered my birthday. Look at this." He tore off the wrapping paper on the top box. It was a large book, glossy cover featuring four airplanes in flight, entitled 'An Encyclopedia of Aircraft.' Inside the cover Amy had written 'Happy 16th Birthday, Flyboy, from your sister Amy.'

His gift from Marie was a long white silk scarf, the kind worn by WWI aces and all the romantic airmen in the movies. The big box carried in by Aunt Clara was a leather jacket, cut in the style made popular during WWII. Petey was grinning, his eyes widened in astonishment. He opened the cards under his plate from his sisters and his Uncle Maurice and then the card from his mother and father that contained a note from Mr. LaFleur showing that flight instruction leading to his pilot's license were paid for. It took all of Petey's self control not to run out of the house and get on his bike to ride to the airfield immediately. He went around the table to kiss his mother and father and his aunt, shake hands with Jack and thanked them all for the great gifts.

"OK, let's eat. Enough excitement. I'm hungry." Pete announced. He reached for the utensils to carve the roast and Angela started passing the asparagus, Clara the mashed potatoes, when the telephone rang. Petey jumped up to get it. It was Amy, calling to sing the birthday song.

"Did I time that right? Are you just sitting down to eat? Have you opened your presents yet?" Amy asked.

"Hi, Goose Girl. Thanks for the great book. Dad just started to cut the roast. Guess what? I got a red car and flying lessons, too. And a cool silk scarf from Marie and a leather jacket from Aunt Clara and Jack. Come on home in the fall and I'll be able to give you a ride over the valley."

Angela looked over at Pete and smiled, conveying with her eyes a silent message to him that spoke of pride and pleasure and acknowledgement of the joy this child gave them.

* * * * *

Amy was annoyed with herself. This was the third time this week she had stumbled and barely caught herself before she took a tumble. It had happened before, but the occurrences were only occasional, never so close together. It crossed her mind that maybe she should stop having a glass of wine at lunch, but she dismissed that idea as soon as she remembered that the unsteadiness had often occurred in the morning.

When David came to pick her up to go to a party, she mentioned that she was very tired and hoped they wouldn't stay long. "We don't have to go at all, Amy. We can order some dinner and watch television." David was surprised to hear Amy talk about being tired. She had always seemed tireless, especially when they were going to an event where they would be with other Hollywood people who could help them with their careers.

"Oh, no, it's OK. I was just thinking we might get back early tonight." Amy brushed off any notion of staying home and missing an opportunity to meet people.

But during the party, as she was standing in conversation near the bar, David glanced over and saw Amy's leg buckle, saw her reach out to grab hold of the wall. He rushed over to her side and took the drink she was holding out of her hand and slid his arm around her. Quietly he asked, "Are you alright? Maybe we should go?" And she answered, "Yes, I think so."

On the way back to the apartment she shared with Cary, who was out of town, David questioned Amy about any other symptoms she had that something was not right. They had been together long enough for him to know about the polio she'd had as a child. After all, her quirky walk was mentioned so often in the press that she felt comfortable telling him that it was really the residual of the limp that had been the aftermath of her bout with polio. She confessed that she was having some problems with extreme fatigue, too. He insisted that she needed to see a doctor to find out if the weakness in her leg and the fatigue were related to the polio.

Over the next months, either David or Cary took Amy to several different specialists and over time the episodes of extreme fatigue and weakness in her leg became more frequent. When it started to affect Amy's ability to work, she became alarmed. Still, she said nothing to her parents in her letters and phone calls, sure that the condition was temporary. When Marie came out to California for a visit, though, it was impossible to hide the truth from her. Marie immediately set out to find who in Southern California was working on any research on polio. It didn't take long for her to get the name of a doctor located at UCLA who was doing a study funded by the March of Dimes.

When they met with him, he took a careful history, examined Amy and diagnosed Post-Polio Syndrome, a condition that had no known cause and no clear treatment regimen. He said to expect slow progression with periods of stability followed by new decline. No drugs had proven to be helpful in managing the fatigue, but some carefully monitored exercise might help. Nothing, absolutely nothing, stopped the deterioration entirely.

Amy was devastated. She saw the end of her hope for a career in films. David and Cary both insisted that she could still do small parts, but while they hotly argued with Amy that it was possible, even they doubted it.

Pete and Angela flew out to the coast to persuade Amy to come home. Though she was plagued by fatigue and using a cane a good bit of the time, Amy was not willing to give up yet. Most of all, she was sure she didn't want to go back to Northampton to be treated like an invalid. If she couldn't appear on the screen she was determined to find some other job she could do in the film industry. This was her milieu and she wanted to stay.

Pete got angry and wanted to insist that Amy come home with them, but Angela observed the interactions between her daughter and David Epstein. She understood, although she wasn't sure Amy knew it yet, that the reason for wanting to stay in California had less to do with the film industry than being with this man her daughter loved. There was no way they would be able to get her to leave him and all Pete's fuming wouldn't make a particle of difference.

* * * * *

Chapter 22

◇◇

Hollywood and
Northampton 1963-64

The Hollywood trade papers were full of stories about the young director who made a big splash with a small budget film that charmed the critics and had the moneymen eager to talk to him about taking on another project. David Epstein had arrived. His gentle way with actors, his willingness to listen to others' point of view, his ability to stay calm in the midst of chaos were qualities displayed all too seldom in Hollywood.

Amy had a part-time job as script girl, working whenever she was not overwhelmed by fatigue. Cary and David had appointed themselves to watch out for her, which was sometimes annoying to her, but mostly she accepted the necessity. When Cary was out of town for a shoot in a remote location, David spent the night at their apartment so someone would be close in case Amy fell.

It had been over four years since Amy and David met and they had been dating more or less steadily since then. He had taken Amy home to meet his family, a close-knit group that included uncles and aunts and cousins, all of whom took to Amy's sweet and sunny character. His mother kept asking him when they were going to get married, but David was determined to make his mark in the film industry before he took that step. He had seen the brutal competitive climate of Hollywood ruin a lot of marriages, mostly because both partners were so involved in the ego draining pursuit of contacts and entrée.

When Amy's health became fragile, his protective instincts rose to the challenge of caring for her. It was a surprise to him to realize how very much he had come to love this *shiksa* with her wonderful smile, her optimism, her ability to weather through bad days, gloomy prognosis and high hopes shattered. Despite the prevailing culture of casual sex in the film world, David and Amy had not become intimate until shortly before post-polio syndrome came into her life.

David's success meant he could move out of the apartment he'd been sharing with a friend since he first came to Hollywood and buy a small house in the canyon. He chose a place that was all on one level with beautiful views of the mountains from the huge glass doors in the living room and master bedroom, beyond which were decks that could be filled with pots of flowers. He took Amy to see it and asked her opinion.

"What do you think of this place? I'm half way to deciding I should buy it." David grinned and raised one eyebrow. They were standing on the deck outside the bedroom, watching the light fade from the sky over the distant mountains.

"David, it's lovely. What a fantastic panorama. You've worked so hard, you really deserve this. Why half decided?"

"You're the other half. Would you like to live here with me? I mean, would you marry me? I know we come from different religions and traditions, but that's not important to me. I love you and I want to take care of you..." David was talking fast, intent on getting his message out. Amy put her hand over his mouth and, when she took it away, replaced it with a kiss.

"I love you, too, David, and I think you are a wonderful man. Are you sure you want to be saddled with a sick wife? Your parents may be horrified. Not only am I crippled, but I'm a Catholic."

"Amy, Amy." David put his arms around her and sighed. "None of that will make any difference. If we love each other, we can work out anything. Please say yes, sweetheart. Just say yes."

Amy looked up at him, her eyes filled with tears. "Yes, David. Oh, yes."

They decided to wait to tell friends until a contract David's agent was negotiating was signed and the house was theirs. First, Amy called her parents to tell them she was engaged to David. Angela answered the phone. Her response to Amy's news was a question. "Does he make you happy?" And when Amy answered, "Yes, Mom, and I love him very much." then Angela said, "All the rest is unimportant. You'll work it out."

Pete came to the phone and asked, "Is he doing well enough to support you?" and Amy laughed. "Daddy, he just finished making a movie that the critics love. Everybody in Hollywood wants to work with him." In response to when the wedding would be, Amy was vague. They didn't have a date yet. It would be a very small wedding. She hadn't even thought about the details. She'd let them know soon.

Marie got really excited and wanted to fly out immediately and take over planning the wedding. Amy assured her she'd call and let her know when it was time to do that, but not yet. Amy sighed when she got off the phone. She turned to David. "She really means well and I'll be glad to have her help. It's just that she always has to be the one in charge. She can't help herself. She has to do it."

When she called Petey, he was enthusiastic. "Good for you, Goose Girl. I can hardly wait to meet this guy. He'd better promise to take good care of you."

Amy giggled. "Or what, Petey? Will you come out and beat him up if he doesn't?"

"Damn right I will. You're my sister and I love you, too."

They decided to drive to Santa Ana to tell David's family in person on a Friday night when many of them would be gathered for the weekly celebration of the Sabbath. David's mother opened her arms wide and gathered Amy to her. "He loves you, I know. That is what is most important."

While his two brothers and their wives were congratulating them warmly, Amy noticed his father's frown. "What about children, David? How will you raise your children? They will not be Jews if their mother is not a Jew. You know that, don't you?"

"We talked about that, Pa, and we decided to raise any children to respect both religious traditions and when they get old enough, they can choose. Lots of people now are getting married without worrying about that stuff. You wait and see. In ten years or so, it will be so common, nobody will think anything of it."

"Well, I don't know about that. I think you don't realize how hateful people can be. I'd hate to see you make a mistake and have to live with the consequences." He got out of his chair and left the room, muttering something to his wife as he passed her.

Amy was a quite upset about Mr. Epstein's remarks. On the drive back to Hollywood, she asked David about it. "He'll come to the wedding, won't he?"

"Well, I may not have mentioned it before, but he was raised Orthodox and only joined the Reform Synagogue when he met my Ma. She'll talk to him. He likes to bluster a bit and play the Patriarch, but he'll be fine. Just give him a little time to get used to the idea. He doesn't know it now, but my sister is dating *goyim*." David's younger sister was a student at San Francisco State.

They started making plans to give a housewarming party and announce their engagement to all their friends then. But first they needed to furnish the house. Because David's family owned a chain of furniture stores, David brought Amy an armload of catalogs and told her to pick out what she liked. She insisted it needed to be a joint decision, so many evenings they sat together in the apartment Amy shared with Cary looking at different styles and choosing what pleased them.

The day after the house purchase was concluded, trucks began arriving to unload their choices. David hired a woman to come in every day and help in the house and he found a service that would take care of the landscaping. He was very busy himself with casting and staffing a new project.

Within the week after closing, the house was livable and they moved in. And within the following week, Amy had a bad bout of extreme fatigue. David was worried that she had pushed herself too far. "Amy, sweetheart, you have to pace yourself. We don't need to do anything in a hurry." He sat down next to her on the soft, comfortable sofa in the living room.

Amy smiled and leaned her head on his shoulder. "Want to hear my news? I went to the doctor today and he says I'm pregnant."

David was stunned. He thought they were being careful. He opened his mouth to say just that and then decided that was not important now. "Amy, that's wonderful. Are you happy? Did the doctor tell you it was OK?"

"David, my love, I am deliriously happy. Having a baby with you is the most wonderful thing that could happen. We have to start planning our wedding right away, though."

"Let's go down to City Hall tomorrow." David covered Amy's face with kisses. He whooped. He stood up and flung out his arms and shouted, "We're going to be a family."

Amy asked Cary for some help planning a small wedding in two weeks and Cary went into high gear. He asked her first if they wanted a rabbi or a priest and when Amy said, "That doesn't matter. We thought maybe a justice of the peace would be best." Cary said, "OK, I know one. He's a nice guy. And I could get a friend who owns a flower shop to make an arch we can set up on the deck at your house. How about that?"

Amy frowned. "I don't know if we can do that. I figure we have to invite about 30 people even if we're just going to have close family. Will they fit on the deck??"

"Sure, it's a very big deck."

In just a few days the whole celebration was planned, family members called, caterers hired, flowers ordered, musicians contracted for. When Amy made the invitation calls to her family, she deflected questions about the timing with a story about moving into their beautiful new home and thinking it perfect for a wedding. When Marie grumbled about needing to change her schedule, Amy got a little exasperated with her. "For God's sake, Marie, you're so smart, figure it out. Why would I want a speedy wedding?"

"Are you pregnant?" Marie asked in a whisper.

"Well, there you go. I always knew you were a smart cookie." Amy giggled, bubbling over with joy.

"Are you sure?"

"Right now I'm sure, but I don't plan to confirm that until the first three months are over, so don't say anything to anybody else. We were planning to get married soon, anyway, but we thought why not do it now? That way the folks who count the months won't be sure whether I was pregnant before the wedding or not."

There was quiet on the other end of the call and for a few beats, Amy thought she might have been disconnected. But then Marie gave a deep sigh. "I'm happy for you.

You don't know how lucky you are. And I'm jealous, too. We've seen a lot of doctors and still I don't seem to be able to get pregnant. It's a big disappointment to both of us. Chris says it's because I work too hard, but I don't think that's it." The tone of Marie's voice changed. "Oh, never mind about my problems. Let's talk about what I can do to help."

"Actually, nothing. It's going to be a very small wedding. Will you be my matron of honor? I'm planning to wear a cream lace dress I bought last year for some big gala here, so whatever you want to wear is OK with me. Cary kind of jumped in and got it together, but once he found a caterer, a florist and a trio, there wasn't much left to do."

"Are you wearing a hat? How about gloves?"

"No hat, no gloves."

"What did Mom say?"

"She said she was happy for me and did I want her to come a couple of days early?"

"Oh. Do you want me to come early?"

"David reserved rooms in a Hilton that's close to where we live. He got one for Mom and Dad, one for Aunt Clara and Jack, one for you and Chris and one for Petey. Sam and Tom are coming, but they'll stay with Cary and all David's family can drive over from their home in Santa Ana. Since the wedding is set for Saturday evening, he got the rooms for the whole weekend, starting on Friday. If you're going to get here earlier, you have to tell me so I can change the reservations."

"I'll have to check my calendar and call you back. Is that OK?"

"Sure, but don't wait. Sometimes the rooms are hard to get during the week."

David called his mother and charged her with the job of calling the rest of their family. She complained a bit about restricting the guest list to close family, reminding her son that there would be some hurt feelings, but then, when David mentioned Amy's fatigue, she said she understood. She never asked about the haste; she never asked about a rabbi. Mrs. Epstein went on her intuition and focused on getting the family together for the celebration.

The florist came up with a cleverly designed bower that could be viewed as an arch or maybe a *hupa* and set it on the far side of the balcony, with the view of the mountains behind it. He set up two rows of white chairs, decorated with silver ribbons and pink flowers, on each side of an aisle and wound silver ribbon through the balcony railings. Then he filled the house with bouquets of pink flowers in silver vases. It looked festive and elegant at the same time.

The Justice of the Peace was becoming more familiar with ceremonies for couples embarking on a mixed marriage. He asked David and Amy if they had any special ideas and whether they wanted the groom to break a glass under his foot. David agreed and that little bit of theatre made his family happy.

Marie, as her sister's matron of honor, entered the balcony first on the arm of David's brother, acting as best man. David's mother and father escorted him down the white carpet that was set from living room to wedding bower and Pete followed, escorting Amy in her cream lace dress, carrying a bouquet of pink peonies. She wore a diamond necklace, a gift David gave her the night before, and the diamond studs she wore in her ears had belonged to her *Memere*.

Everyone there agreed it was a beautiful wedding, small, intimate and tasteful. The LaPointe family and the Epsteins found they had much in common. Conversation flowed easily for the four hour affair. Amy held up remarkably well, although Marie led her away and into the master bedroom to rest when she appeared to tire. The bride and groom were going up to stay near Lake Tahoe at a cabin owned by one of David's friends.

They were planning on five days, but would stay a little longer if David could delay some meetings. They were both eager to have a little while to be together without the pressures of the film community.

* * * * *

On the plane ride home, Angela and Clara sat together, Pete and Jack in the seat in front of them. Petey had a vacant seat next to him several rows ahead, but Marie asked him to switch with her so she could spread out the papers she was working on. He agreed and moved across the aisle next to Chris, who slept most of the way.

Angela and Clara had both brought along magazines to read, but Clara set hers down and turned to Angela.

"I know you worry about Amy, Angela, but I really think her new husband will take good care of her. He seems to be a caring person and very much in love with her."

Angela nodded. "Yes, I think you're right. It's hard, though, to have her so far away. Even when they grow up, it's impossible not to think of them as kids."

"I spent a long time talking to Leah Epstein and she seems to have a lot of affection for Amy. I'm not so sure about her husband." Clara frowned.

"Pete told me he had a chance to talk frankly with Izzy Epstein and he says it's not so much that David's father doesn't like Amy, because he does. He has nothing but nice things to say about her. It's more that he worries if a mixed marriage can work. He talked about community pressures and preserving tradition and stuff like that."

Clara sighed. "Look at my friend, Ruth, though. She and Bob seem to be very happy. If two people really love each other, I don't think religion matters all that much. It's not as if either one of them is fervently devout."

Abruptly changing the subject, Angela blurted out, "Do you think Amy is pregnant?"

"I don't know. She didn't say anything to me. She tires easily, but that's her condition. But if she is, wouldn't that be wonderful? You'd get to be a grandmother."

"Yeah, I know. I wonder if it's OK for her to carry babies with her fragile health. And babies tire out even the strongest of us."

Clara chuckled. "I'm pretty sure David would hire all the help needed. Money does not seem to be in short supply in that family. People don't buy diamond necklaces like the one David gave Amy as a wedding present for peanuts. And Amy told me all the gorgeous furniture in their house was a gift from David's father and mother."

"I asked Amy about that, you know. When she showed me the necklace, I said I hoped he didn't rob a bank or something. And she said his income shot way up after the success of his movie, besides which, he has a trust fund from his grandfather, who was the one that started the chain of furniture stores."

"Well, there you are. They'll be fine, Angela. Don't worry about her. And, if she is pregnant, she's probably waiting until the first three months are over before she tells anyone, just in case she really is too fragile to carry it. After three months, she'll have a good chance of making it to full term."

"I feel so sorry for Marie. For all the trying, she hasn't been able to get pregnant even once. If Amy does produce a baby, it will be very hard on her."

The two women lapsed into thoughtful silence. Then Clara asked, "Do you think she works too hard? Chris asked me something about that one time when we visited them in New York. I was surprised by the question. But, anyway, I didn't have any answer for him. I just said, 'Who knows what's too hard? Everybody's different.' But I did think he was implying that her working hard had something to do with not getting pregnant and I honestly don't think that has anything to do with it."

"Tell me, Clara, what do you think of Chris?"

"I think he's a very nice guy, even-tempered, sociable and so in love with Marie he can't see straight. I'm not so sure she feels the same way about him." Clara's tone was thoughtful and a little hesitant.

"Well, guess what? I agree with you. I think his dream of the future was a nice house in the suburbs with three or four kids. He'd take the train into the city, work hard and come home to a neat house and a well-cooked meal. I don't think he had any idea how ambitious Marie is and, of course, neither of them expected to have any problems with making babies."

The stewardess in her tailored blue suit and perky hat squatted down in the aisle next to them. She was holding a tray of assorted beverages. "Can I interest you ladies in something to drink?" Angela and Clara both asked for ginger ale.

Clara took a swallow. "You know, I wonder if all that drive to excel at her work is just a substitute for having a family or was she always that ambitious? I can't remember ever thinking of her as a businesswoman when she was a young girl."

"Did Pete say anything to you about Marie's new idea? He told me and I was flabbergasted." When Clara shook her head, Angela continued. "She wants to start her own company out in the New York suburbs selling and managing commercial real estate. Imagine that. She says that merchandisers and services have already started to move out to the suburbs because those folks who have bought homes away from the city don't want to come in just to shop for ordinary things. She thinks there are going to be huge shopping centers outside the city. I thought that was crazy, but Pete says she's right."

"Maybe she is. It's different in a small town like Northampton. It's easy for everybody to come down to Main Street. We've got plenty of parking and everything anybody needs is right there. But it must be hard for those folks who moved into places like Levittown on Long Island to take the train into the city whenever they need to buy a new outfit or clothes for the kids."

"*Dio mio,* if she starts a new company she'll never be able to spend time with Chris. I remember when Pete opened the garage, we hardly saw him and when he did come home, he was exhausted. I wonder if her marriage could survive."

"It's for sure she is not like the other girls she went to school with. I can't think of a one of them who has a career. Some work because they have to in order to stay afloat, but usually part-time or teaching where the hours are just right for raising a family. Where does Marie get all her drive?"

Angela laughed and patted Clara's arm. "Look at you, look at me. Aren't we both working at something we love? Haven't we provided the example? Do you know what I think? I think we take notice of her only because her dreams are bigger than ours. And, of course, because we worry about what she's doing to her marriage. If Pete wasn't my champion or I hadn't already had my kids, I'm pretty sure I wouldn't be selling real estate."

They landed at Idlewild Airport on Long Island and gathered inside the terminal to collect their bags. There was a flurry of hugging and kissing Marie and Chris goodbye. Those two grabbed a cab and headed for the city. Jack went off to get his car, parked in a lot some distance from the terminal. He had driven the rest of them down to New York in his new Buick. Angela and Clara set off looking for a restroom. It was still a long drive to Northampton, but better to take a nonstop flight than the nuisance of changing planes somewhere if they had flown out of Bradley in Connecticut.

* * * * *

Amy and David Epstein welcomed a baby boy on December 3 of 1963. He was 7 pounds, 2 ounces, alert and squalling minutes after he was born. Leah and Izzy Epstein were at the hospital, having spent ten of the sixteen hours while Amy was in labor trying to comfort their anxious son. The three of them went to the nursery to gaze through the glass wall at the newest addition to the Epstein family and stood there with tears running down their cheeks.

David talked to Amy's doctor before he went into her room. "Will she be all right? Did the labor weaken her more? I mean more than the average?"

"As far as the birth is concerned, it was normal. I know it must have seemed to you like a long time, but first babies are like that. Because of the post-polio, it will take her longer than usual to get her strength back. Will she have help at home? I think she must." The doctor looked sternly at David.

"Oh, yes. We have a full-time housekeeper and I've hired a baby nurse. Do you think I should hire another nurse just for my wife?"

"No, no. I don't foresee any complications. I don't think it's necessary and she might object to that, anyway. Right now she's asleep. But when we first gave her the baby to hold, she was euphoric. It seems to me she's a positive person. She'll use that to get stronger as fast as she can. Congratulations, Mr. Epstein. You can take your family home in four or five days."

Though Amy was asleep when David stepped into her private room, he decided to sit and watch his much loved wife until she woke up. He was exhausted from waiting so he knew she must certainly be worn out from laboring. While he sat there, his thoughts went to how grateful he was for this extraordinary woman who met every adversity with a cheerful countenance and a belief that everything would turn out all right. Even the obstetrician had noticed it.

Amy woke up and smiled to see David sitting there. "Have you seen him yet? Did you tell them his name?"

David leaned over the bed and kissed her. "He's beautiful, of course. My Ma and Pa were here and they saw him, too. I talked to the doc and he says you came through like a trooper. And no, we all forgot to tell the nurse his name is to be Aaron, so the card on the crib just says Baby Epstein in blue. I'm really surprised my Pa didn't mention it since he was so pleased we were naming him for his father."

"Maybe the next one will be Rose." Amy had decided to name a girl for her *Gran'mere*.

"Amy, my darling, don't you think it's a little soon to be talking about the next one. We haven't even brought this one home yet." David was laughing.

When their pediatrician came to examine the baby, he asked Amy if she wanted him to circumcise the infant right there in the hospital. He said many pediatricians recommended it and believed it was a procedure that was best done immediately.

David thought it was an excellent idea, but he was sure his parents would want to bring in a *mohel*. When his mother had suggested she could help Amy plan a *Bris,* David had nixed that idea immediately. He could just imagine Amy's reaction to a party where she would be on stage for his family when she was still recovering from childbirth. Oh, no, he was not about to let that happen. But he did think it would mollify his mother and father if they could come to the hospital and watch the traditional ceremony. Then, too, if Aaron chose to become a Jew later in life, it would avoid the painful procedure it could be for adults. He talked it over with Amy and she agreed.

David drove his wife and son home paying more than usual attention to all traffic signs and speed limits. He kept glancing over at the sight of Amy holding the infant in her arms and thinking that this was one of the happiest days in his life. No amount of career success could possibly equal it.

The baby nurse was already installed. The nursery was ready. A new rocking chair had arrived just in time. When Amy sat down in it to nurse Aaron, David ran to get his camera to preserve the moment. Amy laughed. "David, you are like a kid with a new toy. Brace yourself, there are going to be days when he'll drive you crazy. Remember, I was witness to Petey's mischief. I'm prepared."

David knelt down on the floor next to Amy, took little Aaron's hand and kissed it. "Whatever happens, I love you both and we'll deal with it together."

* * * * *

In March of 1964, Angela flew to Los Angeles to see her grandbaby. It was a short visit and a happy one. Amy seemed to be doing well. Aaron was thriving, already lifting his head and trying to roll over. She visited the set of David's new movie, went shopping with Amy and had plenty of time to play with the darling boy.

While she was gone, Maurice caught a bad cold and couldn't seem to shake it. By the time Angela got back to Northampton, Maurice was in a hospital in Hartford.

Clara had already gone down to visit him. Pete said, "I'm going down on Saturday. Do you want to come?"

Angela hesitated. She'd been gone for a week and she had a lot of catching up to do. She wondered if Petey would want to give up one of his precious weekend days to make the trip, but when she called him at school, he told her he definitely wanted to go.

Petey was waiting for his letter of acceptance to the Air Force Academy. It would be nice if it came and he could tell Uncle Maurice he was going to be a career military man.

Angela had some misgivings about Petey's decision to apply after Pete had used his political contacts to get Senator Kennedy to nominate their son. After a lot of family discussion about it, she realized this was Petey's big dream.

"I know he's worked hard to get good grades, but Colorado is so far away." Angela was proud of her son, but still, it was hard to let him go.

"Angela, he is 18 years old. It's his decision to make." Pete answered her.

"I know. I know. You're right, but I don't have to like it."

The letter didn't come in the Saturday mail, but Petey didn't seem to be anxious about it. He felt confident that he would get in. Somehow, he knew that this was his destiny, so why sweat it?

Jack and Clara and Simone were at the hospital when they got there. It was a shock to see Maurice, who had always been pink-skinned and smiling. He appeared to have shrunk. His cheekbones were jutting out, stretching his skin. His color was gray. His white hair looked sparse. When he tried to talk, he started coughing and couldn't seem to stop. They stayed for a very short time, maybe twenty minutes, when Pete leaned over and kissed his uncle's cheek, murmuring his goodbye. Angela and Petey followed, making the same gestures. They each hugged Simone, promised to come back, asked what she might need and offered to do anything she needed done.

When they walked out of the hospital, Pete saw Clara waiting for him. "I don't think he's going to make it. He looks really bad."

Clara was biting her lip to stop the trembling. She sniffed back her tears. "My sister is gone. Charlie is God knows where, maybe dead, too. When Maurice goes, I'll be the last one left."

Pete put his arm around his aunt. "Maybe he'll pull out of this. He's pretty tough."

It was not to be. Maurice Billieux died three days later, of pneumonia. He was 83.

Chapter 23

◇◇◇

Northampton, New York and Hollywood, 1964-67

Petey entered the Air Force Academy in Colorado in the fall of '64. He had grown into a tall man, two inches taller than his father. Playing lacrosse and skiing on the Williston team had kept him fit and trim. And, while all his family was proud of Petey's success in athletics as well as academics, his mother and his great-aunt Clara had a lot of doubts about the wisdom of his choice to become a career military man.

For Angela, who had not prepared herself for the emotional jolt of an empty nest, it was a hard time. Pete missed his kids as well, but immersed himself in work and community activities and swallowed his feelings of loss. Angela was less able to hide her anxieties and fretted about her son continuously, even to the point at which Pete complained and they had angry words.

"Merde, Angela, you're driving me crazy. The kids are all adults now. They get to have their own lives, just like we did. They'll make mistakes and they'll learn. Let it go, will you?"

"I don't know how you can say Petey's an adult. He's still a kid. And he's so far away. At least Amy has David to take care of her. Who's taking care of Petey out there in Colorado? Never mind, you just don't understand." Angela started to cry.

Pete, unable to deal with Angela's tears, put his arms around her and patted her back. "Come on, dry your tears. We'll go out for dinner and you'll feel better."

Angela looked up at him, angry now. "You think you can fix everything that easy? I don't want to go out to dinner. I want...I want... I don't know what I want." Her tears changed to loud sobbing. She went into the bathroom and slammed the door.

Pete stood in front of the closed bathroom door. "Angela, what do you want from me? I miss them, too, but they're grown up now. We can do some things we never could before. Why can't you be reasonable?"

She pulled open the door and faced him, her hands on her hips, her posture clearly belligerent. "Look at me. I'm an old woman now, 53. I've got gray in my hair and lines on my face, my boobs are falling and next thing you know, I'll get a fat belly."

Pete was astonished. It took a lot of self control not to laugh at the picture of his still lovely, still slender, still black-haired wife standing there disparaging the way she looked. "Angela, *cherie,* you are very beautiful to me and you will be for all our days together. What's going on here? I don't get it."

"Never mind. You'll never understand. If you're going to take me out to dinner, you have to change your shirt."

* * * * *

In New York, Marie spread out papers all over the table and in piles around her on the floor. When Chris asked her if she wanted to go out to dinner, she didn't hear him. She was entering figures into an adding machine and the sound was annoying Chris.

He got up from his chair, folded the newspaper he had been reading and came to stand behind Marie. When he put his hands on her shoulders, she flinched. "You startled me. What do you want?"

"I asked you if you wanted to go out to dinner and you didn't answer me. I figured you couldn't hear me with that machine clattering."

"No, I'll be done with this in a few minutes. I picked up dinner on the way home. Just give me a little longer."

Half an hour later, Chris announced in a loud voice. "I'm hungry." He went into the kitchen and opened the refrigerator, then banged it shut. "I don't feel like cold roast beef and it will take too long to get that stuff ready anyway. I'm going out to get dinner. Do you want to come with me or not?"

Marie got up from her chair and picked up her purse. "OK, I can just leave it and work on it later. Where do you want to go?"

They walked the two and a half blocks to a neighborhood restaurant, *La Maison Nouvelle,* a particular favorite of both Chris and Marie. Once they were seated, with a bottle of a very nice cabernet sauvignon on the table, Marie leaned back in her chair and raised her wine glass in a little salute to Chris. "This was a good idea, Chris, especially since I noticed today's special is *boudin noir.* So, how was your day? What's new in the world of architecture?"

Chris sat up straighter in his chair and beamed. "I got assigned to the team that's designing a new building at Fordham. It'll be a big challenge to fit what they want into the space between two existing buildings. And there's a faction on campus that's protesting putting in a building there at all."

Marie leaned forward, her eyes bright. "Is this a big opportunity for you to make your name? Will there be a lot of press coverage about it?"

"No. If anybody gets any recognition it will be the guy leading the team and that's not me. I'll do my job and maybe all of us working on it will get a raise if we bring in a design that's acceptable to the board of governors at Fordham. But, sorry, darling, no glory." His expression was a bit rueful. "How are your plans for the new company coming along? Have you met with the bank yet?"

Their dinner arrived in a fragrant cloud and they both took a bite before Marie answered. "Not yet. I want to be sure I've anticipated all their questions and have all the answers ready before I go to the decision-makers. Are you sure you won't mind moving out to the suburbs, taking the train in every day?"

"I've told you all along that I not only won't mind, I look forward to it. We'll buy a house with a lawn and

I'll build us a backyard patio and garden space that will have all the neighbors pea green with envy. We'll give the best parties in town there. I like how your parents have fixed up their yard, but I'm thinking of something much bigger."

They drank their wine and savored their dinner, shared ideas for what they would need in a house and, by the end of the meal, were both feeling relaxed and in accord. Marie tucked her hand into the crook of her husband's elbow and hugged herself close to him all the way home. Chris, pleased with the gesture and the happy look on his wife's face, unbuttoned her jacket and then her blouse as soon as they walked into their apartment. He led her into the bedroom and undressed her slowly, kissing her and stroking her as he did. He knew well how she responded to kisses behind her ear and in the hollow of her throat. It was gratifying to him to hear her gasp, feel her shudder and be assured that she was responding. He stroked down her back and over her buttocks, lowered his mouth to her breasts and hastily removed his own clothes. In seconds he was completely undressed. He backed her onto the bed and followed her down. "Yes?" he asked. "Oh, yes, yes, now, right now." she answered. Their lovemaking left them both breathless. Neither mentioned how infrequently that had happened in the last year.

Chris was just starting to fall asleep when he became aware that Marie was getting out of bed and putting on a robe. "Where are you going, darling?" he muttered.

"I have to finish the stuff I was working on before we went to dinner," she whispered. "Go back to sleep."

"Come back here and let's snuggle."

"I can't. I have to get it done and I'm too busy to do it tomorrow. I won't be long."

"Bullshit."

* * * * *

Marie launched her new company in the fall of 1965. It was a wrench to leave Metropolitan Commercial Properties, where she had started as a receptionist in the summer of 1951. Mindful that it made no sense to make enemies, Marie was careful to hand off that portion of her current client list that was Manhattan-based to another agent at Metropolitan. She had explained her ideas to Mr. Bates in detail and how they would not compete with him. And she was aware of how skeptical some of her colleagues were that she could build a commercial real estate business in the suburbs. When she talked about all the big department stores creating branches outside the city and needing help with finding space, some of them had to struggle to contain their laughter.

By the summer of 1966 no one was laughing.   Two different speculators had started building shopping malls outside the city and had hired Marie's company, Graham Commercial Real Estate, Inc., to manage the leasing of the space. More people were moving out to the suburbs all the time. Astute businessmen assessed the market potential and started making plans. Marie hired a man with connections and an understanding of zoning laws. She set up a division to serve land owners interested in selling or leasing for commercial purposes. The rapid growth created its own challenges. Marie was working day and night.

Chris had the task of finding them a suitable house to buy. He relished the assignment. It was important to him to find a place in an established neighborhood, with trees and sidewalks and a feeling of community. Of course, he wanted it to be well-built and pleasingly designed and available at a fair price. Marie's office was in White Plains, but he was most interested in Tarrytown, a well-established community.   It took three months of looking to find the perfect place. It had everything he believed to be important---trees, sidewalks, a feeling of congenial neighborliness and a lovely "sidewalk appeal."   It was a white center entrance Colonial with a stone fireplace, a glassed-in side porch, a formal dining room, an outsize kitchen, four bedrooms and two and a half baths. The kitchen needed new appliances and he thought he'd put in a slate floor there. The downstairs half-bath needed new fixtures, too. But these things were minor. The yard had space for the large patio he had been planning since they first contemplated a move. He could just see it in his head.

"Come and see the house I've picked out for us, darling." Chris was smiling hugely at Marie.

"Right now?"

"Yes, drop everything and come with me." Chris had appeared at her office on a Saturday afternoon.

He was very pleased when she agreed and even more gratified when Marie loved the house he had found. They stood together in the bare living room and he described his ideas for improving the space before they moved in. Marie could see how excited he was to take on the responsibility and relieved that it would require only that she admire the changes as they occurred.

By Christmas of 1966 they were able to move in and invite Marie's mother and father, her Aunt Clara and Jack and Chris's mother and father to come and celebrate the holiday with them. Having three guest rooms was a great advantage. Chris put up a huge Christmas tree, a wreath on the door and a rope of greens around the stair railings that led up the path to the entrance. Angela insisted on bringing three pies, Clara made cranberry sauce and brought the makings for biscuits which she intended to cook in Marie's kitchen. Chris's father arrived with four bottles of Reisling and four of champagne. He said, "The champagne is for Christmas Eve. We have to have bubbly while we open our gifts."

The four women were working in the kitchen when Angela announced, "I can hardly believe it, but Amy is pregnant again. She didn't say a word to me, but Petey went there for his Christmas break and he called me. He says, so very casually, 'Mom, did you know Amy is going to have another baby?' and I say, 'How do you know?' and he says, 'David told me.' I made him put Amy on the line right away and, sure enough, it's true. She didn't want to say anything until she'd passed the first three months."

Marie felt like someone had punched her in the chest. She could hardly breathe. Her jealousy was overwhelming, her bitterness at the news a surprise. She loved her sister. She was pleased to see Amy so very happily married to David. Why was she so angry at this latest piece of news? How could she feel so hostile to her own sibling? She felt unworthy, a terrible person, a hopeless failure. She bent over the sink, cleaning the inside of the turkey, letting her hair fall to conceal her face. Fortunately the exclamations of surprise and delight from Aunt Clara and congratulations from Mother Graham gave her the few moments she needed to pull herself together.

"I hope she got an OK from her doctor before she decided to do this." Marie commented. As soon as she said the words she realized they sounded wrong. "I mean, I'm happy for her if that's what she wants, but I worry about her health."

"I'm sure David worries enough for all of us and he wouldn't let her have another baby without checking it out with her medical team." Angela answered.

"Yes, you're probably right about that." Marie lifted the turkey out of the sink and set it in the roasting pan, covered it and set it out on the porch, ready to be stuffed in the morning.

Marie had made *tortiere* for supper on Christmas Eve, getting lots of praise from her dad for the tasty meat pies. She used the recipe she treasured, which was in *Memere's* own handwriting and was pleased that they turned out so well. There were sighs of pleasure, exclamations of surprise, kissing and hugging among all of them as they opened the gifts they had for each other while they sipped champagne. Chris gave Marie a silky beaver jacket; which she tried on immediately, preening and vamping across the living room. She got him an elaborate table saw for his basement workshop. They all went off to the Church of the Holy Redeemer for midnight Mass.

After a traditional turkey dinner with all the trimmings served at one o'clock on Christmas Day, Chris's parents as well as Clara and Jack left to drive home. The weather report was for storms coming in the next day and they wanted to get back beforehand. Angela insisted on staying to help Marie clean up and told Pete they could leave early the next morning if the weather held up, but she was not about to leave Marie with that big mess in the kitchen.

The two women worked side by side scrubbing pans, washing china plates, putting leftovers in containers. "Marie, *cara*, I know how frustrated you must feel when you hear Amy is going to have another baby. Have you and Chris talked about adoption?"

"Oh, Mom, not you, too. Chris would like to do that, but not me. If I can't have a child of my own, I don't want to give up my career to raise somebody else's child. It's bad enough to be a failure at something every other woman seems to be able to do. At least my business makes me feel I'm a success at something. Can you understand that?'

"Marie, be sensible. There are lots of women who can't have babies. It's not a failure thing. Where did you get that idea?"

"Listen, Mom, you can't possibly know how it feels. You've had three healthy children. Count your blessings. I don't want to talk about this anymore, OK?"

Angela reached out to smooth Marie's hair out of her eyes. She was more than a little shocked at the anger and misery in Marie's voice. She felt, as she had never felt before, unable to offer help to her beloved daughter. There was no way she could imagine life without her three darling children. Marie bore a tragic burden she would have to deal with on her own.

* * * * *

Clara decided to retire. She was 70 years old and, even though she was healthy and active, she admitted she had slowed down some in the last ten years. She liked working at Harry Daniels'. She was well accepted there by customers and other sales staff, but the long hours on her feet left her tired at the end of the day. She still insisted on wearing heels, even though the podiatrist scolded and muttered about the damage to her toes.

Clara had followed her mother's advice to 'be ready for a rainy day.' For all the years of her working, beginning when she was nineteen, she had 'put a little something aside' so she had a tidy sum in her bank account. Together with her social security income and the income from the investments she'd made with the legacy Ray left her, it was enough to live quite well, with a few luxuries now and then.

Jack had retired two years ago, partly because he'd had a mild heart attack and it scared him. He took up fishing, something he hadn't had time for in the past. There were some very beautiful places to fish less than an hour's drive out of town. He got interested in gardening and hung out at the botanical gardens at Smith, talking to the staff and the students, learning about the properties of the plants he wanted for his garden. He started riding a bike into town to get groceries and run errands after his doctor told him he needed more exercise.

When Clara told him of her decision to stop working, he was delighted, foreseeing more time together, introducing her to the pleasures of fishing and gardening. He had given up importuning her to marry him and accepted the relationship for what it was. He knew his children didn't like it, but they didn't live close and anyway, it was none of their business.

"I'll get you a bike for your birthday and we can go riding together." Jack declared.

"Whoa. I don't know about that. I'd probably fall off and embarrass you right on Main Street."

"We could ride out to Look Park and bring a picnic. We could ride around the Smith campus and enjoy the flowers. It's good exercise." Jack had become a strong advocate for getting daily exercise ever since his heart attack.

Clara agreed reluctantly, but after the first few days of feeling wobbly and a little scared, she came to love the feeling of the breeze on her face, the world gliding by. The two of them explored the little park near the Coolidge Bridge as well as Look Park. Jack got a contraption that fit on his car and could carry their bikes to parks outside of Northampton. They drove to Springfield and explored Forrest Park on the bikes. They tried some parks that turned out to be too hilly or to have paths that were unpaved and too difficult. Pete warned them several times about possible hazards, but they laughed at his cautionary words.

In the spring of 1967, they were riding in Look Park in an area away from the popular tennis courts and playing fields with Jack in the lead and Clara following. She noticed his bike wavering and then Jack falling sideways into the grass. Clara stopped her bike and jumped off. She ran to Jack, crying out his name.

"Jack, Jack, what happened? Did you hit something?"

He was gasping for breath, his hand clutching the front of his shirt. His eyes were wide. He tried to speak but the only sound was a croak. Clara ran for the snack shack which they had passed a few minutes ago and startled the man there with her screaming command, "Call an ambulance right now. My friend has had a heart attack."

Cooley Dickenson Hospital was only minutes away from the park. They were there almost immediately, though it felt to Clara that they had taken a long time. She was sitting on the grass holding Jack's hand and crying. His lips were turning blue.

Despite the efforts of the ambulance attendants and the emergency room doctor when they got Jack to the hospital, he died an hour later. He was 72.

Chapter 24

<><><><><><><><><><><><><><><><><><><><><><><><><><><>

Northampton, Hollywood and Tarrytown, 1967-72

Clara was despondent. Three men she had loved and all three dead. The loss of Jack just as they were beginning to enjoy a pleasant retirement, full of plans for trips they would take to places they had talked about for years, was a hard burden to bear. She thought about each of the men she had loved. Gus, her first love and only husband, was so young, so idealistic, and full of life. She never got to enjoy much of those beguiling qualities about him because he had enlisted less than a year after they were married.

She should have married Ray. When she remembered her reasoning then, she was appalled at how naïve she had been. His death hurt no less than it would have had they been married. Jack was a different situation. By the time she knew she loved Jack, she had come to embrace independence and enjoy the freedom to make choices on her own. It was still the same pain losing him, married or not.

Jack's children treated her with barely concealed hostility and that didn't help. When his daughter found some of Clara's clothes in Jack's house, she bundled them up in large paper sacks and handed them to Clara in the funeral home with a curt, "I presume these are your things."

Amy was too close to her delivery date to even consider traveling to Northampton for Jack's funeral. Since Jack was not related to Petey there was no possibility that he could get leave from the Air Force Academy to attend. But Marie and Chris drove up from Tarrytown, Angela stayed close to Clara each day of the wake, and Pete joined them as much as he could.

Throughout the funeral service at St. Mary's Church, Clara was thinking of how important Jack had been in her life. She remembered how she had started having casual dates with him in 1949, when she worked at McCallum's and Jack was the store manager. Ray was in a coma then and she kept hoping he would come out of it. She remembered the night when Jack drove her to Connecticut in a snow storm, the night Ray died in the VA Hospital. It wasn't until two years later that she and Jack became lovers. She remembered how much she needed his support when Tilly died in '58. Even when she kept refusing to marry him, he was always there. One of her best memories was the wonderful trip to France. All the little surprises he liked to spring on her, the concert tickets, the books, the obscure little restaurants in the country, teaching her to crack open a lobster when they were at the shore, added up to evidence of his love and caring. She would hold these memories close forever.

A few days after the wake, when Angela announced she was going out to California to be with Amy for the birth of her daughter's second child, Clara asked if she'd like some company. Angela was surprised and pleased at the idea. They made plans to stay long enough to drive up to the wine country in Sonoma Valley. When Angela told him about the trip, Pete commented, "I'm so glad she's going to do that with you. It means she's looking forward."

* * * * *

Amy's second son was born on September 7, 1967. He was 6 pounds, 8 ounces, with a head of nearly black hair. They decided to name him Edward, for Amy's

Pepere. Although it had not been a hard labor, Amy seemed exhausted. She tried to conceal her weakness from David and from her mother, too. Neither of them was fooled. The second pregnancy had taxed Amy's physical resources. Amy cried and argued, but David was insistent that there would be no more babies.

With a housekeeper and a baby nurse available, there was little Angela and Clara could do other than give their loving support to Amy. Aaron was already four years old and going to nursery school half a day. David urged them to take Amy's car and visit California in style. He offered to make reservations at convenient hotels in Sacramento and San Francisco so they could explore the wineries and the 'city by the bay.' He recommended restaurants, provided maps and was generally charming and congenial.

"Amy is so lucky to have David." Angela said when she was alone with Clara. "He's a very nice guy and he loves her very much. They seem so happy together. I worry about Marie and Chris. And I'm always reminded of how strained they seem to be together, especially when I get around Amy and David."

Clara looked over at Angela, who was driving. "Those two need to find better ways to talk to each other. They're too polite. I've always thought Chris was a great guy and very much in love with Marie, but she has such a strong personality, I think she overwhelms him. And he doesn't want to hurt her, so he lets her have her way all the time. Sure, it's a sadness that they couldn't have children, but they should be able to let that go and find other ways to be happy with each other."

Angela was aware Clara was talking from her own experience. Despite the death of her young husband, despite having no children of her own, Clara fashioned a life for herself that was marked by deep emotional commitment. It was not the conventional way of life, but it appeared to be a satisfying one.

The two women had a wonderful time traveling around California. They were both attractive, Angela with her black curls flying around her face and Clara, with her close cut cap of nearly white hair. They rode the cable cars in San Francisco, ate exotic Oriental delicacies in Chinatown, strolled through Golden Gate Park, sampled wine all up and down Sonoma Valley and came back to Amy's house to tell her of their adventures. Little Edward was thriving and Amy looked much better every day. Angela reminded them she had a job selling real estate that she loved and that she'd better get back to it.

That trip was the beginning of Clara's travels. She asked the Birdell Travel Agency in Northampton to find her a group going to England that was exploring outside the city of London and at age 71 went walking all over the Cotswolds. When Petey graduated from the Air Force Academy in 1968, she attended his graduation with the rest of the family and then went on to visit the Grand Canyon. She found a group going to Rome and Florence and was thrilled to see the Sistine Chapel and Michelangelo's David. She met people easily and found herself to be a good traveler, never rattled by the unexpected, never complaining about the occasional inconvenience.

Pete and Angela settled into their middle age happy with each other, proud of their kids, financially comfortable and both in good health. Pete's business was doing well. He was known all over town for his willingness to work on community activities to benefit others. He had an easy way about him that made others feel relaxed and willing to help with whatever project he was promoting, whether it was a new park, an after school program or a music festival.

Angela continued to sell real estate until she turned 60 in 1971, when she got a nasty case of the flu that had her down for more than a month. Pete said, "Angela, enough. You've been working too hard and there's no need. I'm going to start slowing down myself. We should be taking more vacation time."

Angela began collecting brochures and maps, planning some short trips they could take. She set out her collection on the kitchen table and told Pete, "Choose." Pete liked the idea of driving up to Quebec to visit Trois Rivieres, where his family had come from. They could stop in Montreal first and visit the Botanical Garden there and, after they went to Trois Rivieres, then could go on to Quebec City.

It took them a while to plan all the details of making the trip. Though Pete had good people working for him at his motor repair and car sales business, he carefully went over all the questions anyone might have while he was gone and promised to call every other day. Angela found someone to check the house and water the plants. She made up copies of their itinerary to send to Marie and Amy and Petey, who was now at Fairchild Air Force Base in Spokane, Washington.

It was a glorious spring day when they left. Pete was driving a new Cadillac and feeling in high spirits. "Angela, *cherie,* we are going to have a great time. This car is very comfortable, *oui*? Who would have thought we'd wind up two sports traveling in style like this." He reached across the seat and pulled her over to him. "You know what? You are still the most beautiful girl in the world and I love you." Angela giggled and patted his arm. "Watch your driving."

The Green Mountains in Vermont are spectacular in the springtime. Watching the landscape turning green was appealing for both of them. Pete became nostalgic. "Remember, Angela, how upset you were when I enlisted after Pearl Harbor? Remember how angry my mother was when I did that? Well, I'm telling you, it was the best thing I ever did. I got thrown in with all kinds of guys. And I figured out how lucky I was to have a family that cared about me. Every time the mail came and I got letters and packages, I noticed how some guys got nothing. And I found out how important it is to have something to look forward to."

Angela shifted in her seat and laid her hand on Pete's shoulder. "It was a bad time at home, Pete. Every time we heard about somebody getting killed, we couldn't help but worry that you would be the next one. We had to do without a lot of things that we couldn't get because of the war. The hardest of all was trying to figure out what was going on. We listened to the radio and read the papers, but nobody could be sure what was true."

"I know what a prick I was at first when you talked about going to work at the defense plant. *Mon Dieu*, was I wrong about that! It was the money you saved that got us started after I came home. We could never have gotten the repair shop without that money." Pete turned his head and smiled at Angela. "We're a great team."

"I'll never forget how surprised I was when you called from New York after you got off the ship and told your Pa you needed to stay there for a few days to get your leg checked out. Do you think he figured out the truth when you asked him to get me on a train to join you?"

Pete chuckled. "I'm pretty sure he knew what was in my mind. And I didn't want my mother to get upset because I wasn't hurrying home. That was a wonderful reunion."

They stopped in Burlington for lunch. Angela had suggested she could make sandwiches to bring along in the car when they were leaving Northampton and Pete had told her not to do that. "It will be good to stop for a while, get out of the car and find a nice place to eat."

After a pleasant lunch in a restaurant overlooking Lake Champlain, they got back in the car. Angela noticed it had gotten much warmer so she removed her jacket. "Only about two more hours to Montreal." Pete announced and looked over at Angela, applying fresh lipstick. He reached over and rubbed the back of her neck. "Tired?" he asked. "No, I'm fine." She answered with a smile.

Pete was singing 'When the moon comes over the mountain' when Angela screamed, "Pete, watch out!" A pickup trunk was coming right at them, driving on the wrong side of the road. "Sonofabitch. What's he doing?" Pete yelled and wrenched the wheel to get over to the side of the road. The pickup hit the Caddie all along the driver's side and the big car struck the guard rail and flipped over, tumbling down the embankment.

A family in an old Chevy on their way to Quebec saw the accident and stopped. A man jumped out of the car and slid down to the Caddie. He could hear a woman moaning. He grabbed the passenger door and pulled, surprised that the door opened. The woman inside was on the floor, covered with blood that seemed to be coming from her head. The driver was not moving. The steering wheel had pierced the guy's chest and he appeared to be dead. The Good Samaritan reached in and turned the key to cut the motor, assured the woman that he was going for help and scrambled back up the bank.

Another car had pulled over and someone yelled out the window, "What happened? Do you need any help?" and was answered, "We need to get an ambulance. There's a woman there who's bleeding a lot. I think the guy is dead."

A man on a motorcycle stopped and said, "I'll go into Burlington and get help." In a few minutes three other cars stopped. One woman called out, "There's a pickup truck back there that seems to be hanging half over the guard rail."

The police and an ambulance arrived a short time later. White-coated attendants carrying stretchers slid down to where the Cadillac had landed on its side, nose facing down the incline. They came back, the stretcher laden, moving carefully on the slippery surface of shale and set their burden into the back of the ambulance. One of the medics observed, "No hurry on the driver. He's dead, but maybe there's a chance for the lady." The ambulance sped off toward Burlington.

* * * * *

Chapter 25

<><><><><><><><><><><><><><><><><><><><><><><><><><><>

Northampton, 1972-1975

Marie was alarmed when her secretary told her that Aunt Clara was on the phone. Immediately, she felt a stab in her chest, a physical response to a premonition of disaster. Her aunt never called her at work. She picked up the phone. "Aunt Clara?"

"Marie, I just got a call from your father's partner, George. The police in Vermont called the business number." Clara was sobbing loudly. She had to get her voice under control. "Marie, there was an accident. Your mother is in a hospital in Burlington. Your father is……" Clara's voice caught. It was a few seconds before she could force the words out. "He's dead."

Marie shrieked, "No....no.....no." Her secretary came running into the office. "Tell me what happened. Where was my mother taken?"

Clara had only sketchy information, but she did know the name of the hospital in Burlington. Marie declared, "I'm on my way."

As soon as she hung up the phone, Marie called Chris at his office in Manhattan, gave him the grim news and announced her intention to leave for Vermont immediately. Chris argued, "Wait for me. I'll get a cab and I'll be there as soon as possible. I don't think you should make that trip alone." Marie didn't want to wait, but she didn't want to argue with Chris either. She'd go home and pack a few things for both of them. Maybe they'd need to be gone for several days.

She scanned her desk and made mental notes of what was pending that would need attention while she was gone, called in two of her best agents and issued instructions, promised to call in every day and left.

Driving home, her mind was churning with questions and decisions that needed to be made. Should she call Amy now or wait until she had more information about Mom's condition? How about Petey? Would she even be able to reach him? She started to cry, remembering that her beloved Daddy was dead. She pulled the car over to the roadside because she couldn't see through her tears.

By the time Chris arrived Marie had filled the tank of her car, packed a few things, left a note for the cleaning lady to water her plants, called to suspend newspaper delivery and was waiting impatiently. Chris arrived by 3 o'clock. He put his arms around her. "I'm so sorry, darling. Let me help you deal with this."

It took about five hours to drive the nearly 250 miles to Burlington, with Chris driving most of the way. When they arrived at the hospital, they met with the surgeon who had operated on Angela to remove bits of bone embedded in her brain. He was not optimistic in his prognosis. "I'm sorry to tell you she has sustained brain trauma. Such injuries are tricky. She may hang on for a long time, but probably not ever recover speech or even basic functions. We just have to wait and see."

When Marie entered her mother's hospital room, she was grateful to have Chris to lean on. The sight of her beautiful, vibrant mother's face, battered to near unrecognizability, with her head swathed in bandages, a respirator over her mouth and nose, tubes snaking everywhere, was shocking. She clasped her mother's hand and kissed her brow. There was no sign of response. Chris led his sobbing wife out of the room.

Aunt Clara had driven to Burlington right after she reached Marie and had reserved a room for them in the same hotel where she got a room for herself. She had not called Amy or Petey or done anything about transporting Pete's body back to Northampton. She had felt sure Marie would want to do that.

Marie wanted to see the police report of the accident before she called anyone. A gray-haired, tall, fit policeman gave Marie the written report and assured her that no one was at fault for the accident. An autopsy would be performed but he felt sure it would show that the driver of the pickup truck involved had a heart attack. His vehicle went out of control, swiping the Cadillac and causing it to break through the barricade and flip over before landing at the bottom of the steep embankment. It was a miracle that more cars weren't affected. The pickup truck driver was dead.

Marie first called Czelusniak's funeral director to arrange for them to come and get her father's body. There was some discussion on the details of the wake, the Mass and the interment which Marie dealt with by deciding to repeat all the details of her *Memere's* funeral, the same style casket, the same music, the same prayer cards.

Chris got Marie and Clara to agree to have a light meal at the hotel. He ordered a bottle of wine and coaxed them to have a drink. Talk turned to calling Amy and Petey. Marie thought it might be best to call David and let him break the news to Amy. Clara would try to track Petey down. All three of them toyed with their food. Clara was somber, but Marie's tension radiated from her. She looked to be ready to jump out of her chair, wanting to do something. It was late, nearly ten o'clock. The restaurant was closing when Chris and Marie parted from Clara.

Just before midnight David called Marie back to say he and Amy and their two boys would be flying cross-country in a private plane owned by a friend of his. He thought that would be the easiest way for Amy to make the trip. He said Amy was devastated but not hysterical. She was holding up better than he had expected.

Clara was surprised to get Petey on the phone on her first try. He asked questions about the accident she couldn't answer. "Just get yourself to Northampton in the next two days and you can ask questions then. I don't know the answers, Petey, but maybe Marie does. You can ask her when you get here, dear. We're all a little shook up. Forgive me if I'm a little scattered. Love you."

The next morning, Marie visited her mother, talked to the doctor responsible for Angela's post-operative care, went to the morgue to sign papers releasing her

443

Louise S. Appell

father's body to the Czelusniak funeral home and left
with Chris for Northampton. She arrived at the house
on Day Avenue and realized she didn't have a key. Chris
fished around in the shrubbery and over the lintel and
finally found the key under the doormat.

"First, we need to find clothes for my father and bring
them to the funeral home. Then, I think I'd better go
over all the arrangements for the wake and the Mass
and be sure everything is all set. Chris, you can help
me by going to the grocery store and getting some food
in here. I don't know where we're going to fit everybody
and we'll have to feed them. Also, please order some
flowers for my Dad's......" Marie's voice broke and she
started crying. Chris put his arms around her and
patted her back, murmuring, "It's OK. It's OK. We'll
get through this."

George, one of Pete's partners, knocked on the door.
Chris answered it. "I came over to see what I can do to
help." Before Chris could answer, Marie came over to
hug George. "I just told Chris to go to the grocery and I
need to go to the funeral home, but we've only got one
car. Can you get me a car off the lot to drive while we're
here?" George was grateful to have something to do.
He suggested he could drive Marie to the funeral home
right away and have a car delivered there as soon as he
got back to the lot.

444

Petey arrived late that night. He'd been able to hitch a ride from Fairchild to Westover Air Force Base on a jet cargo plane. He was offered a ride from the base by some guy coming to Northampton to visit his girl. He was wearing a flight suit that looked like coveralls, but had lieutenant's bars on the shoulders. Marie hadn't seen him since his graduation from the Air Force Academy in '67. She was stunned by how much he had changed. He was a handsome, self-assured 27-year-old man. She'd have to stop thinking of him as her 'baby brother.'

Marie described for Petey the arrangements that she had made and asked if he wanted to suggest anything. "Have you asked the local VFW people to provide an honor guard? I'm sure they'll be glad to do it."

"Omigod, I forgot that completely. Will you take care of that in the morning? The wake starts at 6 tomorrow night and the burial is on Thursday morning. Is it too late?"

"No, it will be fine. There'll be people who are always ready. I'll take care of it. Right now, though, I need something to eat."

Amy and David and their two boys arrived the next afternoon, driven from a private airstrip in Springfield in a hired limousine. Petey hugged Amy, who started to cry. "I can't believe this is happening. It's too cruel."

Marie kissed her sister and led her over to the sofa. "Here's what I've done so far. Tell me if you disagree with something. The wake starts at 6 tonight, but we still have time to make changes if you want to." It was obvious to Marie that Amy was fatigued, but her hair was perfectly done, her slacks were hardly wrinkled and her lipstick looked fresh. David hovered nearby, anxious to rescue his wife if she needed rescuing.

Amy, wiping her tears, listened to Marie describe the decisions she had made about the wake, the funeral Mass and the burial. "Everything is fine, Marie. I don't know how you can hold yourself together to do all that. I told David you would be the general and we would be your troops. What do you want us to do?"

"Just stay by the door at the funeral parlor as long as you can to greet people coming in to pay their respects. I think there'll be a lot of them. Petey and I will be there, too, so when you get tired, just say so. There's a little room in the back where you can rest." Marie looked over at David. "David, you can help Chris dispense drinks to the men who come looking for a little liquid courage. We've already got a box full of liquor to take over there." David nodded, "Of course, whatever you need me to do."

Aaron, dark curls plastered down with some hair product, came over to his Aunt Marie. "What can I do, Aunt Marie? I'm almost ten years old and I can help."

Marie realized she had not yet greeted her two nephews. She put her arm around Aaron and hugged him close. "Of course you can, darling. You can be in charge of the guest book and make sure everybody signs it. And when flowers are delivered you can collect the cards and put them in a little basket. OK?" He nodded and turned back to his father.

David came over and put his hands on Aaron's shoulders. "I'm sure Aaron will do a good job." He winked at Marie. "And, Amy, I think you should lie down for a while. I want to get us checked in at the hotel."

Marie was surprised. "I thought you'd stay here. We've got enough room. I just have to make up some beds in the rec room for the boys, but you and Amy can have Mom and Dad's room, Chris and I will take Amy's room and Petey can sleep in his old room. It'll be fine."

David smiled. "And it will be chaos in the bathroom and the kitchen. No, I already got us adjoining rooms at the Hotel Northampton. It would help, though, if I had a car to use while we're here. Amy thought maybe we could take one off the lot. Is that possible?"

"Sure, I'll call George right now. Amy, you go lie down. I'm going to make some grilled cheese sandwiches. Aunt Clara brought over a big pot of soup earlier today, so we've got something to eat before we go to the funeral home."

Petey had taken the two boys down to the rec room to show them his model airplanes, still hanging from the ceiling down there. Chris went with them and David followed, coming up the stairs in a few minutes with the key to the car George had brought over from the lot for Marie yesterday. "I'm taking our suitcases and going to get into our rooms at the hotel."

* * * * *

Just as Marie had predicted, the Northampton community turned out in large numbers to pay their respects to Pete LaPointe. He had been an active member in most of the business and fraternal organizations in town as well as in local politics and was respected and admired. Marie and Amy, dressed in black suits, and Petey, in his Air Force uniform, greeted a steady stream of mourners, some waiting on the porch for the line to diminish. Aunt Clara appointed herself in charge of watching over five-year-old Edward, who seemed fascinated by the strange scene and asked a continual flow of questions.

Father Dumont arrived and led the assembled mourners in reciting the rosary. Those who were able got on their knees. Soon after that, the VFW honor guard arrived and presented the colors. The Mayor and the entire City Council came, as well as the police chief. Many business owners appeared with their wives. Most of these people knew that Angela was severely injured and expressed their concern. People spoke in low voices, asking each other for details of the accident, stunned at the sudden, violent end of Pete LaPointe's life.

Surprising all the family, Amy stayed at the door greeting mourners for the whole two hours, but when the doors closed and David came to get her, she leaned into him, so clearly exhausted he told Marie and Petey, "I'm taking Amy and the boys to the hotel. After I get them settled, I'd like to come to the house to talk to the two of you. Is that OK?"

"Of course. But do you want me to come with you? I can help with the boys." Marie looked at her sister anxiously.

"No, thanks, I can manage just fine." David smiled. "I'm good at this and the boys are troopers."

When David came back to the house, Marie and Chris, Petey and Aunt Clara were sitting in the living room, talking about the people who had come to the wake

449

and their memories of how some of them fit into their lives. David had changed into gray slacks and a black cashmere turtleneck. He got a drink in the kitchen, declining Petey's offer to get it for him, and responded to questions about Amy's health, reassuring them she would be fine.

He took a deep breath. "Amy and I have done some thinking about her mother. I'm guessing from the information we were able to get talking to her doctor in Burlington that she will need nursing care for a long time. We'd like to move her to a place near us in California. It's a highly respected facility where she'll get the best of care and..." He held up his hand as Marie started to interrupt. "Let me finish...and Amy and the boys-and me, too-- will be able to visit her often."

Marie could barely wait to speak. "But I planned to bring her to a place near me. I think it would be very hard on Mom to be transported that far. And when did you talk to the doctor in Burlington?"

"I called him right away after you called me, even before I gave Amy the terrible news. I wanted to have all the facts I could get. And, Marie, I asked him about moving her out to California. It's no different from taking her to Tarrytown or Northampton, for that matter. She'll have to be accompanied by a trained nurse wherever she's moved. And we can do it by private plane."

Petey looked from Marie to David and back. He shrugged. "Marie, that makes sense. You can fly out there to visit, but it's rare that Amy can make a cross country trip. Besides, you have your business to attend to and Amy has more time to spend with Mom."

Marie glared at Petey and then turned to David. "I have to think about that, David. I understand your point but I'm the oldest and it's my responsibility to see to Mom. But let's get through Dad's funeral before we decide on where Mom should go."

The day of the funeral, the skies were leaden and gray. Marie shook Chris awake. "Goddamit, it looks like snow." Indeed, when the family left the house, light flakes were swirling around in one of those freak spring snowstorms. They stopped briefly at the funeral home for a last goodbye before Pierro Edward LaPointe's casket was closed. The church was filled with mourners, some standing in the rear vestibule. Chris and David and Petey were serving as pall bearers along with Pete's partners, Stanley Borowski and George Corelli. The priest gave a very personal homily, emphasizing Pete's service to the community, his support of the church and his service to his country. Marie sat between Chris and Amy, holding both their hands tightly. Quiet tears slid down the cheeks of the sisters and, when Marie glanced over at Petey, she noticed the glitter of tears on his face as well.

Clara sat in the pew behind them between Amy's boys. She whispered to Edward when he started to squirm. "It's almost over, *chouchou.*"

It was still snowing, although not sticking to the warm earth, as they proceeded to the cemetery. The ceremony was brief, delayed a bit while Amy struggled to climb the slight rise to the gravesite. They all shivered in the unexpected chill. When it was finished and people started to depart, Marie turned to Amy and Petey. "I'm going over to say a little prayer for *Pepere* and *Memere.* They're right there on the other side of the caretaker's house." With Petey helping Amy, all three walked over to the dark red marble headstone.

* * * * *

Back at the Day Avenue house Petey went upstairs to change and pack. Marie called up the stairs, "Petey, do you want some lunch? I've got soup, sandwiches or a bowl of chili." Amy and her family had gone to the hotel to pack and had already announced they would get lunch there.

At the kitchen table, Petey joined Chris and Marie and Aunt Clara. As soon as he sat down, he asked Marie, "What are you going to tell David about Mom? I'm sure he wants an answer."

Marie frowned, "I thought about it all night. It makes me feel like I'm somehow shirking my responsibility, but I agree it makes more sense than expecting Amy to come across country to visit Mom."

"And, anyway, aren't you going to be executor? You're going to have your hands full settling Dad's estate, especially since I'll bet he always assumed Mom would do it."

"Oh, yeah, I'm not looking forward to that."

Petey turned to Chris. "Would you drive me over to LaFleur's airport, Chris? I'm going to see if I can rent a plane or borrow one or get someone to take me up to Burlington to see Mom. I haven't got much time, but it's less than an hour's flight up there and I'd like to see her before I go."

Chris stood and pushed his chair back. "Sure, let's go."

"I didn't mean this minute." Petey laughed. "I have to say goodbye to Amy and David and the kids first."

The Epsteins arrived moments later in a big black, chauffeur-driven limousine. There were hugs and handshakes all around. David turned to Marie. "I returned the car I borrowed to George over at the lot.

We've only got a little time. We want to get in the air and headed back soon. I don't really want to rush you about it, Marie, but we need to know if you've had time to think about Mother LaPointe and made any decisions."

Marie's lower lip trembled a bit. "I thought about what you want to do and decided you're right. Amy wouldn't be able to visit Mom if she was near me and that's not fair. Petey and I are more mobile. So, make the arrangements and we'll talk about paying for it after I go over all of Dad's papers and figure out what's the bottom line. I'm pretty sure George and Stan will buy up Dad's shares in the business, but it's not straightforward, so I really don't know for sure how much money there'll be for her care."

David sighed. Amy's face brightened, clearly relieved. "We were going to get the pilot to take us up to Burlington first if you hadn't agreed to let us take her to California. Now, I'll just go ahead with making arrangements to bring her to us as soon as possible, maybe next week."

When everyone had left, Marie slumped in a chair in the living room, exhausted. "I don't know where to start, Chris. I guess I'll call Dad's attorney today and see how the estate is set up and then call Mom's real estate office and put this house on the market."

"You look pretty much beat up, darling. Let me help you. I can do some of this stuff. You should get some rest now. I'll put the linens in the washer and clean up the kitchen while you take a nap."

When Marie talked to the attorney, she found that her father had planned very carefully, with contingencies for simultaneous death of himself and Angela, as well as contingencies for Angela's care if she were to be disabled at his death. Even in death, Pete was still making sure to take care of his loved ones.

Angela was moved to a rehabilitation/nursing home connected to UCLA. She received the best of treatment and therapy, but never recovered her ability to care for herself or to speak. She seemed to recognize Amy, smiling at her visits and making unintelligible sounds. Marie and Petey visited her four or five times a year and always came away saddened at the sight of their competent, energetic mother encased in a body that was a prison.

Angela Ciccione LaPointe died in her sleep in September of 1975. She was 64.

Chapter 26

◇◇

Northampton, Tarrytown and Hollywood, 1973-1980

Clara knew she was slowing down some. She enjoyed reading and listening to music in her cheery living room more than venturing out to tour the globe. She still went to concerts at John M. Greene Hall and loved Tanglewood in the summer and fall, but the decision to drive to Boston for a performance was not as spontaneous as it had been a few years ago. Despite the fact that she was conscious of eating a healthy diet and walking briskly on the campus of Smith College, her doctor warned her of the legacy of heart problems in her family.

Her friends Ruth Goldberg and Bob Rhoades frequently invited her to dinner or to join them for an outing. They shared her passion for classical music and books and, since their children were now off to college, they had more time to plan Sunday afternoon gatherings. Bob's firm of architects was busy with all the growth in the Pioneer Valley. Ruth had taken a part-time job as a reader at Smith, evaluating assignments for the English department.

It was Ruth who called Clara's attention to a new group called Elderhostel, offering seminars on interesting topics in New Hampshire. "Look at this announcement, Clara. They're seeking older people who want to study a topic and discuss it with other people for three days in an atmosphere of learning. That should appeal to you." It did and Clara Pelletier was one of the first participants in an Elderhostel study group.

* * * * *

Marie's business continued to grow. She became well known for her innovative ideas and was pleased and proud to be mentioned in <u>Newsweek</u> magazine and in the business section of *The New York Times.* When the Today show on morning television was seeking women leaders for a feature story, Marie was contacted and invited to appear. She came across the camera's eye so comfortable and articulate, she was invited back on other occasions when the producer was looking for a businesswoman's voice.

Chris was proud of his successful wife, but also resentful of the amount of time she gave to working. And he was especially chagrined when they planned to do something together and she canceled at the last minute. He got sick of going to a concert or a movie or a Broadway show by himself. He hated the sound of his own voice when he complained of her defection from some event or another.

"Dammit, Marie, it's embarrassing to have to explain to friends when I show up alone. They've started to think we're splitting up."

"Ridiculous. Everybody knows how much it takes to keep a business going, at least all the people who have tried it. I don't do it on purpose. It's just that some emergency comes up."

"Bullshit. I know others who have businesses and they delegate so they can have a life. You think you're the only one who can do anything right. That's the big problem."

"How would you know? You just go in to your office and do whatever somebody tells you to do, get back on the train and come home. You don't have to delegate because you're the one the work is delegated to."

"At least I get to have a life." Chris snapped back at her.

In the fall of 1978, Marie and Chris had tickets to the Broadway musical "Ain't Misbehavin'." It had won the New York Drama Critics Award and a Tony as well. Chris waited in the bar of their favorite restaurant nursing a scotch and watching the door. The bartender came over carrying a telephone. "It's for you, Mr. Graham."

"I'm so sorry, Chris. We just signed a big contract and I have to take these guys out for drinks to celebrate. Go ahead and have dinner, leave my ticket at the box office and I'll try to make it by the intermission."

Chris didn't answer her. He hung up the phone and asked the hostess to find him a table for one. He sat there brooding until it was time to go to the theatre. He was a big Fats Waller fan and he remembered when Marie was, too. The musical was wildly applauded. Marie never arrived.

She was sitting at the kitchen table eating an omelet when he walked in. "How was the show? I'm sorry I couldn't make it, but this contract is a big deal. I just couldn't leave."

"Of course, there was no one else who could possibly play host. You couldn't tell them you were meeting your husband, that you had tickets to a show?"

"Well, not really. They expect me, not some underling. I wish you understood how these things work, Chris."

"You're right. I don't understand. Aren't you supposed to have a life? What about me, Marie? How about my feelings? You don't give a damn about me or ever even give a thought to my feelings, my needs. All you care about is your prestige, your success, your effing business." Chris threw his jacket and briefcase on a chair and went upstairs.

Marie was at the sink, cleaning the omelet pan when Chris came down the stairs, carrying a suitcase. "Where are you going? It's almost midnight."

Chris's face registered his distress. "Marie, I've taken all I can take. I've tried and tried to get you to recognize that this marriage is falling apart. We hardly have a life together anymore. I've loved you since the first time I saw you, but it's not enough. I can't stand to be less important to you than your success. There it is. I want out. I want a divorce."

Marie was stunned. Her voice was barely a whisper. "You can't mean to do this."

"I've been thinking about it for a long time. I'm taking the Mercedes into town tonight. I don't know yet where I'll stay, but you can get in touch with me at work. Get yourself a lawyer. Good night."

Marie sat at the kitchen table for a long time, thinking and weeping. She couldn't get past the notion that Chris should have been proud of her success. Their debts were all paid. They had a substantial portfolio of investments. She had achieved some recognition for her vision in starting her business. Why couldn't Chris be more tolerant of the demands? She never criticized his choices, his lack of ambition. She never nagged him to seek a better position or try to improve his status in the firm. The more she thought about it, the more indignant she got that he wasn't being fair.

The next day was a Saturday and, instead of going to her office as usual, she drove up to Northampton to visit Aunt Clara. "I can't believe he would do this over such a silly thing as missing a Broadway show."

Aunt Clara poured a glass of wine and raised her eyebrow. "Was this the first time you stood him up?"

"Well, of course not. There've been other times when I couldn't help it. Something came up and I just had to call and cancel. So much of my business is built on people knowing me and trusting me. I haven't got a

deputy that can step in and take my place just like that."
Marie snapped her fingers.

"Well, why not? Maybe you should start training somebody to do that. What if you got sick?"

"If I'm sick I show up anyway." Marie's voice reflected her bitterness.

Lawyers met. Agreements were made. Assets were divided. It amazed Chris how fast a marriage could be dissolved. On the few occasions when it was necessary for Marie to see Chris in an attorney's office, she was tight-lipped, unsmiling, and stiff with tension.

Their divorce was final in September of 1979.

* * * * *

It was little more than a year later that Marie got the call from the Lathrop Home to summon her to Aunt Clara's bedside. Ohmigod, she thought, it's been over a year since I've gone to Northampton to visit. How could I have been so thoughtless?

Burdened with grief over the end of her marriage, feeling guilty of neglecting her beloved aunt, Marie quickly made arrangements to leave her office in charge of her deputy and hurried to respond to the call.

Chapter 26

<><><><><><><><><><><><><><><><><><><><><><><><><><><><><><>

Montreal, 1980

Marie was late rising. Yesterday she had finally told Uncle Charley about the accident that killed her father and about her mother's severe disability as a result of that same accident. And she had told him of her divorce. She felt drained, more tired than she had ever known herself to be. She wanted to stay under the covers and hide from the world.

The phone was ringing while she was in the shower. "Dammit, who can that be?" She wrapped a robe around her and called the desk to ask if there was a message. "*Oui, Madame.* You are to call *Mere Superieure* as soon as possible."

Marie reached Mother Superior immediately. "Mrs. Graham, your uncle died in his sleep last night. When Sister Francis went in this morning to help him rise for breakfast, he was already gone to God. You may want to make some phone calls before you come over here today."

"I just finished telling him about all our family and how they fared during the years he was gone. He was supposed to tell me today about himself and..." Marie could not continue. Her throat was thick with tears.

"I think he was only hanging on to hear the end of the story, Mrs. Graham. He's gone now to a better place. We must be joyful for him. Will you come here later this morning and I will tell you our plans?"

"Yes, Mother, give me a couple of hours to make my calls."

It was too early in California to call Amy and anyway, Amy would not be coming. She called Petey and was surprised to get him right away. "Cripes, Marie, I'm sorry. This is a bad time here. The Israelis and the Palestinians are saber-rattling again and this whole base is on high alert. I just can't leave. I'm sorry, sweetheart, there's nothing I can do about it. What do you want me to do? Send flowers? Wire money? What?"

"Oh, Petey, I understand. Sometimes you just can't get away from the job. It'll be OK. Later, I'll probably ask you and Amy, too, to pony up a contribution for this nursing home, but not now. I'll call you later."

The Sisters of the Sacred Heart had already made their plans for the wake, the funeral Mass and the interment of Charles Billieux, their beloved Good Samaritan. By the time Marie arrived he had been removed to a mortician for embalming. The Sisters set up a catafalque in the chapel. Uncle Charlie was to lie there so all in their community could visit him and pray at his bier. One of them would keep vigil through the night. The funeral Mass would be celebrated tomorrow and he was to be buried in the consecrated plot behind the chapel.

There was nothing for Marie to do. She realized how much Uncle Charlie belonged to this group of women. She was an observer. She was a mourner. But her role was limited to that.

The waiting room had a strong scent of linseed oil. A picture of Mary and the baby Jesus hung on the wall. Marie settled on the hard wooden bench anticipating when Uncle Charlie would be brought back from the mortician. There was a small commotion when the casket arrived, as two burly men struggled to get it through the narrow hallway without bumping the walls. Suddenly she remembered she had not called the

Krakow family. She got up and walked over to the desk in the foyer. "May I use the phone, Sister Boniface? I need to call the Krakow family."

"No need, Madame Graham. Mother Superior called them this morning. They'll be here tomorrow."

Marie made her way to the chapel, where two nuns were draping garlands of evergreen around the white cloth-covered catafalque. The casket was open. Marie went over to it and looked down at her much loved uncle. He was wearing a black suit, white shirt and blue tie. His folded hands held a black onyx rosary. Marie remembered it as one that had belonged to her *Gran'mere.* Aunt Clara had brought it to Uncle Charlie when he was in jail.

Marie bent over and touched his hands, kissed his cold cheek. *"Au'voir, cher oncle.* May you be with the angels."

There was nothing for her to do here. She left and drove to Notre Dame Cathedral, made her way to the front of that beautiful and awe-inspiring place to the bank of candles in their dark red holders and emptied her pocketbook of all her change. She lit candles for Uncle Charlie and candles for Amy and then, remembering how dangerous Petey's job could be, lit candles for him, too. She sat in a pew at a side altar, going over in her head the story she had been telling Uncle Charlie all week, remembering and regretting some of her own decisions. When she realized she'd gotten very hungry, she looked at her watch. It was five o'clock. She'd had no lunch. Where did the day go?

The next morning, dressed in her black suit and white silk blouse, the same she had worn to Aunt Clara's funeral a little over a week ago, she went to the chapel in the nursing home of the Sisters of the Sacred Heart. The nuns were assembling. An organ was playing softly. She took a seat in a back pew. Soon the Krakow family arrived and filed into the same pew, coming in from the opposite end. The priest entered with two altar boys. The choir began a hymn of mourning. Marie closed her eyes. Someone took her hand and squeezed lightly. Marie, surprised, raised her bowed head to see Chris beside her. He bent over close to her ear and whispered, "Petey called me yesterday. He didn't want you to be alone. I flew in late last night. I'm so sorry, Marie. I didn't know about Aunt Clara and now this. Let me help you."

The choir began the familiar refrain "Gloria. Gloria." Marie shifted her body to lean closer to Chris. She whispered back. "I'm so glad you're here. Please stay. I need you."

The sweet voices of the nuns in the choir loft rang out "And He shall reign forever and ever."

About the Author

◇◇◇

Louise Appell was born and raised in Northampton, Massachusetts. Her father, Romeo Fortier, was French-Canadian. She graduated from Smith College and went on to earn a doctorate in education at the University of Kentucky, She had a distinguished career in special education as a teacher and university professor before moving to the private sector to lead a team in the development of curriculum materials for people with disabilities. Dr. Appell is the author of several works of non-fiction. This book concludes the trilogy about the fictional Billieux family. She is currently working on a book about a Red Cross "Donut Dolly" and her adventures during WWII. Visit her website at www. Authortree.com/LOUISEAPPELL.

Printed in the United States
215617BV00001B/5/P